CHAPTER ONE

I've always attracted trouble.

My father, when he was sober enough to remember who I was, would always say, "Freya, you were put on this earth to create three kinds of trouble. Trouble for your parents. Trouble for whoever is unlucky enough to fall in love with you, and most of all, trouble for yourself."

Though he might not have been the wisest man, nor the kindest or the soberest, my father always spoke the truth.

I didn't *try* to attract trouble. In fact, I actively avoided it. But somehow, it found me. Like it had tonight.

With the man bleeding in front of me. From a stab wound.

A *stab wound*.

It wasn't just any man bleeding from a stab wound, but one with a crapload of muscles and tattoos, wearing an unmistakable leather vest. They called it a cut, the bikers. The Sons of Templar.

After the night I'd had, after the *life* I'd had, I did not want to have to deal with a bleeding member of the Sons of Templar MC, but I couldn't just leave him there bleeding, could I?

"Shit," I muttered under my breath, rushing over to the man currently hemorrhaging in the middle of the desolate parking lot.

The parking lot outside the club was thankfully well lit, because our boss was actually decent and didn't want us feeling unsafe while walking to our cars. Usually, there was someone available to walk us to our cars. Usually I was lucky enough not to finish my shift while Dante was still on the clock. Dante... an apt name for him since I was pretty sure he was spawned in the fires of hell.

As much as I despised the man and actually felt safer walking to my car when he wasn't around, I would've even taken Dante right then. He might've been a misogynistic, narcissistic asshole, but he had enough self-preservation to know you didn't fuck with the Sons of Templar. Plus, he would've wanted to be in their good books, since I'd heard a rumor that he'd tried to prospect with them and didn't make the cut. Apparently, he was desperate for their approval, for a second chance. Watching him try to act cool and badass in front of them whenever they came into the club was a huge cringe-fest. So if Dante was here, he would've dealt with this, most likely banishing me from the scene because according to him, women couldn't possibly deal with this kind of thing. And he wouldn't want anyone possibly taking away whatever glory would come from saving a member of the club.

But Dante wasn't there.

No one was there.

Just me.

Because I'd stayed at the club writing emails to friends all over the country, catching up on all the messages I'd mentally told myself to reply to later but then had forgotten all about. I'd also forgotten about the fact that Kallum was away, which meant he wouldn't be there to stick around until everyone left, making sure every girl got home safely—which was a huge part of his job. I hadn't been that worried about being there alone in the middle of the night. Our smallish town was pretty crime-free, thanks to the Sons of Templar. There had been some stuff that went down before I moved here, I'd heard about it in whispers. Apparently, almost the entire MC had been murdered by enemies. There had

To everyone who loves an anti-hero.

Editing: Kim BookJunkie
Cover Design: TRC Designs
Proofing: Christine Yates

been some kind of war. It sounded intense and insane and completely fucking dangerous. I stayed away from all of that stuff.

Until now.

"Holy shit," I whispered, dropping my purse and kneeling beside the lifeless man on the ground. The glaring overhead light showed the rapidly growing pool of blood underneath him and that his white tee was stained in the middle of his torso. My hand went to his chest, laying it flat there, holding my breath as I waited for it to rise and fall to show me he was still alive.

"Okay, you're okay," I said to him, blinking rapidly in the low light. "I'm just going to..." What was I going to do right now? The parking lot was eerily quiet, the area surrounding the club pretty much abandoned with the closest house being at least a mile away. Kallum had chosen this location so he wouldn't get any noise complaints or trouble from residents who didn't want a strip club near them. A very smart business idea. Apparently, he hadn't planned for someone being stabbed or shot in the parking lot needing immediate medical attention.

There was no one around. No one but me and the man who was quite possibly dying in front of me. It felt like we were the only people left on the planet. God was playing a cruel fucking joke by giving this guy *me* in his hour of need. I did not do well under pressure. My hands were already shaking, my dinner already threatening to come up, my heart roaring in my ears. Yes, a full-on panic attack was imminent.

Then I looked up from his bleeding torso to where his head was illuminated by the overhead lights. My body jerked as if someone had just shocked me, making me shudder down to my very bones. I'd expected this man to be unconscious. He'd been lying motionless in the middle of an abandoned parking lot, bleeding. He was one of the Sons of Templar. They were hardcore badasses. I'd figured if he was conscious, he would've already sewn himself up with a toothpick and some dental floss.

He was not unconscious. He was laying there, piercing eyes

open, staring at me. Staring into me, it seemed. I sucked in a breath that froze the insides of my lungs. The chill helped. Something inside of me calmed, stilled.

"You're going to be okay," I told him in little more than a whisper. "I'm going to take care of you."

Something moved in his eyes, something that made my skin twitch. Something that shouldn't have been in the eyes of someone bleeding so much. And I definitely shouldn't have been having any kind of reaction to the man except for shock and fear.

I swallowed.

Get it together, Freya. You don't want this guy dying because you were too busy salivating over his intense gaze and his sculpted cheekbones.

It dawned on me then that my hand was still lying flat on his chest. Not pressing against the bleeding wound like I was pretty sure it was supposed to be. Holding my breath, I moved my hand to where the bleeding seemed to be coming from. My stomach lurched slightly as warm liquid coated my hand. I didn't know why I'd expected it to be cold. This was the stuff that had—just moments ago—been running through this man's veins, keeping him alive.

Keep it together.

Keeping my eyes glued to his, I used my free hand to reach blindly into my purse, looking for my phone.

"I'm going to call—"

"No cops," he grunted, his hand darting quickly to circle around my wrist.

I blinked. Not only in reaction to the steel behind his words but also at the pressure around my wrist. He was holding it tight, to the point of pain. To the point where, if he held much longer and much tighter, I'd bruise.

His eyes glittered with something beyond pain. Something dangerous, but they were beautiful. One green and one blue. I'd never seen someone with eyes like that before. Then again, I'd never seen someone bleeding from a knife or gunshot wound before, which was what I mentally told myself to focus on.

"If not the police then we need an ambulance," I argued, his hand still around my wrist. My other hand was pressing into his bleeding wound.

The man's jaw was hard, taut with pain, a thin sheen of sweat covering his face. "Ambulance means hospital. Hospital means cops. No ambulance."

Fuck.

He was still gripping my wrist, and I knew that he wasn't going to let me go until I agreed. I also knew that the leather he wore meant that disobeying his commands would mean trouble for me. A heck of a lot more trouble than I was already in.

I nodded once. "Okay, no ambulance," I conceded.

His grip relaxed on my wrist, but he did not let it go entirely.

My mind should not have been focusing on the fact my skin prickled beneath his grip. And not in an entirely unpleasant way.

"No ambulance. I can't leave you bleeding here, though, so I'll take you home," I decided.

And just like that, I had invited the worst kind of trouble into my life. Into my home.

HADES

It was all my fucking fault.

I hadn't seen her as a threat. Fuck, my entire job, my entire *life* was about identifying threats and eliminating them. And I was very fucking good at my job. There was no place for morality, mercy, or feelings of any kind. I'd learned that the only way you could, the fucking hard way.

For years, I only cared about my brothers. Even caring about them proved dangerous considering how common an early grave was in our lifestyle. Death was a part of being a member of the Sons of Templar MC. Which was just how I liked it. Loved it.

Ending a life meant nothing to me. It made me feel alive. Just barely.

That's what I was right now. Barely fucking alive. Because somehow, I'd found a shred of my humanity. Because of *her*. The memories of her. Of what we had been. Whatever the fuck.

Sure, I knew who she was now. She was the female version of me. Which might've worked in our minds but not so much in reality. We'd initially been friends, tried fucking each other, and now we were something close to enemies. I'd heard it all, about a scorned woman and how they should be feared, but I wasn't afraid of anything or anyone. And everyone was afraid of me.

Except her.

And she was really fucking pissed at me, if the knife in my stomach was anything to go by. I hadn't even been fucking prepared for a fight. The setting of a strip club parking lot in the middle of the night hadn't even given me any clues. Sure, it might've been a weird locale and time for a civilian, but neither of us were civilians, and we didn't keep traditional hours. I figured she was blowing through town and needed some kind of favor. After what I'd done to her, I was prepared to give it to her. For old time's sake. Then we'd have a discussion about how this was the last time we were going to see each other.

Turned out we didn't need to have that discussion. She'd been planning on no one seeing me again. Ever.

"As much as I'd like to stay and watch you die, it's going to be a long and painful process," she'd said after wiping my blood off her knife on the thighs of her leather pants. "And I've got somewhere to be," she continued. I watched her eyes flicker over me under the harsh overhead lights, red-painted lips stretching out into a satisfied smile. "But it's okay. I win."

Then she'd turned on her stiletto heel and walked to her car. Not looking back once.

Fuck, I'd thought I'd turned into a cold and evil motherfucker, but she definitely won that contest. I could leave someone to die a long and painful death, that was for sure. Man or woman. If they deserved it. If the club needed me to do it.

Usually, if the club needed me to do it, they were guilty of something, deserved it in some way. Other times they didn't. I did it anyway. Didn't lose a wink of sleep over it. But there were a handful of people who I couldn't kill, couldn't hurt. She was on that list. Or at least she had been, up until stabbing me and leaving me to die.

She hadn't severed my spinal cord; I had the use of my arms and legs, though I didn't think I could stand up. Fuck, maybe I could've. My phone was in the pocket of my cut, and I definitely could've reached into my cut to call someone from the club. They'd have been there in less than ten minutes, Sarah in tow. They'd be able to save my life. She'd been aiming for my liver, but I'd moved at the last moment, and I was pretty sure she'd missed. Some part of me must've wanted to live, the unconscious part of me, at least. But now I was bleeding on the cold concrete, staring up at a very bright fucking light and contemplating my life. It was very likely that even if I did survive, I'd die in a very fucking similar way at some point in the future.

A future that consisted of a lot of death, violence, and not much else.

I don't know if it was a conscious or unconscious decision, but I didn't reach for my phone. I just stared at that bright fucking light, knowing that eventually, it wouldn't be so bright anymore, and it would eventually get really fucking dark. If I was lucky. If I wasn't, and if a bunch of bible thumpers were to be believed, it would then get all bright, hot, fire and brimstone.

But it didn't get any darker. Or any hotter.

Because *she* found me.

And she made it very fucking clear that she wasn't going to let me die.

FREYA

Somehow, I managed to get him into my backseat. I struggled getting my groceries out of the car, so I had no fucking clue how I managed to move his mountainous frame. I figured it was a combination of adrenaline and the fact that I'd recently started taking Pilates classes.

He was slipping in and out of consciousness, which surely was due to all the blood he was losing, blood that almost made *me* slip out of consciousness. I realized whoever stabbed him could come back, and I really didn't need to faint and get *myself* stabbed, so I held fast.

Thankfully, he'd managed to stay conscious while I helped him to my car and was able to help me get him into the back seat before I scrambled to snatch a blanket from the trunk, covering his bleeding torso with it. "Don't die," I commanded once I'd tucked him in the best I could.

His eyes seemed to glow in the dim overhead light of my car with a glint in them that penetrated me to my very bones. "Don't worry, I ain't fuckin' dying," he declared with a surety that a man with a serious stab wound shouldn't have. Nonetheless, as crazy as it was, I believed him.

That did not stop me from driving like a maniac the ten minutes it took me to get home, though. And it was a fifteen-minute drive under normal circumstances, normal circumstances being me driving ten over. Later, I would wonder why I hadn't just driven to the Sons of Templar compound. Though I'd never been there, I knew where it was, and it was even closer than my place out in the middle of the desert. But I wasn't thinking straight. My mind was scrambled and panicked and, as mentioned before, I did not work well under pressure.

Every thirty seconds exactly—I counted—I asked the man in the back if he was still alive. He responded every thirty seconds, sounding more and more pissed off each time he answered. Which was good, since I doubted that someone had the energy to sound pissed off if they were about to die. It also pissed me off just a little since I didn't think it was polite to snap at someone who was in the process of saving your life and possibly breaking the law by doing so. I didn't point this out to him at this juncture because it definitely wasn't polite to point out the lack of manners of a stab victim currently losing a lot of blood.

He survived the trip to my place, but my nails barely did from the death grip I had on the steering wheel. Thankfully, he was still conscious when we arrived. Although I didn't have to completely carry him inside, he was stumbling and leaning on me enough to coat my forehead in sweat by the time I deposited him on the sofa. My dog, Sirius, trailed us inside, eying the bleeding man warily before jumping on the sofa as soon as I set him down, laying right on his legs and refusing to move.

I didn't know whether it was because he liked dogs—albeit cowardly ones—or because he was too weak to kick him off, but the man didn't protest. Which worked out well since I didn't have time to ask him whether he liked dogs or not. It was clear he needed medical attention, so I grabbed my first aid kit and did my best. My hands shook and my stomach roiled as I worked, but I did as much as I could. The best I could included cutting his shirt off with the scissors in my first aid kit and biting back my gasp not just at the bleeding jagged wound in his mid-section but the mid-section itself. Bloodstained, sculpted, covered in ink.

I again reminded myself that perving at the man bleeding on my sofa was really fucking sick. I'd talk that over with a therapist at a later date. The bleeding man didn't so much as grunt or whimper during me cleaning his wound and pressing a bandage up against it. It had to hurt, like a lot. I did a lot of fucking whimpering when I cleaned out a paper cut. Then again, this tatted, muscled, motorcycle club member didn't exactly look like a whimpering type.

My teeth had been gnawing at the inside of my lip the entire time so I didn't let out any kind of pathetic moan or start crying.

He didn't speak during the process, and neither did I, but that was because I was concentrating on not vomiting all over him.

"Okay, so I've brought you into my home and treated your stab wound with medical knowledge coming straight off *Grey's Anatomy* that I know is not entirely correct, no matter how much of a genius Shonda Rhimes is," I babbled, not looking at him in the eye. My hands were still pressed over the top of the towel I was using to staunch the bleeding, which for all I knew, could have been making everything worse.

"*Scandal, How to Get Away With Murder, Bridgerton.* Though technically she didn't write that, just produced it..." I trailed off, realizing that I was talking about fucking *Bridgerton* with a stranger who was bleeding from a stab wound. A male stranger. With tattoos, muscles, a Sons of Templar cut, and an overall air of menace. Your run-of-the-mill male did not usually want to hear about *Bridgerton* and the overall genius of Shonda, and this was certainly not a run-of-the-mill male—stab wound notwithstanding.

"Anyway, what I was *trying* to say was that we've gone through a considerable amount together," I continued as he raised his brow ever so slightly. "You more than me, of course."

Though I'd definitely be having some sleepless nights thinking about this ordeal.

"And I don't even know your name," I sighed. "Weird since I'm covered in your blood and you're in my house and ... yeah."

He continued to stare at me with those multicolored eyes, with that porcelain skin, that chiseled jaw held tight—likely because of the pain, of course. Not because of ... me.

Oh my god. How narcissistic was I, thinking the Adonis with the chiseled jaw was focused on *me* right now? He was absolutely covered in tattoos, from his neck downward. There was even ink on his face. A small heart underneath his left eye. A skeletal hand holding a rose on his temple. In gothic script, the word 'cursed' curled on top of his right eyebrow. I wasn't sure if they were meant to intimidate or scare away those from regular society, but they did neither of things to me. They fascinated me. The urge to reach out and touch them was almost overwhelming.

"Freya," I blurted out, my heart thundering in my chest, feeling seconds away from a full-on hysterical breakdown. It would not do well to break down with a biker badass in my house. A *still bleeding* biker badass.

He blinked.

"My name," I offered. "It's Freya."

Something in his eyes changed. Giving me a glimpse of something other than pain. Then his eyes shuttered. "Phone."

I stared at him. "I know bikers have some weird names, but—"

"No, phone in my cut," he clipped out, not sounding at all amused. He moved underneath me, letting out a grunt of pain.

He reached over to where I'd carefully placed his cut over the back of the sofa. His hand wasn't shaking. I found that interesting since my hand was shaking, and I wasn't the one bleeding.

"Call Swiss, tell him to come with Sarah to this address," he ordered, his jaw tight.

I nodded once, scrolling through his phone then doing as he said. I didn't know why he wasn't calling Swiss himself but I also figured he was trying to be a tough guy and those words sounded forced and full of pain. The sound of a dial tone echoed through the silent room.

"You fucker, you better be torturing someone or dead. You missed church," was the answer I got.

I cleared my throat.

Torturing someone.

He hadn't said it like it was meant to be a joke.

"Um, hey, Swiss. My name is Freya, and your friend..." Fuck, I still didn't know his name. "The one whose phone this is, with the good hair and a jawline that will ruin your life, he's here and he's been stabbed. And he said no cops or ambulance, but he told me to call you, so I'm hoping you know what to do here because I definitely do not," I uttered in one long breath.

He was looking at me, the bleeding man who had a jawline that could ruin lives. I didn't hold his gaze because he likely thought I was fucking insane.

There was an extended silence on the other end of the phone then a chuckle. *A chuckle.* "Figures that motherfucker would get stabbed then get picked up by a hot chick."

I blinked. "How do you know I'm hot?"

"Baby, I can tell." His voice was saturated in sex, and my body quivered from it. Just a little. I was only human.

Something changed in the room, the energy. I risked a glance to the man on my sofa. His expression had been tight and pissed off before all of this—presumably because he was an alpha male biker with a square jaw who'd gotten himself saved by a *woman*—but for whatever reason, he was seriously pissed now. Likely because I was chatting with his friend about my hotness while he was bleeding without medical attention.

"Get Sarah to this address now," the bleeding man grunted, though it was more of a growl.

Another chuckle came through the phone. "Alright, alright, man, don't get your panties in a bunch. What's your address, baby?"

I was guessing this was meant for me, so I rattled off my address to the man on the other end of the phone with a liquid sex voice that was calling me baby.

"We'll be there in five."

We?

I didn't get the chance to ask any more questions since he hung up. I just stared at the phone, then looked up into one green eye and one blue eye.

"Um, I'll just put this here," I murmured, placing the phone on my coffee table. It was bloodstained. The phone. My fingers.

My hands started to shake as everything really sunk in.

"Freya."

My attention moved back to the man who said my name. In a deep, masculine, throaty voice.

My couch was large. Very large. It had taken me four months to find and it had cost a lot more than a couch should've cost. But it was like a fucking cloud; it swallowed me up and cuddled me better than any man could. I'd covered it in expensive cushions and throws so it looked like something out of a home magazine.

Now there was a man on it. One that did not belong in any magazine. Stark against all the colors and textures. His hair was inky black, mussed in a way that had not taken him hours in front of a mirror, in the way that nature had intended. I wasn't sure if he was pale naturally or from the blood loss, but he was working it in a big way. His brows were as dark as his hair, eyes like carved gemstones against the stark angles of his face. The tattoos, instead of looking like someone had inked them on his skin, looked like he was born with them, like they were part of him.

He was tall, stretched all the way along the length of my sofa, Sirius still on top of his legs. And I'd seen his stomach. Sure, it was a gaping, bleeding wound, but that wound was right in the middle of one ab.

He had eight of them.

Covered, absolutely covered in ornate tattoos. I hadn't gotten to drool over the abs or the tattoos because of all the blood.

It had been established that I wasn't ever going to be a doctor, but I was pretty sure ogling a patient's eight pack was against some Hippocratic Oath.

"Freya."

I jerked, looking up at the man's eyes, realizing I had been staring at his tattoo-covered abs. "I didn't take a Hippocratic Oath," I exclaimed.

He blinked slowly. Once. "You're good."

It wasn't a question. Nor was it a statement of fact. It was an order. He was *ordering* me to be *good* after I'd just nursed his *stab wound.* Sure, he'd flinched a couple of times while I was cleaning his wound while trying to follow a YouTube tutorial of how to treat a stab injury. Other than that, he'd acted like I was giving him a facial. Here he was, still bleeding—though thankfully the bleeding had slowed—still with a hole in his torso, and he was essentially ordering me to calm down.

"Okay, I'm going to..." I pointed toward my hallway. "Don't die."

"Again, not planning on it," he replied.

I nodded once then pointed to Sirius. "Keep watch," I ordered.

Then I walked calmly to the bathroom off my hallway and spent five minutes staring at myself in the mirror, willing myself not to have a heart attack.

I almost failed when there was a knock at the front door, but I managed to force myself out of the bathroom in order to open my front door. Other people were good right now. Even if those other people were men who spoke like sex gods and chuckled when faced with a stab wound. The quicker I opened the door, the quicker I got the bleeding guy off my sofa and my life back to normal.

I stared at the two men standing in my doorway in Sons of Templar cuts. They were tall. Really tall. Muscled. Two different versions of sex gods. Totally different than the sex god on my sofa. One was taller than the other, bulkier and older with greys threaded through his dark hair. He had a goatee, and I had no idea how the fuck he pulled it off, but he managed it. The other was muscled and wearing a tank to show off his smooth, ebony skin with muscles carved like they were made from granite. His eyes were liquid hazelnut, lips full and lush. He had a knife strapped to his belt.

Next to them was a petite blonde woman wearing faded jeans and a Green Day tee, a large leather bag slung over her shoulder. She smiled at me.

There wasn't time for any kind of greeting or pleasantries since they barged right in. "We brought a doctor," the first one yelled as he strode through my house, presumably in search of his bleeding brother.

I stared out at my driveway, the floodlights illuminating my Range Rover, two Harleys and a Mini Cooper. Cute car for a doctor to drive. And she liked Green Day. I liked her already.

Not what I should've been thinking about. And I shouldn't have been staring at my driveway while there were four strangers in my living room. I managed to close the door and walk down the hall, down the steps and back into my living room. I blinked at the sight of the woman kneeling next to—how had I still not gotten his name?—*him*, doing her doctor work while the two club members loitered in my living room, not seeming at all concerned about their friend.

"Bro, you went to a strip club and got yourself *stabbed?*" the ebony-skinned man joked, rubbing Sirius on the head. My dog still hadn't moved from his spot and was not at all worried by the no doubt deadly men in my living room.

"Did you at least kill them, or were you too busy touching up your lipstick?" he continued, grinning at me as I walked into the room.

The other guy was sitting on the arm of the armchair across from the sofa.

"Paid off, though," he continued, eyes going to me.

My stomach dipped as his gaze went up and down my body. It wasn't a leer. I'd had many men leer at me. In fact, it was my job to have men leer at me. I'd actually become comfortable with it. It was no longer a demeaning act, men looking at me like an object, like they had a right to me. At first, for the longest time, it had felt like that. Like I was for sale and cheap. But I'd come to realize that I had the power. I was fucking priceless; no matter how much money men threw at me, they'd never own me. I owned them. Their attention. They were the ones lying to their wives, spending all their money, never taking their eyes off something they could never have.

So yes, I was used to the male gaze. I made money off it. And I was never, ever impressed by the owner of that male gaze until right fucking now.

I was still dressed in clothes from work. Granted, not the teeny G-string or the nipple tassels I wore when I was actually working, but what I wore in and out of the club was what I considered somewhat of a uniform. What I wore everywhere, actually. My clothes made no secret of the fact that I was a stripper. They were always tight, short and revealed of all of my assets.

Tonight was no different.

My skirt was black, as were the boots that finished mid-thigh, showing only a sliver of my tanned legs between the two. The heels on my boots were high—very high— though I'd been dancing on stage in much higher heels for the past few hours. I'd been doing this long enough that I barely had feeling in my feet any longer. Beyond that, I needed the height. Without them, I felt small, vulnerable. The same way I felt without my tight, revealing clothes. They were, in a sense, my armor. I showed a lot of skin, but it distracted from other things.

My cropped tank exposed my midriff, skimming over my D-cups, showing ample cleavage. My arms were exposed, tattoos scattered over them. Not full sleeves, more of a mishmash of things that meant something to me. Memories, moments. A large butterfly on my inner elbow done in watercolor. Script running from my shoulder to my wrist. Little things. They suited me. Or at least I thought they did.

I was used to people looking. Men looking. Women, more often than not, turning their noses up at me, dismissing me as a 'slut' and hating me for whatever reason. Maybe because their husband was staring too long or too obviously, perhaps because they had a whole bunch of internalized misogyny or had some self-confidence issues. Of course, sometimes they were just bitches.

Despite the stares, the attention—almost always negative, because let's face it, the male gaze is always fucking negative—I couldn't leave the house without looking like this. Without my heels, my exposed skin, my hair 'done', my makeup fierce and my nails long, never chipped. As my Aunt Victoria always said, "life is gonna throw some shit at you, honey, no escaping that. No changing that. But you can make sure you always look good while life fucks you over."

This man with the honeyed gaze was redefining the fucking male gaze, and I swear, I blacked out a little before I realized I was staring back at him, slack-jawed. My eyes darted to the sofa, expecting to see my patient either unconscious or gritting his teeth, trying to look tough in front of his hot doctor. Instead, he was glaring. At me. As if I hadn't potentially just saved his life. Or made the stab wound worse depending on how accurate Grey's Anatomy and YouTube were.

His glare doused all the fire from his friend's scrutiny. Every single ounce of it. My blood chilled. My entire body did.

It was an effort, a great fucking effort, to tear my gaze from his, but I managed it, and when I did, the man with the honey eyes was looking between the two of us grinning. Fucking grinning as if his buddy wasn't trying his best to kill me with his glare.

"Can I get anyone anything?" I asked, wringing my hands while watching Sarah work on the bleeding man—how did I still not know his name?—on my sofa.

It would have been rude to ask them to move so he didn't stain the cushions I spent far too much money on, wouldn't it? Yeah, it would.

"A soda? Beer? I could make a quick cheeseboard? I don't have bleu, which is a controversial cheese, but personally, I don't think a board is complete without it. I do have a creamy Camembert and a lovely Wisconsin sharp cheddar, though," I continued, babbling because I had no idea what I was supposed to do.

Did I really just offer to make a cheeseboard while a woman

was performing battlefield surgery on top of my hundred-dollar cushions?

Yes, yes I had.

The man with the hazelnut eyes smirked at me, my ovaries feeling that smirk. "As much as I love a creamy Camembert and a sharp cheddar, I'll have to take a raincheck on that one, darlin'. But trust me, I'll hold you to it."

I swallowed roughly. The man's voice was silky caramel, but something else too. Something that didn't heat my blood but chilled it instead. As attractive as this man was, as quick as he was to a sarcastic quip, he was dangerous. Really fucking dangerous.

Just like the other two.

Well, not like the guy bleeding on my cushions. He was something else entirely. The large, hulking, older man shook his head once. I guessed that was a no, so I guessed it would've been considered rude if I walked to my freezer, unearthed my bottle of Teremana—because "The Rock" was all-around awesome, and he made epic tequila—and slammed four shots.

"I don't know your names," I said in lieu of slamming tequila. My eyes flickered to the blonde head, still bent over the man on my sofa.

"Mine is Freya," I offered.

"Freya," hazelnut eyes said as he considered me. "Suits you."

A blush heated my cheeks at the tenor of his voice. Pure sex.

"Swiss," he said after glancing between me and the bleeding man for a beat longer, eyes finally focusing back on me, sparkling with amusement.

"Elden," grunted the man sitting on the armchair who, upon closer inspection, looked like Jeffrey Dean Morgan. Everyone was partial to either Sam or Dean on *Supernatural*. And yeah, I wouldn't kick either of them out of bed although I was firmly on John Winchester's team.

So in other words, I was attracted to all three very different looking, very dangerous men in this room, and I officially needed to get laid so I didn't ogle at strange men in my living room who meant nothing but trouble.

Three different kinds of it.

"And the pussy who couldn't even stitch up his own stab wound, who was stupid enough to let himself get stabbed in the first place is Hades," Swiss continued.

"*Hades*?" I repeated, blinking at the man still glaring at me from my sofa in that bone-chilling way.

Swiss nodded. "Hotter than Hades, if you're into that kind of thing. Deadlier than the devil himself if you're not." He winked.

He sounded like he was joking, but the way Hades's glare promised that he was really fucking deadly told me Swiss's description was spot on. And I was into that kind of thing, *big time*.

"How in the fuck did you lift him?" Swiss asked, eyes flickering up and down my body in a way that was not at all sexual. It was more communicating my size—or lack of it—and Hades's considerable weight.

I shrugged. "I do Pilates."

His eyes bugged out. "Pilates? No shit." He paused thoughtfully. "Maybe I should get into Pilates."

My mind wandered off, creating images of this man doing Pilates of all things. Naked.

"Okay, I'm done," Sarah proclaimed, standing and snapping off her latex gloves.

I smiled thankfully at her for breaking my thoughts of all of these men doing naked Pilates. Then them doing naked things to me. At the same time.

"You did good," she added softly.

"Thank you," I said sincerely.

"Alright, we'd better get you home to bed so you can get a good night's rest tomorrow. We're exacting vengeance in the morning," Swiss said cheerfully, helping Hades off the couch.

Hades.

I watched the man shrug off Swiss, eyes still on me. They were no warmer than before.

"I can stay, though," Swiss continued. "If you're shaken up from tonight? I know I don't look like it, but *I* can rustle up a pretty good cheeseboard."

Although I didn't think it was possible, Hades's glare turned even more glacial. Even though the other two men were tall, muscled and pretty damn imposing, Hades looked like he could take them both on, stab wound and all.

I swallowed. "No," I replied quickly, looking from Swiss to Hades, then to Elden who still hadn't said a word but was watching the whole exchange intently.

"No," I repeated. "I've got Sirius." I pointed to the dog who was currently pressed up against Hades's leg, looking longingly up at the man who was currently staring daggers at the owner he was supposed to protect.

I was sure a murderer could waltz right in without so much as a growl from my dog as long as he scratched him behind his ears.

"I'm just glad you're okay ... Hades," I said tentatively, barely able to look the man in the eye.

His gaze didn't soften, not even a bit. Nor did he answer, he just nodded once, almost violently. I hadn't thought a gesture as benign as a nod could be violent, but Hades proved me wrong.

The nod, I surmised, was serving as a thank you for all that I'd done tonight since alpha male, biker badasses didn't seem to be able to verbalize things like thank yous. Though other alpha male, badass bikers could discuss cheeseboards, apparently.

Swiss tipped an imaginary hat. "Thanks for your services, darlin'. The club will be in touch for a more ... official thank you." He winked. "Sure I'll be seein' you around since I happen to be Fate's best customer. And now you're a friend of the club, so we'd obviously love for tonight's festivities to stay between friends." His tone was still light, friendly, playful. But something else lingered underneath it.

A threat.

My stomach dipped and all attraction to these men was suddenly doused. I nodded once.

Then they left.

I locked the door behind them, pressing my back against the door while hoping that I never saw them again.

CHAPTER TWO

Life returned to normal after Hades was stitched up on my sofa.

Hades.

Though I'd managed to get his blood out of the cushion and off my sofa—thanks to some hydrogen peroxide and ammonia—I was not able to rid my home of his presence. Of course, having a member of a deadly motorcycle gang bleeding in your living room was not something you just forgot. Then his other two ... friends? Brothers? Comrades? Demigods?

No, that was not something you forgot, especially with the roar of motorcycles being the norm whenever I was in town. But I did my best to get on with things since the club, Hades and his demigod brethren were definitely trouble, and trouble was not what I needed. Trouble was the one thing I was staying away from.

It was supposed to be a fresh start, this town. Somewhere Sirius and I would be able to put down roots after years of drifting from state to state like a fucking tumbleweed. And I liked it here. Loved it. I adored my little house in the desert, liked the fact that Julian at the coffee shop already knew my name, my order and my weakness for almond croissants. And there was the fact he was Australian, so he knew how to make coffee that was "nothing like that dirty water you Yanks drink". On top of that, it was the nectar of the gods and something similar to liquid cocaine. Since I hadn't done cocaine or any other kind of drug in five years, I was glad to have something that almost measured up to it since I worked long hours and didn't sleep often. Hence me having a slight cocaine problem five years ago. Well, it had started when one of the girls at the first club I'd worked at had given it to me when I started having a panic attack about going on stage.

It had helped.

A whole fucking lot.

It helped me take my clothes off in front of strangers and made the reality of what I was doing somewhat softer, less sordid, less humiliating. I was struggling with a lot of other crap then that made me uncomfortable in my own skin, made me clothed in self-hatred no matter whether I was dancing naked on a pole or not.

Now that I was clean—well, I still drank wine and tequila because I wasn't *that* well-adjusted—and I had gone to a therapist to unpack all of my issues, I could get up on stage sober. I could dance, I could take my clothes off and I could give sleazebags lap dances while feeling okay about myself. Good even. Powerful. I knew that my job wasn't what a lot of people in polite society thought to be acceptable, but a crap-ton of people from 'polite society' were also clients who needed an escape from the stifling confines of societal rules.

Two years ago, on a whim, I'd started a YouTube channel for no other reason than I wanted to share my experiences working as a stripper and because I wanted some kind of creative outlet. I hadn't expected to make a cent from it, but I'd done it right because that's just how I worked. I took an online course on filming, branding and editing. I spent a small fortune on a fancy camera and lighting then arranged an aesthetically pleasing background that suited my 'brand': a neon sign of a naked woman's outline dancing on a pole, a bookcase full of steamy, feminist romance books and a rack of the outfits I wore on stage.

I filmed ten videos before uploading a single one. Then I created a schedule and truly started. I talked about my favorite makeup that lasted through the night. How to get the perfect bikini line shave. My favorite perfumes. How stripping on my period always got me the most tips, because despite what they said about the act of menstruation being dirty and forbidden, some carnal part of them loved the fucking smell of blood against expensive perfume.

The title of my channel was 'Stripping Stripped.'

I had five thousand subscribers my first month, ten the month later. Now I was at almost half a million. I made good money off my videos. Uploading one every Wednesday, without fail, I earned thousands a month without any sponsorship. I talked a lot about sex, taking care of intimate parts of your body, how to be safe in the industry. I also did interviews with sex workers, cam girls and porn stars. So yeah, I was doing pretty fucking well.

I was proud of myself. I came from nothing, wasn't educated enough to go to college and I was full of emotional holes, so I used what I had. Now I earned more in a year than most fucking doctors. My car was paid off, and I bought my house with a fifty percent deposit. I invested in cryptocurrency because I knew that my body would inevitably start to sag, then I wouldn't be able to strip any longer. Or before that happened I wouldn't want to strip any longer. And eventually, I wouldn't be hot anymore, my subscribers would get bored with me or I'd get tired of doing videos around the same time my body started to sag.

Whichever came first, I would be taken care of. By me. No one else.

But for the time being, I continued to pull into Fate in my Range Rover, walked through the doors in Jimmy Choos, and shook my well-toned ass for money.

Despite being a small town, Garnett's local strip club was not seedy. The lighting was low, soft. Not to hide a crumbling and stained interior, but to go with the décor. Velvet sofas and armchairs in shades of black and gray. Lamps on every table. A bar with a marble countertop that gleamed. Doors leading toward private rooms which were even more expensively appointed—and constantly monitored to make sure that the girls were never in danger and never doing anything illegal.

Fate operated like a high-end club in L.A. or New York, not a small town in New Mexico. But this particular locale was in a unique location in the state, only forty-five minutes away from a luxury celebrity resort in the desert. And a lot of the celebrities who went there were sexual deviants with a lot of money and a lot of kinks. Not only was our club the closest, it was also the best.

And then there was the fact that the town was home to the New Mexico chapter of the Sons of Templar MC. Before I arrived here, I'd never heard of them. After my first night working, I knew exactly who they were. Muscled, dangerous alphas in leather.

Trouble.

But they were always respectful at the club, tipped like Rockefellers and never got drunk and violent. Surprising, considering what I expected from bikers.

I expected beer bellies, sloppy drunks, exploring hands and blatant misogyny. I'd been nervous around them, even though the other girls spoke so highly of them. The ones who had patronized the club had hit on me, but once I refused their advances, that was it. No anger, no violence, nothing I had come to expect from a man who was refused something he felt entitled to.

It was nice, refreshing.

It took effort to say no to these guys. Not a beer belly to be seen. But I had because I knew they were trouble.

They still tipped well, making conversation when I was around the club bar either before or after my shift. So I wasn't surprised to see the leather out of the corner of my eye while I was chatting to Kallum who was behind the bar. It was early, so I was hanging around the bar in a leather mini skirt and a leopard print halter top that was more of a bra than a top. It was quiet, which was how Kallum and I were able to have this conversation.

"Are you sure you don't mind?" he asked.

I frowned at him. "Mind? You'll be lucky to get him back when you come home."

He put his elbows on the bar and leaned forward, close enough so I could smell his aftershave over the fragrance of the club which was soft, sweet, enticing. Kallum's aftershave was spicy, leathery and pretty enticing too. If you were into that kind of thing. "What about Sirius? He won't feel territorial or protective?"

I laughed. "*Sirius?* Remember when you came to my house, and I texted you to let yourself in?"

Kallum grinned, turning his sculpted, masculine face boyish. "He was so scared he ran away and hid behind you," he recalled, his blue eyes twinkling.

I laughed at the memory. I'd gotten the black lab from a shelter three years ago, thinking he would be good protection. Until the second I got home and he hid underneath the bed for an hour after he was frightened by a bird that had found its way into the house. I loved the little coward.

Kallum's dog, Loki, was a small Papillion, an absolutely ridiculous pet for a muscled strip club owner to have, but he adored him, and so did everyone here.

Kallum was going to take care of his mother in Arizona for a couple of days after she had surgery, needing someone to watch Loki. Kallum was a good son. His mother had moved him and his two sisters from Puerto Rico after his father died, working three jobs to support them, to give them the kind of life she hadn't had. But despite working three jobs living in L.A., she hadn't been able to give her children the opportunities that came with wealth and whiteness. That had made Kallum angry. He'd wanted to provide for his mother and his sisters, be the man of the house. So he fell into a life on the wrong side of the law. He made a lot of money, but his mother had refused to take a cent and kicked him out of the house. He'd continued on that destructive path for several years after that.

He went to prison for armed robbery the day before his twenty-first birthday. His mother forgave him and visited him every day she could. She loved him unconditionally. And because he loved her unconditionally, he made a promise to never break the law again. He also made a promise to himself to figure out a way to allow his mother to retire. A legitimate way.

And he had. After being paroled, he worked his ass off so he could buy his first strip club. Then his second. Then his third. He made them classy, expensive and took care of his girls. His mother wasn't exactly thrilled at her son's choice of career—she'd hoped for a doctor or a lawyer, but that hadn't worked with his record— but it was within the law, and he paid for both of his sisters to attend college.

He told me all of this one night after closing, when we'd found ourselves drinking whisky together after I'd had a bad night with a grabby client. Then I'd told him a little of my life story.

We'd been close since then. Friends. Just friends. Because despite his bone structure, his muscles and his kind heart, I wasn't attracted to him in that way. Even if I was, I didn't sleep with my bosses. Ever. Plus, he was completely and utterly in love with Carmen, a dancer who had worked here for the last three years.

Carmen was a sweetheart, a knockout and totally oblivious.

Kallum's attention had been wholly on me for the duration of our conversation. Until about two seconds ago. Now his attention was focused in the direction of the front door, his eyes shuttered. His form stiffened, creating an air about him that reminded me of his violent past and his ability to turn into a dangerous man if the occasion called for it.

I turned, too, curious as to who could be entering the club this early in the night, setting Kallum off. We weren't technically even open yet, only a few lonely regulars nursing drinks quietly at their tables. Dante was on the door but was probably too busy trying to flirt with the dancers coming in the back entrance to check the front door.

And even if he had been at the door, he wouldn't have said no to this particular patron.

Hades.

Thinking his name was ice in my bloodstream.

It had been over a month since the first time I saw him. Since he was bleeding on my sofa. I figured that the overall drama of the situation made it starker in my mind. That my romantic and dramatic soul had changed the details, changed him to make him more attractive, less intimidating ... just *less*.

But he was more.

More everything.

Taller.

More imposing.

Tattoos etched into his skin yet leaping off it at the same time.

His shadow didn't follow him, it seemed to fucking *cower* before him. His hair was longer, curling up against the nape of his neck, mussed beautifully. I'd thought his skin was pale because of the blood loss, but it was exactly the same. Creamy, beautiful, flawless. Too fucking flawless. His features were all angles, his cheekbones high and sharp, eyes piercing and dangerous. Especially since he was wearing all black. A long black tee underneath his cut, one that hugged his body, hinting at the abs I knew were underneath. His shoulders were large, broad and attached to arms that were fucking perfection.

His jeans weren't tight, but they molded to his powerful thighs, his long legs, and the whole look was finished off with black biker boots. He looked like sin and sex.

And trouble.

I sucked in a harsh breath. His eyes were on me, unwavering with their intensity and unmistakable in their irritation. He did not want to be here, and he did not seem at all pleased by the sight of me. Which was unnerving for me, especially here, especially since I was wearing a barely-there mini skirt, a barely there top, and no bra. My hair and makeup were already done for the night, and I was going for a Bridget Bardot look, so my honey blonde hair was teased into voluptuous curls that tumbled down my back, my smoky eyes smudged to accentuate my blue eyes. I'd applied blush high on my cheeks so they looked rosy and plump. My lips were covered in a nude lipstick, seriously overdrawn so they looked like I had filler when really, I was much too scared of needles to take the plunge.

So yeah, I looked hot. It was my job to look hot, and I was used to men being impressed. It had me off kilter that Hades was not impressed by me, not in the slightest.

Kallum sighed behind me. "These fuckin' guys, think the rules don't belong to them," he muttered not loud enough for Hades to hear.

Kallum had a relationship with the Sons of Templar because they were some of our best customers. And because the Sons of Templar ran this town. If they didn't like him or the club, they'd make sure that he was shut down and run out of town. So he was cordial with them, friendly even. But once we'd become friends, once he trusted me, he began to make it known that he was not a fan of the Sons. At all. Which was unusual because most of the town loved them, even the most conservative of people. The MC kept the town clean, free from violence and drugs, and gave back to the community.

Des, the closest thing to a boyfriend I'd had in a while, even liked them, and his values were definitely conservative. Then again, he had no problem with my job, so maybe he wasn't the most conservative.

I wondered if the Sons reminded Kallum of his past life and that was why he didn't like them. Obviously, I didn't have much time to think on that since Hades had almost made it to us—his long legs making huge strides—and Kallum had his back up, ready to go into some kind of alpha male protection mode.

I reached out to grab his hand, to stop him from rounding the bar and having some kind of standoff, one that might result in him breaking his no violence edict he'd stuck with for about three years now. Three years ago, some client put his hands on Carmen in the parking lot as she was coming in. Didn't particularly like that she had been continually refusing his advances. Broke her nose. Kallum beat the guy half to death.

One of the Sons—Hansen, I think it was—happened to be around at the time. He'd been able to stop Kallum just before he literally beat the guy to death, then he had a little chat with the police, somehow convincing them not to press any charges. The man in question was transferred to a hospital out of town and never seen again. Come to think of it, maybe that was the weird, alpha male, pride-based reason that Kallum didn't like the Sons ... maybe he felt like he owed them something or whatever.

Not that that was something to be thinking about right now.

"It's okay," I whispered to Kallum, his gaze still plastered on Hades. "I ... I know him," I continued, my back burning from the gaze of the man I knew was now standing mere feet away.

Kallum's eyes flared, and he finally moved his attention to me. My hand was still on his. "You *know* him?" he repeated.

I nodded. I hadn't told a soul about what happened that night with Hades and the Sons. Not Des, not even Marilyn, my best friend here. Des would've gotten too worried about me, coming up with some crazy idea to come and move in to protect me, and I couldn't have that.

Marilyn would've caught the glint in my eyes, the shake in my voice, and known it was due to more than the trauma of the event itself. She was some kind of intuitive witch. The smallest tells and she could read my fucking mind. Even the things I didn't know I was thinking.

And I definitely couldn't have told Kallum what happened. He would've fired Dante because of it, and then I'd likely have Dante out for revenge. I didn't need any of that. It'd been better to keep my mouth shut.

"Yes, I know him," I said, louder this time. "Not in any kind of way you'd think," I added when his brows furrowed, and his hand flexed around mine. "I just helped him out with something once."

This did not quell the frown on Kallum's face, but I gave his hand one more squeeze then let him go, turning around before I lost my nerve.

Hades was standing there, watching. Watching the two of us. His jaw was sculpted from stone, his body held tight, eyes narrowed, fury etched in his features. Not just the irritation I'd seen as he walked in. No, fury.

At what, I didn't know. It was terrifying up close. Powerful enough to rattle my bones, making me feel as if the ground was slipping from underneath my feet. I swallowed, tilted my head up ever so slightly, then pasted on a crooked smile.

"Hey," I greeted him, intending to sound carefree, friendly and not at all terrified. Or turned on. Instead, my voice came out all breathy and weak.

He didn't reply to my greeting, not verbally, at least. His eyes once again flickered behind me, to where Kallum was still leaning against the bar, most likely watching.

"We're, um, not open yet," I explained after we'd been silent for what felt like a long time. It was uncomfortable, thick and loaded, that silence. I'd never felt like this around a man before. Unsure of myself. Of how to stand, how to fucking breathe.

"Not here for that," he replied with a clipped edge to his tone.

I gritted my teeth. He made it clear that he would never be here for that and it was structured as an insult. "Well, what can I do for you then, *Hades?*"

His name felt heavy, tasting metallic as it came out of my mouth. His eyes alighted with something as I said it. Something that made heat bloom in my stomach. But it was quickly gone, my body going rigid at the way his expression closed off.

His eyes flickered over me in a way that communicated that he found me lacking. It hurt, that dismissal. I'd strived my entire life not to let the opinions, gazes or insults of others affect me, to not let any of it chip away at my confidence. Considering where I'd come from and the life I'd lived, I thought I'd done really well at gaining my self-respect from inside rather than out. Men did not dictate whether or not I felt good about myself, I'd made sure of that.

Or I had until this very moment. Until this man.

"You look like a girl who likes to party," he said. The words themselves weren't technically an insult, but the way he said them was.

You look like a slut.

When tears prickled the backs of my eyes, I tilted my head up and bit the inside of my lip so they didn't fall. Another thing that I'd never let a man do: make me cry.

My hands were fists at my sides. I ached to scream at this asshole, tell him that feminism existed and that a woman could look however the fuck she wanted to look, could do whatever the fuck she wanted to do with her body and do it all without a man's opinion or input.

But instead, I took a deep breath. Then another one.

It was not smart to get into a screaming match in my place of work. The place I actually liked working at—despite Dante's presence. Kallum was a great boss. The girls were lovely. The clientele weren't all complete sleazebags, and the pay was aces. As cool as Kallum was, I doubted he would approve of me screaming at a member of the club made of the biggest tippers. Plus, he was watching carefully from behind the bar.

Beyond that, I figured screaming at someone in a Sons of Templar MC cut was not at all smart. Although I wasn't scared of them, of him, I wasn't stupid enough to think that wouldn't invite trouble.

And trouble was what I was meant to be staying away from.

So no screaming. I pasted on my biggest, sweetest, fuck you smile and bore my eyes right into his.

"Sure, I'm a girl who likes to party," I replied, my voice high, saccharine-sweet and the same brand of fuck you as my smile.

And I did love to party. He didn't need to know that my version of partying was dancing around in my underwear to the Spice Girls with a glass of cheap wine in one hand and a hairbrush/microphone in the other.

I did not need to correct his opinion of me, though. It didn't matter. That's what I was trying to tell myself, at least.

"The club has parties weekly," he continued. His arms were folded across his impressive chest, standing stock still.

I nodded. As a dancer in this club and a resident of this town, I knew all about the club parties. A couple of the girls danced at them. By invitation only. The club paid well, the members tipped even better. Plus there was the fact that the members were hot as balls and many of the girls I worked with were very keen to become an 'Old Lady.' It was an honorary title around here, despite the club being involved in a lot of illegal shit.

Allegedly.

As of yet, none of the girls had managed to get themselves into an Old Lady position, though many had managed to get themselves in a whole bunch of other positions that were apparently very pleasing.

Very fucking pleasing.

I did my best not to think about any of those positions with Hades in front of me. It helped that he was looking at me in a way that communicated he was not interested in me in that way. In the slightest. Which was unusual for me. I was an attractive woman, not vain, but it was a fact. I'd used that fact to make a living. Men, as a rule, were interested. Most men. But clearly not all men.

Sure, it could be that I wasn't Hades's type. But that did not explain why there was something hostile about the way he looked at me. As if something very particular about me pissed him off.

Which made no sense, since the only interaction we'd had pretty much involved me saving his life, covering up a crime and getting a stain on my sofa. If anyone should be acting pissed off right now, it should've been me.

But that wasn't really my style, and Hades was pretty damn intimidating. So I nodded placidly at his statement about the club parties, not sure whether it was a question or not.

A muscle in his jaw ticced at my nonverbal response. "You have a standing invitation to any one of these parties," he said, voice cold. As if it had been painful for him to extend the offer. "Obviously, you'd be paid well, as I'm sure you're aware. But because of your particular ... history with us, you'd be given a bonus of sorts."

A bonus. Otherwise known as a payoff. A bribe. I was insulted by the fact that he felt comfortable offering one to me, assuming I must've looked like a woman who was comfortable taking and spending blood money.

I tilted my head ever so slightly. "I'm not going to tell anyone."

Something moved in his eyes.

"About that night," I clarified.

"I know you're not going to tell anyone," he replied.

My stomach dropped. There wasn't any warning in his words. No threat there. Confidence. Surety. I wasn't going to tell anyone because if I tried to, they'd know.

"This isn't about that," Hades grumbled. It was very clear he didn't want to be having this conversation. "This is about the club showing our gratitude for what you did."

This was their way of saying thank you. His way of saying thank you. Without actually saying it. I wondered if it was impossible for men like him to verbally thank women like me—or women in general—for saving their asses when they were meant to be badasses who did the saving.

Maybe that's why he didn't like me. Because I made him feel emasculated or some such nonsense.

"You don't need to show me gratitude," I gritted out.

Hades's eyes glittered. "Yes, we do."

I bit my lip. There was iron in his tone. That was all I was going to get. Not a thank you that he was obviously incapable of giving since he was making it clear he didn't respect me. Though he had no right not to respect me, considering he didn't know anything about me beyond what I did for money, how I dressed, and, oh, that I was willing to help a bleeding stranger in the middle of the night.

That was his problem. His issue. This hostility had nothing to do with me. At least that's what I was desperately trying to tell myself. This guy was an asshole, and no matter how badly I wanted to knock him down for his lack of respect and genuine gratitude, it wasn't worth it.

I nodded. "Okay. Thank you for the offer," I said, forcing my voice to remain even, fighting back the tears that burned behind my eyelids.

"You'll come?"

My fingernails bit into my palms as I kept his gaze. As much as I wanted to ask him why he gave a fuck whether I was going to come or not, I kept my expression stoic.

"Sure, I'll come," I lied.

His eyes searched my face, as if he was measuring my words, sensing the lie. But then he nodded once and turned on his heel and left. I watched his large form retreat. Watched the reaper on the back of his cut move. Vowed that I would not get myself tangled up in the trouble connected with that cut, with a man like that. Which should've been easy, since he'd made it clear he wanted nothing to do with me.

HADES

She didn't come.

Fuck if I didn't look for her. Every fucking night.

I was a man who knew people. Considered myself pretty

fucking good at reading them. Better at killing and torturing them, of course. I thought I'd read Freya Barker pretty fucking well. Tits. Ass. Hair. Legs. Face. Not necessarily in that order. I'd noticed all of this while I was bleeding from a stab wound. Because I was a man, and as the majority of the population knew, I was a hot-blooded one. And a man, bleeding from a mortal wound or not, noticed the tits, ass, hair, legs and face on Freya Barker. Lucky for mankind, she liked to show a lot of skin, and her boobs were real. Beyond the fact she was a total fucking knockout, she was somewhat of a goof, talking when she was nervous.

I'd looked into her. The club had to assess the risk. Thirty-two, no record. Father serving time for murder. Mother living in a trailer park in Missouri, working at a supermarket and maintaining a healthy alcohol and drug addiction. Grandparents on her mother's side dead, grandparents on her father's side in that same trailer park. The only other family was an aunt in Arizona. Phone records and social media posts showed that they were close, the only member of her family she was close with.

Freya had finished high school but didn't go to college, left home the moment she turned eighteen, bouncing around the country ever since. Waitressing first then stripping. Earned a good living. A fucking great one, actually. Had a good amount of money in the bank, not much debt. Looked to be pretty knowledgeable about the stock market; even Wire had been impressed. Then there was the fact that she had half a fucking million subscribers to her YouTube channel. One where she talked candidly about the industry, promoted body positivity, female empowerment and makeup shit. Though I wasn't really interested in lipstick or the perfect bikini line shave, I watched four fucking hours of her videos.

Her home here in Garnett was the first place she'd ever bought. She'd had enough for a down payment for years but had only rented before. Looked to me like she was planning on settling here. Didn't want to make trouble. Her upbringing and choice of career made it likely she didn't trust the police.

The fear in her eyes at Fate told me she knew what would happen if she tried to narc—that fear had turned my cock hard in my pants which pissed me off. Every reaction I had to that woman pissed me off. I hadn't reacted to a woman in that way ... ever. The only reason I fucked was for release. So I could exert control over the woman. There was never any connection. I didn't want any pussy to control me. Most importantly, I didn't want anything to lose. Anything or anyone that someone else, our enemies, could use to hurt me.

My brothers, the ones with women—they were happy. They were glad as all fuck to be controlled by pussy. I didn't envy them. Not one fucking bit. I wasn't wired that way. I didn't have goals in my life beyond keeping my brothers alive and killing those who threatened my family. I knew I wasn't going to grow old. Wasn't built for it. That didn't bother me. I didn't have a passion for life, but death, pain, violence ... I had a fuck of a lot of passion for that.

But not life, and certainly not women.

Until her.

"I'm going to take care of you."

They echoed through my skull, those words. Followed me into my dreams. Nightmares. At no time in my fucking life had anyone ever said shit like that to me. No one had spoken to me with such conviction, with a tiny hand on my chest, with both fear and resolve in her eyes.

I'd barely been able to sleep since that night. Pain didn't mean shit, wasn't what kept me up. I was going fucking crazy thinking about her. But I knew it was best to keep away from her. Despite what she did for a living, she was innocent, I could see that. I could fucking taste it. The monster inside of me craved to claim that innocence. To fucking ruin it. But I'd held fast.

Until I hadn't been able to stop myself.

Until I went into that fucking club, saw her bent over the bar, seeing those legs. Those fucking legs. They seemed to go on forever, the heels she was wearing giving her almost another six inches. Then the skirt. The one that was short enough so I could see the cleft of her ass when I walked in. My cock had hardened immediately, and I'd had a near-feral need to surge forward, lift that skirt to her hips, rip off her panties and surge inside of her.

Of course, I hadn't done that. I might've been a monster, but I wasn't that much of a monster. I'd never touch a woman against her will. But something told me, something about the way her eyes had moved over me that night, that she wasn't completely unwilling.

Still, I didn't do that. Beyond that, Kallum would've tried to kill me if I had. And then I'd have killed him. Which I didn't want to do. He wasn't a bad guy. Or he had been a bad guy, and he was trying his hardest to get close to good. Closest he could get was owning a strip club. One where he treated the girls fucking well, paid them better and made sure they didn't get caught up in anything dangerous.

So pretty fucking good in my world.

I didn't want trouble with him. Not until I saw him with her. Saw the casual way she spoke to him, smiled at him. Saw her put her fucking hand on his. Then I saw red. Which made no fucking sense. She wasn't mine.

Except she fucking was.

And she had her hand on another man. She looked like fucking sin. Skin showing. A lot of fucking skin. A lot of fucking hair. A lot of fucking makeup. All ready to dance in front of other men, show them everything, make them imagine fucking her. That didn't bother me. What bothered me was that I was imagining fucking her too, and I didn't want to imagine it. I wanted to do it.

I had no fucking clue why I went to Fate, why I didn't stay away. Because I already knew I wasn't going to let myself take her. Ruin her. But I wanted more of her. Wanted to watch her dance, wanted to imprint it in my fucking brain. Because I was a masochist.

I'd been sure she'd come to one of our parties. Fuck, all of the bitches working at the club were chomping at the bit to get an invitation to dance for us. Either for the money or for the prospect of fucking one of the brothers, becoming an Old Lady.

Freya was not like those other bitches. Because she didn't fucking come. And it drove me crazy. I was close to crushing the glass of whisky in my hand, sitting in the corner, the music thumping, women dancing, people fucking. None of it even penetrated.

I didn't go to her again, though. My resolve stayed.

For now.

CHAPTER THREE

THREE WEEKS LATER

FREYA

I was making a mistake.

That much was clear as I parked my car in the lot of the Sons of Templar clubhouse. I'd almost turned around when I'd stopped at the gates and a young badass wearing a prospect cut had stopped me to ask me my business. I'd almost put on a confused face and asked him for directions, told him that I was an Uber driver... anything to get me out of here and safely back home.

But the problem was, I didn't feel safe at home. Not anymore. Not after what had just happened at the grocery store. Or, more aptly, in the grocery store parking lot.

Going to the police wasn't an option. It wasn't smart, getting the law involved in the Sons of Templar's business. Plus, I was pretty sure that the Sons owned the cops here, so even if I had gone to them, it wouldn't have done any good. And I sensed things would've gotten even worse for me then. My knowledge of the

Sons of Templar had been pretty sparse before I'd inadvertently gotten tangled up with them.

These past months, I'd subtly—or not at all subtly—pumped the girls at work for all kinds of information about the infamous Sons of Templar.

What I'd learned didn't exactly make me feel better about somehow being attached to them, even though it was against my will.

"You can do this, Freya," I whispered, gripping the steering wheel and looking over to the clubhouse.

The parking lot was relatively empty, which I assumed was normal considering it was four in the afternoon on a Thursday. There was a garage to my left which was apparently the best in town, a garage I hadn't used to get my car serviced because I'd heard about all of the mechanics and how they were members of the club. How they were sex on a stick and that most of them were single. And I also had it on good authority that they were life-changing in bed.

Trouble for me.

I had a weakness for attractive men who knew how to fuck. My past meant I had a very complicated relationship with sex. Through a lot of therapy, I'd become as right with it as I ever would be. I was a sexual being. An extremely sexual being. I loved sex, and in almost every relationship I'd been in, I'd wanted it more than the man. It had played havoc on my self-esteem for a while, thinking there was something wrong with me, that I was bad in bed or that men could sense that there was something wrong with me, deep in my bones.

Until Carlos, a short-lived fling when I'd gone on vacation on my own to Puerto Rico. He'd shown me there was nothing at all wrong with my appetite for sex and showed me how much he appreciated it.

It seemed that the majority of men—or the majority of the men I'd dated—loved to pretend they were these testosterone-filled sex maniacs, but most were too lazy, too insecure or too ... whatever to do the legwork. So to speak.

I hadn't found another man like Carlos. Not as attractive, sexual, selfless and gorgeous as that man. I'd seen the Sons around, and I knew I wouldn't be able to control myself around them— especially since I'd gone without sex for the longest time in recorded history these past few months—and the Sons of Templar would lead me down a dark path.

But despite going to a mechanic in the next town over, I'd found myself here anyway.

Before I could lose my nerve, I got out of the car, my heels clicking on the concrete. There was a low hum of music filtering across the parking lot, coming from the garage bays. I didn't look over there, though I felt the eyes of whoever was working there on me as I walked.

The Sons' clubhouse wasn't exactly imposing, but I felt myself being swallowed in its shadow as my shaking hand fastened around the door handle.

The first thing I noticed was the smell. Large parts of me figured it would smell like leather, sex, body odor and cheap whisky. Maybe gunpowder too and the blood from whoever they'd been torturing that day. My imagination had run wild, turning them into violent villains.

But it smelled faintly of disinfectant, lemon scented. The good kind, I knew because I was definitely a Monica when it came to cleaning; I'd tried all of the different cleaners on the market, searching for one that did the job, didn't burn my lungs as I used it, that wasn't terrible for the environment, and gave off that beautiful 'clean smell' that didn't clash with my scented candles.

The smell—the pleasant one—was not the only thing that surprised me. I'd also expected bottles, maybe a few rogue condom wrappers, loud music, gun parts on the coffee table and men in leather everywhere. It was clean, I noticed that first, but before I could take stock of the room, my attention moved to the only man standing in the room.

He had been leaning against a bar, head bent down to the phone in his hand. That head jerked upward as I walked into the room.

There was no escaping now.

"Freya, I knew you'd come eventually. Granted it took a little longer than usual, but I've been haunting your dreams, haven't I?" As he spoke, Swiss grinned at me with fire in his eyes. "Let me guess, you couldn't stop thinking about me, couldn't sleep, couldn't eat and just had to find your way here so you could get some peace? Although that's the last thing you'll get with me."

In any other circumstance, that fire might've done something to me, might've spread to all my limbs. As it was, everything down to my fingertips and my toes was ice cold.

Swiss being the perceptive badass that he was, noted my demeanor immediately, and his smile disappeared, causing his features to change completely. It was chilling, to my bones, to see that transition—he was now a cold-blooded killer.

I actually backed away a couple of steps instinctively as he advanced forward, but he was much too quick, so his hands were grasping my chin before I could even try to escape.

"What happened, darlin'?" he asked, his voice low, menacing, deadly.

His eyes sucked me in, pools of inky black rage. Rage at what, I didn't know. I didn't know what he saw in my eyes to act this way, all alpha male and protective. No one had touched me. There were no physical signs to hint at what had happened. There was something inside of this man that could see my fear, that was trained to see it, utilize it, maximize it, maybe.

I swallowed, unsure of whether I'd made a terrible mistake coming here. If what had happened had occurred in any other city, I likely would've packed up everything and left. I was practiced at doing that, could have my whole life in my car before the sun went down. But Garnett was meant to be different. I liked it here. I liked my boss, the women I worked with, I had friends. I had a coffee shop where they knew my name, order and pastry preference. I had roots here, and I didn't want to yank them out of the ground before they'd had a chance to grow.

Looking into the dark and intense eyes of a definitely dangerous biker, it remained to be seen how big of a mistake I'd made, but it was very clear that he was not going to let me leave. Not now.

The warmth of his fingers against my chin was comforting, grounding, his large imposing presence making me feel secure and a lot less vulnerable than I'd felt about two seconds ago. I'd made my choice, so I had to commit.

"I, um, I was at the grocery store and..."

I trailed off, my mind skimming over what had happened. It seemed detached from my life, as if it hadn't just happened fifteen minutes ago.

The gun barrel was cold against my temple. Shockingly cold. Though the temperature of the gun was not what I should've been shocked by, it should've been the fucking gun at my temple.

I got plenty shocked by that too.

And the fact that it was broad daylight, yet this guy did not seem at all worried about that. And this was not a regular grocery store parking lot; this was a Trader Joe's parking lot which was almost always chaotic, with Lululemon moms and their screaming children, gym bros with their noisy cars. Not men with guns.

"Don't scream or I'll blow your brains out," he said from behind me. His hand was on my hip. The grip was tight, bordering on painful. It was invasive, sinking into my bones, intimate and sickening.

My heart was hammering in my throat, bones vibrating. My trunk was open, obscuring me from the view of the entrance to the supermarket. No one was around, the lot desolate this time of day, which was why I liked shopping at this time. It wasn't busy, aisles weren't clogged. I loved to take my time when I was grocery shopping, leisurely walking through the aisles, looking at the new cookies and coffee creamer flavors, deciding if I was going to be honest with myself and buy five bottles of wine or pretend I wasn't a huge wino and that two would last me the week. Other times, I'd be really honest with myself and buy a whole case of 'Three Buck Chuck.' I'd spend a good ten minutes at the flower display, figuring out what my mood would be for the week.

Grocery shopping was meditative for me. And it was being ruined by some asshole with a gun.

I would've been pissed off had I not been paralyzed with fear.

"I have cash," I whispered, my voice scratchy as I stared at the parking lot, wishing for this to be the moment when a police cruiser drove in. For anyone to drive in.

"I don't want your fuckin' cash," the man with the gun hissed in my ear, his grip tightening around my hip.

His breath smelled like mint, and he had a hint of an accent. Spanish, maybe. If I survived this, I'd need all the details I could glean. I didn't dare try to turn to see his face, but I glanced down and glimpsed snakeskin cowboy boots on the outsides of my bright pink, spike-heeled, ankle boots. If I had to fight, I might've been able to bring my heel down on those boots, hopefully piercing through the flesh.

But we weren't there yet.

I took a breath. Then another. "What do you want then?" I asked evenly.

My past flashed before my eyes with his hand at my hip, with his breath at my neck, the gun giving him power he didn't deserve. Another man taking away my agency, claiming the ability to damage me forever.

If he tried to take me, communicated for a moment that he had intentions of taking more things that weren't his, I'd fight. To the death.

"We want you to give your boyfriend a message," he hissed.

Confusion cut through my terror. "My boyfriend?" I repeated.

"Don't play dumb, bitch." The gun pressed into my temple harder now.

Bile crept up my throat.

"We know you're a Sons whore," he spat, mouth at my ear.

My teeth sank into the flesh of my lip hard enough to dry blood. I forced myself to stay silent, to not correct him on that statement. This obviously had something to do with the Sons of Templar, they were the reason for the gun at my head, but it was likely they were also the reason that the gun hadn't been fired.

"You need to tell them to back off the Segadores Sombríos, or we will finish what Fernandez started." His lips went to my neck, his breath hot and rancid.

My knees threatened to buckle.

"And, baby, we'll make you wish you were dead before we kill you," he whispered.

I prepared myself to lift my foot, to spear it into his boot no matter the consequences. But then his lips left my neck, and I calmed ever so slightly. "You turn around before you hear my car leave this lot, I'll come back and spray your brains all over the concrete."

Then the weight of the gun was gone from my temple, and there was the low click of his boots against the concrete. The ones that he'd promised would be covered with my brains if I turned.

"I don't know how serious he was about that part," I told Swiss, back in the Sons of Templar clubroom after wrenching myself from the flashback that I'd sunk in to while telling him what happened. "I quite like my brains inside my skull and being alive in general, so I didn't turn. But he was driving a 2019 Chevrolet Camaro Yenko. What insecure assholes with small dicks tend to drive, in my opinion."

Swiss, who had been doing the brooding badass stare thing in varying degrees throughout my recount of what happened, smirked. Just a little.

"You noticed the make, model and year of the car the man who had just threatened your life was driving?" he clarified. His voice was low and husky with a hint of teasing to it, but it was mostly still low and deadly.

It relaxed me ever so slightly, so I smiled weakly. "I know cars. My dad taught me."

Thinking of my father made me feel prickly and wrong. Inexplicably, I wanted my father. Which was crazy since not once in the past ten years had I thought of him fondly. Fuck, I wasn't sure if I'd ever thought of him fondly past seven years old when I realized what kind of man my father was. But I loved him. Even after all these years, even after everything he'd done, I loved him. But I had to do so from a distance, because if I let my father too close to me, I'd get burned. Like flying too close to the sun or something.

But in that moment, his presence, the smell of cheap cigarettes, cheaper whisky and some Old Spice, would've calmed my thundering heart in a situation so foreign and uncertain.

"What the fuck is going on?"

Thoughts of my father dissipated, and my attention went from dark eyes to frosty, icy ones. Ones that belonged to a beautiful, pale, furious face.

Hades was standing mere feet from us, presumably having walked in from the hallway behind him. His eyes flit between me and Swiss. More accurately, Swiss's hand which was still on my chin. Swiss saw this, too, and no doubt felt the fury rippling through the air, telling us that everything about Hades was dangerous right now. My stomach dropped and goosebumps peppered my skin from the intensity of it all.

Swiss grinned wickedly.

I stepped back immediately, out of the man's grasp and farther away from Hades whose eyes were now firmly on me.

This was a bad idea. This was a really fucking bad idea.

"It isn't Friday," Hades said, voice tight, thick.

Something inside of me unfurled at his words, the tone, the flatness to them. At the possession in his gaze, a possession he wasn't entitled to. There was a familiarity there, but there was a fury too. Every time he looked at me, it was like he was pissed I was even breathing. Forgetting that he might not even be breathing if it wasn't for *me*.

Then I remembered the way he spoke to me at Fate, the way he'd made me feel. Then I remembered I was pissed off at this guy.

"No, it's not Friday," I agreed, my voice suddenly snippy, no longer shaky and weak. It felt good, made me feel a lot less like a victim. "I'm not here to party with you or get paid *handsomely* by you to take off my clothes. I'm here because somehow, for whatever reason, some of your friends—well, not friends considering the man in question was holding a gun to my head—wanted me to pass along a little message. And in case it's not obvious, I don't like being a messenger, and I certainly don't like having a gun held to my head in a Trader Joe's parking lot because now I'm here instead of at home which means my cookie butter ice cream is going to be melted."

I sucked in a huge breath, having just said all of that without pausing to inhale or exhale. Because I was on such a roll, I did not notice the way the air had completely and utterly changed, hadn't seen the tightness that marred Hades's features, how his fists clenched at his sides and his eyes darkened the more I said.

"Someone held a gun to your head," Hades stated, his voice even, the words coming out slowly as if through gritted teeth.

I nodded, unable to speak.

Luckily, Swiss was here, looking between Hades and me, still smiling despite the subject matter and the air of menace shimmering around Hades.

"They wanted to deliver a message to us," he offered. "Think it was Segadores Sombríos, trying to scare us off the deal."

Hades did not take his eyes off me. "If they were trying to scare us off the deal, why in the fuck did they threaten Freya?" he snapped. I wasn't sure if he was still talking to Swiss since he was still staring at me.

"Because for whatever reason, they thought I was sleeping with someone here," I explained before Swiss could speak for me.

Hades's eyes darkened even further, if that was even possible. "Are you having sex with someone here?"

I froze at his tone, at the threat threaded through those words.

"No," I replied, proud of my voice for not shaking. "Of course I'm not sleeping with anyone here."

"Unfortunately," Swiss muttered.

He must've had a death wish, considering the look Hades directed at him. He only grinned wider at his death glare.

"I don't know why they thought I was connected to anyone here since I'm definitely *not*," I added, interrupting the badass stare off and hopefully stopping Hades from coming to blows with his brother. "Now that I've delivered the message, do with it what you will. I'd appreciate it if I could shop in peace and not get a visit like that in the future. So the next time you talk to this guy, if you could communicate my *lack* of connection to the club, I'd really appreciate it." My gaze swung between Hades and Swiss, both of whom were now looking at me. Swiss was no longer grinning flat out; he was smirking but with something deadly in his eyes.

Hades was nowhere near grinning, and the second my eyes met his, I darted my gaze away like a coward.

I cleared my throat. "Now if you'll excuse me, I've got some ice cream to try to save."

I turned to leave, even though the prospect of leaving the compound and the scary, muscled macho men with guns to go back to my empty house in the middle of nowhere with my cowardly dog was somewhat nauseating.

But I forgot that I was in a room with two alpha male, badass bikers with too much testosterone. Both of them moved, Hades was quicker, blocking my path to the exit with his large form. I held my breath as he moved close to me. Almost too close. Not close enough. His body wasn't pressed up against mine, but he was close enough for me to feel his heat, and there I was, thinking he was carved completely from stone.

He was just as handsome as I remembered. Even more handsome, considering how pissed off he looked. How deadly.

There was something seriously wrong with me.

"You're not going anywhere," he informed me. "Not alone."

I stared at him, my heart echoing through my ears. "Excuse me?"

"I need you to get the location of our friends. Bring them in. I'll be back in the morning to deal with them," Hades instructed, again staring at me while speaking to Swiss.

Swiss nodded then winked at me. "Good luck, darlin'. "Don't worry, we'll take care of you."

He left on that statement, one that sounded like an omen, a threat and a double entendre all in one.

"He touch you?"

My eyes darted back to Hades, whose eyes were running over the length of my body as if he was looking for a gunshot wound I'd failed to mention.

I opened my mouth to tell him no, I hadn't been touched. Then I remembered that grip on my hip. The way it had gone from borderline painful to suggestive of something else entirely.

It hadn't gone further than that, but it could've. He was capable of doing that to me. Confident in using the fear of rape to render me powerless.

I'd thought that Hades couldn't descend any further into a murderous glower. I was wrong. The atmosphere changed with my silence. With what he took from it.

"He fucking *touched* you?" he murmured, barely a whisper. But every word was pointed, every letter a dagger.

"No," I responded quickly. "Or not really. I just, he just..." I swallowed. "I'm sure my hip won't even bruise, but he made it clear that he was more than willing to do ... more," I said lamely, embarrassed by the way my voice sounded weak and full of holes.

The fury in Hades's irises was unyielding, deep enough to drown in. His entire body was held so taut, he was almost shaking.

"He won't touch you. Ever," Hades replied. Another oath. One that had goosebumps erupting on my forearms, on my insides. "No one will."

I didn't have time to unpack that statement and all of the undertones it contained because Hades spoke again.

"I'll follow you home."

I stared at him. "Follow me home?"

He nodded once, the simple gesture somehow violent. "You think I'm lettin' you go home alone after this? The only other option is you staying here."

My eyes went around the room. There was nothing wrong with it. In fact, it was actually much nicer than I'd expected it to be. I hadn't had a chance to properly catalog the interior. You walked right into the living area, with couches scattered in the middle of the room in varying shades of dark brown and in surprisingly good condition. I remembered that almost the entire club had been murdered a year or two ago. They would've been new, the sofas, since this place was the sight of a massacre.

Dread flooded through me at that thought.

Someone had gone to great lengths to erase that past. The sofas were cluttered with pillows, not overly masculine, all in shades of brown and black with geometric designs on them. There were even a couple of chunky throws arranged over the back of the sofa. The coffee table had coasters stacked neatly, some paper-backs and even a candle. Over in the corner, there was a pool table, a small stage and a stripper pole. There was a bar at the back of the room, the wooden countertop gleaming, various bottles arranged on the shelves behind it. To the right was another room, double doors closed with a wooden placard with the word 'Church' carved in it.

The place was very clean, almost stylish, definitely masculine, and even a little endearing to me, but the thought of staying some-where this foreign was terrifying. Something horrible had happened to me tonight, leaving me feeling uneven and a little sick. I needed to be around familiar things, in the place I'd turned into a home. I wanted my dog. But I also did not want to be alone.

Hades was solving that problem.

Maybe I should've asked more questions. Maybe I should've fought this. No matter what kind of physical safety he offered, I knew on some level, this man was my destruction. I sensed that letting him come home with me, allowing him to fill the role of scary protector guy, was going to do something, change something that could never be undone.

"No, home," I whispered. "I want to go home."

He nodded once then stepped aside for me to walk out the door. I did. Then he followed me out.

CHAPTER FOUR

Hades helped me with my groceries. Well, actually, he refused to let me carry a single one, somehow performing the act of bundling them all in his strong and capable arms before depositing them on my kitchen counter. This was done after he'd had me unlock the house so he could do a 'walk through', whatever that was. I was ordered to stay outside while he did that. Because I rarely did as I was ordered, I followed him. As did Sirius.

I got a glower for following him. Sirius got a rub on the head.

It was unnerving, watching Hades prowl through my home, looking for what, I wasn't sure. He went into every room. It was an invasion, but it was also something else. I'd never be able to look at a corner of my home again without seeing Hades's shadow. It was extremely strange, to watch this man in his leather cut—underneath of which was a gun holster, full-on like the ones they wore in moves. I'd peeked as he'd moved through the house—with his imposing presence, muscles and a general air of danger.

My house was unapologetically girly. In a classy, understated way, I personally thought. When I'd first moved here, I put a lot of money into renovations. I'd also paid a good amount of money to make sure the renovations were actually done within my time frame. I'd lucked out, since Kallum 'knew a guy' who also 'knew a bunch of guys' who did good work and turned up when they said they would.

The house itself had a beautiful exterior. It was long and wide, a circular driveway in front of it complete with a fountain in the middle. There were flowerbeds all along the front of the house, flowerboxes underneath the windows. All had been empty when I bought it but were now thriving. You walked up steps to the double doors which opened to a hallway. To the left were my bedroom, an office, a spare room and a filming area. To the right were the doors to the laundry, a bathroom and then down some steps was the open plan living area, a huge kitchen at the back with a butler's pantry and a giant island. There was a formal dining area to the left, and then my living area. French doors opened onto a patio with an outdoor fireplace and a seemingly endless desert.

Yes, the bones of my house were breathtaking. The inside had been bachelor central, so I'd had to make a lot of changes to suit my style. I'd never had the money or the home to do this with, so I went a smidge crazy.

Which meant that I had a pink bathroom. A shower tiled floor to ceiling complete with a waterfall showerhead in brass—all of my fixtures were in brass—and the claw sink was also pink. My hand towels were white, cost a bomb and were gorgeous. A Heartleaf plant was snaking down from a ledge I'd had built especially for the plant. There was a standalone, vintage tub that had been outrageously expensive but was worth every cent since I used it at least three times a week.

I'd even splurged and given myself a princess vanity with a large, circular Hollywood mirror lit up with lights and a plush, velvet chair in front of a desk full of perfectly organized perfumes, lotions and makeup brushes. The adjacent drawers were packed full of makeup.

Then, of course, what was supposed to be a third bedroom was my filming room. Lights, camera and background setup to perfection. I'd purchased a comfortable armchair for when I was editing and a desk with two computer screens where I worked the stock market and edited videos.

The rest of the house was just as girly and glamorous with a Bohemian edge. Even though I hadn't been here long, I'd trusted my gut in thinking I'd found a place to put down roots, so I'd thrown everything I had into making this a home. I'd entertained, had parties, dinners. So I was used to having people in my home, loved it, in fact.

Until right this second.

Until Hades, wearing all black, stood in my pink bathroom looking for intruders, murderers, hitmen.

Because of how I'd grown up, I threw myself into this house, making it mine. So much so that I'd put all of myself into my house. Hades walking through it was like him going through my underwear drawer or seeing me naked. I was suddenly uncomfortable, feeling self-conscious about what conclusions he was drawing about me from my pink bathroom or the red, neon light in my office that read 'Bad Bitch.'

Then there was the fact that since I was following him around during the 'walk through', I was in my bedroom with him. Alone. Not counting Sirius.

I knew I should've been thinking about the people who may or may not be hiding in my house, but all I was thinking about was Hades being in my room, a room where there was a bed, one I'd masturbated in thinking about him for the past month.

My heart suddenly became very loud, very rapid, my palms starting to sweat, and I suddenly had trouble stringing a thought together. Fortunately, Hades was not interested in making conversation of any kind, being solely focused on his job. Whatever that was.

After the 'walk through' I followed back to the front door, him on the outside, me on the inside, without a word said about the décor, not even a raised eyebrow. I'd been so caught up by having Hades in my house, I hadn't even thought of the logistics of what tonight would entail. He'd said he was going to be here all night, but where exactly was 'here'? On my sofa? Or in my office on the daybed that pulled out?

In my bed?

Was he going to demand some kind of sexual payment for the protection detail?

My stomach dropped even thinking about it.

"I'll be out here all night," Hades jerked me out of my fantasy, nodding to where his bike was parked beside my car.

Something inside of me loved the way they looked together, despite the situation I'd found myself in. I knew what the barrel of a gun felt like against my temple because of the man who owned that bike.

However, I had also been closer to death tonight than I ever had before in my life. And although I'd thought near-death experiences made you want to hide in a dark room with a bottle of wine while re-watching *Gilmore Girls,* right now, I really wanted to be fucked by the guy with the cheekbones, the muscle and the ability to kill. Plus, he just so happened to be standing in my driveway.

"You don't have to stay out here." My voice sounded slightly husky, need throbbing between my legs.

Hades clenched his fists at his sides, his brows narrowing and his eyes darkening. I knew he did not miss the sex in my tone and the invitation in my eyes.

Hades didn't answer for a long moment, the tension building in the air, my body taut and coiled, desperate for release. Desperate to give up control to someone. To him. To submit to this man completely.

For a second, he looked like he was going to do just that, right there in the driveway, and I would've let him.

"Yes, I do," he refuted, ice coating his words, his features closing up. "Get back in the house, Freya"

That was an order. It might've even been some kind of threat. Danger threaded through his tone, and not the kind I wanted right now. Not the kind that I could handle.

I held onto his gaze for a moment longer, then I turned on my heel and walked inside. I locked the door. Not because I didn't trust Hades, but because I didn't trust myself. I had a cold shower then I snuggled up with Sirius, a bottle of wine, a family-sized bag of peanut butter M&M'S and *Gilmore Girls*. And I got up at least four times during the night. I'd left my floodlights on, to make sure he wasn't sitting in the dark, even though I got the feeling he might've liked that.

Each time I peeked out my window, he was there, smoking, leaning against his bike. There wasn't a gun in his hand, but I knew he had one. Every time I peeked out my window, his head turned in my direction and we locked eyes from across the courtyard. Like a scared schoolgirl, I darted back to my bed.

Despite the man I suspected Hades was, despite what had happened tonight, when I finally did fall asleep, I slept better than I had in recorded memory. With the enforcer of the Sons of Templar in my driveway, armed and ready to kill someone.

He was gone when I woke up, a young, attractive man covered with a blond crew cut, tanned skin and muscles now there. Not a tattoo to be seen. He looked more like a J-Crew model than a biker. His name was Anderson, he was twenty-two, had a nice smile and chatted about his pregnant girlfriend, Hannah, over the coffee and pancakes I made for the two of us. They were literally night and day, Anderson and Hades. The bright-eyed, young man with an easy smile and the brooding sex god who spelled destruction.

I went about my day as usual after breakfast, including a walk with Sirius that Anderson accompanied me on, chatting with me the entire time, telling me how he got himself involved with the

Sons. Apparently, he'd wanted to join since he was in high school, being a local here and idolizing the Sons like the majority of teenage, wannabe badasses in the area.

He came from a good family who sounded normal and who were horrified over their only beloved son wanting to join a motorcycle club. They'd convinced him to go to college, get out of Garnett, get a degree and see if four years in the real world would change his mind.

He came out of college with a business degree as well as a renewed hunger to join the Sons. His parents were not happy. But they also loved their son, and he quite obviously loved them.

The more I got to know him, the more I liked him. Which was why I really hoped that whoever had made the threat last night did not choose to try to make good on said threat and get this kid—well, badass biker man to most people but when compared with the other Sons, somewhat of a kid—killed or maimed.

As it was, I got my wish.

The day passed without incident, and I got ready for work while Anderson was playing with Sirius or 'walking the perimeter' or eating the banana muffins I'd made earlier.

I waited for some kind of comment about my job from him. Even the best of guys had something to say, an eyebrow raise or something glazing over their eyes when they figured out I was a woman they didn't have to work to get her clothes off of. Not when it was what the woman in question did for a living. Somehow, figuring out a woman was a stripper, brought out the inner sleazebag in almost every man.

So I waited. For some kind of gaze up and down the outfit I was wearing to work—a skintight, white, high necked, sleeveless dress that molded to my every curve and would have shown the label on whatever underwear I was wearing if I hadn't found a very special, barely there pair. I was not a woman who went sans panties. I actually had no idea how women did that. To each their own, of course, but even if I had been that kind of woman,

I wouldn't have been able to go without panties unless I wanted everyone to know my waxing preferences. And unlike a lot of women in my profession, I did still have some hair ... down there.

Anderson did look at me when I emerged from my bedroom at nine that night. His eyes trailed up my snakeskin stiletto boots to the sliver of skin between the boots and the hem of my dress. Then up my body, to my face where they stopped. There was no inner sleazebag though, not even a drop.

Sure, there was a definite kind of male appreciation, but it was detached, and it disappeared from his face in just a handful of seconds. This was a decent man who was most definitely committed to his pregnant girlfriend.

I liked that for her. And for him.

"Ready to rock and roll?" he asked.

I tilted my head. "It's nine and you've been here since I woke up which means you've been my bodyguard for the past twelve hours. Now you're going to a strip club with me where I don't get off until at least one usually two. If not three. And you have a pregnant girlfriend at home. I really don't think you need to come with me."

Even though I'd had an armed, unfamiliar man following me around all day, routinely 'checking the perimeter of my house', I'd all but forgotten I'd had a gun held to my head yesterday. Yesterday.

The power of the alpha male biker.

In the daylight, after a night's sleep, I wasn't afraid of whoever it was that was possibly coming after me. The man with the gun had wanted me to deliver a message. I'd done so. The Sons obviously weren't planning on listening to the message, which meant I was in danger. Maybe. I didn't ask much about it.

I wasn't sure whether that was stupid or naïve of me. Or maybe it was stupid or naïve of me to think a bunch of bikers—albeit sexy, brooding bikers with perfect cheekbones—were going to keep me safe. It was definitely stupid to trust them with my life. But that's what I was doing, wasn't it?

Anderson's boyish face turned hard. "I *do* need to go with you," he countered, his voice suddenly two octaves deeper and a heck of a lot more dangerous. "I'm willing to do anything for the club, to make sure no one hurts it or you. Everything about him told me he was resolute. Devoted. Blindly dedicated to his club. Or cult, since it seemed to have followers willing to do anything and everything without question.

That should've worried me, scared me, made me more cautious. But instead, it intrigued me. Parts of me felt inexplicably jealous of them. It was a family. One that was willing to fight and die for one another.

"Besides," Anderson continued. "I'm only following you to Fate. Hades is takin' over once we get there."

My heart stopped.

"Hades is meeting us at Fate?" I repeated.

He nodded once.

"He's going to be there, at the club, the whole night?" I clarified.

Anderson nodded again, but this time, I swear I saw a hint of a smirk. "The whole night," he confirmed.

Fuck.

———

"Baby, are you okay?" Marilyn asked, looking at me in the mirror. We were sitting side by side, touching up our makeup before we went on stage.

The music was thumping outside as Carmen finished out her set. I was next, and my hand was shaking as I applied a fresh coat of blush.

"Does you being quiet have anything to do with the brooding badass you arrived with?" she prodded, leaning forward to touch up the edge of her blood-red lipstick. It was her signature, along with the beauty spot above those red lips. And the tight curls she wore every day, mimicking her namesake and all-around idol, Marilyn Monroe. Her eyes met mine once more. "The one with the jaw and the cheekbones and the hair?"

I nodded. "The one with the jaw and the cheekbones and the hair and the muscles and the hands," I sighed. "And the tattoos."

She grinned wickedly. "I thought you were going to stay 'far, *far* away from the Sons of Templar'." She mimicked my voice, repeating what I'd said verbatim when they'd come into the club my first week in town.

I groaned, sinking back in my chair, giving up on my makeup. "I was. I am. It's complicated."

She raised a brow. Or as much as she could since she'd had a fresh injection of Botox last week. "I bet it is, honey."

"I have no idea how I'm going to dance with *him* out there," I whispered, glimpsing at the door to where, in five minutes, I was going to have to strut out, shake my ass and take off my clothes.

Hades had, as Anderson had promised, been waiting in the parking lot when we arrived. Leaning against his bike, looking like pure fucking sin. I'd actually released a little sigh when I pulled up beside him. An audible fucking sound that was dangerously and embarrassingly close to a moan. My entire body had tensed up and relaxed at the same time.

As he watched me exit my car, his gaze was visceral. I felt his eyes travel all the way up my legs. All the way. When my eyes locked with his, my stomach dropped. Like all the way to my snakeskin heels. There was heat in it. A fucking inferno.

Then there wasn't.

In an instant, he shut it down. It's how I imagined it might've happened in an airlock when all the oxygen was sucked out. I hoped that I kept a poker face at what this did to me, what he did to me, but I feared I wasn't anywhere as good as he was.

I used a goodbye to Anderson to distract myself, hugging him and promising to set a date for him and Hannah to come over to my place for dinner.

When done, I turned back toward Hades, finding his dark brows furrowed above the glare he directed at me. I'd done something to piss him off yet again. My cheeks heated with the force of that glare, my body responding in a way that was not at all healthy.

Since arriving, he hadn't spoken to me, and I'd done my best to pretend he didn't exist. I couldn't do that now, though.

"We are going to have brunch, and you're going to go into detail about him," Marilyn told me, eyeing me in the middle of my nervous breakdown. "There is no time for details right now." She put her hand on my leg, squeezing for reassurance. She pointed a long red nail toward the stage. "*You* have all the power here. So go out there, show that to him. Make him think you're dancing for him even though you dance for yourself. Men are never weaker than when they're watching a woman take her clothes off."

She gave my leg one last squeeze before letting go.

"You're a bad bitch, you've got this," she continued, her voice confident, sure.

I nodded. "Yes, I am," I agreed.

Carmen came strutting backstage with a wink and a G-string full of cash. Then the song came on.

My song.

"Toxic" by Britney Spears.

Yes. With Britney, I could do this.

HADES

I had no idea how I fucking survived it. How *any* man in this place with his eyes all over her survived it. The only way I was able to keep from killing every motherfucker in this joint was to stay completely and utterly still, my hands around the single glass of whisky I'd ordered. I hadn't taken a single sip, though my body was crying out for the burn in my throat, something to dull the edges.

But even if I'd downed the whole bottle, with her up on that stage, one tiny scrap of fabric away from being completely fucking naked, I knew nothing could've dulled the edges. The only thing whisky would've done was take away the miniscule amount of willpower I was clutching on to.

I'd dreaded coming here. Would've preferred anything else. A dangerous run that had a high chance of some kind of gunfight. An enemy to torture. Fuck, I would've *loved* either of those. I had not wanted to be here and hadn't planned to. Until every fucker in the club volunteered for this protection duty. Well, everyone but Hansen and Jagger whose Old Ladies wouldn't have been pleased with either of them being on protection duty on this particular night. Not that either of them wanted to be in a strip club on a Friday night. They were so fucking in love I'd think it was been pathetic if it weren't for the fact that I was actually happy for my brothers. And I actually liked Macy and Caroline. It was impossible not to.

And, apparently, it was impossible not to like Freya. Which made me want to pummel every single one of the fuckers who raised a goddamn hand.

As much as I didn't want to be here, no way in fuck were any of the other fuckers near her. I'd made that clear when Swiss—the piece of shit—had casually mentioned that he might head over here for a drink and backup 'in case you get stabbed again.' My reaction had amused and surprised everyone, the way I'd slammed my fist against the table.

Hansen had even raised an eyebrow.

Luckily, no one said anything, but I knew that Swiss would have plenty to say when I got back to the club. I figured I'd be able to handle it by then, having had time to lock myself down. But right now, I didn't know shit aside from knowing that I didn't trust myself to move my hands from the cool glass.

Nor could I take my eyes off her.

I hadn't been able to since she'd gotten out of that car in that dress. That fucking dress. With those fucking legs. Those tits. That ass.

That smile.

The one she offered freely to Anderson along with an invitation to dinner and a fucking *hug*. Again, I'd had to lock myself down, watching the prospect's arms going around her. The only reason those arms were still attached to his body was because they'd stayed well north of her ass, and his eyes had been locked with hers. I had kinda liked the fucker before tonight, even though he never shut up about his Old Lady and their baby. The only reason he was on this detail today was because he went on about his woman so much. I figured he was the safest choice around Freya. Even then, my mind had tortured me all fucking day about how quickly another woman could disappear from a man's mind in the face of someone like Freya.

Which was why I'd been busting my ass all fucking day, tracking down the fuckers responsible for this entire situation. And trying to figure out how they'd factored Freya into the situation. They obviously had eyes on us. Bad ones though, to pick Freya as a woman attached to the club. Or maybe they wanted to make a statement and were too cowardly to threaten someone like Macy or Caroline. If that had happened, not only would we find the men responsible, we'd make sure their deaths lasted fucking *months*.

As it was, I was really fucking looking forward to killing the man who was stupid enough to think he could get away with doing that and living another day. We were closing in when I got the message from Anderson that Freya was getting ready for work.

We had to find him tonight, because no way me or my cock would survive another night of this.

Three other women had danced before her. I hadn't seen them. I couldn't tell you the color of their hair or any other kind of physical detail. Then she came on.

Wearing white.

Wearing fucking white.

That should've been illegal.

I'd been planning on staring at the bar, counting the bottles on the shelves, watching the entrance to make sure no Segadores Sombríos came in the door. I didn't need to get in any deeper with this woman. It was the smart thing to do. Safest for both me and her.

But something inside of me reacted, something impossible to control despite the fact that my life only worked because of the way I could control myself, and to a point, others around me.

Until Freya.

Until fucking Freya.

The dress she was wearing was sheer. Lace. I'd situated myself in the corner of the room, as far away from the stage as I could, considering I had to be ready to take down anyone who tried shit with her.

But despite my distance, I could see her nipples, hard and exquisitely pink. My grip on the glass tightened. I was close to breaking it in my palm, but I fucking welcomed that. I needed the pain of glass embedding itself into my skin, anything that wasn't the agony of watching her strut down the stage with her perfect nipples illuminated for the entire club to see.

Her blonde hair was piled on top of her head, so as she rounded the pole, I traced the curve of her neck, imagining my hand around it as I fucked her from behind. Her skin was tanned, smooth perfection. It glistened in the light, and it was fucking hypnotizing.

I knew there was music, I swear I'd heard it moments ago. People had been talking too. Murmuring to each other. Laughing. Talking about what they'd do to the women on stage, the ones they'd never get. I remembered thinking that if I heard them talking that way about Freya, I wouldn't be able to control myself.

But I hadn't needed to worry about that since there was only a dull roar in my ear and everything else had blended into a blur. There was only Freya.

She was afraid of me, that much was clear. And because I was a fucking evil asshole, I liked that. I needed that. Needed her fear of me to mute her down. Otherwise, I'd turn into a fucking caveman.

Since she was terrified of me, I'd expected her to avoid my gaze while she was up there. I'd prayed for it.

But God didn't listen to demons, devils, sinners, or members of outlaw motorcycle clubs. Freya did not avert her eyes like she had in the parking lot or the night prior when she'd lingered by the bar, talking to Kallum, who I also wanted to fucking kill.

No, she only had eyes for me.

They were right, the fucking religious nuts. Hell did exist, and it was Fate, this fucking club. Heaven existed too. And it was also here in this fucking club at this fucking moment.

FREYA

I had not planned on taking Marilyn's advice. Usually, she was great at giving it. But this ... thing, this connection—one sided, of course—was not like anything I'd ever experienced, and I wasn't articulate enough to explain it to her. Certainly not in the five minutes I'd had before I was due to go on stage.

I'd planned on completely avoiding the corner of the club where Hades had situated himself. I'd stripped in front of people I knew before, even a couple of times in front of people I'd dated— which none of them had been able to handle. At first, it was kind of awkward, but I was a veteran now and wasn't ashamed of my body or my job.

The problem was, Hades had a magnetic pull. The second I walked out on stage, it was impossible not to look at him. Not to move for him. Not to breathe for him.

And I was not ashamed. Or afraid.

I was powerful.

It was like sex. That sounded insane, but there was no other way to describe it. Never in my life had stripping been sexual to me. At first, it had been my rock bottom, the only way to pay the bills. Then my secret shame. After that, it became a job. A great workout. The thing that paid for my lifestyle. Yes, it had been many, *many* things. But it had never been sexual.

Until this moment.

Until his eyes followed my every move. Tracing my skin as I moved up and down the pole. The thin lace covering my body was suddenly too heavy, too stifling, too arousing against my hard nipples. My body swayed with the music, pulling off the fabric slowly, sensually. My heartbeat seemed to pulse everywhere in my body, all my muscles coiled tightly, reacting as if Hades's lips were moving all over me, coaxing me to a climax. Although he was in shadows, he seemed to be etched from stone, every detail of his face stark, irresistible.

He had been hunched over his table when I began, clutching his glass, glaring at the stage, glaring at me. For less than a moment. Then I started. Then *we* started. Something moved in his eyes, something sparked. He sat up straighter, let go of the glass, both of his palms flat on the table. He turned so I could see him open his legs ever so slightly. An invitation. I was instantly wet. I must've imagined it, since it was impossible to see such things with the low light from that distance, but I could've sworn I saw the outline of his cock. His very large, very hard cock. That only made me crazier.

I moved like the pole was his body. Like I was involved in some kind of crazed mating dance. It would've felt ridiculous and desperate had I not been so turned on.

Only him and I existed. My skin was damp, clammy and on fire by the time I'd shed my clothes and finished my set. I felt like one fucking touch, the tiniest bit of friction, and I'd explode. It was all I could to do to walk backstage and not launch myself across the crowd to let Hades fuck me right there.

Marilyn, who had been watching from backstage, gave me a wink and mouthed, "I told you so" as she swatted my ass and began her set.

I stumbled to the bathroom on unsteady legs, barely able to lock the door before I pressed myself against it and touched the one area that was begging for attention. I cried out as I came the second my fingers touched my clit.

CHAPTER FIVE

I didn't want to make eye contact with Hades when I finally rustled up enough courage to emerge from backstage. I'd planned on averting my eyes altogether, making an art out of staring at his motorcycle boots. How could I look him in the eye after *that*?

I was all about confidence and owning my sexuality when I was on stage. Hades wasn't scary when I was the one with all the power over him. But now he was plenty fucking scary.

And I couldn't take my fucking eyes off him.

He couldn't seem to take his eyes off me either. Yet there was none of that liquid sex glittering through them. None of that animalistic need from before. Just a familiar fury that I'd never get used to. Never stop reacting to.

"You done?" he barked, the two words rattling my bones.

I couldn't even speak, literally couldn't form words. Instead, I nodded slowly, blinking rapidly at him.

He jerked his head toward the door, not saying anything else.

Somewhere, deep down, it pissed me off something wicked that he thought he could order me around with a jerk of his head and expected me to obey. In any other situation, I would've —or at the very least I might've—given him a piece of my mind then purposefully strutted to the bar to order a drink, making it clear that no man told me where to go with a flick of his fucking head.

But this was a whole other type of situation. So I walked toward the exit, feeling Hades's eyes on me the entire time.

We didn't speak as we walked to the car, not one word. But I felt his presence behind me, his heat. He was close enough for me to smell since he was almost pressing up against me. Almost. He seemed to be being very careful not to touch me. As if we hadn't had some kind of ... moment not twenty minutes prior. As if I hadn't made myself come in the bathroom thinking of his cock thrusting inside of me.

I didn't know if I was glad or disappointed by his silence, all I knew was that I let out a long exhale the second I closed the door to my car. I also looked in my rear-view mirror far too often than was safe throughout the drive home.

Despite having made myself come less than thirty minutes prior, by the time I was back at my place, I was ready to explode. There was no way that we weren't having sex, right? After what had just happened?

I would've loved to call Marilyn to process all of this so I didn't become the first woman to spontaneously combust due to the proximity to a badass biker with a stare that could melt panties. Or drench them.

Unfortunately, the ride from Fate to my place was too short for me to completely unpack with Marilyn. Plus, I wasn't sure I had regained the ability to speak just yet.

I'd call her tomorrow. After all the sex.

There *had* to be sex. As much as I really, really wanted to fight it, fight him, I didn't have the power to. Maybe in the morning I would've regained my wits. Maybe I would be able to straighten things out, banish the biker from my life. But the sun hadn't risen yet.

It was two in the morning, I was pulling up to my house, a man on a Harley behind me, and I was more turned on than I had ever been in my life.

He didn't open my door for me, though I hadn't expected him to. He was just standing there, under my floodlights, a living shadow. A very sexy, menacing, dangerous shadow.

My heels clicked against the concrete of my driveway as Hades watched me approach. My skin prickled with anticipation.

"Prospect is comin' to spend the night," he announced before I'd reached him. "Outside," he continued, his tone like iron. "No invitations to sleep on the couch, the pullout. No hot fuckin' cocoa. He's not hanging around to be your friend. Not coming for shit other than to make sure no one comes and slits your throat in your sleep."

A chill raced through me. Not from the air, it was July in New Mexico. Even at two in the morning, the heat was thick, sticky. But nonetheless, I shivered.

This was not the same man who had sat in the corner and watched me dance for him, that had made me wet with nothing but a gaze and the purposeful opening of his legs.

"We clear?" he grated out when I hadn't spoken in a handful of seconds.

A motorcycle roared in the distance, and my eyes panned to the end of my driveway where a lone headlight made its way toward us.

Suddenly, I was no longer looking at a lone headlight. I was, once again, looking into a cold, icy, intense and unyielding stare. Hades had grasped onto my chin with his fingers, forcing my attention back to him.

My body thrummed under his touch.

"Freya, need to hear that you understand me," he murmured.

I blinked at him, the roar of the oncoming motorcycle nothing compared to the thundering of my heart.

"I understand you," I whispered.

The seconds the words were out of my mouth, Hades let me

go, stepping back two paces. It might as well have been two football fields.

Rejection washed over me like acid, burning away whatever confidence I'd been wearing two minutes ago. He didn't say anything more, didn't address the sexual tension between us. It was as if it didn't exist.

And I didn't storm into my house, swinging my hips in a way that told him I did not need him when I had a perfectly good vibrator in my bedside table. That's what a strong, sexually stable woman would've done. And that's what I thought I was up until two minutes ago.

Hades didn't so much as say goodbye to me when the man on the bike pulled up. He just gave me one lingering look before walking toward the Harley running in my driveway.

I watched them speak a handful of sentences before Hades got on his bike and drove off, not looking back once.

As promised, I gave the prospect a little wave but didn't exchange pleasantries. Instead, I went inside, poured myself a big drink, then another. Then I baked cookies, ate half the batter, eating the rest once they were cooked—except for the three I set on the doorstep along with a mug of cocoa—cried a little, used my vibrator then went to sleep.

HADES

"Please," the man whined.

I stared at him, covered in blood, tears and his own waste. He'd pissed himself before I'd even started on him.

Fucking coward.

If you lived this lifestyle, you had to be at peace with the knowledge that there was a very real chance that you were going to get tortured and murdered. Fuck, all I hoped for was a quick death. But if that wasn't going to be the case, then I would take it like a man.

Unlike this pussy.

"Please?" I echoed, my knife dripping with his blood. I didn't usually like to get this messy, but this man had had his *hands* on Freya. This fucker was the reason her eyes were full of fear, why her voice shook while she recounted what had happened, why her skin was so pale it was almost translucent.

I enjoyed every fucking moment of cutting this asshole to shreds. My body had been taut, wired, ready to fucking explode. I either needed to come or kill. Especially since Freya had emerged from backstage wearing that fucking dress and an expression that made it clear she'd taken care of herself somewhere.

I was barely able to put one foot in front of the other, barely look at her, I'd been so afraid I'd throw her over my shoulder and fuck her against the brick wall in the alley. Then I'd gone straight from her place to this fucking basement. So killing it was.

"You don't get to make demands now," I snarled. "In fact, you never fucking make demands to the Sons of Templar."

Then I sliced off his finger.

Swiss grinned from where he leaned against a bench, where he'd been watching this happen. He was always down here whenever we had a guest. Fucker had a thirst for blood, he got off on pain. Usually, he was more than happy to do it himself, usually with Claw. Until we lost Claw in the war. Swiss hadn't been the same since. None of us had. That pain hadn't made us weak, it had only made us—those of us who still stayed firmly on the wrong side of the law—hungry for more. For more territory. More money. More power.

The Amber club had gone legit, at least when it came to business. But when it came to revenge, they were out for blood.

And yes, I wanted fucking revenge. For dragging Freya into the cesspit that was this world. For putting fear in her eyes. For putting his hands on her.

Finally, the asshole stopped screaming. "Worse than fucking

with us, you fucked with my woman. That's why you die slowly, painfully, and why you'll bleed out like the pig you are."

And that's when I slit his throat.

I stepped back to avoid the spray of blood. Swiss and I both watched the asshole die slowly and noisily. It was damn satisfying to watch.

"So," Swiss said, his eyes moving from the now dead man, illuminated with a sick excitement. "*Your* woman? That sounds mighty serious. I mean, you killed the guy for this broad."

I glared at Swiss, wiping my knife on my jeans before shoving it back into the holster on my belt.

"Fuck you," I spat.

Swiss just grinned in response.

"You know we can't let any fuckers, let alone ones as insignificant as the Segadores Sombríos, threaten us," I continued, looking from Swiss back to the dead guy. "Or threaten our women."

The Segadores Sombríos were a street gang trying to make themselves into something else, trying to cut into our business. We'd sent a few subtle messages that they obviously hadn't got. Thought that we were weak. Now they wouldn't. They wouldn't come for us after this.

"*Is* she your woman?" Swiss asked, a glint in his eye.

Something bubbled inside of me. It was white. Hot. Almost blinding. Something that had me very tempted to put my fist through my brother's face. I had to stop myself from advancing on him.

It had not escaped me that Swiss was very interested in Freya. That he had been almost as single minded as me in wanting to track down the piece of shit who'd threatened her. Even Elden had seemed overly interested in this task, his expression rippling with fury as we recounted what happened at church.

Freya had made an impression. A quick one. A lasting one. And one that piqued at least two of my brothers' interest. Normally, if one of my brothers had his eye on the same woman as me, I'd let them have her. Sometimes, if the woman was up for it and I was drunk enough, we shared her.

But the mere thought of anyone else's hands on Freya's skin ... it made me want to find another guy just so I could cut his fucking throat.

"You seem awfully interested in Freya," I ground out.

Swiss was amused by my fury, his eyes twinkling in delight, his teeth bared in a brutal grin. This was his ideal fucking night, torturing a guy, watching him die then fucking with me.

"Of course, I'm interested in her," he drawled. "She's fucking gorgeous, hilarious, strong and unlike any woman I've ever met."

I clenched my fists at my sides, my body shaking with the need to pummel this fucker.

Swiss saw it. Of course he saw it. He fucking loved it.

"But she isn't interested in me, brother," Swiss added. "Well, she is, at least a little, because she's a hot-blooded woman."

I cannot kill my brother.

"But," he continued. "She's a fuck of a lot more interested in the brooding enforcer who was willing to slit a throat for her." He sighed dramatically. "Another one bites the dust."

"You're full of shit," I sneered. "Nothing is going on with her. She's an innocent who got caught up in this shit because of me, and I needed to make sure she's not in any kind of danger before I leave her the fuck alone."

Swiss's eyes bugged out, and he let out a sound that was dangerously close to a snort.

"Yeah, right. And I can come in missionary without choking a bitch tied to my bed," he quipped.

I flipped him the bird on my way up the stairs, toward her. For the last time.

FREYA

I didn't get the name of the prospect who had spent the night chain smoking outside of my house since he roared off not long after I handed him a coffee. He took it gratefully, thanking me for the cookies and cocoa last night. This one was not as clean-cut as Anderson had been. He was covered in tattoos, including one on his upper eyebrow, looked like he ate steroids for breakfast and would've intimidated the fuck out of me had he not asked for the recipe for my cookies.

He hadn't said anything else, other than the fact his name was Hawk—yes, *Hawk*—and that he had, " to get going," and that I was, "all good", whatever that meant.

Even though it had only been two days of being tailed by men in the Sons of Templar, I suddenly felt vulnerable and exposed, being home alone with Sirius. I'd lived in plenty of different houses, in plenty of different states, in all kinds of different areas. There were times I'd felt uneasy, but I'd never felt unsafe before today. I'd loved the fact that I lived outside of town, on almost ten acres with sparse desert all around me as far as the eye could see. But now it felt isolated and much too far away from anyone who could hear me scream.

As ruthless and dangerous as the Sons of Templar were, I didn't think they would just leave me if I was still in any kind of danger. Honestly, I was surprised they'd done all of this to begin with. The entire point of me driving to their clubhouse after the incident was to make sure I *wasn't* murdered. I hadn't intended it to tangle me up with Hades, for me to feel even more attracted to him.

The morning might have brought discomfort due to the Sons of Templar's absence, but it also brought a heck of a lot of clarity. I would've had sex with Hades last night. Without question. And something told me it would've been earth-shattering. Without fucking question. But something also told me it would've ended in disaster.

I'd had a weak moment, that's it. He held a strange power over me. Maybe it was the leather. Maybe after avoiding bad boys all of my adult life, I finally fell victim to the mystique. Maybe it was the jawline. The hair. The muscles. The stare. The tattoos. The way his voice cloaked over me like velvet. Or it could've been the leather cut, what it represented, and the feeling that he would take care of anything and everything that arose in his presence. That an asteroid could fall from the sky and I'd be okay. He'd take care of me.

Which was wrong on a multitude of levels. I was a twenty-first-century woman; I did not need a man to take care of me. And then there was the fact that he was not a man who would take care of me. He'd ruin me.

So it was a good thing that the danger was over. Hades was now out of my life. He had to be. I'd made that promise to myself after cleaning the entire house with The Spice Girls playing. Then I went for a walk with Sirius around the property, snapping pictures of cacti against the relentless blue sky, uploading them to my Instagram, my personal one which was just a bunch of photos of food, Sirius and the odd selfie. My Aunt Victoria was my biggest fan. She was the first one to like my photos, view my stories and comment. I had been expecting her call after I saw the like on our walk back.

"Are you wearing sunscreen?" she demanded when I answered the phone.

I grinned. "Hello to you too, Aunt V."

"I checked the weather today, and it's supposed to reach the high nineties with no cloud cover," she continued. She was breathing heavily, probably on the Stairmaster at her local gym. My Aunt Victoria was in her late fifties yet in better shape than me. I was breathing heavily after a gentle walk with my overweight lab.

"You wouldn't need to get all that Botox if you just used proper sun protection," she chided.

I rolled my eyes. "I don't get 'all that Botox,' " I argued. "I get baby Botox, once every six months, which is actually quite restrained for someone my age, in my industry."

My Aunt Victoria had known about what I did for a living since my first night. She was there that first night, cheering me on. Which was definitely kind of weird, but my Aunt V was definitely kind of weird in the best way. She had never married, had never had kids and had never moved out of the small town that she grew up in. She and my mother were not at all close, but she had always made an effort with me. Always. She was more of a mother than mine ever was. I loved her with all of my heart.

"And for your information," I continued. "I am wearing a wide-brimmed sunhat, sunglasses that cover up half my face, SPF 40, a white, long-sleeved linen shirt and matching pants. Not an ounce of my skin is exposed to the sun."

I wasn't completely lying.

I was wearing a wide-brimmed, straw cowboy hat and huge, men's aviators that looked absolutely badass. And I was wearing SPF 40 on my face and chest. But I was also wearing a string bikini top, high-waisted denim cutoffs and worn sneakers. What could I say? It was hot as balls, and I loved the look of a natural tan.

"You're full of shit," Aunt V scoffed.

I was a terrible liar. Even over the phone.

"So what's new?" she asked. "Other than you practically begging for skin cancer."

Fuck.

I definitely couldn't tell Aunt V about everything that had happened in the past few days. She would drop everything and get her ass here. Then she would see Hades. She'd see my reaction to him, and it would be a whole *thing*. Even more, I did not want my beloved Aunt V, the only true family I had, to be put in any kind of danger. Nor did I want her to worry about me. She had done that plenty over the years.

So, I couldn't tell her about the man holding the gun to my head, and I certainly could not tell her about the Sons of Templar.

THREE KINDS OF TROUBLE

She'd smell a lie. Though not if I dumped as much information as possible on top of the lie.

"Things are great," I replied, forcing as much sincerity into my voice as possible. "Marilyn and I are planning a trip to that fancy Hollywood resort that is by invite only. She knows someone who knows someone who's sleeping with someone who can get us on the list."

I hadn't told Marilyn that I'd been invited to that resort by the promoters who expressed their hope that I'd post about it to my Instagram, the business one which had over five hundred thousand followers and was full of images that went with my 'brand.'

"The house is finally finished, and I cannot wait for you to come try to convince me to redecorate since it's not feng shui," I babbled. "Sirius loves it here, although he's afraid of lizards. And snakes. And birds that fly too low." I looked at my dog who was eying the sky warily, as if he was waiting for a hawk to fly down and carry him away. As if a hawk big enough existed."

"I can't wait to come and visit, see the house all finished" she retorted, her voice comforting and safe.

"Yes, when are you coming to visit again?" I demanded. She'd come for two weeks to help me move, getting me settled, hanging out. But that was almost a year ago. Aunt V was still working full time as a bank teller and had used up all her vacation days. She refused to let me retire her. I'd been saving money for years to do so, as a thank you for everything she'd done for me. It meant something to me to be able to do that.

"Soon, my sweet, I promise. Now, how is Des? That's someone I can't wait to meet."

"Oh, he's great," I replied. "You'll never guess what he did last week..."

I settled into a comforting conversation with my favorite person on the planet, giving me a much-needed respite from the devil who stalked me through the desert.

A brief respite.

———

I felt uneasy and weird for the rest of the afternoon. While I lied to my Aunt V about the parking lot incident and Hades, the residual trauma from what happened, the lingering fear that I was still in danger and the fact that I was obsessing over Hades despite everything—it was all far too much for me to process. I was totally exhausted. Despite Marilyn's pleading for me to go over to her place for cocktails since we both had the night off, I made an excuse and settled on the sofa, trying to heal myself in the only way I could, with a disaster movie marathon.

Halfway through that marathon, someone knocked on my door. Sirius whimpered once before hiding under the blankets we were both huddled under. I sucked in an unsteady breath, rubbed my eyes, paused the movie then stumbled to the door, not thinking. Which, of course, was a huge fucking mistake.

"What the fuck?"

I blinked rapidly at the form standing in my door frame, blocking out the sun. The voice was low, masculine and extremely pissed off. Dangerous.

"What are you doing here?" I asked Hades, blinking rapidly, my vision tearstained and blurry. I rubbed my face with the backs of my hands, tears still running down my face as I made a very embarrassing hiccupping sound.

Before I could speak, Hades's thumb and forefinger grasped my chin, tilting it upward. "What the fuck happened?" he demanded.

He was pissed off, that much was clear. His eyes, glittering with fury, searched my face, my body, looking for signs of injury.

I felt very uncomfortable under his probing gaze. I'd just been crying hysterically. I was sure my face was splotchy, swollen, my eyes rimmed red. My hair was a bird's nest atop my head, and I was wearing oversized sweats with wine and chocolate stains covering them.

No one saw me like this. The only reason I'd answered the

door was because I thought it was the FedEx guy with my Sephora order.

"Freya, you need to talk. Right fucking now." He was still holding my chin in his hands. My silence was obviously not pleasing him at all, and it was becoming very clear that he was not going to let me go until I spoke about why I was answering the door like this. It seemed like he thought something untoward had happened to me. Which was fair enough since I looked like a fucking mess, but still, most people wouldn't have such an intense reaction. Then again, most people didn't deal with stabbings and violence on the regular. I did not need Hades thinking I was some damsel in distress. Wasn't that kind of thing like catnip to these guys?

Maybe not Hades, though. He seemed like the last thing he wanted was to be the hero, and he was not at all interested in me.

"The end of the world happened," I hiccuped.

His brows furrowed. "That's not an answer."

I sucked in a fractured breath, trying to calm myself down. "Armageddon."

He was still frowning, the cloak of anger he was wearing so thick and palpable, I felt it covering me too.

I blinked, my body calming, my tears slowing. "Ben Affleck. Bruce Willis. Liv Tyler?" I raised my brows in question. "Second to Deep Impact to be sure, because Deep Impact is one hundred percent the number one disaster movie in the world, and no one can change my mind about that."

I sucked in a much more even breath, all too aware of how intensely Hades was watching me. His gaze was no longer deadly or dangerous. Well, not completely, at least. There was something else in his eyes. His jaw was not as clenched as it had been moments ago.

"Anyway," I added, my voice quieter now. "I think that it's impossible to watch Armageddon without crying. The scene where Bruce Willis is talking to Liv Tyler through the NASA intercom thing..." I couldn't finish the sentence without the waterworks starting again, my voice cracking ever so slightly.

Hades's eyes narrowed almost imperceptibly, but I was standing pretty damn close to him. How was it only now that I realized how close he was standing to me? He was still holding my chin.

In his hand.

And I had just blabbered on about Bruce Willis saving the world, my eyes most likely rimmed red, face blotchy and hair a fucking mess. And he was looking at me like ... like I was the most beautiful thing he'd ever seen.

My body hummed beneath his gaze, at his grip on my chin, his smell, how his body was so close to mine. It felt like his shadow was swallowing me whole.

He was still staring at me, still touching me, and I hadn't said a word in like a minute. It was getting hard to breathe. But I didn't move. My body became very aware of the hotness of this man and his proximity to me and how long it had been since I'd had sex. Not to mention that I'd never felt this way in a man's presence ... ever. Terrified, turned on, and like I might melt into a puddle at any moment.

Up until right now, I'd been really sure that Hades didn't like me. Not like that anyway. Beyond wanting to fuck me, though that did not mean he liked me. But he had been staring into my eyes for a good long while now and was still holding my chin. He smelled like man and musk, spicy, unlike any aftershave I'd smelled before. It was the smell of *him*. I wanted it imprinted on my skin. On my sheets. My eyes swept over him, his high cheekbones, his full lips, the veins in his neck that looked as if they were etched in stone. I had yet to find a piece of his skin, apart from most of his face, that wasn't covered by ink. Unfortunately, his chest was obscured by the V-neck tee he was wearing, but the muscles underneath the fabric were impossible to hide. His arms were exposed today, and they were sinewy, muscled, pale perfection. I might've been able to look farther down had he not let go of my chin and stepped back. My body stumbled forward just a little as I leaned in to the space where he used to be.

To my relief, I caught myself before I face planted into his chest. I blinked rapidly, staring at him, watching the expression leave his face. He looked more familiar now, his face harsher, the angles of his cheekbone all the more sculpted and his gaze telling me he was totally unimpressed and pissed off by me.

My fists clenched at my sides, and I bit the inside of my lip to stop from crying all over again. I'd be able to handle this so much better if I was in full glam; looking hot while being rejected was much easier. Or it normally was. Hades cut through all the defenses I'd built up over the years. And I barely knew this guy.

Suddenly, I was pissed off. At myself for having such a reaction to a guy who had been nothing but an asshole to me. I was not that girl. It was so fucking cliché, letting the guy with the sculpted jaw and chaos in his eyes fuck me around because he looked like heaven and hell in a man.

Fuck no.

I folded my arms across my chest and struggled not to react to the way Hades's eyes followed my gesture which made my boobs move upward since I wasn't wearing a bra. His eyes flared ever so slightly, and that felt like a victory. It also felt like something else between my legs, but I was ignoring that.

"Why are you here?" I demanded, my voice no longer shaking with tears mourning Bruce Willis.

Hades's eyes looked over my shoulder into my living room where the movie was paused and where Sirius was hiding underneath the blanket we'd been cuddling under prior to this.

"You need a guard dog," he commented flatly.

I frowned at him. "You need to tell me why you're at my house," I countered.

His eyes went back to me. "Wanted to let you know that you're not going to have a tail anymore. We took care of it."

His voice was deep, menacing and like liquid caramel. I tasted it on my tongue. Or maybe I'd had more wine than I'd realized.

"Took care of it?" I parroted, stepping back instinctively.

Hades noted that, and he stepped forward, his motorcycle boots producing low thumps on my hardwood floor.

My sideboard clattered as candles and knickknacks fell over when I backed into it. Hades had stalked forward so there were mere inches between us. He wasn't touching me this time, though. Nor was he looking at me like he had before. No. He had clocked my fear, sensed it, and had made a conscious choice to magnify it, to intimidate me, scare me in my own home.

Yeah, this guy was no hero.

"Yes, Freya, I took care of it." He spoke in a low tone, still liquid, almost sweet. Well, if cyanide was mixed with sugar. He tilted his head ever so slightly, not taking his eyes off me. "Want to know what that means?"

I was holding my breath, my heart echoing in my ears. "No," I ground out. "I don't need to know what it means."

"It means he ain't breathing anymore," Hades said, as if I hadn't spoken. As if he were enjoying my fear, the tremor in my voice.

I for one was not enjoying it. I fucking hated how cowardly I sounded, how I was letting this man play me like a fucking puppet.

"Just so you know, Freya," he continued, leaning forward, his voice a velvet knife. "No one is going to breathe after they threaten you." He lingered for a moment after he spoke, then he turned on his heel and left.

Left me standing there, staring at the door long after his Harley had roared off.

CHAPTER SIX

THREE WEEKS LATER

I was alone in the parking lot again.

I was late leaving because one of the girls, Natasha, had had a bad night. It was her first night. First nights were always bad. Unless you were high as all hell, which she wasn't. She was young. Barely twenty. I would've thought she was lying about her age had I not known that Kallum did extensive background checks to make sure there was no one underage working for him.

Those background checks extended to everyone who worked for Kallum. Records didn't matter, since Kallum had an extensive one of his own. He believed in second chances. Even third and fourth chances. But he had his limits. No one actively wanted by law enforcement and no one convicted of violence against women. It surprised me greatly that Dante had no outstanding warrants or restraining orders against him. There was something cold about him. In addition to being a sleazebag, there was something else off about him. He was the kind of guy you rejected once, twice, three times then he attacked you in the parking lot for being a 'frigid

ANNE MALCOM

slut.' Of course he hadn't actually done that ... yet. It was only a
matter of time. Because of that, I was glad that Dante had gotten
sick of waiting for Natasha and me to come out and had gone
home. Now that I didn't have members of some kind of street
gang after me, I wasn't as scared of parking lots. It wasn't like I was
going to find another member of the Sons of Templar bleeding out
there. In fact, there hadn't been a member of the Sons of Templar
in this parking lot in almost a month, bleeding or not.

I had not seen hide nor hair of any hottie in leather since
Hades had left me confused, turned on and terrified three weeks
ago. He hadn't made any kind of promises, vows or oaths. He had
absolutely no obligation to me. Fuck, it's not like we'd been dating;
he'd only been around me to make sure I wasn't getting shot in the
head until he could murder the man who had threatened me.

And he'd freely admitted to me that he'd murdered him.

Considering the rumors surrounding the Sons of Templar, I'd
suspected he'd killed people. But suspecting something and
hearing it right from the horse's mouth were two totally different
things.

Staying far away from the self-confessed murderer who got
stabbed in parking lots and had disturbing control over me was the
best thing to do. The *only* thing to do.

Not one member of the Sons of Templar had entered the club
in three weeks. A huge disappointment to the rest of the girls.
They were our hottest clients, and they tipped the best. It was
unheard of for them to stay away for this long. I knew nothing had
happened to them since on more than one occasion I'd heard the
roar of Harleys through town. Just yesterday I'd even been sitting
by the window at Oliver's Café, drinking a cappuccino and
nibbling on an almond croissant as I'd watched them drive by. It
was like a cavalry of Harleys with Hansen, the president, in front
and the rest staggered behind him.

I'd seen him, riding behind his president, hair flying back in the wind, jawline unmistakable. My stomach did a weird little flip, and my skin burned in memory of where he'd touched me. I used my vibrator thinking about him last night. I'd thought about him every night I used it. And afternoon.

I'd eventually forget him. It was a small town, one they pretty much ran, so I'd see them around. Eventually they'd come back to Fate again, and I had to get rid of the narcissistic assumption that I was the reason they hadn't been back. They were outlaws, busy murdering competitors and stuff.

I couldn't help thinking of Hades every time I set foot in the club parking lot. Even as I was walking Natasha to her car. She wasn't shaking or crying anymore, which was a win.

"Thank you so much for tonight, Freya," she hiccupped, fumbling with her keys.

I wiped a tear from her pretty, fresh, young face. Now that she'd cried most of her makeup off, the freckles over her chin were all the more prevalent, making her look even younger and more vulnerable.

"It will get better, honey, I promise." My heart broke for her. She was a young single mother who didn't have any other options, thanks to shitty parents, a shitty education and a shitty hand at life.

She nodded rapidly, sucking in an audible breath, her face clearing under the harsh streetlights. Something passed over her features, something fierce, something that showed me how she'd managed to move out the trailer she had shared with her ex-boyfriend's family, away from the ex who'd beat her, to a completely new town. She was strong, this girl. This woman.

"I know it will," she nodded, surety in her voice.

"And you've got us, all of us. We have your back. You're not alone," I promised her.

She nodded again, tearing up a little more.

"Tuesday night, we're having chocolate cake for dinner,

watching movies, and I'm getting baby snuggles," I reminded her. I'd made the date with her and Harry, her eight-month-old son, because she barely knew anyone here and needed someone on her team.

"Yes, I can't wait," she gave me a small smile.

I leaned forward to open her door for her, watching her get in, then standing there as she drove away. My heart hurt for her. But she'd be okay. I knew that based on the determination I'd seen in her eyes. The strength. She was a fighter.

I sighed, turning back toward my car which was parked across the lot. My mind was on Natasha, on what I was going to eat when I got home and on what Hades might be doing right now. Fucking a club girl, drinking whisky, killing a guy. Then my mind was on how I was supposed to be thinking about anything but Hades.

I was so preoccupied that I didn't see him until I ran right into him. His hands gripped my upper arms. Hard.

Not paying attention while walking alone in a parking lot was a real TSTL—otherwise known as a 'too stupid to live moment.' You know, the heroine who runs up the stairs away from the murderer instead of out the front door? Walking toward the scary noise in the basement? That kind of thing.

I was much smarter than that. Or at least I'd thought I was.

Until my eyes locked with familiar brown ones. "Derek?"

My heart began to beat double time, my stomach dropping as fear crawled from the spots where the pads of his fingers pressed into my bare skin.

"Freya," he greeted, voice warm, welcoming.

"What are you doing here?" I tried to step out of his grip, but it only tightened.

"I needed to see you. Knew that you needed to see me too." His eyes flashed to the now dark sign overhead then back down to me, darkening.

Derek looked non-threatening upon first glance. He was of average height. I was almost taller than him when I was wearing my most modest heels, something he hadn't liked. I hadn't been able to wear my favorite shoes when I was around him.

His dirty blond hair was styled expertly. It took him almost thirty minutes in the morning, and he used shampoo that cost fifty dollars a bottle. He had conventional good looks—square jaw, always clean-shaven. Nose that was perfectly straight, never broken in a barfight or football game. Derek hadn't played football. He was a lacrosse guy. An Ivy League guy. A trust fund guy.

"You need to let me go, Derek," I stated, meeting his eyes, my voice firm and free from fear.

The last thing Derek needed to hear was fear in my voice. He'd like that.

I had no idea what I was thinking when I started going out with him in high school. No ... I did. I was thinking he was the epitome of everything I'd never had when I was growing up. The popular, rich guy. The kind of guy who had dated the head cheer-leader, the prom queen, the girl with two loving parents who lived behind the white picket fence. He had embodied a lot of the things I'd thought I wanted. That I'd let my mother convince me I didn't deserve.

I'd let myself be wined and dined by him. Impressed by his good manners, his good breeding, the fact that he bought me gifts, took me to expensive restaurants. But it didn't take long for me to realize that he was a misogynistic asshole. And that his family was equally horrible, treating me like crap and him letting them. Hence me dumping him.

Misogynistic, trust fund assholes did not like being dumped by women they considered below them. The women they thought they were doing a favor by dating them. Derek had made that clear over the past two years, but I hadn't thought he'd follow me all the way here.

"No, Freya, I'm not letting you go." He pulled me closer, so our bodies pressed together. So I could smell the Ralph Lauren cologne mixed with the hand sanitizer he slathered on after touching anything communal.

"That's where I fucked up before. I let you go. Let you think you know better." He let go of one of my arms so he could stroke the side of my face. I flinched away from his touch. He frowned at this response, but it didn't stop him.

"It's not your fault," he spoke tightly, as if he was forcing his voice to be even, pleasant. "You don't know any better. The way you grew up. The way you live." His eyes raked over my outfit with a mixture of hunger and distaste.

My stomach lurched at that look. At the very real situation I was presented with. I was alone in the middle of the night with my borderline stalker ex-boyfriend.

My head snapped upward, and I glared up at him, at his artificially tanned skin, his classical, ordinary good looks.

I'd been in lust with this man at one point. Then I'd been irritated. Disliked him. Now, in this very moment, with his hands on me and the ownership in his gaze, the judgement, feeling like he had a right to me, I fucking *hated* him.

"I love the way I live," I hissed. "Unlike you, every penny I have in my bank account is money *I've* made. Yeah, some of that money came from taking off my clothes for money, but you know what? It's because of rich, entitled assholes like you that I drive a fucking Range Rover."

Derek's hands tightened around me to the point of pain, but I didn't let that shit stop me.

"You think you're better than me because you were born into a family who has the majority of its 'old money' as a result of slavery," I spat. "You are not special. Throw a stone at an Ivy League college, and I'll find a man exactly like you. Down to the premature ejaculation and entitlement. I'm never going to get back with you. I'll never sleep with you again. I'll never breathe the same air as you again and I'm done being polite about it. If you'd be ever so kind as to fuck off, I've got a life to get back to."

I was mighty proud of my speech and that I'd maintained eye contact with him the entire time, never wavering despite how much tighter he began to hold me, how his eyes had narrowed into slits. I figured that some bruises on my upper arms and having to take out my emotions on a tub of Cool Whip were the worst possible ramifications of this interaction.

But I'd misjudged what would happen when an entitled, spoiled asshole was told no. Worse than that, when he was told the truth about who he was from someone he considered to be below him.

He shook me so hard my teeth rattled, blood rushing into my mouth as I bit my tongue. Hard.

"You fucking *cunt*," he growled, spittle flying out of his mouth. "You're trailer trash that needs to be taught your place."

Then he punched me square in the face. Again, maybe that was another TSTL moment. I didn't have time to analyze that because I fell to the ground. Because I hadn't been expecting it. Hadn't been braced for it, hadn't been ready to defend myself in the slightest. Because I thought this clean-cut guy wearing fucking Brooks Brothers was not a threat to me.

He proved me wrong.

And he quite possibly would've killed me had Kallum not arrived when he did.

———

Kallum definitely would've killed Derek had he caught him. When Kallum's headlights screeched into the parking lot, Derek sprinted off to his Porsche. He had sped off by the time Kallum made it to me.

Kallum had wanted to take chase, but I wasn't really in the state to be left alone in the parking lot. He'd told me all of this after, once he'd carried me to his car and drove me straight to the ER. Things were somewhat of a blur from there. Everything was bright, sterile, loud.

Then they weren't.

A dark shadow descended on my hospital room. A shadow in the shape of a man. Everything quieted, except my heart which thundered in my chest. It took me a couple of seconds to realize he was real, standing in the doorway. That I hadn't begun hallucinating thanks to the drugs Sarah had given me. It was kinda funny that she was the one treating me. Not funny 'ha ha', more … ironic, I guessed. She had been kind, gentle and very generous with the drugs.

Hence me thinking I was hallucinating Hades. But when I blinked four times and he remained exactly where he was, I realized he was really here, in my hospital room. Kallum had gone to my place to check on Sirius after I'd begged him. His jaw had been stiff, eyes narrowed, but he'd finally agreed. That was after his tortured gaze flickered over my face, wearing guilt that did not belong there.

The only reason Kallum had arrived when he did was because he left his phone at the club after leaving early. No matter what I said, he was going to find a way to blame himself for this. For not staying until close. For hiring Dante in the first place. That's the kind of good guy Kallum was.

He also went to your house in the middle of the night to check on your dog and get you toiletries and a change of clothes because you were laying in a hospital bed after being beaten up by an ex.

The man standing in the doorway was not a good guy. I knew that much. But I also knew my entire body relaxed, seeing him cross the distance between us. Even though he exuded fury. With every step. From every bone in his body. His handsome face was painted with it. No guilt. Not an inch of that. No, something else entirely.

He lifted his hand. It was large. I hadn't noticed how big his hands were before. Nice, long fingers too. Those fingers traced a featherlight touch over the area of my cheek that felt tight and hot.

I shivered as he moved his finger down the area of my face that was swollen and bruised from Derek's fist. He traced the bandage that covered the stitches I'd had to get because Derek had been wearing his fucking class ring.

Slowly, gently, he moved his finger across every inch of skin that was battered or bruised. Minutes passed in silence. I must've breathed since I would've passed out if I hadn't, but it seemed like I held my breath the entire time.

I knew I looked bad. They hadn't given me a mirror, and I wasn't strong enough to go to the bathroom under my own strength yet. But I didn't need a mirror. Not when I saw the sorrow in Sarah's kind eyes and the guilt and anger in Kallum's. Especially not with the deadly fury radiating from Hades's entire body. It wrapped around me. Fusing with the anger inside of me. Yet he touched the violence on my skin as gently as if I was a newborn fucking baby.

I didn't know how he'd known I was here. Kallum must've called him since he was the only one who knew what had happened. Sarah had the connection with the club, but I was pretty sure there were doctor-patient confidentiality agreements that stopped her from telling anyone who wasn't an emergency contact that I'd been admitted.

My Aunt V was my emergency contact. There was no way anyone was calling her.

I don't know when Kallum had called him, since he'd been by my side since the second he'd gathered me in his arms, assuring me that everything was going to be okay. The nurse had tried to shoo him away initially. He'd put up a fight, telling her he'd have to be dragged from my side, challenging her to find anyone willing to attempt that. Sarah had then deftly stepped in, obviously having had a lot of experience with pissed off alpha males.

Kallum didn't like Hades. He didn't like any of the Sons. It didn't make sense. Maybe I had asked for him? I didn't remember saying it out loud, but I'd thought of him sporadically.

It's not like I was knocked out or anything. But I'd never been hit before. I'd had a lot of other, terrible, violent things happen to me, so it was somewhat surprising that I hadn't been hit before. Considering all of the things I'd lived through, I figured I would've been able to handle being punched a little better. No woman should ever have to *handle* being hit, of course. In a perfect world, at least. Yet I was all too aware that this world was far from perfect. Though I did think that I was overdue for a period of my life when I wasn't subjected to the violence of men.

Life didn't work that way, though.

"He's dead," Hades murmured, finally lifting his hand from my face.

I felt the loss immediately. His touch leaving my face seemed to be more painful than anything else right now. Of course that made no sense, and I was currently on a lot of drugs.

"You can't kill someone for me," I croaked.

Hades's eyes narrowed. "Yes, Freya, I can. I can kill the man who did that to you."

I blinked at him, my eyes moving over him. "Why?" I whispered, my voice a rasp.

"Because, Freya, you're mine."

The words washed over me like a tsunami, my fingertips prickling, my toes curling. And then, before I could properly digest what he'd said, before I could say a word, I drifted out.

I might've imagined it, but I was sure I felt Hades's hand in mine.

HADES

"I've got Wire on the trace right now." Swiss's tone was clipped, his eyes on the door a few feet away.

I hadn't let them in the room. Freya was sleeping. I'd sat with her, my hand holding hers, the entire night. Aside from the brief interruption by that fucker Kallum. The guy who, up until recently,

I had respected and almost liked. Now I wanted to rip his fucking head off. I hated the way he looked at Freya. The familiarity, the intimacy, the ownership there. Fucking hated that he was holding a bag full of her shit. It was bright pink with a fucking leopard print heart on it. This big fucker with muscles, tats and a glower that told me he was capable of true violence, was carrying a bright pink bag and doing it with some kind of warped pride.

"What the fuck are you doing here?" he'd demanded when he entered the room with the bag, eyes on Freya's small hand in mine.

What the fuck was I doing here?

Sarah had called.

She'd told me what happened, despite it being against regulations or Hippocratic Oaths or whatever the fuck. Sarah had abandoned all oaths since getting involved with us. I had no clue why she'd even called me. How she knew that I'd care. But Sarah was a smart bitch when it came to that kind of shit, had some kind of sixth sense.

My entire body had reacted when she'd told me that Freya had been attacked, beaten. That she was alive but battered and bruised.

Battered and fucking bruised.

If I'd had the name and address of the fucker who was responsible, I would've gone straight there, dragged him down to our basement and made his death last days. Months.

As it was, we didn't have any other information. Plus I needed to see her. With my own fucking eyes. Even if seeing her swollen, bruised face in a hospital bed was a punch to the fucking gut.

It made no sense, the visceral reaction I had to this woman. Why I wanted to rip my skin off my fucking body rather than see her hurt and small in this hospital bed. Then her hand had curled with mine, holding it in a death grip, even while unconscious, and I hadn't been able to think of much else.

Well, other than what I was going to do to the man responsible for this.

Until Kallum walked in.

"I'm here for Freya," I answered his earlier question as my eyes went from the pink bag to his face.

"Freya has nothing to do with the Sons of Templar." He spoke with conviction. Surety. Too fucking sure for my liking. For him to be that sure, he had to know Freya. A lot more than a boss should know his employee.

My eyes flickered to Freya. Another gut punch. The bruises were darkening with every passing hour. Her eyes were still closed, and she looked to be sleeping peacefully. Her full lips were strawberry pink, a dusting of freckles across her nose I'd never noticed before. She looked young, vulnerable, fucking beautiful. Although I would've preferred to cut my fucking arm off, I let go of Freya's hand so I could get up and stand toe to toe with this fucker.

"Freya doesn't have anything to do with the Sons of Templar," I agreed.

He clenched his jaw, gripping the bag in his hand. "Well then, why the fuck are the Sons here?"

"The Sons aren't here. *I'm* here." I made sure to inject challenge into my voice. Plenty of it. I knew that I was an intimidating guy. A terrifying guy. It had nothing to do with my tattoos or my cut that had everything to do with a deep survival instinct that I awakened in people. I fucking liked it. It was very rare that a man didn't instinctively back down from me. On any other occasion I would've respected the man. But not when Freya was involved.

"Freya does not need this shit," he chided, his nostrils flaring.

Fire crawled up my throat. "You have no idea what Freya needs."

His knuckles were white. "I have a much better fucking idea than you do. You don't even know her."

"I know enough that she wants me here. That she needs me here. We gonna have a problem?"

I wasn't just asking him whether or not he had a problem with me, I was asking him whether he had a problem with the club.

That was a whole different fucking ballgame. Kallum had been careful not to get too involved with us since he'd set up shop. We'd been happy with that, since he ran a clean business and didn't cause any trouble. Plus, the entire club loved his fucking girls.

But just because he was quiet didn't mean we didn't do our homework. We knew his history. Knew he'd lived his life on the street, then inside. That meant he knew the rules of the street. He was trying his best to play it straight and narrow which meant politely declining the one business opportunity that we'd presented him with.

Other clubs might've insisted he take the deal, but Hansen wasn't like that. We were outlaws, but we stayed as clean as we could. Didn't drag in people who didn't want to be there. In my experience, that caused problems eventually.

Kallum hadn't wanted to be involved in anything with us.

Probably because he never wanted to be inside again. I got that. But I was interested to see how far that went. If he was willing to throw it all away for the battered woman in this bed. The woman he obviously cared about. The woman who laughed with him easily, touched his fucking hand, who he knew well enough to go into her house and gather shit for her.

I knew I was willing to fucking die for her already, as fucking insane as that was.

There were a couple of long moments where it looked like Kallum was ready to throw it all away for this woman—like any sane or insane man would—ready to go against me and the club to protect her. Something inside me awakened, ears perked, hungry for blood.

But then whatever fire that had sparked inside of Kallum, the kind of fire that was ready to burn the world down for the right woman—it died.

It couldn't be because Freya wasn't the right woman for him— she was the right fucking woman for every man. Maybe he was too haunted by his past, too trapped by his own sanity to set the world on fire for any woman.

For whatever reason, he backed down.

"She asked for this." Instead of handing the bag to me, he moved farther into the room. It took everything inside of me not to stop him bodily as he placed the bag on the opposite side of the bed from where I'd been sitting.

Without looking at me, he focused on Freya, his jaw stiff, brows narrowed. He lifted his hand to gently brush her hair from her forehead.

I had to clench my fists at my sides so I didn't rip his fucking arm off. Eventually, after a goddamn eternity, he moved from her side, walking back around the bed.

"I swear to fuck, if you had anything to do with this, I'll hold you personally responsible," he ground out.

I chuckled. "Yeah, buddy, I'm quaking in my fuckin' boots here," I said because I knew I could take him with one hand tied behind my back and also because I wanted to taunt him. Wanted to see if he'd lose it and give me what I needed.

Blood.

But after a beat, he turned on his heel and left.

It took five minutes for me to unclench my fists, to figure out a way to touch Freya again without brutality. But I did. I sat beside her bed, lifted her tiny hand and secured it in mine.

Then I waited for the sun to rise. Swiss and Elden had said they'd be there by dawn. They'd been on a run but had ridden through the night to get back. I'd shot off a text to Hansen in the early hours, telling him I needed details on what the fuck happened and who the fuck did this as soon as possible. I wasn't meant to be the one giving orders to my president, but he also knew that I wasn't one to be demanding this shit unless it fucking mattered.

Both Swiss and Elden cursed and let out hisses of breath when they'd walked into the room, laying eyes on Freya. I didn't like their fury. There was ownership behind that. They were fucking furious because they cared. Too many fucking men cared about Freya. But for now, I had to lock that down since they were men who could help me track down the one who did this to her.

I'd herded them out of the room in order to speak without waking her up and because I didn't want their fucking eyes on her.

"We tapped the security cameras outside Fate," Swiss filled me in, his eyes dark. "Lucky for us, Kallum pays for a top-notch system, gets it updated and serviced regularly. Crystal fucking clear. Got his face, car, license plate. Derek Ashton. Old money. No connection to us which means it's something personal with Freya."

Nothing in me relaxed at that news. Whether or not it was the club's fault that Freya was in that bed, her face battered like that, it didn't matter. What mattered is that she was fucking there in the first place. If anything, the attack having nothing to do with us was worse because we didn't know what the fuck we were dealing with. The club was a lifestyle, a family, a brotherhood, but it was also a business. Yes, there were some jumped-up cowboys who didn't know the rules to this business, something our chapter knew all too well. But on the whole, there were rules, and most people, even the dirtiest and most ruthless of criminals, the coldest of psychopaths, played by the fucking rules. In business. This being personal made it all the more dangerous for Freya.

"Based out of Texas but just arrived in town last night," Swiss continued, voice grim. "Already went to his hotel. Wasn't there."

I rubbed the back of my neck, thinking about how much I needed coffee since I'd been up all night watching Freya, eyes on her chest, making sure it moved up and down regularly.

"Find him," I ordered. "And find out why the fuck he thought he could put his hands on my woman."

Swiss hadn't so much as cracked a grin since he'd arrived here. The man smiled ear to ear when he was cutting a motherfucker from neck to belly button, but this was different.

He didn't smile or smirk when I spoke, but something moved across his face.

"There it is again, *your woman*." He elbowed Elden who, as usual, hadn't uttered a single word. "His woman," he shook his head. "We've lost another one, I think."

"Go fuck yourself," I scowled. "Then find that fucking prick so I can feel his goddamn blood on my hands."

CHAPTER SEVEN

FREYA

I didn't wake up confused. I knew I was in a hospital. Knew from the smells, the uncomfortable bed, the cheap sheets and the gown. My mouth was dry, my tongue feeling too big for my mouth and my stomach churned.

Not to mention that I felt like I'd been hit by a bus. My ribs hurt. Burned. I didn't move, because I knew if I did, the pain would radiate to my toes. I also couldn't be sure I wouldn't vomit everywhere. So I stayed completely still.

My cheek throbbed, and my jaw felt stiff as if it was made of glass.

Last night was not a blur, although I wished it was. Everything played through my mind in slow motion, every moment of it.

The crunch of Derek's fist on my face. The pain exploding through my cheek, the warm blood on my face, the coppery taste of it in my mouth. The concrete, cold and hard underneath me, the man who I hadn't even considered a threat suddenly becoming my abuser, me suddenly becoming the thing I'd promised myself I'd never be again.

A victim.

Though all of that was very clear, I feared I had imagined the last part of it. That I'd imagined *him*. Despite the fact that there was a hand, large and warm, encasing mine. Even though, above the sterile hospital smell, his scent invaded my senses. Musk. Cigarettes. Leather. Male. Hades.

I'd been awake for a hot minute, but I kept my eyes squeezed shut and forced my breathing to remain even. I wanted to enjoy the simplicity of laying here. Although it was impossible to enjoy the uncomfortable bed, the cheap foreign sheets, the dry mouth and the uneasy stomach, I wanted to enjoy Hades's hand in mine. And even though I was still a little fuzzy from the drugs and general trauma, I knew that this, right here, was going to be the simplest part of my day. The simplest part of my life for the foreseeable future.

"I know you're awake."

My body twitched, the movement beyond my control, an involuntary reaction to the smooth, low voice caressing my insides.

The hand around mine flexed, and I braced for the release, the emptiness that would come when his hand released mine. But it didn't go anywhere. He gripped my hand tighter than before, but nowhere near painful. He was still being gentle with me. That said something about how bad I looked.

Though I wasn't eager to face the day or face my reflection, I couldn't stop myself from opening my eyes when I was promised with Hades as the first thing I saw.

He did not disappoint.

His hair was mussed, liked always, falling effortlessly across his eyebrows like an inky silk curtain. His eyes moved, alighting when they met mine, simmering with intensity. The green one an emerald, the blue one pure ice. Some of the fury remained from last night. A lot of it, actually. But there was something else too. Something I couldn't put my finger on.

His skin seemed even paler beneath the florescent lights, making every one of his features that much more striking. Cutting.

I wasn't sure if he'd been here all night, but he sure as fuck didn't look like he had.

"You're a sight for sore eyes," I rasped, my voice low and scratchy. "Literally." I gestured to my left eye, the one that felt tight, uncomfortable and tender.

The slight movement sent pain ricocheting through me. I tried to hide my flinch, but Hades saw everything. Though I hadn't noticed it initially, he had been relaxed. Or at least as relaxed as a man like Hades could be. The second I flinched, his body turned taut, as if someone had yanked a string attached to all of his muscles.

I let out a mewl of protest as he let go of my hand to move to the call button. Hades's glower deepened as he most likely misunderstood that sound as a whimper of pain. It was probably better to let him think that it was because I couldn't stand him not holding my hand.

"I swear to *fuck*," he muttered, getting up and pacing, his eyes on me.

The words were saturated with frustration, with fury.

For me.

As much as his presence comforted, unnerved and distracted me, it also confused the ever-loving fuck out of me.

I shifted, trying to yank my body upward in the bed so I wasn't laying down flat with him towering over me.

Hades stormed over to me as I let out a hiss of air between my teeth.

"Don't fuckin' move until the doctor gets here." His hand was on the center of my chest, gently holding me down. He didn't have to exert pressure because I was laughably weak right now. Weak due to the beating, the shock of Hades being here, acting like the possessive male, and weak because I hadn't eaten since lunchtime yesterday. It felt like I hadn't had water in fucking *weeks*.

So I didn't fight him. Though I did glare at him. I did it regardless of the fire that spread through his body from where his palm laid flat on my chest, thumb and pinky barely brushing the tops of my breasts. The touch itself wasn't sexual. Or at least it wasn't meant to be.

His palm stayed there as I breathed, moving slowly up and down with his eyes locked on mine. I'm not sure how long we would've stayed like this had the doctor not rushed in, ruining the moment.

I would've ripped his head off had he not been the guy with the drugs. He'd checked my vitals then let me know that there were a couple of ribs broken and a lot of bruises that would heal on their own.

I was to be discharged later in the day. There was no mention of an interview with the police, something I found odd. I was sure the hospital had a legal obligation to contact the authorities after someone came in with such injuries. But maybe I watched too much *SVU*.

The nurse came in straight after, bringing water and food which she urged me to eat, which I only finished because of Hades's watchful eye and the thin line of his lips that told me he'd force the food down my neck if I didn't.

Then she offered to take me to the bathroom. Hades himself took my hip and helped me across the room. I didn't make eye contact with him, but I pressed into his comforting hold, relishing the hard lines of his body. He had carried my pink bag in first, leaving it hanging on a little hook for me.

Though it was infinitely embarrassing, he was waiting for me when I came out. I felt well enough to walk under my own power, and I definitely should've done that for independent women everywhere. Instead, I let Hades walk me back to bed.

The nurse lingered for a bit, her eyes on Hades with a little too much interest for my liking. Though it didn't matter what I did or didn't like since we weren't together. We weren't dating. We weren't sleeping together. We hadn't even fucking kissed.

I'd saved his life that one time.

He'd sat by my hospital bed, holding my hand the entire night. He'd vowed to kill the man who did this to me. He had already killed the man who'd held a gun to my head.

But he wasn't my boyfriend.

My head hurt enough without trying to dissect what the fuck Hades was to me.

Finally, the nurse left, and she didn't leave her number in his cut or something that would've hurt more than another punch to the face. Well, maybe not *more* than a punch to the face, but it was comparable.

As much as I had wanted her to leave, I became suddenly and terribly uncomfortable in the room alone with Hades. I was thankful that in the bag that Kallum had dropped off at some point when I was unconscious and Hades was here—I really would've loved to see that—there were some PJs. I tried my best not to think about my attractive, alpha male boss going through my pajama drawer. My pajama drawer was not chaste. It contained a lot of silk, a lot of lace and a lot of lingerie. I was grateful to see that he hadn't chosen to put any of that in my bag. Instead there was a pair of silk, bright pink, oversized pajamas that draped over my skin like butter and smelled like my fabric softener. They calmed me. Grounded me.

I also felt a fuck of a lot more attractive after washing my face, applying my skincare and spritzing on perfume. I owed Kallum one. A hundred, actually. For a man with muscles, tattoos and an air of menace, he somehow knew to include the essentials of my skincare routine. It was hard to do with my face how it was, and it was hard for me to see myself like this, but I'd bit my lip until I tasted blood and forced myself through it.

Hades had been prowling around the room like a caged animal while the nurse had been doing her thing—in between checking him out—but now he'd stopped. He stopped to look at me, sitting cross legged in the hospital bed, propped up by the three extra pillows that he had obtained at some point. I'd been considering my phone which was sitting on the table, wondering if there was someone I should call. Not Aunt V. No way. Maybe Marilyn. Her strong, comforting presence was always helpful. Hades was going to leave sometime, and I wasn't strong enough to be alone.

When he spoke, I thought it would be announcing his exit. But I was wrong. Really wrong.

"I've got a lot of things I want you to tell me about, but first things first, I want to know what the fuck you were doing in that parking lot alone at three in the morning. Kallum and I are going to have a fucking conversation about why in the fuck he doesn't have someone watching over you."

My stomach dropped at the chill in Hades's voice, what was left unsaid. The probability that the kind of conversation he planned on having with Kallum would involve violence.

I was sure that Kallum had experience taking care of himself, but I was also sure he'd never come across a man like Hades. Because another man like Hades didn't exist. The urge to protect my friend was overwhelming, so I spoke quickly without thinking.

"Dante doesn't like waiting," I said, moving in the bed. My ribs protested, and my cheek throbbed. I'd never been hit before. Boy did it *hurt*, though the pain was not what I was focusing on right now. It was the growing, deadly glare on Hades's face.

"Dante doesn't like waiting," he repeated as he folded his huge arms in front of him as a vein bulged in his neck.

I shivered, actually fucking *shivered* at his tone. It was flat, emotionless. Or it should've been. Something about his eyes, though. The way his hands were fisted at his sides and the way his body was too still to be human, made it clear that there was emotion in there.

"Um, yeah," I shrugged before I remembered everything hurt. "Dante is kind of an asshole. He doesn't take his job very seriously, but honestly, I feel safer walking to my car alone than with Dante. Well, except for last night."

Okay, that was the wrong thing to say. Totally fucking wrong thing to say.

"Dante is going to be looking for new employment starting now," he seethed. "After he recuperates."

I blinked. "Jesus, Hades, you can't just make all these badass threats of violence about everyone you think deserves it."

"Look at your fuckin' face Freya," he bit out. "He deserves it."

I held in my flinch at his tone. I felt delicate today. Like tissue paper instead of the usual steel. Hades didn't know me very well, but when he looked at me, I felt like he saw my insides, so I knew that he'd noticed how vulnerable I was. Fuck, anyone would notice, considering I was in a hospital bed after being beaten up by my asshole ex-boyfriend.

Anyone would've treated me a little more delicately. A lot more delicately.

Hades was not anyone.

And he was not treating me delicately. I didn't even think this man was capable of that.

"Why are you doing this?" I asked, my voice much wispier than I'd intended. "Why are you here in my hospital room, glowering, dripping dangerous hotness everywhere while promising vengeance? You barely know me. We're..."

I didn't know how to finish that sentence. All I knew was that it felt dangerously normal to have Hades here, his presence casting a shadow over the stark white hospital room.

"How about we talk about what I do and don't know about you later? Right now, we're going to focus on you telling me everything you know about the fuck who did this."

I fingered the cheap polyester sheets, avoiding his eye contact. Yes, I would love to chop off Derek's balls and then make him eat them. Well, the dark parts of me wanted to do that. But most of me, the lighter, more squeamish and more well-balanced part of me figured karma would find him. Maybe reporting this in a town where his parents couldn't buy off the police meant he might actually get some justice.

Maybe not.

I'd report it no matter what, because if Derek was capable of doing this to me, he'd probably already hurt other women, or he would in the very near future. I'd do my very best to make sure he didn't. But giving Hades information that he'd use to most likely kill him would weigh too heavily on my conscience, so I wasn't doing that.

"Give me your fucking eyes, Freya," Hades demanded, frost in his voice.

Without my brain being in control of them, my eyes immediately darted to his. My skin tingled under the force of his stare.

"You know this fucker," he deduced after looking at me for a long moment.

Shit, was I that transparent, or was he that fucking good?

Whichever one it was, I knew there was no way I could lie to him.

"Look, it's not a big deal," I rushed out, still trapped in his gaze. "I have an ex. He doesn't like being my ex, but I didn't like being cheated on, talked down to and being in his presence, so I dumped him. He'd never been dumped before. He's rich, entitled, attractive like he was made on a hot guy conveyer belt, all the stuff is there. You appreciate it at first, but once you get close enough it's just … boring, I guess." My eyes moved over his face. The ink covering his face. The slight crookedness of his nose. The different colored eyes, glittering like gemstones.

"He's nothing like you," I whispered. "There was no conveyer belt with you. You were handmade, my friend." My cheeks burned, realizing what I'd just said.

Oh my god. Don't just sit here gaping and turning red. Say something.

"Anyway," I continued, waving my hand, going for nonchalance. "He sometimes, kind of … follows me. Finds me however it is rich guys with lots of resources and no real job figure out how to find people. Usually, he tries romantic gestures. You know, flowers, gifts, the whole thing. But when I don't accept and tell him in no uncertain terms to go away, he gets mad. Never anything like this, of course. This is a whole new level of assholery. In the past it was just words. Insults, that kind of thing..."

I trailed off, deciding not to tell him about the time he'd slashed my tires and spray painted 'slut' on the side of my car since he was getting more and more still, and that twinkling kind of intensity that had been there when I was talking about him being handmade was now nowhere to be seen.

This was a completely new kind of intensity.

One that should have absolutely terrified me. Which it did. Kind of. Mostly it just turned me on.

All the way on.

"He follows you," he said slowly.

I swallowed at his tone, the way his words made the air thicker, making it almost impossible to breathe. Not trusting myself to speak, I nodded once.

He looked like he was going to say some things. A lot of things. Not quietly. I waited for these things, the ones that protective alpha males spouted. The questions about why I hadn't gone to the cops. I had, but with my nomadic lifestyle, my chosen profession and the fact that Derek's last name held a bunch of sway, the reports hadn't gone anywhere.

He didn't ask questions nor demand to know why I hadn't tried to do more. Instead, he uttered something that might've knocked my socks off, had I been wearing any.

"You're movin' in with me."

I blinked. "Excuse me?"

"You heard. Once you get discharged, you're gonna pack your shit. Or better yet, I'll get Scarlett over to pack your shit since you need to rest. She'll know what you need. Or you can make a list.

Anything she forgets or doesn't get, you tell me, I'll go out and buy it."

"Scarlett?" I repeated, wondering if my meds were kicking in again.

He gave me a brusque nod that seemed to be more like an impatient twitch. "Old Lady. In town for the week. She knows girl shit."

Just when he looked like he was about to move forward and drag me somewhere—which I got the feeling he was about to do—and I lost all of my faculties under the magic that was his touch, I held up my hand.

"Wait, this is getting far too alpha male for my liking, with all of this telling, the clipped words and the brooding stare." I tried to make it sound like the brooding stare wasn't at all impressive, but it really fucking was.

His jaw flexed, and he folded his arms across his chest.

Do not look at his biceps. Do not look at the flexing muscles and think about them wrapping around you. Oh, you've gone and fucking done it, haven't you, you horny bitch.

"No," I snapped, both to my hormones and to Hades.

"No isn't an option," he returned.

"No is most certainly an option," I argued, sitting up even more in bed. If he hadn't been standing so close and I was feeling strong enough, I would've grabbed my bag and stormed out. But he was standing much too close, and I wasn't feeling strong enough. So I did my best with furrowed brows and a 'don't fuck with me' look.

"I barely know you," I pointed out before he could keep on saying shit that was really, *really* pissing me off. "I am a grown woman. A grown woman who got the shit beaten out of her by an overzealous male last night. One I knew a fuck of a lot better than I know you. In ordinary circumstances, I would not react well to someone deciding I'm going to move in with them. Especially if that someone has a penis. I'm reacting even worse right now."

Hades's glower intensified tenfold. "I would never lay a hand on you."

An oath.

Something at the bottom of my stomach flipped. In a bad way and a something else kind of way. I could not allow myself to get caught up in that feeling, and luckily, the fire burning a little higher in my belly helped.

"I know you're not going to lay a hand on me," I conceded, my voice firm, sure. I believed it with every cell in my body. Which was incredibly stupid and naïve considering just last night I'd been sure that Derek wouldn't lay a hand on me either. Needless to say, I believed my own words and his.

"I also know that I'm not moving in with you," I continued. "For a variety of reasons. Some of which I've already mentioned, like that I barely know you. You're part of a club that I have absolutely nothing against but I'm not at all interested in getting caught up in. Beyond that, I have a dog who likes his home. *I* like my home. I like my mugs. My shower. My entire beauty routine is there. My sheets are divine. I feel safe there. Plus, the entire idea is completely ridiculous and not something that happens in real life."

"What about that?" Hades gestured violently to my face, so much so that I flinched. That only caused his jaw to harden further. "That," he murmured again, nodding his head to my face. "That is something very fuckin' real that happened in your life last night. Something that, by the sound of it, is very fuckin' likely to happen again based on your description of this asshole. And that's something I refuse to let happen to you ever again."

Another oath.

"Eventually, I'll take care of this fucker," he vowed, causing my blood to run cold.

There was no mistaking what he meant by that, nor was there any mistaking that the dark part of me was satisfied and turned on by his words.

"I don't plan on that takin' long," he added. "But it could take longer than I want. And this piece of shit has been stalking you for years, so he's not goin' to stop. Not until you're dead. He's going to come back. You live in the middle of nowhere with no one to hear you scream. Your dog is terrified of its own shadow. You're unprotected." He paused, his eyes moving over me, something moving inside of his mind. "If you're not willin' to move in with me, I'm comin' to you." He raised his brow ever so slightly in challenge.

I bit my lip, forgetting that it was bruised and swollen. It smarted, but I was glad for the pain. With the pain came clarity.

This biker in front of me was making it very clear that he was going to do everything in his considerable power to make sure I didn't get hurt again. And although it was absolutely ridiculous to consider him moving into my home, into my sanctuary, it was also ridiculous to think that Derek was going to leave me alone. Plus, there was no way I was going to move into a strange place with a man who terrified and fascinated me.

Hades was right about him. I knew that the second his fist landed in my face. For whatever reason, he wasn't going to stop until he killed me. And I had no protection. I didn't believe in guns. I barely knew how to throw a punch and my dog would do nothing if an intruder came through intent on murder.

Sure, I could buy a gun, learn how to shoot, I could take a kickboxing class—which I was totally going to do—I could run again, but none of those were permanent fixes. I already knew that if this went to court, his father would know a judge or a senator who'd get him off with little more than a slap on the wrist. That would be after my entire life was dissected, and I'd be made to look like a cheap whore.

So instead of arguing more, I nodded and whispered, "okay."

CHAPTER EIGHT

"Okay, so you know that there's a man in your living room, right?" Marilyn chirped after she'd strutted into my bedroom, a large Chanel tote slung over her shoulder. She had been to visit me just before I'd been discharged from the hospital with Kallum in tow. Tears had filled her eyes as she'd muttered curses about men, about how every single one should have their cocks cut off. I'd never heard her speak with such anger, with such animosity before.

It had hit me in a place very deep down, a very vulnerable place where nobody other than my Aunt V had reached in such a visceral way. I'd managed to hold in my tears, fearing they wouldn't stop once they started.

Fortunately, Marilyn wasn't one to linger in painful, emotional moments, and she'd straightened her spine then opened her bag to prepare to do my hair. She painted my nails too. There was no need for makeup considering I was wearing various shades of purple and pink already. Plus, anything touching my face hurt. It even hurt to smile too wide.

Kallum had leaned against the wall with his arms crossed, glowering. I wasn't sure if it was because he was a protective, kind man and seeing a woman, a friend bruised and battered like this, fucked with him. Or if he was still harboring guilt for having employed a fuck-stick like Dante. Or because there was some protective, alpha male showdown going on with Hades who was off 'getting his shit.' Anderson had been lounging in the chair in my room before Marilyn and Kallum arrived. Both had looked at Anderson— Marilyn with obvious interest, Kallum with a glower.

Kallum had given Marilyn a ride so he didn't get the chance to say whatever may have been burning inside of him. I'd dealt with enough males in the past twenty-four hours.

Hades had arrived not long after they left, with Marilyn promising to come over once I was home.

And here she was keeping her promise.

"A man wearing a Sons of Templar cut and wearing the absolute fuck out of it is in your house," she fanned herself with one hand as she put her bag on one of the chairs at the end of my bed. Then she ruffled Sirius's head. He'd been incredibly fascinated by Hades when he'd first walked in with me. But he quickly became incredibly protective of me once he'd gotten a good look at me and the tentative way I was moving around the house. He had not left my side since.

I felt awkward with Hades in my house, unsure of what to do with myself. Suddenly, my cozy, colorful, chic home felt strange and foreign. I felt uncomfortable inside of my own battered and bruised skin, staring out all of the windows I'd loved so much yesterday. And all the yesterdays before that. I'd adored the fact that I could look out every single window and not see a house or the evidence of a single soul.

Now, I felt exposed and unsafe. Or I definitely would've felt like that had Hades not been here.

But he was here.

I was totally fucking glad he was here. That was supremely anti-feminist of me, but sometimes when your ex beats you half to death you need a scary, sexy, dangerous biker lingering in your living room with a gun.

I'd offered him every kind of liquid I had in my fridge, including cold-pressed celery juice and kombucha. He'd declined everything without even looking at me. He was too busy looking at all the entrances and exits with a furrowed brow. I figured that the locks weren't up to his standard. I must've been annoying the shit out of him since he ordered me to lie down in my bed. Or maybe he'd noted the way I was holding myself and had barely slept last night.

Whatever it was, I'd been glad for the command and had let him walk me into my bedroom. He'd glanced to the bed once with an empty expression, then he had walked out without a word. I hadn't known how to take that. I didn't have enough energy to think about how to take that. So I ran myself a bath and stayed in there for forty-five minutes. Then I'd put on my very expensive and comfy sweats which I'd thought were a rather ridiculous purchase since sweats weren't supposed to be expensive, but I was incredibly happy I owned them now since I wanted to look effort-lessly and impossibly glam.

Hades had not entered my bedroom again, though. Not even to ask me if I needed more water or pills or something to eat. Then again, he wasn't here to take care of me in that kind of way. He was here to make sure I wasn't horribly murdered.

Marilyn, thank God, was here to take care of me in that kind of way.

"I'm aware of the man," I told her, pausing the *Real Housewives* and sitting up in bed. She had started unpacking everything that was bursting out of her Chanel.

"Oh, as long as you're aware," she replied, raising her brow while handing me a jar of edible cookie dough and a spoon. I grinned, shaking my head, taking it gratefully.

"Well, he kind of owes me one," I hedged, opening the jar, avoiding eye contact.

She continued unearthing snacks with varying degrees of sugar from her bag. "I'm going to need to know why a member of the Sons of Templar owes you one and why the fuck you haven't told me about it," she replied, holding up what I knew to be a very expensive bottle of Pinot Noir from New Zealand. "I'm also going to need to know how many pain killers you're on, so I can pour your wine accordingly. The good ones you get a big glass, the really good ones you get an even bigger one." She winked.

"You should pour it readily and heavily if we're going to have this conversation," I admitted with a sigh.

Marilyn grinned. "Oh, yes, I suspect we're going to need a lot of wine." She began walking toward my bedroom door. "I'm going to go get glasses and drool all over that man again. I'm also going to put together a cheese platter to balance out the sugar." She nodded her head at the snacks covering my comforter which Sirius was sniffing thoughtfully. "I know you well enough to know that you have the fixings for an excellent charcuterie platter in your fridge at all times."

Marilyn did know me well enough to be right about that. Two things I always had in my fridge: ingredients for a charcuterie platter and French champagne. She knew me and my house well enough to leave and come back in twenty minutes with an excellent looking cheeseboard and two very generous glasses of wine.

I knew her well enough to know that it did not take her twenty minutes to pour wine and put together a cheeseboard. This was not her first rodeo.

I also knew her well enough to know that she loved men, hot men. And Hades was beyond hot. Fortunately, I also knew that she loved me more than she loved hot men, if only by a slim margin. She was protective. Behind the red lipstick, the perfectly curled, perfectly colored hair, the slim-cut red suit and rockstud Valentinos, she was a bad bitch. Certainly brave enough to take on someone like Hades if she thought he was a threat to me. It was very likely that she had given some threatening speech to him in the kitchen. On any other occasion, I might've grilled her about what she'd said to him, but Hades would not have been in my kitchen on any other occasion.

So instead of doing that, I took the glass of wine and waited for her to arrange our little feast on the bed, sneaking a slice of cheese to Sirius before I shooed him off my bed and back to his bed in the corner of the room.

Marilyn held up her glass. "To the super bad, super-hot, super scary biker and his team of equally super-hot and scary bikers finding that motherfucker and burning him alive," she toasted cheerfully.

My stomach dropped ever so slightly at that visual and the prospect of Derek's death weighing on my conscience for the rest of my life. But I gritted my teeth and clinked my glass to hers, taking a heavy swallow.

"Now's the time to spill," she informed me, picking at the Brie.

I took a breath, then another sip, and then I spilled.

And spilled.

Everything. From the night we met till now. Everything including my confusing feelings for the man. Including the fact that sometimes I thought he might have confusing feelings for me too. Except when it seemed like he didn't; when it seemed like he didn't like me at all.

"Holy fuck," she uttered.

I nodded.

"Holy fuck," she repeated.

I nodded again, as this entire situation really did warrant two holy fucks.

"I don't know how it happened," I admitted as she refilled my wine. The story had needed a lot of it. "I moved here because it's small. Tranquil. Quiet. A place for me to settle. Peacefully. Where there's no trouble."

Marilyn quirked her brow. "Honey, you're a stripper with an ass that won't quit, moves that I've never seen before in my life and eyes that tell anyone looking that you're a great fuck. On top of that, you're a YouTube sensation, some kind of whiz with the stock market and make more in a year than a fucking surgeon." She gulped her wine. "There's no way you can exist anywhere in this world without at least a little trouble. And I'm not talking about the asshole who did that." She nodded to my face, fire in her eyes. "I'm talking about that out there." She pointed in the direction of the kitchen with her wine glass.

"But I don't think he likes me," I whined, hating the way I sounded. I also fucking hated that I was somehow still interested in whether a guy did or didn't like me after what had happened to me last night.

"Honey, he likes you. He's prowling around out there like a caged lion. You can feel it in the fucking air, his fury. I only know that because I'm plenty fucking furious too. And I love you. It's only people who care about you that can get *that* mad about you getting hurt."

I bit my lip. That made sense. At least a little sense. I'd been battling with why in the heck his reaction to this was so damn strong. Yes, Anderson had seemed pretty fucking pissed off, his normally casual expression turning rock hard, his eyes filled with rage. But he hadn't demanded I move in with him and his pregnant girlfriend, nor had he been willing to move into my home with me.

"It makes no sense. Him being here. Him being all intense. I don't get it."

I waited expectantly as Marilyn just stared at me.

"What?" she demanded after a few beats.

"Some insight would be great," I grumbled.

"Honey, just because I happened to be born with the same parts does not mean that I know what the fuck men are thinking. I may know a lot about them through sheer experience, but I know nothing about *that* kind of man." She did the pointing with the wine glass thing again. "I don't think another man like that exists. The world would tilt on its axis or something."

I sighed. "Yeah, you're right." Oh, and you can't tell Des," I ordered.

Her brows furrowed. "I won't tell Des because *you* have to tell Des."

It was my turn to furrow my brows. "I do not have to tell Des. Des will do something stupid."

She didn't speak immediately because she knew that seeing my face, Des would get angry. Very angry. Then he'd be likely to do something stupid.

"Des does not need to know," I stated firmly, my stomach turning even thinking about him seeing my face.

"How are you going to hide it from him?" Marilyn asked. "It's going to take weeks for that to go away. And one week at the very least for makeup to be able to cover it."

I sighed, the small realities of this situation rushing at me. "I'll make excuses. Tell him I'm sick or something. Can we please not talk about it right now?" My voice went up at the end, too high. Bordering on shrill. That was only because I was forcing it not to shake, struggling to keep the tears from escaping.

Marilyn's face softened, and she reached forward to pat my hand.

"For now, let's drink wine and eat food we don't need, watch trash TV and try to forget about men, good and bad."

"Good plan," I agreed. "You're staying the night, right?"

"Of course I'm staying the night," she said. "I brought my toothbrush and nothing else because I know you've got great PJs and even better skincare."

I relaxed back into my bed, glad that, at least for tonight, I didn't have to sleep alone in my house with Hades under the same roof.

HADES

Being in her space was hard.

Fucking hard.

It was full of shit I didn't understand, a sofa with too many cushions, throws and other crap. Candles everywhere. Rugs. A bed that looked like nothing I'd ever seen. A bed I wanted to fuck Freya in. Every way I knew how to fuck a woman. And I knew how to fuck a woman in a lot of ways. I wanted to invent new ways to fuck Freya.

I'd been here before, and I'd been smart enough to shut down any and all kinds of feelings about Freya or her house. I didn't have that choice now, though. Not with Freya looking like she did. Not with her walking around, teeth gritted, trying and failing to hide the pain she was in. I didn't miss the way her black and blue face paled as she looked around her living room, seeing it through new eyes. Eyes that bore the evidence of what a violent, entitled, self-centered piece of shit could do when he was presented with what he couldn't have.

Now her home, the one that she'd worked her ass off to purchase, the one that she probably loved due to its solitude and peace, was now just another place he could ruin. A place where he could hurt her.

Her house made no goddamn sense to me, and it pissed me the fuck off. It pissed me off that I knew what the inside of her bedroom looked like, but I didn't know what the inside of her pussy felt like.

Then there was the friend. The one I'd seen at the club. Amazing tits. Full figure. A knockout in every way that would've made most men instantly fucking hard. Any man who hadn't seen Freya.

She had come in with her own key, which told me she was a close friend. Then there was the speech that told me she was a good friend.

"Hey, Sons of Anarchy," she'd called from the kitchen.

I had been on the phone with Keltan from Greenstone Security, telling him I'd really fucking appreciate him getting his guys out here by tomorrow. He'd been about to give me trouble, but then I'd told him what happened to Freya. He'd gone silent for a beat then told me he'd be flying out here to oversee the installation personally. And he'd get his guys on the case, tracking down the piece of shit responsible. He wouldn't be there for what happened when we caught him. Sure, if it was his woman, he would've been. But Keltan mostly worked in the gray areas. He wasn't all the way in the black like the Sons of Templar were. Like my chapter was.

My chapter ignored every fucking rule and law except the ones we made for ourselves. Which made us very fucking dangerous. It also made it so people did not talk to me the way that Blondie just had. Nor did anyone crook their finger at me like they were expecting me to obey that gesture.

I had no fucking idea why I'd told Keltan I'd call him back then walked over to the breakfast bar.

She'd had a look on her face that made my steps almost tentative. Fucking almost.

"I'm not going to ask why you're here," she said as she rummaged around in the kitchen. "Because all that matters is the fact you're armed and adept in the art of killing."

I didn't respond to her. I hadn't needed to.

She popped the cork on a bottle of wine then moved across the room to a shelf full of tumblers to get two wine glasses.

"I'm not adept at killing, but I sure could get there if I was presented with the guy who did *that* to my friend." She tilted her head toward the hallway where I'd banished Freya then headed back to the breakfast bar.

I was glad this chick was here because I was a fucking coward. Because I could barely look at Freya. Because I didn't trust myself in the same room as her.

"I've got a feeling you've got that covered, though," she added as she poured the wine.

I nodded once, my body already heating at the thought of what it was going to feel like being covered in that asshole's blood.

"Good," she said. "I haven't got the entire lowdown on what's going on between the two of you, but I'm preparing for that." Her eyes flit down to the wine glasses. "But I will tell you something. There is more than one way to hurt a woman. Unfortunately, men are plenty adept at doing that in a variety of ways. And I'll promise you that if you hurt her in any single fucking way, I'll do to you what you're planning on doing to the man who put his hands on Freya."

Something cold and uncomfortable moved in my stomach. "I have no intention of hurting Freya. I don't plan on getting close enough to her to do that."

The woman gave me a look that called bullshit. "Baby, you're plenty close enough to do more damage than that asshole ever could."

With that, she somehow effortlessly bundled two glasses and a large tray filled with cheese in her hands then sauntered out.

CHAPTER NINE

FREYA

Marilyn was a married woman, which meant that she could not move in with me for the entirety of this ordeal.

After spending the night, she did stay for half the day, leaving only to pick us up a variety of pastries and coffee for breakfast. Marilyn's cooking skills were limited to heating up leftovers since her husband, Jed, did all of the cooking. And the cleaning. And the worshipping of the ground that she walked on. He owned a construction company and was as buff and as macho as you could imagine, but he was a fucking marshmallow for his wife. The one who he considered to be one hundred percent woman despite full knowledge of her past. It was because of his devotion and adoration to her that he wasn't bothered by the fact that his wife was a stripper. When they began dating, he grew to know her well enough to understand that she needed that job, for her mental health, her sanity. He still supported her wholeheartedly.

Jed was a unicorn.

Jed also came over to see me, bringing more wine, flowers and a lasagna. The second he saw my face, his contorted, and he took me into his large arms with a tenderness I didn't think aforementioned arms were capable of. Then he kissed my head with that very same tenderness.

Jed was a fucking unicorn.

Before leaving, Jed took Hades outside to have a very long and likely testosterone-filled chat. Marilyn, Sirius and I had spied on them from the window. There was a lot of glowering, a lot of arm folding ... basically, the swinging of proverbial dicks. Then, after a tense few minutes, there were nods and one very strong looking handshake.

Afterward, both Marilyn and Jed left, promising to be back soon, Marilyn with more wine and Jed with more food.

Leaving Hades and me alone in my house. For about ten minutes. Then Anderson rolled up and Hades muttered about, "having to take care of club business," leaving without looking at me.

I didn't see him for a week.

He came back to my house. I only knew this because Anderson told me. Somehow, Hades had managed to time his arrivals and departures around my sleep schedule so that we didn't lay eyes on each other.

I missed him. A lot. Missed the security of his presence, although I knew that he wouldn't have left me with Anderson if he didn't think I was taken care of. And I was taken care of. The day after Hades disappeared, some very attractive men turned up at the house with a lot of complicated-looking technical equipment.

"Are you guys in a club or something?" I asked Keltan, the stunning looking man with a sexy accent and a large wedding band on his left hand. He'd introduced himself as the owner of Greenstone Security, the company who was apparently installing a state-of-the-art security system in my house. Which he'd explained after doing the alpha male, furious stare at my face. Which looked fucking terrible. The bruising had only gotten worse, and it was difficult to look in a mirror.

His expression shifted to one of confusion. "Say again?"

"A club," I repeated, waving my hand at him and then to the three men who were working on something in the vicinity of my French Doors, nibbling on the cookies I'd offered them when they arrived.

"A hot guy club," I clarified. "One where you all seem to find each other and only talk in alpha male grunts and phrases. Average men need not apply."

Keltan chuckled. He had a really nice laugh. I wondered what Hades's laugh sounded like. Felt like. I wonder if the man even laughed. Surely, he had. He was human, and every human laughed, cried, bled. I'd only seen the latter, yet I found it impossible to imagine him doing the other two.

No, he wouldn't laugh like Keltan. He would not have that air about him, an easy kind of presence that felt warm, comfortable, nonthreatening. Nonetheless, I felt myself longing for that. For him.

And that afternoon, six days after the security was installed, as if I'd wished him into existence, he arrived. The roar of the Harley had both mine and Sirius's ears perking up. Sirius didn't have to worry about things like dignity, so he went sprinting to the front door, pouncing on Hades the second he walked through it. And it took me a lot of willpower not to do the very same. Instead, I put down the book I was reading, got up from the sofa and met him in the arch over the hallway leading to my kitchen and living area.

Sirius was pressed to his side, so he was barely able to walk. It took a lot of willpower for me not to do that too. In fact, I had a totally ridiculous urge to run into his arms and never leave them. Despite his jaw droppingly sexy arms, they weren't exactly the kind of limbs that invited a woman in. They were the kind of limbs that warned people away, that did unsightly and terrible things to others.

My eyes traced over every inch of him, drinking him in like I was dying of thirst. Across his angular face to the strands of

midnight hair that framed it, then down his muscled neck, along
the span of his broad shoulders, down his sinewy arms then down
his lean torso. I held my breath and decided not to go lower than
the belt. My body was battered, broken and bruised. Everywhere
but below my belt. So instead of torturing myself over what lay
beneath his belt, I forced my eyes upward. Right to the patch on
his cut that read 'Enforcer.' I might have been ignorant about the
outlaw lifestyle, but I knew enough to understand what that patch
meant. It was meant to scare me away, to communicate that this
was a man unafraid to hurt, maim and kill those who crossed him
or the club.

The patch did not scare me. Nor did the cut, even though I
knew both should. It was the man. The man terrified me.

"You're back," I stated the obvious, my voice breathy and
weird.

His eyes moved over my face, his jaw set, body taut. "I'm
back," he agreed.

I moved uncertainly from foot to foot. My feet were bare. I
didn't know what to do without shoes on. Without my heels. Even
my bright pink slippers with the fluffy bows on them would've
been welcome at this juncture. At least my toes were painted
bright pink. Marilyn had been over today with her pedicure kit and
brownies that Jed made.

I was still in too much pain to put any kind of makeup on,
though. It would've been fighting a losing battle anyway. The
swelling had gone down, and there were only small butterfly
bandages on the cut on my cheek, but my bruises had developed
these past few days. Sarah had come over earlier today with her
doctor's bag, with her kind eyes, with gentle squeezes on my hand
telling me that I was going to heal just fine. On the outside, at
least. I figured that my insides would take a lot longer.

This past week had been one of the strangest and hardest of
my life. I didn't spend much time—or any time—thinking about
what I'd do if I was beaten up by an ex-boyfriend again. Theoreti-

cally, I figured I'd handle it like I handled everything else in my life: by putting on some Shania Twain, some heels and getting the fuck over it.

But I had struggled to get out of bed for a week. Sure, my schedule might've made it so I was never going to be up at dawn, but I had always jumped out of bed, excited for the day, in love with life.

Until this week. I'd wanted to hide in my sheets and never come out. Or at least hibernate under them until I wasn't reminded of what happened every time I passed a reflective surface. Every time I moved a little too fast or reached too high for a glass, my healing ribs reminded me that they were still broken.

It reminded me of a feeling I'd done a good job of shutting out over the years. The feeling of being violated, of my body no longer being my own.

But that feeling dissipated with Hades standing in front of me. It didn't completely disappear, of course. He wasn't a wizard, but the weight on my chest lightened by about three hundred pounds.

I held my breath at the silence between us. At the electricity crackling between us. I'd had a lot of free time over the past week, considering I couldn't work, couldn't film and I could only spend so much time on the stock market. I was lucky that I had a month's worth of videos filmed in advance, in case of emergency. Not that I'd expected that emergency to be a black eye and four stitches in my cheek.

Hades lifted his hand up to my face, and for a moment, I thought he was going to touch my bruised face. I even leaned into it, despite recently thinking that I wouldn't want a man to touch me for a long time.

But he just hovered his palm in the air for a few moments then brought it back to his side, as if he'd thought better of it. His eyes were glaciers, his jaw granite.

"I, um, so..." How exactly did I ask him whether he had

successfully found and killed my ex? That was something that I'd found I was actually able to completely avoid thinking about. Don't ask me how I'd managed that since it was a pretty fucking big deal, but I did.

Until Hades stood in my living room, towering over me, drowning out the late afternoon sunlight with his very presence.

"Did you, have you..."

"Found him?" he finished for me.

I pursed my lips, unable to speak, so instead, I nodded.

"No." The single word burst from his lips with fury.

I let out a breath I hadn't known I was holding, my entire body relaxing.

"You're relieved," he observed. His tone was flat, his expression still taut. There was no judgement in his tone, nothing at all.

I looked to my bright pink toes then back up at those ice chip eyes. "I guess I am," I admitted. "Don't get me wrong, I don't want him to get off easy. Not in the slightest. But *I* want to get off easy." I paused, thinking of the effort it took me to get out of bed this morning. "Or as easy as I can in this situation. I guess I'm not ready for his death to be on my conscience."

His jaw ticced. "It's not going to be on your conscience, Freya. It's going to be on mine." His words were firm. As if he were speaking them into law.

I sighed, thinking about how this was not going to be a conversation I was going to win and how I really did not want to argue with Hades right now. Not when he was finally back. I wanted him here, right here, for as long as I could have him.

"I was just about to make dinner." I gestured to the kitchen. "Um, I hate to eat alone and like to cook with company. Sirius is a terrible conversationalist and really only hangs out for the scraps." I spoke quickly in a weird tone because I was very nervous. "So do you want to maybe have dinner with me?" I couldn't help fidgeting as I asked. "I've got beer. And wine. And tequila. And ESPN, at least I think I do. Surely there's some kind of fight or game or manly kind of event on there."

I was babbling I needed to stop babbling.

"I'll stay," Hades said after a long moment, eyes never leaving mine.

"Awesome," I sighed. "I'll just..." I pointed to the kitchen. He followed me there, instead of going to the couch to watch something manly.

He followed me to the kitchen, leaned against the island instead of perching on a bar stool, then took the beer I gave him.

"You can sit," I offered.

He shook his head. "Tell me what you want me to do."

I gaped at him, and my stomach flipped. What I wanted him to do was lift me up onto this counter and eat my pussy. But I couldn't say that.

"Excuse me?" I rasped out.

Something moved in his face, something that I felt low in my stomach. Something that made me think he might've been thinking the exact same thing as me.

"With dinner, tell me what you want me to do to help." His voice was flat, but there was an edge to it, like a serrated knife.

"Oh!" I said. "You really want to help with dinner?"

He nodded.

"Okay, how's your knife work?" I asked, knowing my mistake the second I uttered the words.

The corner of Hades's mouth twitched. "Fucking excellent."

My stomach dipped. And just like that, Hades was helping me with dinner.

———

Halfway through cooking, Hades got a phone call, scowled at the caller ID, rubbed his hands on a kitchen towel then left the room.

He didn't come back until the food was finished. I'd set the table, put my speaker on low and brought him a fresh beer.

He'd walked back in just as I was carrying our plates.

"Club business."

That was his explanation.

It intrigued me but it wasn't my business, so I didn't press the subject. We probably wouldn't have been eating anything if he'd stayed in the kitchen for the duration of the cooking process.

Hades sat down at the table as I set his plate down. I'd given him a heaping serving, guessing that he needed it to fuel his muscles and deadly instinct.

"Enchiladas," I stated the obvious. "Vegan enchiladas. Well, almost. There's cheese."

I pursed my lips, forcing myself not to continue babbling.

"You're a vegan," he didn't phrase this as a question, his expression blank and his tone flat as he stared at me then down at the plate of food.

Now, Hades might've been a cold, dangerous man, but he was very expressive. Even when he wasn't. Somehow, I knew that the careful flatness of his voice was not due to a lack of emotion.

"Yes, I'm a vegan," I confirmed, handing him a fork and napkin.

He took both of them, looking at me the entire time. It was definitely unnerving, his eyes on me as I settled at the opposite side of the table. Hades frowned at me while I did this, as if he did not like my choice of seat. But I did not trust myself sitting right beside him. Our arms brushing as we ate, thighs pressed together. No, it would've been torture. And I likely would've dropped food all over my shirt and made a fool out of myself. Yes, across the table was much safer.

He also could've been looking at me in that way because he was a red-blooded, American, alpha male who existed on red meat, Jack Danielsm and the blood of his enemies, yet I was serving him a vegan meal. Granted, it was a kick-ass vegan meal consisting of spicy sweet potato, black bean enchiladas and rice. Complete with margaritas. Made from scratch. The secret was freshly squeezed limes, agave, Grand Marnier and a lot of tequila.

"I'm a vegan on weekdays," I continued speaking because the way he was looking at me was making me all squirmy, and I couldn't eat under his scrutiny, no matter how hungry I was or how good the enchiladas were. "On the weekends, I'm just vegetarian because I love cheeseboards. And French Toast. And full-fat lattes. Sometimes if I go out for brunch on a weekday, I cheat too. And then I have a cheeseburger once a month."

Hades raised a brow ever so slightly. "You eat a cheeseburger once a month," he repeated.

I nodded. "I know, it's terrible. I'm not really a vegan, obviously. I definitely shouldn't be calling myself one, but..." I shrugged. "Whatever. I definitely can't call myself a vegetarian because of the cheeseburger thing. But have you *had* a cheeseburger before?"

The corner of his mouth turned up in something that could only be described as a smirk. My insides did a backflip, and desire flooded into my stomach—and my panties.

"Yeah, baby, I've had a cheeseburger before." He scooped a bite of rice onto his fork and took a bite.

Baby. He'd just called me baby.

Endearments such as that were throwaway to bikers, I knew that. It didn't mean anything. But I was sure that Hades had never called me baby before, I most certainly would've noticed. I hung on his every word like some kind of pathetic, lovestruck teenager.

I loved the way it sounded coming out of his mouth. Loved the possession in it.

Or maybe I was just imagining that.

My neck flamed with heat, and I struggled not to crawl across the table and kiss him.

"So you understand," I forced myself to get back on track, my voice thick. "I just can't deprive myself."

Although he remained stone still, his eyes flickered; his expression turning into something else entirely. I didn't have words to describe it, but I felt it in my entire body, shaking my bones and drenching my panties. "Yeah, I can't either."

I thought he was going to toss his silverware onto his plate then proceed to sweep both of our plates to the floor so he could fuck me on the dining room table.

He did toss his silverware on the plate, and it did land there with a clatter. He also stood up. But he did not sweep the plates to the floor like they did in the movies. Instead, he turned on his heel and walked off.

I was left turned on, confused, rejected and not at all hungry. But I ate the food anyway. Because I had no clue what else to do.

————

I cleaned up the dinner, carefully putting Hades's portion in a glass Tupperware container and placing it in my organized fridge. Everything in my house was meticulously organized and cleaned because I'd had nothing else to do this past week. Apart from walking Sirius, I hadn't left the house. Not even to get coffee. Marilyn had come every morning with pastries and caffeine, and Jeb came in the afternoons with all of the groceries I could ever need. And I did need a lot, considering Anderson had eaten every meal here. He hadn't grumbled about the lack of meat. In fact, he'd demanded the recipe for my meatless nachos after he ate three servings.

Kallum had also come over a couple of times, his facial expression similar to the one he'd been wearing at the hospital. He'd made it very clear that he was not pleased with Anderson and the Sons of Templar being involved in any of this. But because I still looked fucking terrible, he was still tiptoeing around me. What was it about the sight of a bruised woman that made men decide to *then* treat her gentle? After the damage was already done?

Because I had wonderful friends, I hadn't needed to leave the house, which was good because I really, really hadn't wanted to. I didn't want to deal with the stares, the well-meaning questions from people I'd been so proud of being friendly with before this happened.

So, because I hadn't left the house, my pantry and fridge were bulging with food that not only Jeb had made, but things I'd baked too. Baking was my solace. The measuring, the mixing, the eating of the uncooked batter ... it was a sacred tradition that was only overindulged in when I was feeling particularly out of control.

Despite all of the vegan and non-vegan baked goods in my kitchen, I spent the evening making cookies. Because I didn't know what else to do, where else to go. Sirius was nowhere to be seen, and I hadn't heard the roar of a Harley after Hades had stormed off, so I deduced that he hadn't left me alone. I wasn't going to be so pathetic as to go running around the house looking for him, though. He'd made it clear he didn't want to be around me.

I was doing my best to pretend that I didn't want to be around him either. It had worked rather well until he and Sirius had come into the kitchen well after midnight, well after I'd made three batches of cookies.

I'd just finished putting away all my dishes because I did not like waking up to a dirty kitchen.

And it was then, in that moment, that something snapped. I wasn't sure what. Maybe it was the fact I hadn't properly dealt with what had happened to me. I hadn't cried. Not a single tear. Had barely uttered a word about the entire experience, not even to Marilyn who'd made it clear she was there to listen, to provide a shoulder. Or at the very least, a large glass of wine.

Thus far, she'd respected my silence and ignored the elephant in the room. She hadn't wanted to push, but maybe if she had, I would've been able to spew all of my emotional trauma all over her instead of all over Hades.

"Why don't you like me?" I demanded, putting my hands on my hips, glaring at the man wearing all black who was probably armed.

The tone, the glare and the unmistakable female battle stance were likely unwise in the face of a muscled biker—a muscled, *armed* biker—but I had a bad temper. Always had. I tended to look on the bright side, almost always. But when I got pissed off, like really pissed off, there was no stopping me or my temper. It had gotten me in trouble on more than one occasion.

I didn't let him answer. Instead, I began pacing, glaring at him. "I mean, first of all, I *saved your freaking life*," I snapped, holding one finger up. "I ruined one of my favorite towels saving your life." I held up another finger. "I did not demand any kind of thank you or reimbursement for that." I abandoned the finger thing but kept pacing. "Then I went about my life, doing my best to keep out of your way despite you coming into Fate and being *mean* to me. I wasn't mean back. I'm never mean back. Because I'm a nice person. I write thank you cards. I help old ladies get their groceries into their cars. I donate blood. I never correct the people who talk down to me, assuming I never finished high school because I'm a stripper. That includes you, by the way."

I pointed at him, not registering the way his face had changed since I had started talking. I was too far gone for that. "No. I'm a good person, even though the majority of people I encounter, present company included, are assholes. So you have not one single reason not to like me, whereas I have plenty not to like you. Yet I still do." I pursed my lips before I said anything more. Before I said that I liked him. That I pleasured myself thinking about his hands and lips all over me.

"I did not force you to move in here," I continued, fury still coursing through my veins. It was either yell at him or cry in front of him. Obviously, I chose to yell. "You were the one who went all macho and alpha, deciding that you were going to move in here. And you haven't even *been* here." I threw my hands up. "Because you obviously can't stand to be around me. Because you don't like me. And that's fine, that's totally fucking fine. You don't have to like me."

Then I just ran out of gas, standing in the middle of the room panting, heart thundering, my limbs suddenly feeling heavy and my soul suddenly feeling lighter. I'd just yelled at Hades. I'd just yelled almost everything I was feeling at him, and he'd heard me. I'd made him hear me. I made it impossible for him to ignore me.

I didn't know much about Hades, but I knew some things. I knew that he probably wasn't used to being yelled at. By a woman, no less. I assumed that he was going to yell back. Fuck, I hoped that he yelled back. Hoped that he would not be yet another person walking on eggshells around me.

But he didn't yell.

Nor did he walk on eggshells. No. He stomped on them. His strides were long and quick, but so was my retreat. I would've gone farther had my back not slammed into the wall.

"I have too many reasons to fucking like you," he murmured, caging me in with his arms.

I held my breath, staring at his face, the angles of his jaw, his full lips, stark against his blanched skin. His eyes were roving over my face with pure hunger. Pure fucking need. Mine responded in kind.

Fervently.

He moved one of his arms from the wall to slowly brush down the side of my face, gently tracing the bruised skin.

His touch was an inferno. I must've been breathing, because if I wasn't, I would've passed out. My heart must've been beating, because if it wasn't, I would've been dead. Regardless of these facts, it felt like every single cell in my body paused. Everything stopped working under the weight of Hades's stare, under his gentle yet rapacious touch. It was as if he was the commander, the conductor of my body, and he demanded that it sing for him. Scream for him.

"I like you too much, Freya," he growled, his voice tearing away at the loaded silence between us. His eyes were on my lips. The ones that felt swollen, desperate for his, eager to taste him on my tongue. "That's the fuckin' problem."

Then he stalked off.

Again.

He spent the rest of the night chain smoking outside, leaning against his bike. I knew that because after I eventually found the use of my legs, I'd managed to get my night-time routine down, slipped into my bed and fell into a fractured sleep. I kept my curtains open a crack so I could see his dark silhouette whenever I opened my eyes. I saw everything else when I closed them.

CHAPTER TEN

We were watching *Game of Thrones*.

Not a word had been said about my little outburst the night before or what Hades had said after it. But he was here when I woke up. And he was still here when Marilyn arrived. Hansen—the bald, attractive, muscled president of the club—had come by, being gentle and kind to me before heading out to the patio with Hades to have a man huddle. He'd stayed for cookies and coffee and showed me pictures of his kids.

Hades had sat there with four cookies of his own, not offering any conversation. But he was there. He'd been here all day.

Things weren't awkward between us. They should've been, but they weren't. Things were energized, that much was clear. The majority of the day, there'd been buffers. Marilyn. Jed. Hansen. Even Sirius, needing his walk, which Hades accompanied me on while letting me babble about all kinds of shit that didn't matter.

I'd come back to shower, to put on jeans that looked amazing on my ass and could pass off as casual. And a thin-strapped cami with lace around the top and the bottom. No bra.

Because I was done with this. With him getting me worked up and nothing coming of it. Yeah, I probably should've waited a little longer for my body and soul to heal before I seduced the dangerous biker, but I was going insane.

So I put on the outfit, did my hair. Makeup was still a crapshoot.

Hades had gone still when I'd walked into the kitchen, getting ready to make dinner. His eyes had stayed pinned to my chest for five seconds—I'd counted—his jaw marble. Then he'd stalked outside to smoke.

He'd sat across from me at the dinner table silent. I had been too turned on, too nervous to even babble. The only sounds were the music coming from my speaker and the clattering of our utensils against our plates.

When we were done, he'd snatched my plate from underneath me and refused to let me help with the dishes.

"Find somethin' for us to watch," he'd demanded.

Find something.

For us.

I'd never been more nervous. It's what I imagined an inexperienced teenage girl might've felt like. I had never been an inexperienced teenage girl, never gifted with that giddy, overwhelming yet exciting fear.

I was not a girl. I was a woman. A smart one. Which was why I chose *Game of Thrones*.

Hades finished the dishes, refilled my glass of wine then sat on the other end of the sofa. Sirius immediately hopped over and pressed himself as close to Hades as physically possible. I pouted at my dog over my wine, very jealous of his ability to show his affections to this man without fear of rejection.

With great difficulty, I moved my attention from the hot, tattooed, muscled man cuddling with my dog on my sofa.

I'd picked the episode carefully. It was one I'd watched before. More than once. The episode that included the scene where Daenerys, the small, blonde queen takes control of Khal Drogo, a large, dangerous, deadly man. I really hoped it would tip Hades over the edge.

We watched in silence, Hades not asking questions about the show or why we hadn't started at the beginning. He just watched. My body was coiled tight from tension and Hades's close proximity. I kept moving on my side of the sofa, watching Hades out of my periphery. His attention seemed to be wholly on the show, and I couldn't very well stare straight at him, so I pretended that my attention was also wholly on the show.

Then the scene began.

My grip around the stem of my wine glass tightened, and my breathing became shallow. Suddenly, I regretted this. I regretted this very fucking hard.

Okay, watching a graphic, very well-done sex scene with a dangerous, sculpted, muscled, sinful biker sex god in the same room as me had to be the most embarrassing thing in the entire world. Not the kind of embarrassment that you had when you watched a graphic sex scene with someone who was related to you, where you pursed your lips, looked straight ahead and non-verbally agreed to not say a single fucking word nor acknowledge what was going on, hoping it would fucking end.

No, not that.

Something else that sent heat up my neck to my flaming cheeks. Then more heat down, all the way down between my legs. I swallowed, refusing to look in the direction of the man who was no longer watching the scene on the television. His stare was zeroed in on me. Sirius, as if he'd sensed the sexual tension in the room and it was inappropriate for him to be sitting here, chose that moment to jump off the couch.

Without the canine barrier between us, the air became thicker, hotter, heavier. I could barely breathe around it. I didn't want to breathe, to accidently puncture this moment.

"How long has it been since you've been fucked, Freya?"

My heart stopped beating. My skin flamed with fire, my body was thrumming with need, with shock at what he'd just asked me.

I'd been sure something was going to happen. Something like Hades getting up and walking out to chain smoke in the driveway again. Another kind of rejection, more walls being erected between us.

But not this.

"It's been ... a while," I admitted, picking at lint on my jeans, uncomfortable with this conversation, with this man, and uncomfortable with the hunger that had been steadily building since the first night I met him

His stare was unyielding. Even though he was at the other end of my large sofa, it seemed like he was right next to me.

Right fucking *there*.

His Adam's apple moved visibly as he swallowed, his eyes devouring me. There was no second guessing it now, Hades wanted me. He really fucking wanted me. Sitting here with bruises covering my face, no makeup, in more clothes than I usually wore, he wanted me.

"How long has it been for you?" I rasped.

Hades went still. I shivered as the air changed.

"Go to bed, Freya," he ordered. "And make yourself come thinking about me."

I stared at his back as he left for the front yard, frozen by his voice, the words, the gaze that turned my nipples hard and left my panties soaking.

HADES

I deserved a fucking medal.

Granted fucking sainthood.

To be just a few feet from Freya, her pebbled nipples pressing through the thin fabric of her shirt, her lips pink, full, begging to be wrapped around my cock. Her pussy already wet for me.

Drenched. If I'd pulled down her pants, bent her over the sofa, she'd be ready for me. She'd clench around my dick, and she'd scream my fucking name.

Oh, how I wanted to make her scream.

But I didn't.

I wouldn't.

I'd made an insane vow to myself that I wouldn't taste the inside of her cunt until I'd worn the blood of the fuck who put those bruises on her beautiful face.

I might've been an outlaw, a demon, an immoral piece of shit, but I kept my vows. Especially when they came to death. I'd also been fucking certain it wouldn't take this long to find the piece of shit. He was a trust fund pussy with no idea who was after him, yet somehow, he'd eluded us. He'd made me torture myself, depriving me of Freya.

After she'd stumbled to her room, face flush with arousal and disappointment, I'd almost followed her. Truth is I would've had my phone not rang.

"We got him," Swiss snarled.

It seemed, on this night, the devil was looking out for me.

The second a prospect roared into the driveway, I left, hurtling toward my vengeance. Toward my vindication.

———

He was bleeding and tied to a chair in the basement when I got there.

I glared at Swiss who just shrugged. "You said we couldn't kill him, not that I couldn't have some fun with him."

As I stepped closer, the piece of shit opened his mouth, and blood poured out along with a muffled, wet groan. His tongue had been cut out.

Swiss shrugged. "He was talking too much."

I stared at him, the blood-soaked, urine-drenched piece of shit.

My fingers trailed across the knives laid out on a tray beside him. "I've put a lot of thought into your death," I said, looking at him. His eyes were wide with pain, with panic. He was staring at death, and he knew it.

"I was going to make it last for days," I continued. "Weeks. It was just going to be me and you down here. I was going to fucking bathe in your blood." I gripped a knife I'd imagined cutting his balls off with, the urge still strong.

But I let it go.

"The problem is," I said, taking my piece from my holster. "That takes away the time I have with her. Freya."

He stilled at her name.

I smiled. "Yeah. Freya." Her name was ambrosia, even in this windowless room that smelled of death and piss. "I'm not going to waste time killing you since it's time I could spend fucking her." Then I lifted the gun and shot him in the face.

Unfortunately, time had to be spent getting rid of the asshole's body. Time had to be spent because he was an asshole who, unfortunately, would be missed. Money would be spent looking for him. So we had to make sure that no one found him. That there was nothing left to be found. It was also a good way to educate Anderson on the finer and more gruesome aspects that came with wearing the patch.

We'd all been convinced that he was going to pass out or vomit, but the kid held fast. He didn't even fucking pale. Didn't look away. His eyes actually lit up, showing me he was worthy of the cut.

My hands were still covered in blood when I disarmed the alarm at Freya's house. It was the middle of the night. The curtains in her room hadn't even moved when the other prospect left, so I knew she was dead asleep.

I was going to wake her up with my mouth on her pussy. My cock was rock hard even thinking about it. My cock which had been hard as I'd been cutting her fucking ex to pieces. It was sick and evil, and I shouldn't have even fucking been here. But I was sick and evil, so I was fucking here.

My hand paused on the handle of her bedroom door. I'd go in there. I'd finally taste her. She'd come around my cock. I'd feast on every inch of her fucking skin. Even though I'd make it last for as long as possible, even if I made it last for fucking days, it would eventually end. I'd have to leave. My job was done. There was no justifying my presence in her life. No reason to stain it with my sins, stain her with them.

My hand released the doorknob, and I walked back into the living room, poured myself a tequila, slammed it then went back to my room and took a shower, letting the blood wash off, making myself come thinking of her cunt.

FREYA

I didn't see Hades the next day. Not fucking once. I'd woken up excited, giddy, with fucking butterflies in my stomach. *Butterflies.*

I'd decided my bruises had faded enough for me to put on makeup. They fucking had to be. That had to have been the reason why Hades didn't want to fuck me last night. He hadn't wanted to look at the bruises another man put there. An alpha male thing. Or maybe he hadn't thought I was ready, hadn't wanted to take advantage of me. The latter was much less likely. That was a good guy thing to do. Hades wasn't a good guy. And I fucking loved that.

So I'd taken a shower, a long one. I'd exfoliated, shaved, used my fancy body wash. Then I used a fancy moisturizer and curled my hair in loose waves that tumbled down my back. I'd had to use more makeup than I typically would've for daytime, but it covered all of my bruises. The cut on my face was still visible, but I looked good on the whole. My blue eyes glowed with happiness, excitement. My lips were full, thanks to a plumping lip gloss that was like filler in a tube.

Matching underwear was a must. Pink. Light pink. Silk. A bra that showed my nipples. Underwear that barely covered the small triangle of hair on my pussy.

Then I slipped on a t-shirt dress, one that clung to my every curve and finished well above my knee. Yes, I looked good. Great. Fuckable.

But Hades wasn't there when I walked out. Anderson was. He was sipping coffee at the breakfast bar, Sirius at his feet. When I got closer, I saw that he was reading a baby book.

"Morning, Freya," he greeted, looking up with a grin.

"Morning," I replied weakly, walking toward the coffee he'd thankfully brewed. It was nothing on Oliver's, but I needed something.

"Where's Hades?" I asked with my back turned. I could almost make my voice casual, even, but no way could I control my face.

"Club business."

As much as I liked the prospect, I currently wanted to wring his muscled fucking neck.

Club business. The blanket statement that could be used for any number of things and something I couldn't ask questions about.

The door opened and closed, and my body froze despite not hearing the telltale roar of a Harley. "Put that filter coffee down right now," Marilyn's voice came from the archway. "It's an insult for it to be in the same room as the nectar of the gods."

I forced a weak smile on my face and turned toward Marilyn.

"Woah, you look fucking amazing!" she whistled. Her eyes flickered to Anderson, familiar with him now. "Good thing that I wagered that there would be a man with muscles and a cut sitting in this kitchen." She placed a coffee cup in front of Anderson then a paper bag that no doubt contained pastries. He beamed at her. She winked.

I gratefully took my coffee from her.

"You putting on mascara requires celebration," Marilyn decided. "After caffeine, after pastries, we're going to the mall. We're going to spend a lot of money then have tacos and margaritas for lunch."

———

Hades came back just after Marilyn left. Anderson had some kind of powwow with him in the driveway before he came in. Anderson had thoroughly enjoyed our day today, surprising both of us. Though he was technically our bodyguard, he'd spent the day as our very alpha shopping partner. We'd had a ball, buying things for Hannah as a reward for putting up with Anderson spending so much time with a younger woman. A stripper at that.

Then there were the baby clothes. They'd just found out they were having a boy. Marilyn and I might've gone a little wild, fueled by the margaritas that we'd had for lunch. Then we'd gone to Anderson's little house, a bungalow on the outskirts of town with flower boxes and a perfectly mowed front lawn.

Hannah was a beautiful brunette with freckles covering her tanned face, glowing in her seventh month of pregnancy. She was warm, welcoming and kind, not jealous in the slightest and did not resent me for taking her fiancé away from her. We spent two hours there, watching her unwrap the gifts with glee, helping with the nursery decorations and drinking iced tea to sober us up.

Hannah promised to come over for dinner the following week with Marilyn and Jed. Jed doing all the cooking, of course.

After Marilyn left, Des called me and told me he was coming over and dragging me out of the house if I didn't meet him at the usual place at the usual time.

I put on a new dress. It was silk, flowy and whimsical, empire-waisted with a butterfly print. I'd paired it with slouchy, tan boots and styled my hair in a messy updo. I'd even put on false eyelashes.

I almost felt like myself again. Of course, I hadn't been able to stop thinking about Hades, but there was no controlling that.

The door opened and closed, and I held my breath as my energy changed. Sirius trotted forward without hesitation.

I tried my best to fiddle with my hair in the mirror, not looking at Hades.

"Where are you going?"

His voice washed over my skin like silky caramel, covering me, engulfing me. My pulse immediately quickened, and memories of last night consumed me. He hadn't even fucking touched me, yet it felt like he'd ruined me somehow.

I straightened my spine, narrowing my eyes at him in the mirror. "I have a date."

He went still. "A date."

As I swiped on my lip gloss, his eyes followed the action. My body instantly responded to that look. Big time. With great effort, I screwed my lip gloss closed.

"Yes, a date. Though I figure you heard me the first time."

"I heard you the first fuckin' time," he grated out, folding his arms.

I tried—and failed—not to look at the way his biceps bulged from the gesture.

"Who are you going on a date with?"

I sighed. He was standing in my way, and it was very clear that Hades was not going to move until I answered the question. Even then, I didn't like my chances. I weighed up jutting out my hip, narrowing my eyes and telling him it was none of his damn business, but I figured that wouldn't go well, and I knew that I didn't have enough sass to go against all that was Hades.

"Des," I replied.

His eye twitched. Arms stayed folded. "Where did you meet *Des*?" He spat out the name with distaste.

I bit my lip. Hades wasn't exactly a man to show emotions beyond fury. But I sensed the tiniest bit of jealousy. It was ugly of me to feel satisfied by that jealous look, but Hades awakened things in me. Need. Desperation. Ugliness.

"Des is my man. Wednesday nights are our nights. We have other dates, too, but we never miss a Wednesday." I paused, looking back in the mirror to adjust my hair. "Up until recently. For obvious reasons. I didn't tell him about what happened because he's very protective of me."

Hades's fury was palpable. "Why the fuck did I not know about Des until now?"

"Because it's none of your business," I replied.

I held my breath as Hades stepped forward, his cut brushing against me. "You are all of my fuckin' business, Freya."

My knees shook. Somehow, I found the strength to step around him. "I'm leaving, Hades. And you're not telling me otherwise because Des means a lot to me. So you're going to do your job, the one that you're so focused on, and make sure I don't die." I'd leaned in to whisper that into his ear then stepped away before I forgot what I was doing.

And my own name.

"You're going to follow me," I continued, forcing authority into my voice. "You're going to sit in the restaurant, and you're going to stay in a corner, only watching. I don't want any alpha male stare-downs. What I really don't want is you walking up to Des and saying something insane like I'm yours. Because you've had plenty of fucking opportunities to make me yours. And you didn't."

On that note, I turned my back on him and walked out my front door.

He followed me.

———

"Des!" I ran into his arms, settled and safe once they closed around me.

He smelled of drug store aftershave and mint. There was a long squeeze before he pulled me back to arm's length, his dark brown eyes focusing on the cut on my cheek. His thumb brushed over the skin.

"What happened, kiddo?" he asked, his voice and the deepening lines on his face conveying his concern comforting.

"Oh, nothing," I scoffed. "I had a little too much to drink, got up too fast, caught the corner of the coffee table." The lie came out smoothly because I did not want Des to know the truth. I did not want a sixty-eight-year-old man deciding he had to exact vengeance.

Des did not look sixty-eight. He barely looked fifty-eight. His black hair only had a hint of grey to it, neat and closely cropped to his scalp as it had been since I'd met him, since he'd enlisted in the army when he was eighteen.

His ebony skin was smooth, and the creases in it only made him all the more handsome and distinguished. He was tall. Taller than me, and he always wore his veteran cap with the American flag on it paired with an old blazer on top of faded jeans and Chuck Taylors.

Despite his heart problems, he still worked out three times a week and was in great fucking shape. He most likely could've taken Derek, but I didn't want him to.

"Ah, well, next time, make sure you remove all sharp objects from the area when consuming wine," he teased with a wink.

I relaxed as he bought my lie. Yet that sense of relaxation evaporated as a flash of black caught my eye and I saw Hades in the corner, his eyes intent on us. His gaze was heavy, difficult to carry. My lips turned up in satisfaction, having achieved the impossible, shocking Hades.

Des held out his forearm. "Shall we?" He nodded to the table that was always reserved for us on Wednesdays at the best Italian place in town.

I took his arm. "We shall."

Though I was focused on Des the entire night, though I did

not look in his direction once, I knew he watched us. For the entire fucking night.

—————

Hades followed me home, his headlights shining in my rearview mirror. My hands had been clenched on the steering wheel, my stomach swirling with nerves. I didn't know why. How many times had I been sure, certain that something was finally going to happen between me and Hades? How many times had exactly nothing happened between me and Hades?

Okay, maybe not nothing.

The man hadn't even touched me, yet I felt more connected to him than I had any other man in the world.

Tonight ... tonight somehow felt different. I hadn't missed the way he watched me throughout the entire dinner with Des, causing me to struggle to concentrate on the man in front of me, the one I loved and had missed dearly.

There was something else tonight. We'd reached a bottleneck. Something had to give. Something had to fucking explode.

I was shaking when I got out of my car, the sound of my heels against the concrete ringing in my ears. Hades's bike turned off, but he didn't get off immediately. There was no thump of motor-cycle boots, no heat against my back.

He didn't enter my house until I'd retrieved a bottle of red and a glass. He was a shadow against the lights.

"Des," he grunted. "Explain."

I sighed, trying my very hardest not to smile as I poured myself a glass of wine. The look on Hades's face when he saw Des was nothing short of priceless. I'm pretty sure no one had surprised the badass biker like that in a long time. It had been extremely satisfy-ing. Not just that, but I was satisfied that I'd made him jealous. Of course, Des had no knowledge of this, but the second I agreed to meet him for dinner, I decided to play it up. I needed to feel like I wasn't completely insane or pathetic. Because I was developing feelings for Hades. The attraction I felt toward him grew every single day.

The need for him.

Every night, after listening to him close his bedroom door— usually it was in the very early hours of the morning, considering the hours we both kept—my hand found its way between my legs, and I made myself come quietly, stifling my whimpers as I thought of his large, strong hands all over me. Thinking about the way he would dominate me. What his cock would feel like inside of me.

"Freya."

I jerked, staring into a glacier blue and an emerald green eye. There was a spark in them, as if he could read my mind. Which, of course, he couldn't. That was crazy.

I swallowed. What had he said? Oh yeah, he'd asked about Des. A safe subject, talking about a sixty-eight-year-old man to get my mind off this thirty-something man—or he could be forty. Sex gods seemed to be ageless.

"I met him in a grocery store," I answered, refusing to meet his eyes. "He was behind me in line. I had a bunch of stuff, like a *bunch*. More than I should've had for a woman who lives alone, but it was that time of the month, and I'd just watched the Food Network for like six hours straight and ... yeah." I picked up my glass, lifting it to my lips to take a sip because my throat was suddenly unbearably dry. "Even though there were all of those self-service lines open, he came behind me with some antacids and seltzer water," I continued, finally feeling brave enough to meet Hades's eyes.

There was no longer anything glacial about his stare. Nothing at fucking all. It was an inferno.

"He struck up a conversation," I pressed on, my voice shaky. "He asked me what I was planning on cooking that night. I told him. Ratatouille. I have this great recipe from my Aunt Victoria. She uses..." I didn't bother finishing that sentence, realizing this was not the point to talk about the secret to my Aunt Victoria's Ratatouille. "Anyway, we got to talking. It became clear that his night consisted of nothing more than a bottle of gin and a frozen dinner his daughter left for him when she was visiting. She lives in New York with her asshole husband. He loves her, and it was clear that he missed her, that she was all he had in the world." I swallowed, not meeting Hades's eyes. "He didn't tell me that part out loud, I could see it in his eyes. He was lonely. Lonely enough to stand in line at the grocery store just so he could talk to people in front of him for a handful of minutes. It broke my heart. So I invited him over for Ratatouille. Then he told me about how his wife had died five years ago. How most of his buddies had died in the past decade. He got to know Sirius." I shrugged. "We hit it off. We made a standing dinner date. Once a week. Sometimes more. Breakfast too. Late breakfast. We'll go to the movies sometimes. I cook him dinners for when we're not together. I've met his daughter. She's lovely. Met her husband. He is an asshole. Des is my best friend, well, tied with Marilyn."

Hades blinked at me. Once. Twice. Three times. Then my wine was plucked from my grasp and slammed down on my kitchen counter before Hades's arms yanked my body to his. I didn't have a moment, not even a second to process what was going on. He was kissing me. Kissing the fuck out of me. Months, a fucking lifetime of need poured into one kiss. It was an out-of-body experience, except I was very fucking aware of every single cell in my body, every single limb, every nerve ending.

"This is happenin'," he growled, his mouth against mine, hands pushing the skirt of my dress up to my waist so he could palm my bare ass. "I can't control it anymore, Freya. Can't control myself. This is fuckin' happenin'."

I harshly sucked in air, breathing in everything that was him. My body was pins and needles, electric shocks, an inferno.

Why was I fighting him again?

"I can't wait for your pussy to clench around my cock," Hades murmured, his soft lips at my ear, a hand pulling at my hair.

Oh, I was fighting him because I was fucking insane.

Yeah.

No more fighting.

It was at that moment, that exact moment, the doorbell rang. The fucking *doorbell*.

"I do not care if that is Dolly Parton herself, finally coming to her senses and deciding to a duet with me like I asked her to when I was eleven years old," I hissed.

Hades's eyes flared then he kissed me once more, deeply, with infatuation. "I'll get rid of whoever the fuck it is and kill them if they don't get the message."

When he turned to leave, I grabbed his hand, forcing him to pause and turn. "If it is Dolly, make sure you don't actually kill her. The world really does still need her."

The corner of his mouth twitched, then he smirked. Smirked. That might've been the most attractive thing I'd seen up close. Or from afar. Or ever.

"Okay, baby."

I nodded, hoping that I wasn't showing exactly what it did to me, hearing him call me baby.

I stood in the middle of the room, watching him walk away, watching the grim reaper on his back ripple slightly with his movements. As much as he wore the fuck out of that cut, I could not wait to see him out of it. The entire time I'd known him, he'd worn that thing. Even though he'd been 'living here' for over a month, I had yet to catch him just out of the shower or in workout gear, and I had really tried my darndest. I had come to the conclusion that he must've slept in that thing. If he ever slept at all.

It dawned on me then, hearing the low murmurings coming from the front door, that I was going to sleep with Hades. Well, not tonight. I did not plan on sleeping a fucking wink. We were going to have sex. I should've been utilizing this time by using breath spray, spritzing perfume, fixing my hair, aiming to look effortlessly desirable.

But no. I'd just stood in the middle of the room, breathing heavily, waiting for Hades to come back to me.

Like an idiot.

The door slammed, my mouth suddenly going dry as motorcycle boots thumped on my hardwood floors. Why didn't I get a glass of water? My palms were suddenly sweaty, and my heart started to pound in my chest.

Why was I nervous? Oh yeah, because I'd been waiting for this since the moment I laid eyes on this guy.

This guy, who appeared to be a lot more pissed off than he had been moments ago. The smirk was nowhere to be seen.

"I've got to go," Hades announced.

I stared at him, my chest still rising and falling rapidly. "You've got to *go*?" I repeated, my voice breathy and needy but also with an edge. He had been driving me insane for weeks, and finally—*finally* —when I was about to get the relief I needed, he had to go?

No fucking way.

His face was blank, but I noticed his hands were fisted at his sides so that the veins in his forearms were chiseled from the sinewy muscle. That was the only sign that this was pissing him off even a little.

That was not enough for me.

"Club business," he ground out. "Got a prospect outside. I'm leavin' a weapon on the kitchen counter. You go to bed, you take it with you." His eyes traversed over my body with a hunger that left goosebumps in their wake and had me sure he was going say "fuck club business", cross the distance between us, rip my clothes off and fuck me right here on the floor.

I was ready to stake my life and my purse collection on that.

But he stayed where he was.

"I'm hopin' this isn't gonna take long," he raked a hand through his onyx locks. "If it does and I'm gone until after you go to bed, you're not to go into your bedside drawer, you're not to make yourself come. The next time you come is going to be around my cock."

I blinked at him, the words, the pure sex and sin in them sending shockwaves through my body. Being momentarily blinded by my desire, I forgot about the fact I should be totally and utterly pissed at that statement.

Hades, being the villainous badass that he was, took advantage of that and turned around and left.

And just like that, I went to bed with my dog and a gun and no one else. Despite how much I wanted to, needed to, I did not open my bedside drawer to grab one of my many vibrators to relieve the tension in every limb of my body.

Because I was obeying Hades.

Parts of me hated him for it. Hated myself for obeying him when I was supposed to be a strong, independent, sexually free woman. If I wanted to come, then I was going to make myself come.

But I didn't.

And Hades did not come home that night.

CHAPTER ELEVEN

I purposefully woke early the next morning. Before Hades got back from club business. Whatever 'club business' meant. Whatever it was that tore him away from me just when we were finally about to have sex. Whatever had kept him out all fucking night.

Or the club business could've wrapped up promptly yet he'd decided to go back to the club to get laid by someone else. Someone less complicated ... or whatever.

We weren't married. We weren't even dating let alone together. He just happened to be living at my house because someone connected to his club may or may not try to harm me and because my crazy ex-boyfriend may or may not come back to beat me up or worse.

He was well within his rights to get laid by a club girl or whoever if he wanted to. It was with that at the back of my mind that I got up before the sun and went to a spin class with Marilyn. She was surprised to see me there since she'd been inviting me for months, and not one single time had I taken her up on the offer. I was certain she'd made a deal with some kind of demon or super-natural entity making her able to dance until three in the morning then get up three hours later to do an hour of torture disguised as exercise.

Though I had to admit, it was a good way to take out my anger, frustration and all the excess energy coiled in my limbs. My ribs had protested ever so slightly since they weren't completely healed yet. They definitely weren't healed enough to go back to work. The doctor said it might be a few more weeks, and Kallum refused to even consider me coming back until I was completely healed.

I showered at the gym, something I'd never done in my adult life. I had no idea how often gym facilities were cleaned—although this place was pretty swanky, especially for a small town—and there were things like foot fungus. Then there was the fact I had a very rigorous skincare, makeup and hair care routine that took me over an hour with a whole bunch of products. Obviously, I couldn't commence said routine in front of a poorly lit gym mirror without ample counter space or outlets, nor could I lug all of the products required for said routine in a small gym bag.

There were ample, very good reasons why I hadn't showered at a gym, especially when my house was a ten-minute drive from the aforementioned gym. But now I had someone to avoid and punish just a little. So I made it work.

After a bare-bones skin and hair care routine, I had breakfast with Marilyn. She had some chia seed pudding thing. I had Nutella French toast. What was the point in killing yourself for an hour working out if you couldn't eat Nutella French toast? Plus, I needed carbs and refined sugars in order to get through the day.

My phone had begun buzzing on the surprisingly spacious counter at the gym while I was drying my hair. My stomach dropped the second I saw his name on the screen. I had programmed the number in there when he'd demanded I save the numbers of all the club members. He'd never called me, and I'd never called him, so some pathetic, needy, desperate part of me itched to answer it immediately. Fortunately, that part of me was very small, so I held back. I ignored his call. And the one after that. And the three texts.

Marilyn glanced down at my buzzing phone halfway through our meal. "Someone is really insistent about getting hold of you before eight in the morning," she commented evenly.

I swallowed my toast. "Mmm-hmm."

She quirked an expertly manicured brow. "It doesn't happen to be that hotter than Hades," her eyes twinkled as she said that, "biker who has been attached to your shadow lately?"

I sighed. "It may be."

Her face lit up. "Excellent. I would say you finally got laid, but if that were true you wouldn't have been getting your sweat on with me this morning, nor would you have showered and cut your morning routine in half in order to avoid going home."

I sipped my coffee. "How did you get all of that so early in the morning?"

She waved her hand. "I'm psychic. I'm good at picking up the details." She put down her spoon and eyed me with intensity. "You haven't had sex yet, but you've come close. *Really* fucking close. Since he's been in your life, in your home for a decent amount of time, you've been wanting him, which I'm sure feels like forever. He's a hot-blooded man, so he's wanted you since the moment he saw you, and he's obviously battling with some demons since he's a big bad alpha male who is used to just taking what he wants." She took a break to sip her tea.

"And that's a compliment, honey, that he's fighting all of his instincts for you," she continued. "Because he respects you. Thinks you're too good for him—which you are. You're too good for all of us. He's a bad guy trying to do a good thing. But since he's a bad guy to the bone, in all the worst and best ways, he's not doing the noble thing of leaving you alone which makes your coupling inevitable and only makes him grow more attached to you every second you spend together."

I gulped my coffee, desperately wishing it was a mimosa.

"You're attached to him because you're a unique woman with a huge heart, and he's hot as balls," she stated softly. "But that's not why you're attached to him. You see the bad, and you want to dig beneath it, to find the good. And the bad excites you. Because unlike your other boyfriends, you know that his kind of bad will never be used against you, only against the motherfuckers stupid enough to even think about laying a hand on you."

And on that, she leaned back, flipped her hair over her shoulder and crossed her legs. "I'll bet my vintage Chanel that he'll be walking his fine ass through that door," she pointed a long nail to the entrance, "within the next ten minutes. I'm surprised you even managed to get any breakfast, honestly."

I blinked at her, amazed, impressed and mystified.

It was at that moment, the door to the café opened and the air pulsed with intensity thanks to the large, pissed off, sinfully hot biker currently prowling through the café.

"Are you a witch?" I whispered across the table to Marilyn.

She just grinned wickedly.

There wasn't any time to digest everything she'd just said or to debate her magical powers because Hades was here, pulling me out of my chair.

Pulling me out of my fucking chair.

He didn't exactly drag me out of it because my body kind of moved of its own accord, but he did most of the work. While holding my upper arm, he reached into his cut, somehow got cash out of his wallet one handed, then threw way too many bills on the table.

"Get your shit," he demanded, nodding to the bag I'd set on the vacant chair beside me.

"You can't just—"

"Here you go, sweetie," Marilyn interrupted, leaning over the table to snatch my bag before holding it out to me, smiling smugly.

I glared at her. "You really are a witch."

She only winked and wagged the bag at me, which was actually really impressive considering she was doing it one-handed and that bag was heavy as all hell.

As much as I wanted to sit my ass back down, attach myself to the chair and refuse to leave—only a little bit of that was due to the three bites of French toast that were left on my plate—I knew when I was outnumbered and fighting was futile.

Instead, I snatched the bag and stumbled ever so slightly as the weight of it transferred from Marilyn to me. Hades, quick as lightning, grabbed the bag from me without so much as flinching, then he proceeded to drag me out of the restaurant.

Okay, drag might've been a little dramatic since I mostly walked out of my own power, but still. It was only after we'd left the main street and were down an alley where he'd parked his bike that I thought to stop walking and snatched my arm from his grip.

Or at least tried to.

Hades only stopped walking because he literally would have had to drag me otherwise, and that was obviously crossing a line for him. But his hands tightened around my upper arm, almost to the point of pain. He was making it clear that he wasn't going to let go of me.

The tightness of his jaw and the chill in his gaze told me he was pissed. Really pissed. Join the fucking club, buddy.

"What are you doing here?" I hissed.

"I tracked your phone." He didn't let go of my elbow.

I kept trying to pull it from his grip, but I barely moved. "You tracked my phone?" I repeated, my voice sharp. "That is an invasion of privacy."

"You've got about a million fuckin' apps on there already that are already invading your privacy," he fired back. "What I'm doin' is try to keep you safe."

"I'm at brunch!" I screeched. "The only thing you're keeping me safe from is from ordering a second serving of French toast that I'm ninety-nine percent sure has crack in it because there is no other way they can make it taste that good."

I thought my voice held the right amount of outrage and strength in it, but it didn't have its intended effect since some of the chill left Hades's eyes and the corner of his mouth twitched.

"Don't you smile at me when I'm planning on being pissed off at you for a great deal longer," I demanded.

I saw the twitch again.

"Fuck you're cute," he muttered, yanking me forward so our bodies pressed together.

I let out an embarrassing little sigh as they did which caused his eyes to darken and his head to dip lower so our lips were almost touching.

Almost.

"I'm not trying to be cute," I whispered. "I'm trying to be otherworldly and threatening."

His mouth twitched again, and it was even more attractive up this close. "You are definitely not from any world I know," he murmured as his eyes raked over my face. "And you most definitely are a huge fucking threat."

Something in his words told me that was a compliment. A big one. A scary one.

"Get in your car, Freya, and get your ass home," he ordered softly.

In about two seconds, my ass was in my car and on my way home.

———

He did not fuck me when I got home, like I'd expected he would. Like his eyes had promised he would. As if he'd timed it, his phone rang the second we both walked in the door. To be fair, he did look like he was ready to kill whatever guy or gal dared call him. To be fair, I was also ready to kill whoever had dared to call Hades when it seemed like this was going to finally fucking happen between us.

Then I'd been ready to kill him for glancing down at the phone, seeing who was calling and then fucking answering it. I knew it was ridiculously unreasonable for me to get as pissed off as I did, but I was a woman frustrated. Severely sexually frustrated. So I did get pissed off.

Pissed off enough to stomp off to my room, shutting my door very loudly after I entered it. Not quite a slam—only teenagers slammed doors. Adult women shut them with passion. I ripped off all my clothes with the same passion. Not the kind of passion that I'd been expecting them to be ripped off with, but what could you do?

A small, romantic, foolish, sexually frustrated part of me expected Hades to storm into the bathroom as I showered, get in fully clothed, free himself from his jeans and fuck me senseless.

Although I'd showered at the gym, I took another one. I needed another one. A cold one. One to wash off the thin layer of perspiration covering my entire body. I even treated myself to a top-level shower. One including the exfoliating, the shaving, the hair mask, the pumice stone, all of it. The kind of shower that was usually reserved for Sunday nights so I could follow it up by slathering myself in expensive body cream, putting on my hundred-dollar face mask, then covering my hands in Vaseline while indulging in a *Real Housewives* marathon.

Once the shower finished without any kind of orgasm or intrusion by Hades, I did put on expensive body cream, but I didn't follow that with any of the other steps. Because I'd glanced at my phone, read the text from Macy and made a decision. A decision that had me blow drying my hair, something I preferred to pay someone to do because I had a lot of hair, and I could never get it looking as good as the hairstylist did.

But I was pissed off, determined and turned on. Apparently, that was the recipe—at least my recipe—for the perfect blow-dry. Then I spent thirty minutes applying the 'no makeup' makeup look. The kind that made my skin look dewy and flawless, my lips look impossibly pink and full, and my lashes look long and lush.

Next, I put on a sundress. It was technically getting too cold for a sundress, but I had a plan. It was white, simple and not exactly my style. I'd bought it because I knew I'd need it sometime, whether I had some kind of picnic to go to or if I had to torture an alpha male. A short skirt, visible midriff and ample cleavage were all well and good for making a man want you, but it was the impossibly fitted, perfectly tailored sundress that made men go wild.

Especially when paired with a pair of wedges that wrapped up my calves.

I dabbed perfume on my wrists, then behind my ears, staring at myself in the mirror. The bruises were a slight shadow underneath the light makeup, just barely visible. My cut was still red and angry but muted by the concealer I'd dabbed on. Yes, I looked good. Fucking great. My eyes then flickered to the door, the one that was still closed.

I had taken my sweet ass time in here, and there was no way a phone call lasted that long. He wasn't coming in. Sure, I could've strutted down to the living room and made the first move. I'd done it before. I liked the power of it. It was a confidence booster, that was for sure. I abhorred most of the conventional rituals surrounding dating. Rituals that gave men all of the power, that made women submissive, that left them sitting by the phone or led them to spend two hours in their bathroom.

But I wasn't going to do that with Hades. This wasn't about power. We were both powerless in this. I knew that he had been battling it, the attraction, this thing between us. I knew that it was unlike anything I'd ever experienced with a man, and it scared the shit out of me. Nothing about this was conventional.

I pulled the door open with the same passion that I'd recently closed it. My gaze flickered out the window, facing the driveway. His bike was still here. Of course it was. I hadn't heard it roar off, and I'd been listening for that. But Hades wouldn't roar off, not while my life was still in danger. Although I didn't think it really was. I had not seen or heard from Derek since that night. No heavy breathing phone calls, no threatening notes on the windshield of my car.

I wasn't sure if he'd scared himself off or if he thought he'd killed me. Or maybe he had been following me and realized that I was constantly in the presence of some kind of armed, alpha male wearing a patch that declared them an ultimate badass. Derek would definitely be threatened by that. He was not an alpha male. He got manicures weekly. Not that a man couldn't be an alpha male and get manicures, but Derek was not.

It was terrible of me, but I'd pretty much forgotten about Derek. Sure, he was front and center when I jerked awake from nightmares where he'd done a lot more than beat the shit out of me, but other than that, I barely thought of him.

My mind was preoccupied, fixated on the guy who was meant to be protecting me from Derek. My mind was also focused on teaching the aforementioned guy a lesson. The lesson being me leaving the house while he was still, presumably, on the phone.

Earlier, I'd put my purse on the sideboard in my entryway, my keys in the jade bowl in the middle of it. I couldn't hear Hades murmuring on the phone from the direction of the living room, so I figured he was taking Sirius to 'walk the perimeter' as he did sometimes. Or he was chain smoking on the patio as he did often.

"Where are you going?" a cold voice demanded.

I jumped, my keys clattering to the floor. Hades was leaning against the door jam, staring at me. There was challenge in his eyes, like he'd caught me doing something I shouldn't have been doing. Like he was going to punish me for something.

Fuck did I want him to punish me for something.

I bent down to retrieve my keys, Hades's gaze following me the entire time. That did nothing to tamp down the fire burning inside of me.

"I'm going shopping," I answered, my throat dry.

"Shopping," he repeated, in his predictably flat tone. There was no inflection at the end of the word, but it was a question, none-theless.

"Yes, I'm going shopping, Hades," I snapped, forcing my tone to be snippy because I didn't want it to be all breathy and turned on. "Because Macy and Hansen are having a party."

I had never met Macy, but I'd seen photos of her after while I was stalking her and all the Old Ladies on social media. I had no idea how Macy had gotten my number or knew anything about me, but I knew that I was going to her party.

"Because Macy has a boho-chic thing going that is absolutely fucking amazing," I continued, showing off just how deep my digital stalking had gone. "Because Scarlett dresses like a sex goddess. Because Macy told me Gwen and Amy are coming, and I stalked their social media, and I think they may be the most glam-orous creatures to walk planet Earth," I rambled on. "I know you're going to say that you've seen my closet and I have plenty of clothes, that I couldn't possibly need another outfit for a party, but don't you say that. Don't you dare." It was around now that I began pointing at him.

I didn't know how a conversation about shopping led to me babbling in a semi-shrill voice while pointing aggressively at a dangerous man in a Sons of Templar cut. Then again, I had no idea how I got tangled up with the Sons of Templar in general, let alone had one living in my house.

I was breathing heavily by the end of my tirade, my face contorted into a frown I feared was not at all cute. Hades, for his part, looked calm and placid.

There wasn't even a slight rise of his dark brow to communi-cate that he was starting to think I was fucking crazy.

He just stared.

I started to sweat, and my hands fisted at my sides.

The silence rang between us. It was a thick silence. A really fucking thick silence, full of tension, and extremely sexual. I couldn't breathe beneath the weight of his stare, and my panties became drenched from the promise in his eyes. He was going to cross the distance between us. Grab me. Plaster his mouth to mine. He was going to taste like sex and man. Then he was going to tear off my clothes and fuck me hard, brutally.

I would've bet my life on it.

But instead, he opened his mouth and said something I never thought I'd hear him say.

"Let's go shopping then."

CHAPTER TWELVE

"So?" I questioned, twirling. "What do you think?"

I felt oddly uncomfortable twirling in front of this man. Yes, I'd spent a huge chunk of my adult life twirling in front of men, but I was usually attached to a pole and half naked. I'd never flushed this much since ... ever.

I was modeling yet another sundress. This one was black. Halter neck. Backless. It clinched in at my waist, skimmed over my body and finished just below my knees. I was in bare feet, so I was twirling on my tiptoes to help with the effect. This was the first one I'd tried on, one of only a handful that was hanging in my dressing room.

It felt incredibly weird walking around Nordstrom—we'd had to drive thirty minutes to the next town, thirty minutes of near silence—with Hades beside me. With all the expensive shoes, the purses, the low playing elevator music ... he stood out, that was for sure. A large, menacing man wearing a biker cut in all black. Yeah, he stood out alright. Every woman—and a decent amount of men —we walked by had checked him out, big time. The salespeople had looked at him tentatively, as if they were expecting him to hold up the joint or something. I'd made sure to meet their eyes with an angry, judgmental stare, causing them to quickly avert their eyes. I was not unused to sales assistants at expensive stores giving me those kinds of looks, especially with the way I dressed. I dressed like a stripper. One who wore Jimmy Choos and carried around a Chanel purse, but a stripper, nonetheless.

I'd learned to let such looks bounce off my hard exterior despite the number of times I'd wished to have the *Pretty Woman* "big mistake, *huge*" moment. But I'd taken the high road. I barely noticed it anymore. Yet I felt strangely and weirdly protective over this man, who had been willing to walk into Nordstrom with me. Not that he needed me to protect him.

He'd taken to the experience like he took to everything, like this was something he did every day. No male shifting from foot to foot, no eyes darting toward the exit, looking for the closest escape.

Sure, he wasn't picking out outfits for me or anything, but he was attentive. Staring. At me. I doubt he noticed a single woman— or man—who had checked him out since we'd arrived. Not one.

It was almost impossible to concentrate on shopping. Which was a big fucking statement for a girl like me. I'd grasped a handful of dresses, barely paying attention, then hightailed it for the dressing room.

He'd followed me. All the way in, down the row of doors, to the one I selected at the end where there were a bunch of mirrors and a seat, presumably for the husbands. There was no husband in the room I chose. There was no one in any of the dressing rooms, as far as I could tell. It was late morning on a Thursday, not exactly peak shopping hours. That was one of the best things about having a job like mine, daytime shopping without any of the crowds.

But right now, twirling in my dress in front of Hades, some crowds would've been welcome.

The dress was utter perfection. Surprising since I'd just snatched it off the rack, the first one I'd tried on. That never happened. Ever. It had to be Hades. Hades, the magical, badass, sexy man. His powers apparently extended to the women's department at Nordstrom.

It showed off my ample assets, but not in a way that would be inappropriate for a family barbeque. Though this was a Sons of Templar barbeque, so I didn't think it required the same kind of outfit as the WASP barbeques I used to attend with Derek.

Ugh, *Derek.*

I did not need to think of him at that moment.

When I was brave enough to look up at Hades, I melted. I truly fucking *melted.*

I couldn't say his eyes had softened because there was nothing soft about this man. I was pretty sure it was impossible for anything about him to be soft or tender. And although I had thought that's what I wanted, I realized I hadn't known what I wanted. What I needed. Until that very fucking moment.

"Freya," he said through gritted teeth. It was a warning. One that made me take two steps back without even consciously thinking about it.

Hades followed me. All the way back into my dressing room. He slammed the flimsy door shut behind him. Everything was moving in slow motion, my heart thundering against my ribcage. In my throat.

Somewhere, far away, in another world or maybe in another dressing room, women entered, chatting.

Hades and I stared at each other for a split second, for an eternity, before he approached me. Or maybe I approached him. Either way, his hand was at the back of my neck, bringing our bodies and mouths together. We crashed against each other. Tongues. Teeth. Desire that had been building for weeks, fire that had been simmering for months. It wasn't just an inferno now. It was something else entirely. A fucking explosion. Destroying everything in its path. Even now, in the state that I was in, I knew that nothing would ever be the same after this.

Then again, nothing had been the same since the night we met.

And I was totally fucking okay with that.

"Fuck," he hissed against my mouth, his other hand at my ass, bunching up the dress. "I knew you'd taste like this. Like goddamned destruction."

There was no time to digest this, no time to explore the heat in his eyes. No, he was kissing me again. He was devouring me fucking whole.

And I let him. Gladly.

Something ripped. My sanity, maybe. More realistically, it was the thin strap of the dress. Hades jerked the fabric covering my breast away as if it was nothing, his palm kneading my bare ass.

I moaned in a way that was much too loud and much too sexual, but I couldn't control it.

He bent down and put my nipple in his mouth, tracing his tongue over the sensitive skin, his teeth grazing against me. I tore my fingers through his hair, itching to yank it out by the root. My body writhed against the wall, and I feared I was going to break it down. Men had explored my nipples with their mouths before, and it had been nice, but nowhere near as stimulating as every porno made it seem.

Now I was questioning every man who'd come before Hades and wondering whether every porno producer was actually a woman who had, at some point, been fucked by Hades or a some kind of alpha male.

My climax started building, my body tensing, readying to explode. Solely from his lips on my fucking nipple. Although I knew that the orgasm that I was a handful of moments away from having was going to be fucking awesome, really fucking awesome, I did not want my first orgasm with Hades to be from his lips on my nipple. I wanted his cock in my pussy.

"Hades," I huffed out, pulling at his hair in a different way now. "The first time we have sex cannot be in a dressing room at Nordstrom." My voice was breathy and not at all convincing, considering his mouth was on my nipple and his fingers were probing the edge of my panties.

"I know," he murmured, removing his lips from my nipple.

But his fingers did not move.

No, they *did* move.

They moved *inside* me.

First inside my panties, then inside of me.

I gasped, my knees giving out. Hades somehow held me up while his fingers worked expertly inside of me, coated in my need for him.

"I didn't want the first time I get inside your cunt to be somewhere I couldn't make you scream without getting us arrested," he murmured in my ear, fingers still moving inside of me. "I had plans for you, Freya. To own you. To take every part of you." His mouth moved upward, tongue slipping into my mouth. He tasted of man and sex.

"I wanted to taste every part of you," he continued against my mouth, putting another finger inside of me.

I gasped, no longer caring that we were in a public place, that there were women trying on clothes mere feet from us. That there wasn't a solid wall anywhere around. That a world beyond this fitting room existed.

Nothing existed except him.

Hades.

"I wanted to control everything about the first time I was inside of you," Hades growled, his fingers still moving, coaxing me to climax. "But then you babbled about going shopping. Then you looked at me like you were imagining my cock inside of you. Then you came out in that fucking *dress*." He pulled my hair to expose my neck. His lips landed on it, teeth grazing my carotid artery. "You stole all my control. I don't have a choice."

Somehow, some way, his fingers left me, my legs wrapped around his hips, my panties were pushed to the side and his cock surged inside of me.

All the way inside.

I screamed. It was muffled by his hand against my mouth, but it was still a scream.

It was exquisite. Overwhelming. I'd never felt so full in my fucking life.

He didn't remove his hand straight away, as if he knew I was about to fall apart, as if he sensed that even his large hand against my mouth might not come anywhere close to muffling the sound of my next orgasm.

The conversations of people beyond the door were nothing but a faraway echo.

"I don't have a choice whether or not to fuck you right now, Freya," Hades murmured, his lips at my ear. "I'm going to come inside you. You're going to clench around my dick. I won't get to see every inch of you as you do so. I won't get to hear you scream the way I want. but that's gonna happen later."

Then he started thrusting. He stared at me as his hips moved, his hand still at my mouth, muffling my moans of pleasure. Veins in his neck pulsated from restraint. And I knew he was restraining himself right now. This was a muscled fucking sex god. He was fucking me with one-tenth of his strength, of his hunger, his desire. I heard that in his voice, saw it in his eyes, in the way he was holding himself.

If this was one-tenth of what he was capable of giving me, I had no idea how I'd survive him.

But I couldn't think about the future right now. All I cared about was Hades's cock plunging inside me, his hand on my mouth, my teeth grazing against his fingers, fingers that tasted faintly of me.

My second orgasm came fast, quick, and it was earth-shattering.

"Yes," Hades hissed, still fucking me, holding me up, taking all of my weight since the flimsy dressing room partition definitely couldn't take it. "That's my girl," he rasped, his voice animalistic. "Come for me."

He kept going, my body exploding with aftershocks, his body refusing to let me settle, to let me come down. His eyes were locked on me the entire time. It was an out-of-body experience, having this man—the one I'd touched myself thinking about for weeks—fucking me in a Nordstrom dressing room, fucking me like I'd never been fucked before.

And I'd never felt more in touch with my body in my entire life. Never felt more like a woman in my entire fucking life.

I came apart again, coming for the third time. This time, I brought Hades with me. He let out a low growl that sounded like it came from the back of his throat. I couldn't tell whether it was a roar or a whisper. All I knew was that I felt it in my pores.

I felt *him* in my pores.

———

I did not walk out of Nordstrom with a dress. However, I did walk out of Nordstrom with a man who had just made me come. Three times. Although his hand was settled on my lower back and his cock was back in his jeans, I could still feel him inside me. Because he was still inside of me.

Not only had Derek never come inside of me, but he'd also never fucked me without a condom. That was not something I did. Ever.

Nor was it something I forgot about in the throes of passion. The throes had never been intense enough for me to forget about sexually transmitted diseases or unwanted pregnancy. Sure, I was on the pill and had been since I was a teenager, but that did not mean I couldn't get pregnant. Multiple girls at clubs I'd worked at had told me stories about unplanned pregnancies that were the result of sex with a man who hadn't wanted to use condoms. I'd told myself I would only forgo condoms when I was okay with having a child with the man I was fucking. There was not one single man who'd ever fucked me that I had wanted to have a child with.

I snuck a look at the man who was driving my car. Something he'd demanded because apparently it was impossible for a man to sit in a passenger seat and let a woman drive.

God forbid.

I didn't mind even the slightest right now, considering his hand was on my thigh. High on my thigh. Plus, I was busy thinking about his cum. Then I was thinking about a dark-headed baby in his muscled arms.

Fuck.

No. I needed to slow down. I'd had sex with this guy once. *Once.* Now I was imagining what our *child* looked like? Fucking insane.

Hades looked at me when I cleared my throat. It was not the first time he'd done that, looked at me. We hadn't spoken since we'd gotten into the car. Actually, we hadn't spoken since he'd gotten out of *me.* Not because things were awkward. Because there wasn't much else to say.

Well, now there was something to say.

"We didn't use a condom," I blurted out. My cheeks flamed. I couldn't believe me, of all people, was embarrassed by that. Not twenty minutes ago, this man had been inside me.

"No, we didn't," he agreed.

"I don't have sex without a condom."

His grip tightened on my thigh. It almost hurt. And I liked it.

"I don't want to hear a word about you fucking anyone but me," he shot back.

The corner of my mouth turned up in amusement. "I don't plan on fucking anyone except you," I admitted, laying my cards on the table. There was no point playing hard to get here, not when he already had me.

"I'm clean," he said, still gripping my thigh tightly. "Can get tested when we get back, show you the papers before I fuck you again. And, baby, as long as you've got no objection to it, I need to fuck you raw."

Now, he might not have been a traditional gentleman, but the offer was remarkably polite in my opinion. But the reality of that meant that I would have to wait at least two days for Hades to fuck me again. The mere thought of it made my skin crawl and my stomach constrict in need, despite the fact his cum was still dripping from me. Yes, I could've insisted on a condom. It was my right as a woman, and I'd scoffed at all the men who'd whined about how condoms numbed things. But I was a woman who'd never been fucked without one.

It might have been foolish of me to take an outlaw at his word, but I didn't give a shit. For better or for worse, I trusted Hades. My gut told me he wouldn't do anything to hurt me.

"No, I don't have any objections," I rasped out, barely able to speak.

His hand moved even higher up my leg, so high that it brushed the edge of my very damp panties.

My teeth sank into my lip hard enough for me to taste blood. Hades returned his eyes to the road, but his jaw was granite.

Neither of us said a word during the rest of the drive home. His finger just kept brushing the side of my panties and that soft area where my pussy and my upper thigh met.

I wasn't even sure that he'd put it in park by the time we got back to my place. I wouldn't have even noticed if he'd driven through the house and parked in my living room at this point.

We barely got the door closed before he was inside me again. Sirius, who had cheerfully run up to us when he'd first heard the door, had taken one look and politely left us to it.

Now I was bent over the sideboard, my palms flat on the surface, Hades fucking me so hard that everything on the sideboard clattered to the ground. I barely noticed. All I noticed was that I could watch Hades fuck me thanks to the mirror I'd placed above it.

"Look," he hissed, his hands bunching my hair, yanking it so my chin jutted up and my eyes found his icy ones in the mirror. "Look at yourself," he ordered. "Look at how beautiful you are with my cock inside you." He kept thrusting, and I cried out, looking at myself. My face was flushed, my eyes glowed, and yeah, I looked good.

"Remember the way you look right now," he grumbled. "Remember it."

It was a command. One that went deeper than just being surface words. He didn't just want me to remember how I looked, he wanted me to remember *him*. Because he was already establishing that he'd be something to remember.

I might've held onto that a little tighter if my grasp on reality hadn't picked that moment to explode into a million tiny particles with my orgasm.

I didn't think about it later either.

Which was my mistake.

———

"I think this qualifies as a cheeseburger day," I said to the ceiling.

We had made it to the bedroom. Just not the bed. We were laying naked on the lush, fluffy rug that took up half the room and had cost a small fortune. That was something that they—the proverbial 'they'—didn't tell you about adulthood: how expensive nice rugs were. It was worth every penny right at that second as we used it as a mattress. I was lying flat on my back, breathing heavily, waiting for my heart to return to its normal rhythm. Hades was beside me, also lying on his back, not staring at the ceiling. I could see him from the corner of my eye, looking at me. We weren't touching. No cuddling. But I was glad about that. I was already covered in him. Drenched in him. Practically drowning.

"A cheeseburger day?" he repeated.

His voice was low, throaty and warm. Warm. I hadn't thought Hades was capable of speaking in such a way. Or maybe he was speaking the exact same way he had before, but I was different now.

It seemed that there were going to be two versions of me: B.H. and A.H. Otherwise known as *Before Hades* and *After Hades*.

"Yes," I sighed, still looking at the ceiling. "If there is ever a time for a cheeseburger, it's after..." I struggled to find the right words. "So many orgasms I can't even count. After the absolute best sex I've had in my life. The kind of sex I didn't know existed. The kind of sex I couldn't possibly tell anyone about because they'd think I was making it up."

Fuck.

I really hadn't meant to say all of that. It was the sex. It had done things to me.

Heat crawled up my neck. Now I was still looking at the ceiling because I had no other choice but to stare at the ceiling. I couldn't possibly look at Hades's handsome, angled, masculine face after spewing out that very embarrassing and dorky statement.

But he took the choice away from me as he lifted from his back onto me. He rested his forearms on either side of my body, not giving me his full weight. But he gave me his full stare, and it crushed me. In a good way.

Though his features couldn't possibly have changed in the past few hours, like his voice, it was softer now. The edge was still there, of course. This was not a man who could lose his edge.

I could not predict what Hades was going to say at any given moment, but what he said next would never have even entered my mind in my wildest dreams.

"Okay, baby, I'll go get us cheeseburgers," he murmured, kissing my nose. "You're going to stay here. You're not going to shower. You're going to open a bottle of wine. You're going to do that without putting on any panties. You can wear a robe. Nothing else." His eyes bore into mine. "Is that clear?"

"Yeah," I whispered. "Clear."

He kissed me then, his mouth moving slowly over mine, his hand trailing down to cup my pussy. "And I've gotta say, I love what you've got going on down there," he murmured, stroking the hair between my legs. "You ever get rid of it, we're gonna have problems."

"I'll never get rid of it," I promised, forgetting that I was not supposed to take anything off my body, or in this case, keep it on my body, at the demand of a man.

"Good." He cupped me hungrily, then he went to get us cheese-burgers.

Because I was high on Hades, on what had just happened, it didn't enter my mind that before this, Hades had never left me alone in the house. Not even for ten minutes. It didn't enter my mind to wonder why that was. I just went into the kitchen, opened a bottle of wine and waited for him.

HADES

I should not have come back. I knew better. I'd finally got to taste her pussy, got to feel her cunt around me. Everything I'd been torturing myself with. So there was no reason to stick around.

Except there was.

There were a thousand fucking reasons.

Freya's skin flushing as she babbled on about how fucking good the sex was—and the sex wasn't just good, there wasn't a word to describe what it was. Freya talking about cheeseburgers. The smell of her hair. The way she fucking spun around in that dress, looking tiny without her shoes on. The hair on her cunt. The tight, velvet grasp against my cock.

Yeah, there were about a thousand and one reasons why I came back to her house, holding a greasy paper bag, unwilling to go anywhere else.

The dog met me at the door. Another fucking reason I came back. I liked her fucking dog. Glancing to the floor by the sideboard with all the shit on it—shit that didn't make sense mixed with shit I fucking liked … pillows, candles, fucking all of it—my cock went hard at the memory of this afternoon. At Freya's face, flushed, full of ecstasy and full of fucking me.

"Hey," she whispered. She was in her robe, standing up from the sofa.

I dropped the cheeseburgers on the counter.

"Take off the robe, bend over the couch," I snarled. "I'm gonna fuck you, then we're gonna eat cheeseburgers."

Her robe dropped to the floor.

I fucked her, and then we ate cheeseburgers.

CHAPTER THIRTEEN

FREYA

"This is your fault," I snapped at Hades, emerging from my closet for the five hundredth time.

He was lying on my bed with Sirius on top of his feet—now allowed on my bed because we were done with all the fucking, for now at least—completely naked, his hands behind his head, the sheets covering him from the waist down, looking absolutely delicious. My sheets were white, my ornate headboard also white with gold hardware. My side tables were mirrored, and both had large glass lamps and fresh flowers on them. White flowers.

Hades was not wearing his cut, nor what I'd come to think of as his 'badass uniform', but he still emanated darkness while lying there. He produced shadows wherever he went, and those shadows swallowed me whole.

"You are the reason I didn't get a dress," I continued when he didn't respond to what I'd said. I frowned in my mirror, trying my best not to look at him in the reflection. Then I'd get distracted, and we were already running late.

Macy and Hansen's barbeque had started thirty minutes ago,

yet I still wasn't dressed. Because the perfect dress was still in Nordstrom, ripped and ruined, and I couldn't go back to buy it since we'd ruined the dress and hadn't paid for it. As if I hadn't felt naughty enough.

"You want to go back to get the dress?" he asked from his spot on the bed. He hadn't started getting ready because he was an evil creature who could just throw on clothes and look devastatingly handsome in about five minutes flat.

"If we go back there, we might get arrested," I grumbled to the mirror, frowning at the dress I was wearing. It went down to my ankles, was floral, halter neck, with a small cutout in the mid-section and lace trim at the bottom. I'd paired it with a baby pink cashmere cardigan. Both were remnants of my life with Derek. I'd kept them because they'd cost an arm and a leg, plus they came in handy when I was in the mood to look like I wasn't a stripper.

I'd thrown them on in a panic after everything in my closet seemed wrong.

"They could've had video cameras in the dressing room," I groaned, my skin heating at the memory of what we'd done in there.

"They don't," Hades said.

I frowned. "How do you know they don't?"

"Beyond the fact they'd be sued up the ass, I had our guy hack into their system, check to see if they had any footage of that area. Had him wipe anything from that area just to be sure."

I blinked. "You had a guy hack into the Nordstrom security system just to make sure there was no compromising footage of us?" I clarified.

"I did."

Jesus fucking Christ. What did one even say to that?

I had no idea what to say to that, so I just frowned at myself in the mirror.

"What are we going to say when we get there?" I asked, staring at Hades in the mirror.

"About what?"

I picked an imaginary piece of lint off my dress, nerves suddenly crawling up my throat. "About us," I answered, not looking at him anymore. I sucked in a breath. "I mean, I don't know your dating history because we haven't really talked about that. But my guess is, based on the time I have spent with you, that you're not really a relationship kind of guy. That maybe you're more into..." I searched for a word that wouldn't piss him off.

"Fucking," he finished for me from his spot on the bed. My eyes met his, and he was watching me intently. In a way that made my stomach coil.

"Yes," I agreed, both loving and hating the sound of the word and what it meant coming from him. Coming from him naked in my fucking bed.

"Fucking," I said it again because I liked feeling dirty with him. He must've liked it too because his eyes flared, and he sat up slightly in bed. "And you're very good at it," I added. "Very good." Fuck. This was not going well. "Um, and I don't think there is a single thing wrong with just fucking or being sexually free. But I'm a thirty-two-year-old woman."

Fuck.

I'd just told him my age. That wasn't something that he needed to know. Sure, Hades looked like he might've been a few years ahead of me, but it was impossible to tell. His porcelain face was almost lineless, and the only sign of age was in his eyes, displaying the only evidence of the years he'd lived, the lives he'd taken. I wasn't ashamed of my age, I looked great for it, and I'd never had a complex about it, but still.

I straightened my shoulders and played with the bun I'd piled my hair into. "As a thirty-*something*-year-old woman, I'm not interested in just fucking. Even fucking that's as magnificent as we've had."

I bit my lip, already regretting what I was about to say. It was all too tempting to give Hades everything and just take whatever he was willing or capable of giving me. I certainly would've done that in my twenties, but not now. "I need a relationship. I don't need labels or even anything serious right now. I'm more than aware that we barely know each other. But one thing you should know about me is that I don't bullshit. So I'm telling you how I feel without the bullshit."

I sucked in a breath then turned to face him. I took a couple of mental pictures of him lying there, sculpted abs on show, the thin scar representing the night we met marring his otherwise perfect torso. Hades, in my bed, with my dog, looking like he belonged there.

"I like you," I mumbled quietly, forcing myself to keep eye contact. "I like you a lot. And I don't know how it works in the club. I'm not really experienced with the outlaw world, but I do understand that fidelity isn't something always practiced. Then again, it's not something many regular men practice."

Fuck, I was babbling. Again.

"If you, by chance, like me too and want something more than fucking, I would need you to not fuck anyone else." I had to look away from his penetrating stare, hating that I did not sound like the articulate, strong adult I'd considered myself to be.

I felt incredibly awkward and exposed standing there in a dress that covered me more than most of my wardrobe, Hades still staring at me. He was naked and lying down, yet he held all the power.

He let me stand there, emotionally sweating from the fear that I'd just fucked everything up. After what felt like an eternity, he got out of bed and strode over to me. I'd thought it would be incredibly hard for a man to stride like a badass while naked.

Hades managed it.

In a big way.

He thrust a hand into my hair at the base of my skull then pulled my body to his. I sighed in relief as my clothed body pressed against his naked one.

"Freya, there is no way I will have my cock inside anyone else but you," he murmured.

My body sagged ever so slightly. I'd heard the rumors about 'club girls', about them being around specifically for tension relief. I hadn't judged them, not even a little bit. But I also wouldn't have trusted myself around them if I knew that Hades was fucking them at the same time he was fucking me. Not that that would be their fault. But jealousy had never known reason.

"You guessed right. I don't do relationships," he continued.

My previously relaxed body coiled up tight, shame and rejection washing over me like a tidal wave.

His hand moved from the back of my neck to cradle my jaw. "I don't know how to do a relationship," he added. His voice was not gentle, but I knew he was trying to be. "What I do know is that now that I've got a taste of you, I'm not fuckin' lettin' you go." His hand squeezed my hip to make his point.

Fuck, way to put a gal on an emotional rollercoaster in the space of thirty seconds.

"What does that mean?" I questioned quietly, unable to hide my insecurity.

"What it means is that you're on the back of my bike."

I blinked. Although I was relatively ignorant about the outlaw lifestyle, I knew that 'you're on the back of my bike' was biker speak for 'you're my girlfriend.'

"Okay, if I'm going to be on the back of your bike, I need to change my outfit." My voice was all breathy, my body feeling so light I was afraid if he weren't holding me, I might've actually floated away.

"Okay," Hades said.

"You should get dressed too," I reminded him, my eyes flickering down his naked body, marveling at it once more. Hunger built at the base of my belly. A gal did not get used to a body like his. I had yet to trace every single one of his tattoos, obsess over every detail. We'd been busy. "I know that you guys are all about freedom and breaking all the rules, but I feel like even the Sons of Templar might frown on you arriving naked."

His mouth twitched. Almost a smile. I considered that a victory.

With great effort, I walked back into my closet to find an outfit that was motorcycle appropriate.

Once I was safely inside, I did a girly little dance, sans the scream.

———

Though I'd lived somewhat of an interesting and rather transient life, I had never found myself on the back of a motorcycle, so I had no idea how to dress for it.

There was a lot of pressure riding on this barbeque. I wanted to look like me but the absolute best version of me. Hades had never talked about his parents, not that we were at the point of talking about families—thank God—but I was going to take a shot in the dark and say he wasn't close with them. Meeting the club was his version of meeting his parents. The men I wasn't worried about. I did well with men on account of my dress sense, my boobs and my occupation. However, I did not usually do as well with women. On account of my dress sense, my boobs and my occupation.

Though I'd figured—I'd hoped—the women of the Sons of Templar would be different. That I wouldn't experience the judgement that had come with meeting the parents, the friends, the family of every boyfriend before Hades.

Not that Hades was my boyfriend.

He was my *Old Man*.

The thought made me smile. It also released a lot of the tension in my body, making it possible for me to move through my closet and pick a pair of tight leather pants that laced up at the front and a cropped tank top. I finished it off with some spike-heeled, red Louboutin ankle boots. I considered it to be the perfect 'meet the outlaw bikers' outfit. It was also a perfect outfit to communicate my style. Expensive, revealing, and just a little trashy.

When I walked back into my bedroom, Hades was dressed. I got the idea that he'd been dressed for a while, since he was sitting on my bed, stroking Sirius with one hand and frowning at his phone which was in the other. I watched him for a little while, wondering what he was doing on that phone. He had been tight-lipped about the Derek situation the entire time he'd been living here. I hadn't even asked because parts of me didn't want to know. The other parts of me didn't want him to leave. Now, the thought of him leaving was absolutely terrifying. It was also terrifying that I wanted my biker Old Man of five minutes to move into my home.

Someone or something must've been looking out for me because Hades looked up from his phone before I could commit to a full-blown freak-out. His gaze flickered from my toes to my head, paused on my tits, then finished on my face. It was full of fire.

I waited.

For the comment.

The one I always got from men I was dating asking, "Aren't you going to put a shirt on?" Or, "Don't you think that's a little…" trailing off, not actually saying the word 'slutty' because that would've made them an asshole. Even if the man in question had been attracted to me because of my fashion sense.

Most men expected me to change the way I dressed—and my occupation, but that was a whole other story—the second they considered me theirs. It was all well and good for me to dress like that to capture their attention, but once I had it, they didn't want other men ogling what was theirs.

Hades was definitely a possessive kind of guy. The kind of guy who would not take lightly to ogling. Classic alpha male behavior.

"Fuck, baby," he muttered, standing up and crossing the distance between us. It was like he had to make up for all the time we'd been in the same room without touching. Which did not bother me, not at all.

Hades did not say anything else other than those two words. He hadn't needed to. The way he looked at me made it very clear that he appreciated my outfit a whole lot and nothing about it bothered him.

"We need to go," he said, squeezing my hips.

"We do," I agreed.

He did not step away or release me to let me go or walk toward the door.

"We really need to leave," he said again.

"Yes, we're late already."

Still, he did not let me go.

"Freya, baby, you're gonna have to be the one to step away because if I move, I'll throw you on the fucking bed, bury myself in your pussy and we won't leave this fucking house." He gripped me tightly as he spoke, his body dangerously still.

I swallowed roughly, staring into his hypnotizing eyes. My body responded to his words, the promise behind them, and the evidence of how horny he was pressing into my stomach. How in the fuck was I meant to have more willpower than Hades?

For a long, long moment, I seriously considered staying exactly where I was and letting nature takes its course. Despite all the sex we'd had in the past twenty-four hours, I was desperate for more.

But I was also desperate to find my way into Hades's world. Into the Sons of Templar. I wanted to meet his people, the people he considered his family. He'd been living with me—as my protector, staying in a different bedroom—for over a month, and I hadn't seen any of the famed Sons of Templar, despite the few who had been on my protection duty.

Hades had obviously decided that he didn't want anyone else in his world interacting with me. I hadn't exactly wanted to interact with a whole bunch of people anyway; I hadn't wanted to meet people while covered in bruises, looking like a victim. But now that my bruises had healed almost entirely, I was ready to face the world looking like myself.

So, in an act that I should've gotten a medal for, I stepped back. Hades watched me do so with his jaw set. "Walk out, now," he seethed. "Don't fuckin' stop until you get to my bike. I'll meet you there." His words were forced, and he was still watching me like a predator.

My stomach flipped as I did as he'd ordered.

Eventually, he came out, got on his bike. And I got on the back.

———

"You're here!" a feminine voice screamed at me the moment we entered the backyard of a beautiful home. It was like mine in that it was in the middle of nowhere, the sprawling desert surrounding it. The driveway was full of Harleys. There were a few fancy SUVs as well, several with car seats. I hadn't gotten to gape at the beauty of the home's interior because I'd been too overcome with nerves, but it was definitely more boho than mine, and impeccable. I noted and appreciated the *Lord of the Rings* paraphernalia scattered around the place, the shiny KitchenAid appliances. Despite my nerves, the warmth of the home washed over me. This was a *home*. The photos, the smells. The sounds of people and music filtering through the open doors.

It was getting chilly in the desert, and I wasn't wearing enough clothes, but I didn't feel a hint of it.

Not with Hades pressed against me.

We hadn't walked in holding hands or anything, Hades was definitely not a hand holder, but I'd rode here on the back of his bike. I still smelled of him, he still smelled of me. There was no mistaking it.

And then I was holding someone else's hand. Or more accurately, they were holding my hand.

"Oh my god, I can't believe it's taken me this long to meet you," the woman clutching my hand yanked me into her small frame for a hug.

I was not a person who hugged strangers. Sure, I gave off that vibe since I was friendly and warm—or at least I liked to think so —but hugging strangers, or even hugging friends, was something I just didn't do. It brought back things I did my best not to think about.

But there was something about this hug. No, something about this *woman*. She smelled of vanilla perfume. But with an edge. Hugging her didn't make my skin crawl. It was warm, comforting, just like the home itself.

Eventually, she released me, but she still held my wrists in her hands.

She was stunning. Petite, wearing a long-sleeved, maxi dress that molded over every inch of her body. For a woman that small, she had curves. She was also wearing sky-high wedges that still didn't put her at my height. Her hair was cropped into a pixie cut which totally suited her. Like perfectly. She looked like a bohemian fairy princess, and her eyes were glowing with warmth. Well, they were until they darted to the man still standing at my side.

"You," she snapped, letting go of one of my hands so she could point her finger accusingly at Hades. "You have kept her from me for too long." Her eyes then went back to me. "I fucking love your channel. *Love* it. Everything about it. I'm a little star-struck right now. My bikini line has been forever changed thanks to you." She looked to Hades once more and made a shooing motion with her hand. "You can go now. I want to talk about things a lot more inti-mate than my bikini line, and Hansen gets pissy with me when I do that in front of other men."

I don't think I'd ever seen anyone *shoo* away a fully-grown man. And I hadn't thought anyone would ever be brave enough to shoo away Hades. Unless they weren't overly attached to the hand that did the shooing.

Amazingly, Hades shooed. But not before he yanked me out of the woman's—I'm assuming Macy's—grasp so he could kiss me. Not on the cheek. Not on the forehead. Not a chaste peck on the lips. No, a kiss. French. As. Fuck. For about one point five seconds I was worried about the audience, about the woman I'd just met standing inches away from such a sexual kiss. Then I forgot the woman existed. I forgot anything existed except Hades, his kiss and the hands that found themselves on my ass.

Eventually, he pulled away, which was good since I never would've, and things could've gotten even more inappropriate.

Hades did not let me go entirely, though. I was still pressed against his body, his head tipped down, his eyes on my face. "You gonna be okay, baby?" he murmured against my mouth.

If I hadn't already been liquid, I would've melted.

Instead of answering, I pursed my lips and nodded once.

Still, he didn't let me go completely. He just stared at me in that way that made my insides turn inside out. In a way I hadn't thought he would do outside of the bedroom let alone in front of witnesses.

"Later," he murmured, too low for even the woman to hear. "I'm going to fuck you so hard that your screams will echo through the fucking desert."

Cue girly stomach flip.

He squeezed my hips a little tighter before he stepped back and walked away. Both Macy and I watched him walk into a sea of leather, doing some chin lifts and back slaps with various men wearing cuts. Some I recognized, some I didn't. Children tore around their feet.

There were women, too, but I didn't get to take a good look at them or try to spot the infamous Gwen and Amy because the woman demanded my attention.

"Holy fucking *fuck* that was hot," she fanned herself. "I mean, I'm married, happily. Very happily. To a man who pleasures me every night. And I know that sounds like a lie because we've been married for years now, and people who are married for years aren't supposed to have daily orgasms." She paused. "Well, not from each other, anyway." She winked. "But as it's very obviously become clear to you, these men are an entirely different breed."

Both of our eyes went to the sea of leather for a hot minute before the woman demanded my attention once more. "I swear, I never thought I'd see the day when *Hades* brought a girl home." She put a hand on her heart. "And I cannot tell you how glad I am that it's you. I mean *you*, Freya Barker."

"And you're Macy?" I guessed.

Her eyes went wide. "Oh my god, yes! Did I not mention that? I'm such a dork. I've been so excited for you to arrive. Hansen made me have two sangrias to calm myself down, but that kind of backfired." Her eyes went to the kitchen counter, which was overflowing with plates of food. I'd placed a batch of cookies and wine amongst it all right as we'd walked in. I might've been raised in a trailer park, but I knew it was good manners to arrive at someone's house bearing gifts.

"Let me get you a sangria, then I'll introduce you to the rest of the girls. They've been *dying* to see you." She leaned forward and squeezed my hand. "Welcome to the family, honey."

Her words, spoken softly, almost offhandedly, punctured my heart. I had to bite my lip to hold back my tears at such a simple statement. Something that no one had ever uttered to me before. Not Derek's family, who had known me for two years and purposefully said my name wrong every time I went to their house. No one.

———

"Okay, so you were kidnapped." I pointed at the gorgeous brunette with the emerald eyes and outfit that somehow did not have a single stain on it despite the fact it was crisp white, she had two kids *and* she was drinking red wine.

"And so were you." I pointed at the red-haired knockout wearing heels higher than even I'd worn. Her outfit, like Gwen's, looked like it was supposed to be on a runway somewhere. They oozed style and class in a way that wasn't intimidating.

"Your husband is your high school boyfriend back from the dead," I pointed to Caroline, the stunning woman with the shocking red lipstick and the impressive journalism career.

Each of them nodded.

"Holy fuck," I said, taking a large sip of my drink.

"Right?" Amy smirked, taking a large sip of her own drink.

"The courting process of the Sons of Templar seems to err on the side of the dramatic," Gwen chimed in with a warm smile and an accent I couldn't get enough of.

"The first time I met Hades he was bleeding from a stab wound. And then he moved in with me because my ex beat me half to death. We've already had our fair share of drama, and we've only been sleeping together for less than forty-eight hours," I explained.

Amy's eyes bugged out while she made a choking sound at the back of her throat. Gwen leaned forward and helpfully pounded on her back while taking another sip of her own drink.

All of the other women chuckled at Amy's reaction, waiting for her to get a hold of herself.

"Sorry," she croaked. "I swear, I thought you said that you only had sex with him forty-eight hours ago."

"I did say that," I nodded.

"You're serious?" Caroline asked, her expression one of disbelief.

"Serious," I replied.

"You've had *that*," Amy pointed directedly at Hades who seemed to be in some kind of man huddle with Hansen, and who, of course, looked over the second she pointed, "in your house for over a *month*, and you only just started having sex? How did you survive?"

It didn't sound believable when she said it like that, especially not when Hades was standing there with the desert backdrop, looking all ... *Hades*. Yeah, sure all of the other men, especially the husbands of these women, were so attractive I had the urge to poke them with a pin to make sure that they bled, but they had nothing on Hades.

His eyes went from Amy to me. They were intense. Unyielding. Even across the throngs of people at this party, his gaze was physical. My need for him was overwhelming, and it took a long time to get myself under control, to remember I was supposed to be in the middle of a conversation.

"I have no idea," I admitted, still staring at Hades. "I have no idea how I survived before him."

CHAPTER FOURTEEN

"I had fun," I told Hades.

No, I *sang* the words. I may have indulged a little too heavily in the sangria that Macy had been serving. To be fair, it was Macy's fault. She kept refilling my glass the second I finished my last sip. Then Gwen had done the same. Then Amy. It was a miracle that I was still standing. But of course, there was all of the food. Which I had also heavily indulged in. All of the gorgeous, slim women had done the same, so I felt comfortable actually eating with them. It was a rare thing with women who looked like that, to see them eat all the gauc, salsa, queso, and chili in sight. Then the brownies. The brownies that should've been illegal. I had not felt awkward, completely sating my appetite.

With the majority of women who looked like that, dressed like that, I would've nibbled daintily, weary of the judgmental stares and the sparse plates that would barely be touched by the end of the night.

There had been none of that. It had been very clear that these women devoured food in the same way they devoured life. They swallowed it fucking whole.

It had been like a drug, being engulfed in that family. It had felt effortless. They'd all known what I did for a living, and they'd asked about it with real interest, with not an ounce of judgement. Amy had even demanded that we go down to the club someday so I could give them a class on how to properly work a pole.

I agreed because there was no way in hell that you said no to Amy Abrams. I said yes because I was eager to be in their company again. I was also eager to introduce them to Marilyn, who I knew they would adore, and she would adore them right back. We had also agreed to try to plan a shopping trip. In the space of one day, I'd found myself a boyfriend—or Old Man—and a badass girl posse.

So I was tipsy and singing as I traipsed around my living room. The leather pants were long gone, narrowly avoiding a Ross from *Friends* situation after everything I ate, suddenly making them shrink two sizes. The tank was still on, but I'd changed into a pair of Juicy Couture shorts that had a wonderful elastic waist.

Hades had been putting away the leftovers Macy had forced us home with—they traveled surprisingly well in the saddlebags of his bike—while I was dancing around, feeling happier than I'd felt in as long as I could remember. Apparently, he was done in the kitchen, standing a few feet away with his eyes on me.

"Do you know how sexy you look?" he asked, arms folded in front of him as he evaluated me.

No, he *growled*.

Then he prowled toward me. I was instantly up in his arms, him gathering me up like I weighed nothing. "I have to have you, right fucking now."

Another growl.

My panties were already drenched. They had been since the moment he laid his eyes on me. In two of these long strides, I was sitting on the edge of my dining room table, my legs splayed apart.

Moments later, my panties were ripped apart—*ripped apart*—and his mouth was there. On me. On my fucking clit. Tongue moving expertly, he ate me. He *feasted* on me.

My body sang for him in ways I hadn't even known were possible. His hands were on my upper thighs, holding them apart, the pads of his fingers pressed into the delicate skin hard enough to leave bruises. At least that's what I'd hoped. Even though I was still wearing bruises that another man gave me, I was greedy for more. I wanted marks on my body that hadn't come from pain. No, I craved bruises from pleasure. The most exquisite kind of pleasure that the human body could experience.

I must've transported outside of my body as I came because when I opened my eyes, Hades was no longer there. He was standing, poised at my entrance, readying himself to fuck me.

My clouded mind sharpened, and I moved my leaden limbs upward.

"No," I called out, using his torso to pull myself all the way up to sitting. He let out a hiss between his teeth as my pulling motion pulled him closer to me, so he was almost inside of me. My body convulsed, and I almost abandoned my plan. Almost.

Hades was holding himself taut, the veins in his neck protruding with the effort it was taking him not to surge inside of me.

"No?" he repeated, one of his dark brows arching. Of course, he was never going to do anything against my will, but he also knew very well how much I wanted him.

"No," I mumbled, lips inches from his. "I want you."

His eyes darkened. "Baby, you're about to have all of me," he rasped, the words caressing my skin.

"I want you," I repeated. "In my mouth."

He stilled completely, eyes on my lips. There was a battle in his eyes. His cock was pressing up against me, I was wet, fucking soaked for him. But I had managed to have sex with him countless times, had him go down on me countless times, without me returning the favor. Such things were almost unheard of. It was almost always the other way around. I had wanted to, but we'd always gotten carried away. Hades always took control.

Hades found some of that trademark control now as he stepped back. I gritted my teeth against the loss. Then I prepared to get down on my knees. Hades stopped me. "No, baby."

I frowned in confusion until he moved us across the room toward the sofa where he nabbed one of the cushions and threw it down on the hardwood floor.

To protect my knees.

My knees were on the pillow in mere seconds, then I held him in my hands, staring. Hades was big. Not something that was surprising. He was gorgeous. His dark hair was groomed, which had been a welcome surprise. When I cupped his perfect balls, he let out a groan of pleasure.

My heart thundered at the power I had over this man. This dangerous man.

I just looked at him for a moment, holding him in my hands. His abs were tight, taut, his entire body like stone.

He raked a hand through my hair, running it softly through the strands then holding on tighter.

I took one more look at this magnificent man with a magnificent cock, then I took him in my mouth. Though I was on my knees, doing things to him, I'd never felt more powerful in my life. After a few minutes, he bent me over and fucked me harder than I'd ever been fucked.

And I loved it. All of it.

TWO WEEKS LATER

"Club party tonight, babe," Hades informed me, watching as I cleaned the last of our bowls.

Not that there was a ton to watch. Even before we'd become what we were, Hades was remarkably tidy. Disturbingly so. Before we started sleeping in the same bed, I'd barely known he'd been in my house. Not a single dish, a rogue coffee cup, nothing. No signs of a man being in the house. Not that I'd ever lived with a man, but I'd heard plenty of women complain about their boyfriends and husbands leaving the seat up, hair in the sink and dirty underwear all over the floor.

Now that we were sleeping in the same bed, using the same bathroom, I'd expected to find some of those things to complain about. But with Hades, there was nothing to complain about. In the bedroom. The bathroom. The kitchen counter. The kitchen floor. The dining room table. You get the picture.

"I can't," I told him, wiping my hands, not looking at him.

"Can't?" he repeated.

"It's my first shift back tonight, I told you that," I lied. I knew very well I hadn't told him that. I'd been a total coward about it. Not because I was ashamed. Because I was scared. This ... relationship had been perfect these past weeks, one that felt like it had lasted for a year and a moment at the same time. I was aware of how insane that sounded. I was a stripper dating an outlaw with an ex-boyfriend after me. On the surface, it seemed like there was nary a place for perfection. Especially with someone like Hades who was technically pure male perfection yet was simultaneously the embodiment of chaos and trouble.

I'd never felt like this. So thoroughly protected. So thoroughly understood. Even though he didn't know about the darkest parts of me, it was like he sensed them.

Then there was the sex. The fucking sex.

I had discovered the reason why he was referred to as an outlaw: because sex like that was definitely criminal.

Our relationship had existed in somewhat of a vacuum since my bruises had begun healing. I'd been unable to work or film, and my routine had become all jacked up. It was like my house had become our little private island, with us occasionally venturing out to club parties and things like that. Of course, Hades slunk off at varying times for 'club business', which I sometimes wondered about. I didn't wonder long, though, because whenever he came back, he was on me. His hands. His mouth. Then he was inside me.

It had been an orgasm-filled vacation. I couldn't recall the last time I took a vacation. Every single day, I had worked in some form or another. Dancing. Editing. Filming. I hadn't let myself stop because I'd feared if I stopped, it would all go away. That I'd fall into poverty like tripping on a crack in the sidewalk or something.

The time to sleep, to have sex, to bake, to cook, to have coffee with Marilyn, to walk Sirius, have more sex, reorganize my closet, deep clean the house, have more sex ... it had been exactly what I'd needed.

All it had taken was my ex to beat me half to death.

But the honeymoon—so to speak—was over now. I needed to work. Needed to get back to my routine. Back to myself.

Hades picked up an apple, tossing it in his large palms as if he was considering it. Except he looked at me while he did so, as if he was considering me.

"You did not tell me," he finally replied. Not an accusation exactly.

For the first time since his lips landed on mine, I got a cold, uncomfortable feeling in my stomach.

"Here it is," I snapped.

"Here what is?" Hades asked, leaning against the kitchen counter, taking a bite out of the apple.

How in the fuck did he make eating an apple look sexy?

I could not let that distract me.

"Here is the part where, now that we're together, you feel like you own me, body and soul—"

"I do own you," he interrupted, having swallowed the bite of his apple.

I narrowed my eyes, forcing myself not to give in to my body's reaction to his words, the tenor in which they were spoken and the expression on Hades's face as he was speaking them.

THREE KINDS OF TROUBLE

"We're going to circle back to that later," I informed him, my voice sounding husky and vaguely turned on instead of the sharp, pissed off tone I'd needed. "The 'here it is' was about the moment we start to become a thing where suddenly you have a problem with what I do for a living," I explained, watching him take another bite, getting inappropriately turned on by Hades eating a fucking apple.

Then I remembered that I was meant to be on a roll, and this was kind of an important point to bring home.

"Me being a stripper was fine at the start, when I was just the woman saving your life. Fine when I was the woman that you needed to protect or whatever that was, fine when I was the woman you were fucking in fitting rooms, but now that I'm ... something else, something that you feel the need to own..." I blew out a frustrated breath, raising my brow pointedly before I carried on.

There was no longer any kind of sexual amusement or intensity in Hades's eyes. Nor was he eating the apple anymore. He'd abandoned it because apparently you can't eat an apple and stare at a woman with brooding intensity at the same time.

Something was pissing him off. Probably what I was saying, but I was on a roll.

"Now that you think I'm yours..." Cue an even more intense brooding stare, clenching of the jaw and an overall menacing vibe. Cue my body responding totally inappropriately to those things. "Now that you *think* I'm yours, you think it's time to change things," I continued

Hades's brows narrowed.

I soldiered on. "Because a woman you're dating certainly cannot be taking her clothes off for money. Not now. Not when I've got you to take care of me, right? And let me tell you something. That's not happening." I held my finger up to make my point, but I feared it looked like something a suburban mother did to her ten-year-old.

Hades continued to stare at me for a handful of seconds once I was done speaking. Then he leaned forward, grasped my wrist and moved my still extended finger to his mouth which he opened, using it to slowly suck on and kiss the aforementioned finger.

My knees turned to jelly.

Once he was done sucking on my finger, Hades tightened his grip on my wrist and used it to tug me forward so our bodies pressed together. He lifted his other hand to grasp the back of my neck, tilting my head upward so our eyes locked.

"Lot to unpack there, babe," he said, his voice raspy and thick. I could've poured it into a cup and drank it in one sip.

"First, I'm going to tell you that from that first moment, when I was bleeding on the ground and your face hovered over me, you were not the woman saving my life. You were *my* woman. Nothing else. Never have been anything else."

My insides melted.

Melted.

His hands moved from my neck to caress my jaw so his thumb could run over my bottom lip.

"I do want to take care of you, Freya," he murmured, eyes on my lips. "In every fuckin' way possible. And I plan on doin' that in every way I know how. Even though I'm not practiced, not in the slightest at taking care of another human being, I know how to protect you. Know how to avenge you." His hand, the one holding my wrist between our bodies, suddenly let it go so he could skim the sides of my body until he palmed my ass.

I sucked in a breath, one that smelled and tasted exclusively of Hades.

"I know how to fuck you," he continued, fisting my dress then yanking it upward so he could touch my bare skin.

"But I'm still figurin' out how to take care of you," he confessed, gripping my ass in his hands. "What I'll tell you is I don't give a fuck about your job. I'm not gonna ask you to change anything about your life except to make a little room for me in it.

You want to keep stripping, I'll support it." His hand moved around my body to my hip and then farther, creeping inside of my panties. "I have one request, though. You can show off these magnificent tits, that magical ass, but this..." he slipped his fingers into the area that was already soaking wet. "This cunt, this is mine. Other men can see every inch of you, they can watch you, imagine what it would be like to touch you, to fuck you. But I'm the only one who gets to see, eat and fuck this cunt."

He lifted me up onto the counter we'd just eaten at, shoving my legs apart.

"What you do with your body tonight is up to you," he added, tearing my panties off. "But what I do with it right now is up to me. And I'm going to eat your cunt then fuck it. You're not going to shower. You're gonna go up there tonight smelling of us, still feeling me inside of you."

Then he made good on his promise.

THREE DAYS LATER

I'd forgotten.

Throughout the wonderful, stimulating, overwhelming and arousing weeks Hades and I had been together—really together— I'd forgotten. I'd forgotten that the reason Hades was here, in my house, was because he was protecting me from my psychotic ex who he was sure was trying to kill me.

I wasn't convinced that anyone was trying to kill me since all had been quiet on the Western Front for some time now.

Which was, of course, when everything went to shit.

I had known something was wrong the second I arrived home. I'd been out shopping with Marilyn, an event that would've lasted all day had it not been cut short by Marilyn's sister unexpectedly coming to visit, and Marilyn loved Jed far too much to let him deal with her sister alone.

I'd expected Hades to be at the club because that's where he'd told me he'd be when I left him this morning. But his bike was parked in my driveway which was why I'd sent the prospect still following me around home. After having to shop with us for the scant hour we'd been out, he looked incredibly thankful. Figured. These men could handle all sorts of scary, deadly, icky stuff, but they were complete babies when a few stores were involved.

Sirius did not meet me at the door, my first clue that something was really wrong. Although he was one hundred percent Team Hades, he still loved me. He always met me at the door with a wagging tail and the dog version of a smile. Even if he'd been out walking with Hades, I'd have heard him bark a greeting in hello from across the desert.

The only sound in the house was the closing of the front door. It echoed through my house and through my head. Alarm bells started to go off, my spidey senses telling me that something was wrong. Really wrong.

"Hades?" I called out, my voice shaky and low.

No response.

The inside of my home suddenly felt like a tomb, and despite the heat that I had turned on this morning, a chill crept into my bones. My hand shook as I got my phone out of my purse and fired a text off to Swiss. I had all of the emergency numbers on my phone now, and everyone had my number, but they were under the threat of death not to use mine for anything other than a complete emergency.

I'd felt silly texting him, telling him to come to my place because something felt wrong. He'd likely arrive and give me shit for being such a drama queen, then Hades would do his whole threatening glower thing, and I would roll my eyes and convince Swiss to stay for dinner.

Although I had no concrete reason to think that wasn't going to happen, I had a strong feeling that there would be no dinner, no teasing.

My heels clicked on the floor as I walked slowly toward the

kitchen and living room, waiting, hoping, praying for Sirius to emerge so the foreboding covering my entire body would disappear.

Sirius did emerge. Laying lifeless at the bottom of the steps leading into my kitchen and living area.

I let out a strangled cry, the phone I'd been clutching with a death grip clattering to the floor as I rushed to kneel beside Sirius's body. My hands trembled on top of his fur, and my throat closed up with grief. I couldn't touch him. Because the last time I'd touched him his tail had been wagging, and he'd been slobbering all over my hardwood floors. The last time I'd touched him he was alive. I did not want him to be dead the last time I touched him.

"The dog isn't dead," a voice said, and my eyes flickered to a woman standing in my kitchen. She was drinking a glass of wine. Her nose was bleeding, and her eye was starting to swell shut. Despite those two things, she was beautiful. An unusual thing to notice about a strange, injured woman standing in my kitchen, drinking my wine and holding a gun. Did I forget to mention that part?

Yeah, a gun.

Her dark hair was a mess of curls, framing her face. Her features were dark, too, large eyes open a little too wide to be sane.

"Just drugged," she added, nodding to Sirius. "I would never kill a dog."

I stroked his head, my heart thundering as I forced myself to stand up. "Where is Hades?" I asked. My voice was even which surprised me because I did not feel even. At all. But I knew this woman was a predator. She could smell weakness. Sensed it. If I crumbled here, then it was game over for me.

She grinned, sipping the wine. "This is a good bottle. Pinot from New Zealand. Some of the best."

I gritted my teeth and wished I hadn't refused to let Hades take me to the gun range so I could carry one in my purse. My purse which was laying somewhere beside Sirius, who was drugged.

Drugged, not dead, I'd reminded myself.

"I'm a big fan of yours," she told me. The woman with the gun. The woman who had drugged my dog, the woman who had done something to Hades. Who Hades had tried to fight by the looks of it. It seemed impossible that he had lost said fight. He'd definitely lost because if he had won, she would not be standing in my kitchen. Hades was impossibly strong, impossibly deadly and a man who could take care of anything. So Hades was not okay. And I was alone with a crazy human holding a gun.

CHAPTER FIFTEEN

"Where is Hades?" I repeated. Demanded. My heart was pounding against my chest, panic crawling up my throat.

"He was getting chatty, so I had to put him to sleep for a bit too." She nodded her head over to the sofa.

My eyes went there, and my heart dropped even further. Hades was slumped over, as if he'd just fallen asleep watching the game or something. That would've only been possible if Hades was the kind of guy who watched games with a beer in hand and a belly protruding from his tee. Hades was not that kind of guy. Hades was a guy who fought a woman with a gun, and for whatever reason had lost then been drugged.

Every cell in my body called out to me, urging me to go to Hades so I could put my hand on his chest, feel the rise and fall of it. Maybe let some of his courage and strength seep into my body.

But I couldn't do that. The woman was watching me with eagle eyes. It was my job to figure this out, to protect Hades and Sirius.

"I wasn't expecting you home," the woman remarked casually. "I watched you walk into Nordstrom with your girl and your shadow, figured you'd be hours." She tilted her head, regarding me.

"Oh, I apologize. My bad," I snapped at her. "I'm so sorry for interrupting your plans." It was a mistake to get ornery with the woman with a gun, but it was either pissed off or hysterical.

Surprisingly, she didn't seem pissed off at all. In fact, she grinned. Wide.

"Don't apologize, you're being here makes this all the more delicious." She spoke to me as she rounded the kitchen island. I walked backward, slowly, hating to leave Sirius but needing to get to Hades.

"What are you doing in my house?" I demanded. She was a big fan, she'd said. Had she somehow found out where I lived after becoming obsessed with me? That sounded insane and narcissistic, but I couldn't think of any other reason why she'd be here.

"What do you want with me?" I implored, getting closer to the couch. I didn't dare take my eyes off her.

She stopped walking then. "With you?" she asked.

I nodded once. "Yeah, with me. Since this is my house, and it's my dog you drugged and..." I trailed off, desperate to look at him but not willing to let her out of my sight. "And you were talking about my channel," I finished weakly.

"Oh, yes, I can understand how you could assume that," she nodded, the gun still held casually at her side. "But I'm not here for you, I'm here for him. More accurately, I'm here to kill him." She lifted the gun and pointed it at Hades.

My eyes went to Hades, instantly moving so I could get between the barrel of her gun and Hades's prone body.

The woman's eyes flared in surprise at this as a stirring on the sofa stole my attention.

Hades's jerked, eyelids fluttering then opening wide. He went from unconscious to disturbingly alert in a manner of seconds. He was on his feet in a couple more seconds, looking like he was going to rush toward me when the woman spoke.

"Nuh, uh," she tsked, still pointing the gun at him. He stopped in his tracks, and my stomach lurched.

"So happy you could join us," she cooed, her voice saccharine sweet. "Freya and I were just chatting."

"Freya, get the fuck out," Hades seethed, eyes hard and voice cold. He wasn't looking at me, he was looking at the woman.

Even in a terrifying moment such as this one, something about the look on his face irked me. There was a stony fury there. One that was deep and familiar. This was not just some stranger in my house, and this was not about me. This was about them. This was about only one of them making it out of this room alive.

"You are free to leave whenever you'd like," the woman agreed. "I was telling the truth when I said I was a big fan. I really don't want to have to hurt you." The gun was still pointed at Hades's head. "But if he tries any of his shit, I will unfortunately have to kill you to punish him." Her brows furrowed ever so slightly. "Then again, it really does seem like the surest way to hurt him."

She sighed, focusing on Hades. "I was so sure that you were like me, that you were unable to love, that we were perfect for each other. Then you had to go and fuck that up. Then you had to live when I'd been certain you were dead. And I had to come all the way back here to finish the job. I've got a lot going on right now, you know. This is *very* inconvenient."

She was speaking so casually, as if we were all sitting across from each other at dinner, not in some deathmatch or whatever the fuck this was. This woman was one hundred percent insane. And she seemed to be an ex-girlfriend of Hades's.

Her eyes landed on me then, and her gaze on my skin was repulsive. "I will say, it was a happy surprise to see that you were fucking Freya Barker," she chuckled. "When I said I was a big fan, I mean really, I am. It's nice to meet you in person."

I sneered at her, shaking my head in disgust. "I wish I could say the same."

She grinned, showing perfect, white teeth. "Oh, fire. I like it. I'm sure that's why he likes you. More than *likes* you."

I was watching this woman like a hawk, looking for a moment, any moment I could get the gun away from Hades's head. I couldn't remember how long it had been since I'd walked in the door, since I'd sent the text to Swiss. Five minutes? Ten? How long did it take to get from the clubhouse to here? Ten minutes? Fifteen? And that was only if Swiss got my text immediately and wasn't busy choking some girl or whatever the fuck it was he did. Only if he'd taken my text seriously and was riding over here armed and ready to kill a bitch.

Three was a good chance that he wasn't, and I could not keep stalling in hopes that he was. Hades and I could very possibly die if I didn't think of something soon. Presumably how to kill a bitch.

I'd never had a violent bone in my body, even toward those who had hurt me in the most permanent of ways. Now, looking at the woman who had drugged both my dog and my Old Man, I was more than ready to claw her fucking face off.

"No," the woman decided. "No, I can't kill Freya Barker, even if that would punish Hades deliciously. Us girls have gotta stick together." She winked at me.

I glared at her.

"Freya, leave," Hades gritted out.

I didn't move.

She sighed, the woman with the gun. "As riveting as this honorable routine is, I've got a plane to catch. I've got to wrap this up. Hades, don't worry, I'll get the brain on the first shot." Then she steadied the gun, looking more purposeful.

I acted on instinct then, my life flashing before my eyes, Hades's life flashing before my eyes. There no reason, no tactic to it, only the desperate need to keep Hades alive.

I charged.

The only reason it worked was because the crazy woman was not expecting to be out crazied and charging an armed woman without a weapon or any kind of brawling experience was definitely crazy. My hands went for the gun, then we went tumbling to the floor.

Hades reacted fast, really fucking fast. But *it* happened faster. As we slammed to the floor, struggling for the gun, my finger found the trigger, and it went off. Loud. Loud enough to rattle my teeth.

Something warm covered my face.

Hades was there then, pulling me backward, the gun in his hand now. It all happened slowly, in my head, at least. In slow motion, my eyes looked down at the woman.

The dead woman.

The one I had killed.

———

Things got a little chaotic once Swiss arrived, just seconds after the gun went off, after Hades had searched my entire body, looking for wounds. There were none. The blood and brain matter I was covered in was not my own. He'd let me go only because I was desperate to check on Sirius. Obviously, Swiss had taken my text seriously, arriving with Elden, Anderson and Hansen. All of whom were armed and quite obviously ready to go to war.

"Late to the party. Fuck," Swiss teased, holstering his weapon and pouting. *Pouting* at the woman lying dead on my living room floor.

I was sitting on the floor with Sirius's head in my lap, face and eyes dry even though I was sure I'd been sobbing. Maybe that had just happened on the inside. Whatever the case was, I was grateful since there were a lot of stoic badasses here right now, and I did not want to be the crying, hysterical woman.

"Fuck," Hansen hissed, walking over to where I was sitting on the floor.

"She killed the fucking *dog*?" Swiss asked in horror.

"He's not dead," I snapped, my hand on Sirius's torso, letting the even rise and fall of his breathing stave off the grief and panic.

"I'll call a vet," Anderson offered, phone at his ear.

"I'll take care of her," Swiss volunteered, nodding to the dead woman on the floor.

"Someone needs to check on Hades," I told Hansen from my spot on the floor.

Hansen's eyes went to Hades, looking for a wound of some sort.

"I'm fuckin' fine," Hades ground out, eyes on me.

"No, you're not," I seethed. "She, whoever the fuck she was, drugged you, and I want to make sure it wasn't some kind of lethal, slow-acting poison."

Hades looked like he was going to argue, but I pointed at him from my spot on the floor. "So help me God, if you try any macho masculine shit, I will scream. I'm holding it together by a fucking thread right now. You're going to get checked out."

Hansen watched our exchange with a raised brow. Hades glared at me.

"Fine."

The word was a victory, or it would've been if I wasn't holding my unconscious dog in my arms. If I hadn't just killed a woman, and if I wasn't covered in her blood.

———

Sirius woke up. After a checkup from a vet—one who made house calls and didn't ask questions—he was declared healthy. The vet had said that Sirius might be groggy and confused for a while, but the drug would have no lasting effects. I was going in for a checkup tomorrow too. Just in case.

Hades was also fine, according to Sarah, who I believed to be a fucking saint. Swiss, as promised, had 'taken care' of the body. After a badass powwow, the Sons of Templar left my house.

Hades had wordlessly taken me into my bathroom, slowly peeled off both of our clothes and got us both in the shower. The water turned red as the blood washed from me. I'd watched it with detachment, my body cold despite the steaming hot water, despite Hades's body pressed against mine. He washed me with tenderness and care, in a way that wasn't at all sexual. Then he'd taken me out of the shower, dried me and wrapped me up in a terrycloth robe. It was the warmest robe I owned, yet my body still shivered underneath it.

Hades didn't speak until we were back in the bedroom, after I'd checked on Sirius, curled up happily on the bed. When he spoke, the tenderness that existed in the shower stall was nowhere to be seen.

"Freya, why in the fuck didn't you leave when I told you to fucking leave?" He was seething, holding my hips tight. He hadn't stopped touching me since the gun went off. I was grateful for that since I was pretty sure that his hands were holding me together.

My body was trembling under Hades's touch. The harder I tried to make it stop, the harder I shook. I tried to focus on Hades, his eyes, his downturned lips, his milky skin. He was pissed off. That was good. Pissed off was something I could work with in that moment. That meant I could also be pissed off instead of falling apart.

"Why the fuck would I leave?" I replied with bite.

"Because I fuckin' told you to."

"Because you *told* me to?" My brows all but flew up into my hairline. "Well, if I'd done what you told me to do, you may not be standing here right now." As pissed as I was, the mere thought of what could've happened had the world tilting beneath my feet.

"If things had gone a little bit different, and I mean if that bullet was a few fuckin' inches to the left, you'd be dead," he forced out. "I'm gonna do my best to make sure you're never in a situation like that again, but if shit happens, you're gonna do what I fuckin' say."

"Did you hit your head at some point tonight?" I scowled, rolling my eyes, anger completely and utterly taking the place of the shock.

"This is not a fuckin' joke, Freya," he scowled, making it clear that he was not amused. His hands tightened. "Need to hear you tell me you get me on this."

"I will not," I scoffed, stepping out of his arms so I could fold my arms and say with my body what my tone and face were saying. He was really starting to piss me off.

Hades was having none of that, striding over to hold me once more.

As if a switch had been flipped, I broke. All the strength I'd been clutching with a death grip vanished. "You want me to walk away when we're in a situation like that?" I countered, my voice shaking. "That's never going to fucking happen. I may not have the skills, I may not be brave and badass, but I'll never leave you when you're in danger. I'll fight for you. Despite what you try and order me to do. I'll fight for you."

Hades froze at my words, something I couldn't define passing over his face. Then he pulled me to him, pressing his lips to mine.

I relaxed into the kiss, lost myself in it. I would've been willing to drown in it had he not pulled back.

"I'm an enforcer," he murmured against my lips. "My job is to fight for the club. Kill for the club. Die for the club if need be. I fight for them. My brothers. No one has ever fought for me."

My heart shattered then, into a thousand and one tiny pieces. He spoke in that same deep tenor I'd grown accustomed to, iron ever-present in his voice. There was nothing soft, nothing vulnerable about his voice. But I knew him well enough to hear them. The cracks. The deep chasms between them.

I lifted my hand to cup his jaw. "Honey, you've never had me before. I'm going to fight for you."

Emotion swirled in his eyes. Emotion that shattered those thousand and one tiny pieces into another thousand and one tiny pieces.

"Who was she?" As much as I'd wanted this moment to last

forever, this question had been burning in my throat, and I couldn't hold onto it for a moment longer.

Hades sighed. He'd had to have been expecting it. Dreading it, by the looks of it. "Someone from my past."

I waited for him to expand, but he just kept staring.

"Honey, she almost killed you. I *killed* her..." My voice broke a little on that, and Hades's jaw contracted, but I held it together. "I'm going to need a fuck of a lot more detail than that."

His eyes searched mine, as if he was searching for a way out of this. Or maybe he was trying to figure out how much to tell me.

"Everything," I stated firmly. "I need everything, Hades."

"She was the one person I cared about ... before you," he answered after sucking in a deep breath. "Because she hated the world just about as much as I did. Because she was a fucking knockout at sixteen, and I was a teenage boy who wanted to fuck because I thought that would make me a man."

He paused, looking at me from beneath his dark lashes. "You sure you want to hear this ... now?"

I gritted my teeth. No, I really did not want to hear how the woman who had been lying dead in my living room up until about an hour ago was the only person in Hades's young life that he'd cared about. And, by the sounds of it, the girl he'd lost his virginity to.

"Yes, I'm sure," I had to force strength into my voice.

Hades did not look happy about this, but he nodded once then began talking. "We fell into the same crowd. She did even worse shit than me, which was sayin' something. But she'd also been through shit worse than me. Shit she never talked about, shit that I later learned took away her ability to be human."

My stomach roiled at his words.

"She had me tangled up in her shit for a long time." He stared off into the distance, like he was back there. Faraway.

"Before I patched into the Sons. Sure, we're outlaws, we do some fucked up shit, but we have rules. She's a high-ranking member of a cartel. Those fuckers have no rules. I knew she'd get me killed. I didn't want to die. She took me explaining that to her as rejection. It didn't end well."

I raised my brow in a 'no shit' gesture.

"Hadn't seen her until a few months ago. The night I met you." He reached out and took my hand.

I gaped at him. "The night you met me? The mean the night you were stabbed?"

He nodded once.

"*She* was the one who stabbed you?" I screeched.

He didn't reply, which was all the confirmation I needed. "We've been together all this time, and you didn't tell me your psychotic ex-girlfriend tried to kill you?"

"Not exactly something you slip into conversation," he remarked dryly.

I glared at him. "I don't know … how about, 'hey babe, remember that night we met? A girl didn't like the way I broke up with her, so she tried to end me. For good.' " I waved my hand. "Something along those lines would've worked *swell*."

Hades rubbed the back of his neck. "If I'd tracked her down and killed her like I should've, then we wouldn't be having this conversation right now. You wouldn't have to live with this for the rest of your fuckin' life."

My anger dissipated immediately. It hadn't disappeared completely; I was sure it would reemerge at a later date. But for now, I reached up to cup Hades's jaw.

"Oh, for fuck's sake! I swear, if another alpha male tries to place blame on himself for not being supreme ruler of the universe, I'm going to scream," I rebuked. "I will not let you take the blame for this just because you didn't kill your ex-girlfriend after she stabbed you and left you for dead." A dark smile stretched across my face. "There's a sentence I never thought I'd say."

Hades examined me then. Examined me as if he was trying to

see inside of my head. "You're okay." Not a question exactly. An observation.

I remained quiet for a moment, doing some of my own self-examination. "Not entirely," I admitted. "But you're okay. Sirius is okay. I'm okay. Those are all ingredients to me being on the road to okay." I frowned at him. "As long as you're not going to do some noble, alpha male shit and decide to leave me because you don't want me to have to deal with your world."

His eyes blazed, and he squeezed my hand. "I'm not fuckin' noble, Freya," he bit out. "And I'm not goin' anywhere."

An oath.

I relaxed.

"Then I'm definitely going to be okay."

———

Hades had not wanted me leaving the house after that. He was in full-on, alpha male, protective mode. I couldn't breathe heavily without his body stiffening and his eyes narrowing as if he was waiting for me to dissolve into a blubbering mess, trying to figure out how he'd catch every single one of my tears.

It was nice, comforting even. But it also made me feel all the more breakable knowing he was waiting for me to break down. I needed to be around someone different. Someone who had called late the night before.

"Coffee," Macy said as a greeting. "Tomorrow morning. I'll also come over later on in the afternoon with wine or tequila or both, but I feel like you need to talk to someone sooner than that. So coffee. As soon as you wake up. Call me. You won't wake me up because I have children, and those little devils are up before dawn." This was followed by a long pause. A loaded one. "You're going to be okay. And you did the right thing. Love you, babe."

"You too," I returned, a little stunned. Stunned that she'd said all of that without so much as taking a breath. That she'd known exactly what I'd needed to hear, that she'd said 'love you' in an offhand, casual way yet really sounded like she meant it.

And that was why we were sitting at Oliver's at seven-thirty in the morning with pastries and very strong coffees. I'd barely slept the night before, even with Hades's arms wrapped around me, with Sirius's weight at our feet, with all of the adrenaline rushing out of my body. I knew Hades had barely slept either because every time I'd jerked out of a nightmare, his arms had tightened around me. He never said anything, just held me close. It had helped. A whole bunch. But there were some things even hot, alpha male bikers couldn't fix entirely. Sometimes you needed a hot, hippy biker babe like the one sitting across me with understanding in her eyes. The one who had just shared her heartbreaking story with me, the one that made me feel a heck of a lot less alone and doomed.

She'd made it through killing a guy—not to mention losing her parents—yet her eyes were full of light and happiness. She had a family, a life. No mental breakdowns on record. There was hope for me yet.

"I can't believe I'm in a world where death and violence and breaking the law is a way of life," I mused over my second coffee.

She patted my hand. "You feeling like running yet?" The question was serious, and there was not an ounce of judgement there.

I considered the question. Running had always been my default. Escape was easy and something I was familiar with. I could've run. I could've left this place behind to find a small, quiet town—one without a resident motorcycle club—and build a quiet life. I could've found a job that did not require me to take my clothes off, which would in turn help me attract a man who was not going to break the law or murder people on a regular basis.

If I'd wanted to give up Hades and the fabulous women like Macy who came with him.

"No," I proclaimed adamantly. "No. I'm not thinking about running."

The mere prospect of existing in a place where Hades wasn't

seemed impossible. Just thinking about it made my heart beat faster and made my skin feel tight and uncomfortable.

"I love him," I whispered to my muffin.

"Well, *duh*," Macy muttered when she'd finished chewing her croissant.

"I have no idea how this happened," I looked at the ceiling, as if I'd find the answer there. "He's not who I'm supposed to fall in love with."

"Yeah, right," Macy snorted. "Women *never* fall for the evil, dark-haired, psychotic man. There's *nothing* attractive about that."

I grinned. My body grinned. Bloomed. That's what it had felt like, these past months with him. That I had emerged from the winter of my life. That first night, the one where he was bleeding on the parking lot, was the first chilly morning of spring. There hadn't been any visible new life, no beauty, the skeletons of before still stood stark and overwhelming. But somehow, while I wasn't looking, new life began to grow.

I began to grow. To flower.

With a man who never in a million years would look like he could foster or nurture new life. But he had.

"There's something about the villain," Macy continued. "When the antihero, the scoundrel, is ruthless and deadly to everyone but you." She noticeably shivered, her cheeks flushing. This woman with years of marriage under her belt, with children, blushed talking about her husband, her villain. "There's something about that. And it takes a certain kind of woman to tame a villain. To love a scoundrel. They don't live their lives like other men. Certainly not like any kind of hero or prince. But they love you that much deeper, fuck you so much better and make your life that much more amazing."

I blinked it at her. "I couldn't have said it better myself."

She smiled. "When you're in the thick of it, you barely know which way is up, and the only thing you do know is that you need him. And he needs you, Freya. I cannot pretend I understand

Hades because I don't. He's the darkest horse in our fucked up little stable. His heart may be black, but it's there. It's big. And it's yours. When a man in a Sons of Templar cut loves you, really loves you, it's for life." She tilted her. "And he loves you. In his own way. He's going to battle with what happened last night. With the guilt, blaming himself. He may be different than my Old Man in every other way, but in that regard, they're the same. You're going to be okay, though."

I smiled weakly. "How do you know that?"

"Because, bitch, you've got me. And Caroline. And Scarlett. And the whole fucking club. You're not alone."

Her words echoed through my head, rebounding through my body and settling in my stomach, flourishing. They kept me warm.

I was not alone. I had Macy across from me. Hades at home. Marilyn. My Aunt V phone call away. Des. Kallum.

I was not alone.

CHAPTER SIXTEEN

ONE MONTH LATER

HADES

"Baby, me and Macy are going to my place," Freya informed me, clutching the sides of my cut.

She was not afraid to touch me in public. Actually, whenever she was talking to me, she had her hands on me. Not because she was a possessive bitch or because she was thinking ugly thoughts about the club girls that had come before her. No. She was friendly to the club girls. Every single one of 'em. In a genuine way. A warm way. Freya's way.

It was the same thing in the way she touched me. Freya's way. The way that made my cock turn to stone the second she laid her hands on me. Fuck, the second I laid eyes on her.

It didn't help that she was wearing low-slung jeans that clung to her every fucking curve, that the shirt she was wearing did the exact same thing while showing off her entire mid-section. She was walking sex. Though not a fucker in the room would dare stare at her for longer than a second. Not if he wanted to keep his eyes. Men looked at her when she was on stage, and there was nothing I could do about that except fuck her in the bathroom of the strip club the second she left the stage. And I'd done that. More than once.

"She wants to see my filming setup, and I was thinking of doing a little feature on Old Lady life for my channel," Freya continued, her voice the sweetest fucking thing I'd ever heard.

Her ocean eyes darted to Hansen who was holding his beer and watching our interaction with obvious amusement and satisfaction. "As long as you're okay with that?" she added quickly. "I know that the ways of the club are meant to be all mysterious and hush-hush, but we're not talking about that. Mostly we'll be talking about beauty routines, outfits and shoes."

Hansen grinned. It was warm and easy, and for a split second, I hated him for it. "I'm okay with it," he replied. "Mostly because I know that my wife would likely skin me alive if I said anything different."

Freya beamed at him. "Great!" Her gaze moved to me. "Okay, well, I'll see you at home later then?"

Home.

Fuck. That was a knife to the heart.

"Okay, but you're gonna have a prospect on you," I forced the emotional shit away, keeping my voice to be cold and dismissive. She didn't blink at my tone because she was used to it from me. She trusted me. Despite the fact I was lying to her.

I was a piece of shit.

But that had been established long ago.

She rolled her eyes but did it with a grin that made my cock even fucking harder. My grip tightened on her ass, causing her eyes to flare with need, with hunger. I nearly threw her over my shoulder to find the nearest bed I could fuck her in.

I resisted that urge. Barely.

"Alright, I'm heading home now then." She licked her lips,

knowing she was driving me fucking crazy.

I just nodded because I couldn't fucking talk.

She grinned again then placed her hands flat on my chest, tilting her head up toward me. She was short, even in the heels she always wore—which she even wore to the fucking grocery store—so I had to bend down for her to lay her lips on mine.

She tasted like strawberries and fucking Freya.

Again, I restrained myself from fucking her right there.

Her eyes were lazy when I finally pulled back. "Later," she murmured.

"Oh, fuck yeah, babe," I promised, my voice low.

She winked at me, lingering with her body pressed against mine for a beat before she turned her back on me. Fuck if it wasn't a pathetic thing to think, but I missed her already.

As Freya walked away, Swiss came from behind the bar to stand next to me.

"A woman with an ass like that and that kind of fire in her eyes..." He didn't finish that sentence, his eyes lingering on her ass for much too fucking long. Finally, just before I was about to rip his head off, he looked back at me with a knowing grin. "A woman like that is gonna ruin your life, brother." He chuckled as he walked forward and clapped me on my shoulder. "And there ain't a damn thing you can do about it."

She'd already ruined my life.

I'd eventually ruin hers too.

FREYA

I'd known something was wrong the second Hades had walked into the house.

He hadn't said anything. He hadn't needed to. Something had changed about him. Something that made my stomach drop and my blood chill with fear. He hadn't touched me when he walked in. It was a loss, or at least that's what it felt like. For the past few months, whenever he walked into a room, his hands would be on me, his lips would be on me. Even if he'd only been gone for five minutes.

Hades might not have been a man of many words or a traditional kind of romantic, but he said fucking everything in those little gestures that weren't little at all. A huge chasm opened up inside of me when he walked into the house, ruffled Sirius's head absently, watched me work in the kitchen for a minute then walked toward the living room. I hadn't even spoken; I'd had no clue what to say. My spatula was frozen in the air as I watched him walk slowly across the room, to the open doors, lighting up a smoke as he stared out into the desert. He hadn't moved from there.

I'd done my best to act normal, to seem cheerful, but my smile was weak, and my hand shook as I iced the cake I was making for Natasha's son's birthday. I'd wanted to abandon the cake, run up to Hades and demand to know what was wrong, but I knew that would come off desperate and insane. I also wanted to pretend that I was imagining things, that it had nothing to do with me, and if I finished this cake, gave him time, everything would be okay.

I finished the cake.

Everything was not okay. Even Sirius, who followed Hades everywhere the second he entered the house, knew something was wrong and was tucked up in his bed in the corner of the room, staring at the man in the Sons of Templar cut chain smoking on the patio.

My steps were unsteady as I made my way toward him. I hadn't wanted to go there, to him. Something in me told me something very bad was going to happen when I made it there. That it was going to hurt. But it was impossible not to go to him. Hades was a magnet, and I was drawn to him whenever we were in the same room. It was impossible for me not to gravitate toward him, not to touch him.

He didn't look at me when I stopped beside him, just a couple of feet away. We might as well have been a fucking ocean apart. He didn't put his smoke out like he normally did whenever I was near. Nor did he hook his palms around my waist and drag me to his body like he also usually did when I was near but not near enough. He just continued smoking, continued staring off.

I supposed I could've said something. Asked him what was wrong. I would have in a different world, with a different man. So I didn't speak. I just watched him, my heart in my throat, my fingers and toes numb.

Finally, he finished his smoke, leaning forward to snub it out in the rose quartz ashtray I'd bought especially for him. He emptied it every day without me saying a word. It had had one butt in it from this morning since Hades was trying to slow down. Now it was full.

"It's done."

I blinked at him. His breath smelled like cigarettes and whisky. A lot of it. His eyes were clear, and he hadn't stumbled when he'd walked through the house. Hades drank beer and whisky. Wine with me sometimes. But I'd never seen him drink in excess. I'd also never seen him kill anyone, yet I knew he did that semi-regularly.

He could've been drinking more than usual because he'd just come from the club party. But it didn't feel like that. It felt like he'd been trying to drown something, numb something.

"What's done?" I asked, hating how much my voice quaked.

"The asshole."

I didn't need to ask him to clarify; the asshole could only mean one guy. The guy who beat the shit out of me, the guy who had inadvertently played cupid between me and my biker. But I had the sinking feeling that he wasn't going to be my biker for much longer.

"It's done meaning..." I was pretty sure I knew what he meant, but I was walking on eggshells.

"Meaning he's dead," he said flatly.

I flinched. It didn't affect him. Not outwardly, at least.

I'd known this was going to happen. I'd done my best not to think about it and when I had, I'd felt vaguely sick about the entire situation. Strangely, hearing about it right now, knowing that it was done, I felt … nothing. I felt nothing regarding the death of the guy I used to sleep with at the hands of the guy I was currently sleeping with. The guy I currently loved and would always love.

"He's been dead for two months."

Now I felt something. I stared at Hades, gaped at him, actually. His expression was as blank as his voice.

"Two *months?*"

He nodded, staring out at the desert in order to avoid my eyes. He eventually turned to face me, to really look at me. I flinched again at what I saw in his eyes. Rather at what I didn't see in his eyes. The man he'd shown me since he'd fucked me in that dressing room.

"Why didn't you tell me?"

Then I saw a flicker. It was small, but it was there. "Because I didn't want to leave you."

I frowned. "Why would you have to leave me after you told me?"

His eyes widened ever so slightly. "Why?"

I nodded.

"Because the only reason I'm fuckin' here is because you think I'm protecting you from a guy who's been dead for two goddamn months," he hissed.

His words knocked the wind out of me. So much so that I took a step back.

Hades narrowed his eyes at the distance I'd put between us, then at the horrified and hurt look I was sure was on my face. Because horror—and mostly hurt—was coursing through my veins right then.

"The *only* reason you're here?" I whispered, hating the sound of my voice. Where was my anger? My sass? That's what I needed right now. A fuck of a lot of sass.

Hades's face transformed then. Almost completely. "Fuck," he muttered, stepping forward.

I held up my hand to stop him. He ignored that, grasping onto my wrists and yanking me forward.

As much as I really wanted to be pissed at him, I didn't fight his embrace. No, I gave myself permission to relax into his arms.

"Baby, fuck, no," he murmured against my hair. "You are the reason. You are the reason I didn't fuckin' die in a parking lot. You are the reason that I've found a reason to actually look forward to wakin' up every morning. You are the reason I've lied for the past two months, no matter how fucking sick it's been making me feel." He pulled me back so he could cup my jaw, searching my eyes for something. "That's seriously what you're upset about right now?" I inched back so I could glare at him. "Seriously? Of course, that's what I'm upset about right now."

"I killed him," he told me, his voice chilly once more. "I killed the man who put his hands on you. Then Swiss cut him to pieces, and we dissolved his body in acid. Left no evidence."

I screwed up my nose, the thought of all that turning my stomach. "Really?" I snapped. "I have so much cake batter inside me right now, and I don't want to experience it coming back up."

When I pulled from his arms, I tottered ever so slightly on my heels, which wasn't common for me. His face shut down again.

"What the fuck?" I snapped.

"I just told you, in detail, how I murdered a man you used to sleep with," he replied in a clipped tone.

"Yes, too much detail," I exclaimed, rubbing my bare arms. Sure, there was a chill tonight, but the goosebumps coating my skin had nothing to do with that.

"That doesn't bother you," He phrased this as a statement; it wasn't structured as a question. "That I'm a criminal. A murderer."

I frowned at him. "I've known that's what you were since pretty much the first moment we met."

Apparently, my response did not help the situation.

Like at all.

"I've fucked this all up," he muttered, brushing his hands down his face.

"Fucked what all up?" I demanded.

"You!" he exclaimed, as close to shouting as I'd ever heard him. "I fucked *you* up. Brought you into a world that you don't deserve to be in. One you don't belong in."

It would've been less painful if he'd slapped me in the face.

"I don't belong?" I croaked.

His answer was a curt nod.

I shook my head. Then I started to pace. "My entire fucking life, I've never had a home. Certainly not the one I was born into. The second I could, I left that place. And for well over a decade, I've been drifting around this country, looking, desperately searching for where I fit."

I turned to glare at him for a second before I continued. "Sure, I'm an easy-going gal, albeit one with a very complicated skincare routine, but other than that, I'm pretty laid back. I can have fun anywhere. I could win a gold fucking medal at pretending I fit in. But never, not once, have I felt the way I feel with you." My voice broke ever so slightly, but I sucked in an unsteady breath and pressed on. "The way I feel in this town. When I'm at club parties. When I was at Macy and Hansen's barbeques. When I'm on the back of your bike."

I stopped pacing and turned to look at Hades. To glower at him. I had no other choice since it was either glower or burst into tears. And I could not give him that.

"Jesus, Freya," he muttered, looking about as sheepish as he should look. "I didn't mean it like that. No one belongs on the back of my bike except you."

I would've fucking loved that sentence had it not come right after he said all the other stuff. "If you didn't mean it like that, how exactly did you mean it, *Hades*?" I spat out his name like an accusation, like a weapon.

I had needed a weapon. I'd come into this woefully unarmed.

"I mean that I won't do this to you," he pinched the bridge of his nose. "I won't fucking drag you into a world that you shouldn't even know exists. You're so much fucking better than that."

"Stop," I hissed. "Stop justifying keeping me at arm's length because you think of yourself as some kind of demon and me as some kind of angel. Newsflash, buddy, angels don't take their clothes off for money. Angels don't dress like this." I waved my hand at my body.

Hades's eyes followed my hand as it moved down my body, tracking it in a way that made me lose my train of thought. "In my world, angels dress exactly like that," he argued.

My skin prickled, and desire flushed through me. His voice was pure sex. It might've distracted me had this subject matter not been hitting the core of me.

"This isn't a joke," I snapped. "And this isn't something you can use your sexy voice to make go away. I'm sick of you putting me up on some kind of pedestal, sick of you making yourself into the enemy just because you have a few scars, a few marks on your soul."

The liquid in his eyes turned to stone. "I have more than a few marks on my soul, Freya."

"My uncle molested me when I was a kid," I revealed, careful to keep my voice flat and emotionless, forcing down the telltale shake that meant tears weren't too far away.

For a long, long time, I hadn't been able to say that out loud. Not to anyone, not to my first therapist or my second. Certainly not to any boyfriends. I'd spent a great deal of time pretending that period of my life didn't exist, though that was a difficult feat due to the consequences that came from it. Such a large, life-altering trauma shouldn't be so easy to escape from, but I'd made an art out of shutting that part of my life away, locking it behind steel doors.

Eventually, I came to realize that unhealed trauma only got

sharper and sharper the longer it festered, infesting everything healthy and beautiful in the present. So I got a third therapist, where I said it out loud for the first time. I'd choked the words up as if they were razor blades, my entire body quaking as I spoke, tears flowing uncontrollably. Similar things happened when I said it out loud after that too. It took years for me to be able to say the words without any evidence in my voice or on my face of what it had done to me. I'd healed somewhat, but I was nowhere near brave enough to slip it into any kind of conversation or talk openly about it on my channel. Which had made me feel like a fraud since my brand was all about honesty and openness, sharing things people were afraid to.

But this was too tightly entwined with all of my fragile wounds. It still made me feel dirty, unclean, ruined.

"It started when I was seven," I continued, leaving for that faraway place I needed to go to when I spoke about this. My words sounded muffled in my head, like I was underwater. Hades was muddled in that same kind of way, too, his features blurred as if my mind was protecting me from seeing that information reflected on his face. There was no way I would've been able to continue if I truly processed the way he was looking at me.

"I didn't tell anyone at first. He told me that it was something that everyone did but no one talked about." My palms were clammy, and my heart was roaring in my ears. Panic was setting in by talking about this, reliving it. But I needed to. For Hades. Mostly for myself.

"I knew it was wrong," I continued. "That this could not be something that everyone did. Certainly not my friends at school. Because if the same thing was happening to them, there was no way they could smile, laugh, go on with their lives. But I felt trapped. I didn't know what to do, so I just ... let it happen."

"You didn't let it happen. *He* made it happen, there's a fuckin' difference," Hades's seethed.

I flinched at his voice, which penetrated through all of my

layers. I'd never heard him sound so raw, so carnal before. I couldn't acknowledge that, though. Not right now. Instead, I just nodded slowly.

"You're right. As an adult who has gone through a lot of therapy, I'm aware that none of it was my fault, but I felt like it was at the time. I felt like I was dirty, wrong, weak. He made me feel that way. Until ... what he was doing got worse."

I didn't expand on what that meant because by the way the air felt, Hades knew exactly what I meant. And I also felt that if I went into further detail, I'd vomit all over the patio.

"That was then I started fighting him," I rasped out. "Told him I'd tell if he didn't stop. He kept threatening me, telling me that he'd kill me. I believed he would, too, but I also knew, in my young brain, that it wouldn't be long until I'd want to be dead, so I told."

Though I wasn't letting myself really look at Hades, I knew that there was a certain kind of reaction a man like him would have to this kind of news. He'd had a certain kind of reaction to what Derek did to me before we'd even started sleeping together. He cared about me more now than he did then, so I knew his anger would be even more intense.

"Before you go into alpha male, badass mode and demand to know where he is so you can track him down and kill him, he's dead." I inspected Hades's eyebrows, still refusing to focus on the entirety of the man, to see whatever lay behind his eyes. "When my father found out, he killed him. His own brother."

My mind turned prickly and fragmented under the proximity of those poisonous memories. It took a moment for me to gather myself, to find a way to continue. Hades had not attempted to fill the silence. He hadn't touched me. Comforted me. Which was a good thing since even his hands on my skin would've sickened me at that very moment. I could barely handle living inside of my own skin.

"My father was not a good parent," I said finally. "He drank too much. Sometimes the drinking made him angry, other times completely apathetic. I grew up thinking that at best, my father hated me, and at worst, he didn't think or care about me enough to hate me. I was an inconvenience to him. When I finally told my parents, my mother immediately thought I was making it up for attention."

I rolled my eyes and rubbed at my arms again, wishing I could scrub away the trauma, grow new skin.

"My mother didn't like me much either, you see," I shared after a long pause. "My father, though. He knew it was true. I had no idea why. Maybe because he'd sensed something was wrong, seen something rotten inside of his brother."

It took everything I had to chase away the image of the man who'd ruined my entire childhood, the man who still haunted my nightmares on the odd occasion.

I sucked in a heavy breath. "Maybe he'd paid more attention to me than I'd thought, noticing the way I'd curled in on myself, stopped trying to get his attention with pictures I'd drawn. That I'd stopped taking care of my appearance." The words were coming out quickly now. "My mother didn't notice any of that. I know my Aunt V would've seen it immediately. She might not have been able to figure out exactly what was wrong, but she would've known something was off. After the very first time, probably. And she would've..." I didn't want to finish that thought.

"Anyway." I waved my hand dismissively. "That didn't happen. She wasn't around then because my mom had had a falling out with her and refused to see her. There's no point in all going through the 'what ifs.' For whatever reason, my father believed me. He didn't say a word to me or my mother. He just turned his back on me, walked into their bedroom, then came out with his gun. My mom was screaming at him by then, trying to stop him. But he pushed her into the wall, only looking at me."

My voice was even further away now as I descended into the memory of that day. One of my very worst memories. I had a lot of bad memories from that period of my life to be sure, some arguably worse than that moment. Like the actual abuse. Those weren't just bad memories, they were horrific. Terrible in ways I was only able to articulate by shaking and crying, spewing the ugly, rancid words at parents who had never cared about me in the first place. Then my mother screaming at my father, saying that I was lying. That I was dramatic, a needy little bitch.

Then the sound of her hitting the wall. My father's rage, his eyes on me, showing me something that I'd never seen during the ten years of my life.

Love.

It was poisoned, of course. By the rage, by his thirst for blood. By the guilt.

Then my mother was laying on the floor.

Her lip was bleeding.

He must've hit her.

I didn't remember that part. But I did remember what my father said as he stood over my mother.

"I'm going to kill him," he proclaimed soberly, in a voice I'd never heard from him. "Then I'm going to go and turn myself in. I'll sit in a cell for however long the state decides, and I'll do it fucking happily since I did one thing right. One fucking thing. You'll take care of that girl." He pointed at me with the hand that wasn't holding the gun. "You lay a fucking hand on her, I'll know. And I'll make sure that if I ever get out of there, I'll kill you too."

Tears were running down my cheeks. Cold tears, like they'd sprung from insides that were frozen. Like my heart was frozen.

My father walked out. He didn't look at me when he did. Not even a fleeting glance.

I knew now that it was from the shame of what he'd let happen. The kind of man he'd been to me.

"I never saw my father again," I told Hades, slowly coming back to the surface. "He did just as he said; he drove over to my uncle's trailer and shot him in the face. Then he went to prison for murder. He did not say a word in his own defense during the trial.

I didn't go, but my Aunt V told me years later. I don't know whether he was trying to protect me, my honor, or trying to keep the shame a secret. I don't know. I do know the judge took one look at him, his history, and sentenced him to twenty-five years."

I imagined my mother might've screamed, cried or done something equally dramatic when the verdict was read. She had been there every day, pretending to be some kind of loving, devoted wife.

"He's been up for parole a couple of times," I looked down at my cuticles, still not letting myself see whatever it was that Hades was communicating with his eyes and body language. "He was rejected. He won't see me either. I tried when I was younger. Wrote him letters. He never wrote back. I'm not sad about that. I'm sure he's full of shame over what kind of father he was to me. That he let his brother into my life, let him ruin it in ways that he and my mother never could."

I shrugged. "It used to bother me, only because I thought it was supposed to. I believed that I was supposed to try and contact him, have some kind of relationship with him. But the only way he was ever a father to me was killing the man who hurt me. I don't think he was capable of anything else. He couldn't give me anything except more pain and disappointment. So I'm good without him."

I paused again, like I was running some kind of marathon I hadn't trained for and needed to keep stopping to catch my breath.

"My mother doesn't speak to me. She hates me. Blames me for opening my mouth, for putting my father in prison. "She told me that every day. But she didn't lay a hand on me. She made sure I was fed, clothed, taken care of in the most basic of ways. She was afraid of my father. Even though he was locked up, she was terrified of him."

Again, I stared at Hades's eyebrows, not strong enough to look into his eyes. I had a few miles left to go before I could do that.

"But she was a smart and vindictive woman, so she knew that

she didn't need to lay a hand on me to hurt me. To damage me," I sighed, thinking of those terrible years after my father was sent to jail. The ones that remained open wounds, still bleeding.

"I'm indifferent to my father, but I dislike my mother. No, I hate her." My voice was ugly and angry now. "Sure, I'm supposed to be better than that. I'm supposed to feel sorry for her, recognize that her life empty, miserable and sad. But I can't do that."

I sucked in a long, deep breath, letting the oxygen seep into the limbs that felt numb and heavy. Parts of me felt lighter, but there were parts of me that felt more weighed down than before I began.

It was one thing to say all of this, to let it all hang out, to show Hades the dark parts of me. But now I had to deal with what happened after. After I'd shown him the damaged parts of me. In the time it took for me to recover from saying all of that, to find even footing in the present after lingering too long in the past, Hades did not say a word. The silence stretched on, yawning forward, creeping into the crevices inside me.

He wasn't going to speak. Either because he didn't know what to say or because he expected me to say more. Despite the fact I'd shared with him more than I had with another living soul, I did actually have more to say.

"So you see, Hades, I'm ruined," I admitted, my voice little more than a whisper. "In the most visceral of ways. In a kind of way that makes it impossible for me to be with anyone who isn't. I need someone who understands monsters, who understands and knows how to live amongst the ugliness of this world."

I sucked in an unsteady breath, finally looking at Hades properly for the first time. "I need you."

He didn't hesitate then, pulling me into his arms. Our bodies pressed together, his heat chasing away the chill in my bones.

"Baby, you've got me," he promised. "You've fuckin' got me."

He didn't say anything else. There was no need to. He'd just given me everything I needed.

CHAPTER SEVENTEEN

"So can we agree that you're not going to try to push me away again?" I mumbled into his chest. It was later. Much later. Hades had made love to me.

Made. Love.

I was sure that's what it had been. Before, I'd been absolutely certain that the only thing Hades was capable of was fucking me. And I was more than okay with that. I loved the way he fucked me, loved how I felt owned, every inch of me. Loved that he branded me with his touch, with his lips, with the bruises on my hips from him grasping them so tightly, the red marks on my ass from him slapping it. The sensitivity in between my legs after he'd fucked me hard.

Yeah, I was more than okay with the fucking. The whole 'making love' thing had always grossed me out. That had to do with my past, no doubt, and the unhealthy way I was introduced to sex. It also had to do with the fact that when *he*—I refused to let myself think his name, it gave him too much power—touched me, he did it slowly. Gently. Lovingly. So whenever someone, especially a man but even a woman, tried to touch me in that warm, casual way, I recoiled.

Aunt V hadn't been able to hug me until I was twenty-five, and even then, I'd had to grit my teeth to hide my disgust at the intimacy of it all. At the way my insides felt filthy and wrong, willing to do anything to escape my skin.

Even after all the therapy I'd had, after all the healing, I'd made peace with the fact that I'd never able to be touched like that without that rancid, horrible feeling. That I'd have to fake intimacy with men. That I could only orgasm while a man fucked me hard and dirty. For years, I hadn't even been able to come without shame and filth washing over me before the aftershocks had even subsided. For a long time, my sexuality had been a wrong, filthy thing.

Until Hades.

After I spilled my guts, he made me come twice, both times with a gentle touch. First with his mouth, his lips worshipping my skin, my pussy. My hands had fisted the sheets of my bed and my back had arched off the bed with the power of my orgasm. It had felt clean, wonderful, beautiful.

Then he crawled slowly up my body, his eyes on me the entire ascent. His warmth was overwhelming, the weight of his body on mine overpowering in the best possible way. As soon as he poised himself at my entrance, his lips hovering over mine, seconds away from filling me, he shifted us. He turned us so I was on top of him, his hands tight on my hips, positioning me above him so his cock was brushing against the sensitive skin he'd just devoured.

I couldn't tear my eyes away from his, could barely breathe under the weight of the emotions enveloping me, of what the simple gesture meant. Hades was not able to read my mind, of course. But he could read me. He understood my pain and trauma because I'd laid it out for him, all of it. And he'd realized what this might be doing to me, with everything so close to the surface. So he gave me control. All of it. Giving me agency over something intimate and carnal, he gave me his submission.

And I loved it. I moved against him slowly, my palms on his

chest, the ink seeming to reach out and swallow me. His hands were on my hips, tight, but not guiding, not pulling me. They were just holding as I rode him, as I brought us both to earth-shattering climaxes.

Now, I was laying on his chest, absolutely exhausted, both emotionally and physically. I'd never felt so raw, so exposed. Every single corner of my body and soul had been exposed, I no longer harbored any secrets. It felt freeing yet terrifying. Now that I'd given him everything, I needed to know he wasn't going to take it all away.

Hades didn't reply to my question right away, drawing circles on my naked back.

"You gave me somethin' tonight, Freya," he finally said. "Something that you ripped out from inside you. You gave it to me despite the pain it caused you because you didn't want me leaving you."

I didn't say anything because I was too busy trying not to cry.

"I'm gonna do the same," he continued, his voice rough and low. "And then, you're gonna decide whether you want me to go or stay."

Dread washed over me. "I'm going to want you to stay no matter what."

Hades didn't try to argue with me, just continued to draw circles on my back in silence, working toward what he was going to tell me. What he was going to expose.

I waited, hungry, desperate to peer into the darkest corners of his life, to feast on his mysterious past.

"Monsters are not born, they're made," he stated after we'd been marinating in silence for minutes.

I turned my head to stare at him, not liking where this was going. "You're not a monster," I disagreed, my voice tight.

"You don't know enough about me to make that statement."

I pouted at the coolness in his tone, refusing to back down from his practiced bad guy stare. He was trying to scare me, with all that brooding intensity. Sure, it was a touch scary before I'd gotten to know him, and it would definitely be scary if I was someone who had gotten on his bad side, but I was on Hades's good side. Despite what he was implying here, he had a good side. A wonderful side. But he was making it clear that I wasn't going to be able to change his mind. At least not right at that moment. I would change his mind, though. With time. Hopefully we had time.

"I had a good childhood," he told me, obviously choosing not to debate with me over whether or not I knew him well enough to deem him human instead of a monster. "People meet me, they figure I was fucked from the beginning. Think that to be the person I am now, I must've never known true happiness. But the only way to truly create a monster is to give them love and happiness, so they know how it tastes, then snatch it away from them completely. Make it so that sweetness rots on your tongue and you have to live with that taste in your mouth for the rest of your life."

He shifted slightly to trail the side of my face with his fingertip. No one had ever touched me that gently in my life, and I sure wasn't expecting it from a man who had seemed incapable of tenderness.

"Some people are dealt shit from the day they're born," he murmured, searching my face as if he were committing me to memory. "Very fuckin' few of those people manage to rid themselves of it. To rise above it and turn into something magnificent. In fact, I would've thought such a feat was impossible had I not met you."

My heart jumped to my throat, warmth spreading to the very core of me.

"I had what you didn't," he continued. "I had a mother and a father who loved me, loved each other and gave me a safe and stable home. Until they didn't. Car accident. On their way home from date night."

He shook his head. "Yeah, can't get any more cookie-cutter,

American dream than people who have a 'date night' once a fuckin'
week. My parents, they came from shit, both of 'em. Mom had a
family who was bad news. Real bad fuckin' news. To the point
where she changed her name to escape 'em. Didn't know that until
later, of course. Dad had once had a family, but he was an only
child. Parents had him later in life and both died within six months
of each other before he turned five. No brothers or sisters, uncles,
what the fuck ever on either side. No close friends either. Not
close enough to take in a ten-year-old orphan anyway."

I had to struggle to keep my tears at bay. I knew I couldn't
weep for Hades, not now when the story had only just begun. Not
even after, when I'd heard the worst of it.

"Went into the system," he continued, his hand once again
tracing circles on my back as if he needed some kind of anchor.

"Again, not many adoptive parents want a ten-year-old boy
who's angry at the world, hating everyone for being strange and
unfamiliar. So I went to group homes. Some were okay. Most
weren't. Problem was, I was too old to be adopted, too old to
forget the life I'd had before. If my parents had died when I was
much younger, growin' up in that shit would've been much easier
because I wouldn't have known any better."

He lingered in that 'what if' for a moment, the same way I'd
lingered in the possibility of Aunt V taking me away from my life
before the worst could happen. Then his eyes shuttered, and he
shook it off.

"But I did. It turned me bitter. Angry. Fuckin' furious. Made
me decide that I would not care about another fuckin' thing in this
horrible world. When I was older, it made me want to hurt people.
Fell into crowds lookin' for someone exactly like me. Had nothin'
to lose, nothing to keep me human." His eyes seared into mine. "I
did some fuckin' bad shit, Freya. I killed people. A lot of them.
And I didn't feel bad about it. I loved it. I still do."

I shivered from the coldness of his voice, the truth in it. I was
in the arms of a killer. He hadn't hidden that from me, not once.

He'd expected me to recoil, to banish him from my life. I'd expected it too. But I only held him tighter.

"I want you, Freya. More than I've wanted anything in my fuckin' life. I can't bring myself to leave you. But I'm not going to stay with you, pretendin' that I'm something I'm not. I'm a monster. I know it. My brothers know it. There's a reason I wear the patch I do. Because I do things even the worst of them couldn't stomach."

Hades was still gently drawing circles on my back. I was still tucked into his side. Warm. Safe. Satisfied.

"I don't care." I craned my neck to look into his eyes as I spoke, wanting him to feel the truth in my words. "I don't care about what your patch means or what you have to do because of it. That you think yourself to be some kind of monster—"

"I *am* a monster," he interrupted.

I gritted my teeth. Fucking alpha males.

"Fine, okay, you're a monster," I conceded with a pout. "But you're *my* monster, Hades. Monsters need to be loved too." I took a breath then repositioned my body so I could meet his eyes. "I love you, Hades. With blood on your hands, with death on your soul, with demons in your eyes, I love you." My voice was barely a whisper, but the words came out heavy.

Hades's face changed completely, contorting from what I assumed was shock. I wasn't sure why he was surprised since I'd done a terrible job at hiding what I felt for him. Hades was shrewd, he could read my tiniest subtleties. He had to have known.

But maybe he hadn't, maybe the hatred he'd felt for himself made him blind to the love anybody else felt for him.

He wasn't going to say it back, I'd known that. I had expected his silence. To stop it from smothering us, I pressed my lips to his and climbed on top of him. He kissed me back immediately, with all of the words he couldn't say, with everything he felt but was still trying to fight.

He then fucked me with passion, with need.

With love.

THREE WEEKS LATER

When I got the call, I was unloading groceries from my car. A lot of groceries. Even considering my standards. Surpassing PMS groceries or movie marathon groceries. The weight of them in my arms was overpowering enough that my biceps burned. Regardless, my heart warmed.

Expanded.

They were groceries for two people. For us. We were an us, Hades and me. The fighting had stopped. Against ourselves, against each other. We had both accepted that this was a battle neither of us could win, and we just ... settled in.

Although I wasn't in danger anymore, Hades was still here. Every night.

It should've freaked me out, that we had only just technically started dating and he was already living with me. He had been living with me before we'd started dating. That was not normal. Not even a little. Nor was it healthy. Or the way regular relationships progressed. But I was not one to live a 'regular' life. Nor was Hades.

So, whatever.

Sure, I was freaked-out, but not by our situation. I was freaked out by my feelings for Hades, that I could feel him under my skin in a very permanent way.

That's what I was thinking about as I carried the groceries into the house, grinning stupidly. My phone had been ringing while I carried them, and I somehow managed to get it to the crook of my shoulder to balance it against my ear, balance two very heavy, reusable grocery bags in my elbow and kick my car door shut with my foot by the time I answered.

When I heard the words on the other end of the phone, I froze, a dull roar invading my ears. I must've spoken. Or at least, I think I did because I ended the call before my phone dropped with a clatter to the concrete.

Sinking down on the ground in the middle of my driveway seemed a little dramatic and something a heroine did in a movie rather than something a regular person did in real life, but I couldn't help myself. I wasn't in control of my limbs. I just kind of ... fell to the ground. The shopping bags tumbled from my hands, rogue oranges and apples rolling lazily down my driveway. I snatched a bottle of wine before it could go too far, thankful for the cool, solid glass around my fingertips.

I was especially thankful it had a screw top otherwise I might've really damaged my nails, trying to pry the top off. As it was, it came off without much effort, and I started drinking. Wishing the liquid sliding down my throat could change things.

———

I wasn't in a catatonic state when they arrived, but I was definitely drunk. Drunk enough that I didn't care I was sitting on my ass in the driveway surrounded by groceries, chugging the last sip from the bottle of wine I was drinking.

The roar of their bikes was delightfully loud, almost loud enough to drown out my thoughts. But not quite. That's what the wine was for. I was actually disappointed when the roar disappeared. It wasn't long before he got to me, crouching down so he was at eye level. The sight of his worn leather boots was welcome.

"Freya."

Hades grasped my chin in his fingers in order to tilt it up to look at him. His face was tight with worry, eyes hard with a fury that told me he was already ready to hurt whoever was responsible for me being in this state.

"I need you to tell me what happened," he articulated slowly. He was forcing his voice to be even, trying to remain calm. I knew that.

My eyes flickered behind him to where Hansen was standing wearing his own version of badass concern.

"Oh, shit," I groaned. "Tonight is our double date dinner. The dinner is..." I held out my arms to the food that was decorating my driveway. "Ruined," I finished. "We might have to reschedule," I whispered, meeting his eyes.

"Freya." There was agitation in his tone now.

"My father died," I mumbled, the words tasting strange, sounding even stranger in the air. "In prison. He'd been sick for a while, apparently, but I didn't know. Because he didn't want me to know, didn't want to say goodbye." I hiccupped. "It's stupid to be upset about it. I mean, I didn't even know him, not really. I didn't even *like* him. I don't know why I'm making a scene. Ugh, this is so embarrassing."

Hades's finger pressed against my lips in his version of 'shut up, you hysterical female.'

"Stop," he urged me. He said it so softly, yet with such force, that I did exactly as he said.

The next second, I was in his arms. His chest was warm and hard and safe. "What about the groceries?" I whined.

"I'll take care of them," he promised.

What was left unsaid was, *I'll take care of you.*

———

Hades had done as he'd promised. He took care of the groceries. And me. There was no comment about how I'd consumed a whole bottle of wine on pretty much an empty stomach. He did give me a large glass of water, but a generous glass of tequila followed that.

I was sitting at the breakfast bar, sipping tequila, contemplating the tiles on my backsplash, when Hades walked in. He had been gone for a while, cleaning up my mess. Now my phone was pressed against his ear, and he was murmuring something I couldn't hear.

When he approached me, he leaned down to drop a kiss on my neck. "She's right here," he said into the phone.

It took me a couple of seconds to take the phone he was holding out to me, but eventually I did.

"A man answered your phone," my Aunt V remarked quizzically.

"I know," I replied, staring at the man in question.

"He sounds attractive." I could hear the delight in her voice.

I smirked. "He is."

"You haven't told me about this man," she accused.

My smirk turned into a smile, something that had seemed completely impossible just a few moments ago.

"And because you haven't told me about the man and because of the strange and horrible things you must be feeling right now, I'm coming there," Aunt V reported, her voice a tad softer now.

The softness reminded me of my hard edges, the ones that had been sharpened by today's news. My smile faltered, but just a little.

"You can't come here," I groaned, looking at Hades and wondering what he'd look like through my aunt's eyes. I was desperate for her to meet him, just to give him a little more permanence in my life. Yet I was terrified that she wouldn't approve. Not that my Aunt V had a judgmental bone in her body, but still.

"You have your job," I pointed out. "Your routines."

"Fuck the job and fuck my routines," Aunt V scoffed. "I have a niece to visit. And I have a man to meet. I've already booked my flights and a rental car. I'll be there by tomorrow."

My body relaxed at this news. It had been months since I'd seen my aunt. Months of huge, traumatic life changes. And wonderful life changes, like the one I was looking at. Today's news had shaken me to my core, and despite the amazing people I was surrounded with, I needed my Aunt V.

"For now, you let that gorgeous man take care of you, and I'll be there tomorrow so he can take care of us both," she teased.

"I love you," I whispered into the phone.

"Love you too, sweetcakes."

When I put down the phone, Hades was still staring at me. "My Aunt V is coming tomorrow," I told him.

"I gathered."

"She wants to meet you," I added.

He folded his arms. "She told me as much on the phone."

My mind immediately went to what they might've talked about. My Aunt wasn't into bullshit, so it was surely colorful. Hades hadn't struck me as someone who'd be good on the phone. Damn, I hadn't ever talked to him on the phone. That was totally weird.

"Is it weird that we haven't spoken on the phone?" I blurted out.

Hades regarded me evenly, like he wasn't thinking I was completely insane. "No."

"Okay," I replied.

He kept looking at me like he was waiting for me to break down. But the problem was, I had already done that.

"You're going to go and sit on the couch," Hades instructed, as if sensing that I had no idea what to do with myself right now. "Then, you're going to put on that show you love about the bitch who drinks too much coffee."

I raised my brow at this because he knew very well what *Gilmore Girls* was called. I actually suspected he liked it, but to utter the name of the show must've been tantamount to forfeiting his badass card.

"I'm going to make us dinner," he continued.

My brow raised farther. Hades had never made me dinner. Sometimes he helped chop things, but then he distracted me with his mouth, with his hands, with his cock. Then we never ended up eating anything but each other. I did the cooking. And I was more than happy doing the cooking. I loved the simple act of feeding him. Taking care of him.

"You can cook?" I asked.

He didn't reply to this. "After we eat, you're going to have a bath. After that, I'm going to fuck you. Then we're going to sleep. When we wake up, you're going to see your aunt."

I stared at him. The man in my kitchen, laying out exactly what I was going to do with my night so the future didn't seem so icky or uncertain.

"You got me, Freya?"

"I got you," I whispered.

He nodded at me. "Then get your ass on the couch."

I didn't say anything else. I just got my ass on the couch.

———

"This is something I should've asked a long time ago, but what exactly does the club do?" I asked, drawing patterns on Hades's chest with the pad of my finger.

There were scars peppered all over it, intermingled with the tattoos. I wondered which had come first, the tattoos or the scars. His body was covered with both of them. There was the neat line on his abs which was what I considered 'my scar.' Then there were the ones that weren't so neat, the jagged, painful-looking ones that made me feel vaguely sick. Ones that I'd stared at and wondered about often. Ones that hinted at what exactly his life as the enforcer of the Sons of Templar MC entailed.

I'd figured that sleeping with an outlaw and being submerged in his world would be a bit more jarring. Sure, there was the crazy ex I'd killed in the living room, but that wasn't exactly an outlaw thing, that was more of a Hades thing.

"This is something you want to talk about right now?"

Right now being the day I'd found out my father had died and had consumed a fair amount of wine and tequila. I'd also consumed two bowls of the pasta that Hades had cooked for me. Then there was all the sex. It had all been fucking wonderful, the pasta, the sex. But it had only worked for so long.

I was painfully sober. And I really needed to think of something in my present—what would hopefully be my future—instead of the man who would only ever remain my past.

"Yes, this is something I want to talk about right now," I affirmed. "Something I need to talk about right now."

Otherwise, I'd be thinking about my dead father and why he hadn't wanted me to know he was dying. Why he hadn't wanted to mend fences with his only daughter who was the whole reason he was in prison.

Yes, distraction was crucial right now.

Hades didn't hesitate, didn't ask me again if I was sure or if it was just the grief talking. He trusted me to know myself.

"The club runs guns," he said.

"Runs guns?" I echoed.

He nodded.

"Can you explain what that is?" I asked. "Because I'm taking it includes you running with a bunch of guns, like in a relay race or something, and I know that's not right. Plus, I also had a lot of wine, so my brain is a little hazy. And on top of that, I'm not really hip on the outlaw lingo, so you're gonna have to spell it out for me."

"Sons of Templar has a connection with Russians," Hades explained patiently. "They ship the guns to us in pieces. Club picks up the containers, each chapter receives their quota, assembles the guns then we deliver them to our contacts."

I digested that. "So you sell and distribute black market guns?" I clarified.

"We do."

"And you do other things too?" I asked.

He paused, looking pointedly at me. Just briefly. "You don't have more to say about the gun shit?"

I considered that. "No." I adjusted so I could fully look at his face, finding that it was carefully blank. "What more do you think I should ask?"

"Thought you'd have somethin' to say about criminals using those guns to do evil shit."

"Criminals can buy their guns at Walmart to do evil shit," I shrugged. "You're not responsible for the sins of others."

"I'm responsible for my own, though," he muttered.

I frowned at him. "What else? What else does the club do?"

"Security," he stated after another pause. "Work as muscle if needed. Don't tangle ourselves in drugs often since it gets messy, but there has been an occasion or two. We don't fuck with women, with children, but that's about it. That's where our line is. Anything else, anyone else, is fair fuckin' game."

There was no shame in his voice, no regret. He wasn't trying to scare me off with the truth. He was just telling the truth. No sugarcoating, which I was happy about.

I thought about everything he'd said. About the guns. About the violence. It was probably a lot more complicated than what he'd just condensed into a handful of sentences. I then thought about Macy. Hansen. Jagger. Caroline. Their kids. Gwen and Amy. Swiss. Elden. Anderson. The brotherhood. The family. The home for the misfits that society looked down on. Yeah, I could relate to that a whole fucking bunch.

There were a lot of things I could've said right then. I could have asked a bunch more questions, demanded to know every detail. But that wouldn't change anything. It wouldn't change how I felt about Hades. Wouldn't change what I felt about everyone I'd met connected to the club.

"Okay," I said finally.

"Okay? Hades asked. "That's it?"

I settled back into his chest, sighing. "Yeah, that's it."

I got the feeling he was going to say something else since his body was still taut and tense. But after a few seconds, he settled back into the mattress and his arms tightened around me.

"Okay, he murmured, his lips in my hair.

Then I fell into a dreamless sleep.

———

"You're here!" I screamed, running down the driveway and damn near yanking my Aunt V out of her car.

"I'm here!" she screamed back.

We hugged for a long time. I relaxed into her smell, Chanel No.5, the only perfume she'd ever worn. Her grip was tight, firm and soothing. I realized that it was the very first hug we'd shared where I was completely relaxed, where I wasn't waiting for it to be over.

She let me go and something shifted behind her glassy eyes, making me wonder if she'd noticed it too.

"You look amazing," I told my aunt honestly, my eyes running over her petite frame. She was shorter than me, even wearing heels. Which she always wore. No matter what.

Her auburn hair was hair sprayed within an inch of its life and pulled back off her face so it tumbled down her back. Her makeup was immaculate and subtle, her skin glowing thanks to a lifetime of SPF and a religious skin care routine. There were lines on her face, though shallow and only adding to her beauty.

She was trim because she exercised daily and followed a strict diet. Every one of her slender and manicured fingers held a gold ring, glittering with one gemstone or another. She wore all black today, which is what she always wore when traveling. Said it was effortless, comfortable and classy. She definitely looked that.

"Me?" she scoffed, her eyes running over me. "Look at you. You're glowing, honey!" Her shrewd gaze then found its way to the man who hadn't sprinted out of the house like a madman the second her car pulled into the driveway.

"Holy fuck," Aunt V murmured under her breath.

Aunt V, as a rule, didn't swear. There were exceptions, and Hades was the ultimate exception.

He was wearing black, as always, and his Sons of Templar cut. I hadn't asked him not to wear it because I'd sooner have him peel off his skin or remove his tattoos. His cut was a part of him. I'd wanted him to meet my aunt exactly as he was. Aunt V was a smart woman; she'd see exactly who he was which was completely wonderful.

"Aunt V, this is Hades," I gestured to my man, suddenly nervous.

"Hades," she parroted.

He nodded once.

"No, God didn't have a hand in this," she waved her hand up and down his body. "Only the Devil himself is smart and wicked enough to craft something so succulent."

I blushed. "Aunt V, you can't call my serious, badass and macho boyfriend *succulent.*"

She scowled at me. "I'm old, I can say whatever the heck I want." She returned her focus to Hades. "You're the young man who's been taking care of my Freya?"

Hades nodded again. "Yeah," he confirmed. "And you're the reason why she's Freya."

I blinked, tears suddenly welling up in my eyes.

Even Aunt V looked dumbstruck.

My hand immediately found Hades's. I knew he wasn't a hand holder, but I needed to touch him at that moment, and it was the best I could do. He didn't let go of my hand, he squeezed it hard.

Aunt V took a couple of seconds to recover. "I love him already," she told me, her voice shaking just a little. "Now!" She clapped her hands. "Put those muscles to work and get my bags."

Hades was not a man you asked to fetch your bags. Kill a guy? Sure. Steal nuclear codes? Definitely. But bring in bags? No.

Hades squeezed my hand once before letting it go. Then he went to get my aunt's bags.

"He's a keeper," she winked, linking my arm in hers before walking us into the house.

"Yeah," I smiled my heart feeling close to bursting. "He is."

———

The subject of my father didn't come up immediately. Aunt V was busy.

Talking to Hades. Gawking at him, not hiding the fact that she was gawking at him. Cooking dinner. Going for walks with Sirius and me. Having lunch with Marilyn. Going with us to a club party —which she fucking loved and where she also didn't hide her gawking over every sexy man—making and drinking margaritas. She was busy catching up with me, immersing herself in the life I'd built here. A real life. The kind I'd never had. She was busy distracting me from the knowledge that my father had died serving a prison sentence that everyone in my extended family blamed me for. Apart from her, of course.

The topic had to come up at some point. It was bubbling inside of me, and there was no one else in this world I could talk to about this. Hades would listen without any kind of judgement, with his quiet strength, but I didn't want him to see that part of me.

Which was why, while he was at 'church', Aunt V and I settled outside with the outdoor fire roaring and fresh margaritas, and I readied myself to open those wounds. The ones that would sting like the salt on the rim of my drink was rubbing into them.

"Why didn't he want to see me?" My question came out as a whisper, the words leaving my mouth in a puff of frigid air. "Not even in the end? When he knew that he was never going to get out? Why didn't he want to see me before he died?" I had tried to verbalize the words with strength, but it was impossible to utter such things without exhuming the pathetic and desperate longing I'd had for my father's love that had been buried inside of me for all of these years.

"Because he made a mistake," Aunt V replied, the reflection of the fire dancing in her eyes. "There are men, very rare men, who can handle their mistakes, can face them and learn from them. Then there are the more common ones, like your father, who are delicate and dangerous when it comes to three things: when they're rejected, when they're bested and when they make a mistake."

She sighed. "And he didn't just make one mistake with you, he made many. What happened to you, that was the culmination of all of his failures as a father, as a man. He was too weak to face them, so he couldn't face you. Not because he didn't love you. Because he hated himself."

She squeezed my hand. "Honey, I hate this for you, but the one and only half-decent thing your father ever did was what landed him in that prison. The three meals a day, the place to sleep, that was his only reward."

She sipped her drink, and I did the same, licking at the salt while all the open nerves inside of me stung.

"The years he spent there, the likelihood that a man named 'Big Jim' made him his girlfriend, the illness that crept into his blood and killed him, that was all punishment for everything else he did," she continued, fury fresh in her voice. "For the way he failed you. Mourn what you should've had in a father. Mourn that you never got what you deserved. But never mourn for him, sweetheart."

She cleared her throat, staring out at the desert.

"I'll always blame myself," she admitted quietly. "For not seeing it. For not getting you out of there. For not fighting for you." Her voice cracked toward the end, with a thinness that I'd never heard from the woman who had always seemed so solid to me.

Now it was my turn to squeeze her hand. "No," I ground out firmly. "Don't you dare. You are the reason that I got through those years."

"You wouldn't have had to get through anything if I'd taken you away from there," she argued.

There it was, the blame she'd carried around for decades. Dragged around with her. That she'd kept hidden deep inside, letting it eat away at her.

The worst kind of blame, that kind felt by everyone who had experienced or witnessed something horrific, wondering what if it had been different? What if I had made it different?

"My mother would never have let you, you know that," I told her what she already knew. "Not because she wanted me, but because you did. She would've sunk her claws in deeper, leaving more scars just to spite you. You did the only thing you could do, the best thing that you could do, giving me light and strength and positive memories." I squeezed her hand harder. "You gave me you."

We didn't speak about anything else, and she didn't try to argue further. We just watched the stars and let the tequila stave off the worst of our pain.

———

I didn't usually answer calls from unknown numbers, but I was distracted. By happiness. By Aunt V chatting as she cooked dinner for Hades and me. We were sitting at the breakfast bar drinking wine, watching her because she'd demanded that we not do a damn thing to help her.

Hades had been a presence throughout Aunt V's visit. Not a constant one, letting us have our time for the most part. He disappeared to the club most days, not coming home until late, crawling into bed with me then making me come quiet and hard. He'd do the same in the morning, and the routine continued.

I'd asked Kallum for the week off, and he gave it to me because he was that kind of guy. The night before her second to last night, I took Aunt V on my 'date' with Des. Not surprisingly, they hit it off big time. A part of me had become hopeful over the way they'd teased each other as if they'd known each other for years, at the twinkle in Des's eyes as he spoke to my Aunt V. I hadn't said anything, didn't push it, not with people as bull-headed and stubborn as them. I just sent out a silent little prayer for two wonderful, deserving people to find their happy endings.

Tonight, Aunt V's last night, Hades was with us. Because he knew what it meant to me. Because he knew how hard it was for me.

He didn't speak much, but that didn't bother Aunt V. She fucking loved it, actually.

"You should've heard her last boyfriend," she'd bantered as she chopped onions. "Spoke because the sound of his own voice made his dick hard." She screwed up her nose. "A man who is comfortable making his actions speak instead of his words is the one who wins. The other one is hopefully living a terrible life."

I bit my lip as I regarded my wine. Aunt V obviously didn't know that Derek wasn't living *any* kind of life. She also didn't know that he'd beat me up. Nor did she know how Hades and I had actually met. Not much shocked my Aunt V, but that would shock the fuck out of her and sentence her to a lifetime of worrying about me.

She was perfect knowing what was important, which was that I loved Hades, and he would protect me with his life.

"You know, it is painful, *criminal* even, that you have a playlist with the title 'World's Greatest Music' yet Madonna is nowhere to be found," she commented sharply.

I grinned as my phone rang.

"Hello, Freya's house of pain, how may I help you?" I greeted.

"You *cunt*."

My smile froze on my face as I recognized the voice hurling that disgusting word through the phone.

"You *stupid* fucking cunt," my mother added. "It's your fault he died in prison. Your fault that he was there in the first place, by lying like the little bitch you are."

I had, from time to time, considered what I might say to my mother given the chance. While I'd been quite comfortable never speaking to her or seeing her again in my life, part of me had wanted the confrontation. Wanted to face her as a strong, healthy, successful woman. To look down on her and show her that she had not succeeded in breaking me. That she had failed in so many ways. I'd tell her that I became this despite her, that her life was sad and lonely, and her opinion of me meant less than nothing.

I'd planned to be sharp, strong, articulate. I'd meet her wearing an emotional suit of armor so there wouldn't even be even a tiny space of skin for her to hit, to pierce it, to make me bleed.

I was suddenly given that chance, to commence the speech that I'd sometimes rehearsed in my head while I was in the shower or out on walks. Yet I didn't say a word. Not one. I just held the phone to my ear, smile still frozen on my face.

Hades stilled the second my mother screamed the second sentence at me. The phone hadn't been on speaker, but he was sitting close enough to me to hear every vile word.

The phone was no longer at my ear. Hades slammed his wine glass down on the counter so liquid sloshed over the top and stained the surface like blood.

He only listened for a handful of seconds.

"You don't know me," he said in a clipped tone. "You don't need to. All you need to know is that if you ever contact Freya again, I'll hunt you down and hurt you. You will regret ever being fucking born."

Then he hung up.

My Aunt V and I just gaped at him.

"I like him, a lot" she announced after a handful of seconds of silence.

"Me too," I whispered, leaning over to squeeze his thigh. His hand covered mine.

We had a wonderful night. I did not let my mother ruin it.

HADES

I'd known this was happening.

It was clear that Victoria cared about Freya. A great deal. In the way a parent might. A lot fucking more than either of her given parents had. With a ferocity that made me feel grateful. Infinitely grateful that Freya had someone who shared her blood who was fighting for her, who would go to battle for her without hesitation.

She wasn't afraid of me, which was impressive and jarring. I'd been used to people being afraid of me my entire adult life. Even my brothers, though they hid it well.

I didn't relish women being afraid of me, but I couldn't change it. Maybe that's why I had never tried to have any other woman except club girls, chicks who knew the score.

Freya wasn't afraid of me either.

No matter what I said to her, she took it in stride. Fuck, she'd known I'd killed people before I started fucking her. I told her I killed her piece of shit ex, and she didn't kick me out of the house. She still hadn't kicked me out of the house, not pointing out that there was no longer a reason for me to be living there. I hadn't fucking pointed that out either.

I hadn't been able to bring myself to go back to my shithole of a house. Or to my room at the club, where I'd slept a fuck of a lot more than the house I owned. The clubhouse used to be the only place I felt at home. The closest thing I had to happiness had been at that club. Or more accurately, in the bloodstained basement where I could make people scream.

But Freya's home, with the candles, the throws, the pillows. Her fucking sheets. All the shit she had in her bathroom. I never wanted to fucking leave. It soothed me more than the fresh blood of my enemies.

With her Aunt V there, it had become something else entirely.

Happiness radiated from Freya's fucking pores. I'd thought all I liked from people was their pain. Their suffering. I'd sucked it from them like a goddamned vampire. But it was her joy. That was my fucking life force.

Being alive hurt less when I was around her.

I fucking loved her.

With all of my wretched soul. If I even fucking had one. I loved her.

Victoria was shrewd. She saw fucking everything. So when Freya went to the grocery store because she'd decided that we needed more wine and would not hear of anyone else going, Victoria made the most of the moment. It had taken everything in me not to go with her, but I'd managed. Neither of us insisted we go with Freya because we both knew she needed the time to herself.

I was smoking outside, trying to lock myself down after hearing the venom that creature spat through the phone. The words that had wiped every ounce of joy from Freya's face and replaced it with a pain so visceral it cut me to pieces. Freya recovered quickly because she was Freya. Because she was used to having to heal from these kinda fucking hits.

Victoria wordlessly lit up beside me. Though she was lighting up a joint.

"My niece is a marvel," she exhaled into the desert.

"I know," I replied immediately, even though I knew she was nowhere near done speaking.

I felt her gaze on me as I continued to look out on the desert.

"The fact that she survived that house. Survived what happened—"

She broke off, and I could practically feel the jagged edges of her broken heart. Fuck, they drew fucking blood because I was already cut the fuck open from when Freya had told me what happened. I'd barely fucking survived hearing what had happened to *her*. Even though I'd survived a lot of fucking shit. Done a lot of fucking shit. I hadn't thought it was possible for anything to shock me anymore. Didn't think I'd care about anyone's sorrows or misfortune because none of them were unique.

But *Freya* was unique. She was one of a fucking kind. And her sorrows? Fuck. They cut me in places I hadn't even known existed in me.

I could feel the love that Victoria had for her niece. It was etched in her, as was the pain.

"Every day I wonder how in the heck she manages it," Victoria shook her head. "She does because she's a marvel." She paused, still looking at me. "She loves you. She has never loved a man before because the only model she had for male love was a father who killed for her. He didn't show her anything else but that. The only fond memory she has of her father is that he killed the man he should've protected her from in the first place."

"It's a gift, what you've got, that love," she continued, her voice thick with smoke. "I'm sure you already know that. You're a smart man. A smart man wouldn't fuck this up. Wouldn't ruin this gift." She took another hit. "Unfortunately, love makes us stupid. I don't give a fuck about the way you live your life. I've got the idea it's a dangerous one. But there's nothing more dangerous than hurting Freya. 'Cause I'm an old woman. I've lived a good life. I'll happily kill you, and I'll do it slowly if you let harm come to her. If you're like her father, if you choose to show your love by avenging her after the damage is already done."

Her words hit truer than a bullet to the heart.

Sirius, who had been laying at my feet, lifted his head in the direction of the door then ran barking toward Freya who was walking in with two bags.

She beamed at us. "I know I was supposed to get wine, but I got distracted. With ice cream!" She held up her reusable grocery bags in triumph.

My heart clenched, and I knew what I had to do. I had to destroy this woman. Because I'd damn her otherwise.

FREYA

Something had been off about Hades since Aunt V left. I knew she'd talked to him, had recited the kind of speech a protective father might. Though with her own unique spin. There was no stopping her from doing that, and I hadn't really worried about it since I figured a man like Hades would be able to handle my aunt and her speech.

But maybe I'd been wrong. Maybe Aunt V had been scary enough to put off the biker who wasn't afraid of anything.

Or maybe it was something else entirely.

I didn't push him because I knew pushing a man like Hades could only end badly. If he wanted to talk, he'd talk. Sure, he didn't do much of that in general—compared to me, at least—but when he had something to say, he didn't beat around the bush.

So I waited. For him to either tell me what was going on or for the situation to work itself out. The former terrified me, so I prayed for the latter.

But God was apparently on another call or I didn't have her number, because it all came to a head one night when I didn't have work and he didn't have club business. A night when there were no parties, barbeques or family dinners. It was just us two, sitting on the patio after eating dinner and drinking a lot of wine. The fire was raging, the stars above us and Sirius at our feet. I felt safe, comfortable. Embraced.

We hadn't spoken much throughout the night, though I was used to that. Hades had spoken to me in his own way. With his hands at my hips as I cooked. His lips at my neck, hands sliding under my shirt, tweaking my nipple. They said a picture was worth a thousand words, but there was nothing like the man you loved brushing against your panties with his thumb for the entirety of a meal.

Though I couldn't translate the thousands of things he told me with his hands, I never would've thought any meant goodbye.

"What do you want out of life, Freya?"

The question filtered through the crisp, thick, night air, hanging there.

We had talked about a lot, Hades and me. Almost everything, actually. The past, in all of its ugliness, and the realities of our present. But the future, the future was a big, looming cloud that we never mentioned.

Although the future was surely a topic that couples typically discussed, it had been well established that there was nothing typical about us as a couple.

Despite feeling overwhelmed by the dread weighed on me, heavier than the night sky itself, I forced myself to relax.

"I used to want a normal life," I answered, my voice low. "A golden retriever. A never-ending pile of laundry. Regular Pilates classes with girlfriends who complained about their husbands. I would complain, too, but secretly be head over heels in love with my husband. I wanted there to be a local coffee shop where as soon as I walk in, the barista greets me by name and asks, 'the usual?' " I paused, thinking of Oliver. "I do have that. I have a lot of things that I never in a million years would've thought I wanted." I looked into the fire, feeling too uncertain to look at him. "I've spent my whole life trying to avoid trouble because my father told me I attracted it. That has always stuck with me, what he said. That I'd bring trouble to my family, myself and the man unlucky enough to fall in love with me."

Hades didn't say anything.

"I guess on some level, I always thought what happened to me was somehow my fault. Including what happened to my father. So I looked for normal because I thought I'd hurt less people that way, that I wouldn't hurt the man I fell in love with." I paused, the words I hadn't been brave enough to say thick on my tongue.

"But then I found out something. Rather, I found someone." I licked my lips. "And I've come to learn that trouble, with the right man, is all I want out of my future."

Still he said nothing, the sound of Sirius's snores the only noise punctuating the silence. Hades was obviously waiting for me to say something else. For more.

I bit my lip as I realized I'd forgotten to mention one important thing. The most important thing.

"I want kids," I announced. "Oh, do I want kids. I want to be there when they come home, make them snacks, help them with their homework. Fill this house with them."

I smiled, thinking of dark-headed children running around our home. It wasn't mine anymore, this place. I didn't know when that had happened. We'd never had a conversation about it, it had simply become ours. Somehow, it was no longer the place where I'd killed Hades's ex-girlfriend before she killed him. It wasn't the place where I'd recovered from my own ex beating me. It wasn't even the place Hades had his stab wounded stitched up. It was just ours. Hades had stayed despite my not needing 'protecting' anymore. The clothes that I washed then wordlessly put away in my closet. Our closet. He saw them in there because Hades saw everything, but he didn't say a word.

He hadn't needed to.

Because this was our future.

Or at least I had thought it was.

Hades's arms had loosened around me after I told him this. I hadn't realized it was because he was also thinking about dark-headed children running around the backyard. Not until he sat up and not so gently pushed me out of his arms and stood. My body chilled at the abrupt change in atmosphere, in temperature.

I stood, too, because I wasn't fond of the distance between us.

"I don't want kids," Hades informed me, his eyes fixed on me, his expression communicating that I should not come any closer.

I blinked at him. At the words he'd spoken. The ones that were set in stone. Hades never said anything that he didn't mean. And he meant this. In a very real and very heartbreaking kind of way. He meant this.

I was an idiot.

It wasn't as if this came as a complete surprise, knowing the man Hades was. The life he'd led. The scars imprinted on his soul. He had never once hinted that he'd wanted to be a father, and before tonight, I'd never outright said I'd wanted to be a mother. Some stupid, pathetic part of me had just assumed that because he loved me, we were unbreakable. We'd gone through so much already, probably more than any couple on the planet—or any couple outside of the Sons of Templar, considering the romantic history of the club—I'd never imagined that something as ordinary as struggling over who did and didn't want kids could ruin us.

Sure, the fact that he was an outlaw and lived a dangerous life had kind of hinted that his environment was not a kid-friendly one, but the club was warm, welcoming, a family. Even his president, who no doubt was deadly and badass, was a husband and a father. These men were a dichotomy. They had so much violence, danger and rage inside of them, but they had equal amounts of love. It was impossible not to see. The children in their lives were adored, were happy and protected. I'd been delighted and ecstatic, thinking about our dark-headed child having that exact same thing.

I'd been a fool.

"I want kids," I reiterated. My words were not as firm and loud as his had been, but they were also set in stone. I wanted desperately to abandon that want, to sacrifice that for Hades, to tell him that he was enough. That he was more than enough. And he was. In so many ways. But I wouldn't be able to stay with him without eventually resenting him. Without being overcome by grief when I looked at Hansen and Jagger and their children.

"I already knew that," he sighed.

"You knew?" I spluttered.

He nodded.

Of course, he already knew. He knew everything about me without me having to utter a word. With maybe a couple of exceptions. Although I'd never verbalized that I wanted kids, I hadn't exactly hidden that part of myself. He'd seen me with Macy and Hansen's kids. With Jagger and Caroline's baby. He'd probably seen the need on my face when I'd inhaled that beautiful baby scent while I was cradling her.

"You knew, yet you didn't say anything," I whispered.

He nodded once.

I fought against the tears pressing at the back of my eyes. "Why?" I rasped. "Why when you knew—"

"When I knew that this, us, was eventually going to end?" he finished for me.

My stomach dropped. I couldn't even entertain the thought of us ending.

"Because, Freya, I'm greedy. Because I wanted to take whatever fucking scraps of happiness I could get with you." He grasped the back of my neck, yanking me forward until our foreheads touched.

I wanted to flinch away from him, to fight him, scream at him, but I knew that my time with him was draining quickly, and I had to hold on to what I had left. Even if that was like trying to hold water in my fist.

"Because I'm not a good fucking guy," he hissed, his mouth inches from mine. "I knew it would ruin you. That I would ruin you, break your fucking heart. But I couldn't stop myself. Because I want you to feel me for the rest of your life. I want you to wear my fucking scars into the future I know doesn't involve me."

There were a million things to say then. I wanted to scream at him. Curse him to hell for making me fall in love with him, for not leaving before he'd grown roots in me. But I knew better. Hades hadn't had control over this either. This pull we had for each other. And even if he had, he wasn't the good guy, he wasn't going to do the noble thing and leave before he could do any permanent damage. He wanted that. He wanted me to wear the memory of him like he wore his tattoos.

So I didn't scream. Didn't curse. Didn't kick him out.

I surged forward, wrapped my legs around his waist, and I

kissed him. He caught my hips, holding me close, tugging at my hair as he kissed me back.

"Fuck me," I demanded against his mouth. "Fuck me so hard that I forget."

Hades fucked me. So hard that I forgot that we were over. That my life was in ruins now. That I'd wear him on my insides forever.

———

We were tangled up in each other hours later, covered in sweat, in pain. My breathing was rapid yet shallow, my heart thundering. All of my limbs were numb, my eyes heavy. Hades held me tight. Neither of us spoke. There was nothing left to say.

I hadn't wanted to go to sleep. Hadn't wanted to close my eyes while Hades was still here, while his arms were around me, while our scents intermingled. I didn't want to have to open my eyes in a world where none of that would be anymore. But he'd exhausted me, perhaps for this very purpose. Because no matter how hard I fought it, sleep finally claimed me.

Hades was gone when I woke up.

CHAPTER EIGHTEEN

THREE MONTHS LATER

"You can't leave," Marilyn admonished, glaring at me while I packed my suitcase.

"I have to," I grumbled, looking down at it. I was trying my best not to look around my room. At all the boxes piled up with the life that I'd thought was going to be so permanent here.

"What you have to do is tell him," she argued.

My eyes snapped up, narrowing at her. "Tell him? So he can do what? Change his mind about something that he's been certain about his entire life? So he can abandon the life he'd created for himself to have a long and happy life with me?" I shook my head. "Things would never work that way. Even if he tried to do the noble thing, which I doubt he'd do, he'd end up resenting me. He'd end up hating me." I sucked in a breath. "I wouldn't be able to handle that."

"How are you going to handle this," she waved her hand at me, at my body which betrayed no signs yet, though it would soon, "alone?"

"I'm not going to be alone," I reminded her. "I'll be with Aunt V."

As soon as I'd found out, I'd called her, hysterical, which was rare for me. She'd been calm, quickly laying out a plan for us. She'd immediately asked me where I would want to be, where I'd feel safe. Of course, the only place I'd felt safe was here, in the arms of the man I loved. But I would never be in his arms again, and I couldn't stay in this town knowing that.

We'd decided on Colorado. The mountains. The clear air. In the small town of Falcon Springs where I'd spent a couple of months before I'd moved here. It was pretty. Peaceful. Safe.

And my Aunt V, who hadn't moved out of her hometown in sixty years, was preparing to pack up her house, her life, for me.

"Honey, that is wonderful, but your Aunt V is getting older," Marilyn said softly.

Anxiety surged in my gut at the truth in her words. I'd never thought of my aunt as being old. In my head, she was this fabulous, ageless creature thanks to her spunk, her energy, her personality. But she *was* getting older. As much as the thought sickened me, she wasn't going to be around forever. Eventually, I would be alone.

"It's not up for discussion," I declared finally.

A crease formed between Marilyn's brows. She was not on board with this plan, obviously. But she was not going to change my mind. She had a wonderful husband who loved her more than life and would lasso the moon then yank it down to Earth if that's what she asked for.

As empathetic and wonderful as she was, she couldn't possibly understand the turmoil I was going through right now.

"What are you going to do when this kid gets old enough to ask about his father?" she demanded.

"I don't know!" I screamed, throwing down a handful of night-gowns that wouldn't fit very soon. "I don't know what the fuck I'm going to do then. I don't know what I'm going to do when I stare into his eyes on our baby, because we know that his genes are super dominant, so mine won't stand a chance. I don't know how I'm going to raise him or her without his presence." I sank down on my bed, suddenly unable to support my own weight, suddenly unable to hold it together for a moment longer.

The tears had started coming, and they did not stop. Not for a second. It was a fucking flood of all the emotions I'd been trying to hold in for the past three months. It had taken a Herculean effort, not shedding a single tear during the most painful breakup of my life. It had also taken countless batches of cookies, dozens of cakes, muffins and brownies. It had taken two-hour walks with Sirius. Many, *many* glasses of wine. Arguably more shots of tequila. Daily spinning classes with Marilyn.

Then it had taken a positive pregnancy test, meaning the wine and the tequila had to stop. After that, there was no time for tears, there was only time for plans. For action.

"Honey," Marilyn cooed, sitting down beside me on the bed before pulling me into her arms. She smelled of Tom Ford perfume which upset my stomach just a little since morning sickness was a bitch, but I needed it. The loving embrace of my strong, kind friend. A hug that didn't make my skin crawl. Because of Hades.

"I know I'm making a huge fucking mistake," I sobbed. "This place is the only place I've ever felt at home. You're my family. I'm going to miss you so much." The tears descended faster than Marilyn could wipe them away.

"Baby, we'll visit. Often. You know you won't be able to keep Jed away. And we're doing our surrogate thing next year which means I'll be moving in with you so I don't accidently kill our child. You'll be an old pro by then." She winked, uncharacteristic moisture in her eyes.

I fought to control my own tears, but now that the floodgates had opened, it felt impossible to close them. It felt impossible to leave my friends, this house, this town.

Him.

I hadn't seen him. Not once.

Not at Fate, where I'd stopped dancing when I found out I was pregnant. Not that I had anything against mothers who continued to work when pregnant.

Those two lines turned my world upside down. Those two lines represented the end of a long and significant chapter of my life. One that had been good to me but one that needed to be over. Honestly, I'd been waiting for a solid reason to retire for a long time. A baby was a pretty fucking solid reason.

When I met Hades, I'd thought—I'd hoped—my life would look different than this. But that's not the way life worked. And I was lucky. I had friends all over the country. And I was financially free.

"I'll come here every week," Marilyn assured me, stroking my hair. "To check up on the place, or to escape from Jed if he's making something that's not in my meal plan for the week." She winked.

I smiled weakly. Although some would say it wasn't fiscally responsible, I hadn't sold this house. Hadn't rented it out either. But I could easily swing the mortgage payments along with the rent on the place I'd gotten for me and Aunt V in Falcon Springs.

There was no way I could possibly leave this place in my rearview mirror completely. Not with the roots I'd grown here. Not with the memories stained into the foundation like blood. Not with the fucking blood that had literally been spilled in it. No, I couldn't sell it any sooner than I could sell a piece of my soul.

"It's going to be okay," Marilyn reassured me.

I didn't say anything to her because I didn't believe her. It wasn't going to be okay. But I had to do it anyway.

HADES

TWO WEEKS LATER

I killed Freya's mother.

Right after I left her bed, I drove fourteen hours straight, watched her trailer for a few hours, chain smoked, then walked in and shot her in the head. I didn't leave any evidence. Getting away with it was not something I was worried about.

I wasn't worried about anything. I thought of nothing on the ride home. Someone with a soul might've been sick. Been overcome with guilt, disgust in themselves. No feelings plagued me except a sick longing for Freya. Had I killed her mother in order to make it impossible for me to go back to her? Freya was not one for vengeance. She had accepted me killing the ex, but I knew she would never forgive me for murdering her mother. I hadn't done it for her. I'd done it for me. Because I was a selfish piece of shit who couldn't stand the thought of someone who had a hand in Freya's suffering to still draw breath on this Earth.

I'd killed her because that's the kind of man I was. That's the kind of monster I was.

Then I went back to the club, went back to the life I'd had before Freya. I fucking dared anyone to mention her name. Even Swiss, the fucker with a death wish, wasn't brave enough. No one went to Fate for that same reason.

When I couldn't sleep, I'd park my bike at the end of her road and just stare at the faint lights of her home. The one she'd given to me. I'd stare and smoke for hours until the night was chased away by the fucking sunlight.

I had done that every night for months until there were no lights. She was gone. That was what I was supposed to want, but it made me want to rip my own fucking heart out just so it wouldn't have to beat anymore.

Luckily, club shit got busier. We'd been getting more shipments in as the Russians upped our supply. And with more shipments came more shit. Which was what I'd guessed the phone call was about when my cell rang. No one called or talked to me unless shit was going down.

"You better be calling because you've got the location on the assholes trying to move in on our shipment routes," I spat as I answered my phone.

It was not a good thing for the club that things were so chaotic in the arms business right now. It was a fucking great thing for me, though. If I didn't have people to hurt, things to do, people to kill, then I'd do something fucking stupid, like track down Freya and drag her back here.

"Yeah, I've got their location. Already gave it to Hansen an hour ago," Wire said.

I clenched my fist. "If you gave it to Hansen a fucking hour ago, how am I not at that fucking location?" I gritted out the question that I should not have been asking Wire but asking my fucking president.

"Because I also told him something else that had him putting Swiss on that particular task," Wire replied, surprising me with that information. Despite being thousands of miles away, the motherfucker knew everything. And I knew by the sound of his voice that he was about to tell me something that was going to really fucking piss me off.

"Don't kill me."

Yeah, it was really going to fucking piss me off, since he'd said that with absolute sincerity.

"What is it?" I demanded.

"No, first you have to promise that you're not going to kill me," Wire asserted.

I gritted my teeth and looked for something close by I could smash. There wasn't a second of the day where I didn't want to smash something. I was angry, furious, all the fucking time which was not something I had any experience in. Before her, I never got angry. Never got anything. Then she went and fucked it all up. Shouldn't this shit have ended by now? Or at least dulled?

I had a feeling that it wouldn't dull until I was dead. That was my sentence, for thinking I could have her, thinking I could hurt her without consequences.

"I'm ain't promising shit," I told Wire, tempted to drive down there just so I could wring his fucking neck. I'd liked him before, but now I didn't like anyone. Most of all myself.

"Okay, well, then I'm hoping that the news itself will have your mind on other things rather than my untimely death," he retorted.

I let out an audible breath into the phone.

"I've been checking in on Freya," he said quickly, sensing he was not long for this Earth.

Everything in my body froze.

"Gwen and Amy practically held guns to my head," he continued, signifying that he was probably tweaking on the energy drinks he consumed like they were water.

"And I know you're one tough motherfucker, but even *you* would crack with those two bitches breathing over your shoulder."

Though he might've been just a little bit correct, I could barely focus on anything else other than the name he'd just uttered. The name that no one in the club dared speak around me, not even Macy.

"They liked her. A lot. Everyone did," Wire added. "And I thought, given the club's history with women, I thought it would be best for us to keep track of her. You know, until..."

He trailed off, and I gritted my teeth. *Until you get your shit together and bring her home.* I knew that was what he'd left unsaid.

Yeah, that's what all the other motherfuckers had done. Gotten their shit together, figured out how to be a monster in a cut while being something else entirely for their woman. I wasn't like them, though. I wasn't going to bring her home.

But he wasn't calling me to try to convince me to do that. No one was going to do that unless they had a death wish. Wire was calling for a different reason. And I knew it wasn't a good fucking one.

"Is she okay?" I barked into the phone.

Anderson looked up from the book he was reading across the room. Newly patched, yet he somehow had the balls to read a book on breastfeeding in the fucking clubhouse. I hated the motherfucker. Hated him for his happiness. His family. I hated all of them. And I would burn the fucking world down if anything had happened to Freya.

"She's okay," Wire answered quickly. "More than okay, depending on how you look at it."

"You better stop dancing around whatever it is you have to fucking say," I hissed.

"Okay, well I've been keeping track of her credit cards, her phone location, pretty much everything that Uncle Sam keeps track of in addition to a few things he isn't smart enough to look at. Something came up on her health insurance. A visit to an OB-GYN. So I did some more creative digging and broke a few dozen laws. Got her records." Wire finally took a breath. But then he said five more words, rocking my fucking world. "She's almost four months pregnant."

My heart stopped beating. But that couldn't have been right since I hadn't fucking had one since the moment I'd left Freya in her bed, naked and asleep.

Almost four months ago.

I threw the phone at the wall where it smashed into pieces.

THREE WEEKS LATER

FREYA

"Ms. Barker?"

I turned around to look at the man who'd called my name. He was wearing an expensive suit, was tall, clean-shaven and handsome. I did not recognize him, yet he knew my name, setting off my internal alarm bells.

He couldn't have been a police officer, or any kind of government worker for that matter, because his suit was expensive. Tailored for him specially. No one in the government made enough money for bespoke suits.

My guard went up immediately, and my gaze went around the grocery store parking lot, barely a car to be seen. It was two in the afternoon on a Wednesday. After the lunch rush, before the moms who brought their kids after school had arrived. A lull. The larger chain grocery store down the street was more crowded, but I'd wanted to go to the expensive health food store, so I was here.

Alone.

I swallowed. This was a safe little town. A large majority of its residents were retired and nostalgic for an old America that didn't exist anymore. It almost existed here, in this small town with only a handful of big-box stores. It was becoming more popular with the cashed-up, younger generation who were filtering in to open trendy boutiques and artisan coffee shops—where the coffee paled in comparison to Oliver's, and they had yet to remember my name or my order.

Yes, this was a safe town. There was a perfectly normal explanation as to why this man knew my name and was approaching me in a quiet parking lot.

"Can I help you?" I asked, straightening my spine after closing the trunk of my car.

His gaze flickered up and down my body. I was wearing chunky heeled boots and a fitted tank dress, so the small swell in my stomach was clearly visible. I'd 'popped' overnight after my stomach had remained almost completely flat for four and a half months.

When his eyes stayed on my stomach for a little too long, I gripped my keys tightly in my palm. I was supposed to go for the eyes, that's all I remembered.

"I'm going to have to ask you to come with me," he said when his gaze returned to my eyes.

It was not a request. The man had spoken in a cold, even, authoritative tone. He'd given me an order. Like he was someone entitled to order me to do such things. My stomach dipped. Maybe the government had started paying law enforcement more. My mind immediately went to Hades, to his club. Fuck, as much as I'd thought about their illegal activities, I'd never entertained the possibility that they'd get caught.

"Are you a police officer?" I asked, willing my face to stay even.

"No, ma'am."

My brows narrowed. "Are you affiliated with a government agency of any kind?"

His eyes didn't leave mine. "No, ma'am."

"Well, then I'm not going anywhere with you," I declared, suddenly pissed off at this man and men in general. What the fuck was it that gave them the deluded sense of entitlement to do shit like this?

"I'm going to have to insist."

Something unfurled in the pit of my stomach. I glanced around the parking lot. Still desolate. Had I not learned my lesson about shopping at times when everyone else was somewhere else?

"I'm going to have to insist, *harder*," I shot back through gritted teeth. "No."

He sighed. It was long and audible and told me he thought I was a huge inconvenience. "I didn't want to have to do this, but..."

He pulled open his suit to reveal the gun that was tucked neatly into a holster. Fear crawled up the back of my neck and something else too. The holster, the gun—it reminded me of Hades, who was thousands of miles away and had no idea what was going on. Who could not save me or our child.

It was up to me right now. Could I run? Not so well wearing these heels and carrying extra weight. It was very unlikely that this man in the expensive suit was going to shoot me in the back, so maybe if it was just me, I might've taken that chance. But it wasn't just me anymore. Even if the risk was slight, it was there. And if he didn't shoot me, he could make chase, I could trip, something could happen, and I could lose the small swell in my stomach that meant more to me than anything.

But getting in that car could be much, much worse than potentially getting shot in the back. Not knowing what to do, I stepped forward and got in the car, praying I'd made the right decision.

Because no one was coming to save us.

———

We drove for two hours.

The driver, otherwise known as my kidnapper, did not speak to me. I spoke. A lot. Demanded to know where he was taking me, who had sent him. He remained tight-lipped, so I eventually gave up. There were water and snacks in the side pockets of the car. Fancy water. The Fijian kind. Fancy snacks too. Gluten-free, refined-sugar-free, happiness-free. The car itself was even fancy. It appeared that whoever had kidnapped me was rich.

My assumption was confirmed when we pulled up to opulent gates that opened for the car and we drove up a winding driveway to a house nestled in front of the mountains. Not a house. A mansion. There were no neighbors to speak of, and the last house I'd seen had been at least fifteen minutes ago. I was in the middle of nowhere.

HADES

"What the fuck?" a female voice screeched from the direction of the door.

I didn't turn because the daylight would burn my fucking corneas. I didn't need to turn to find out who was standing at the clubhouse door anyway.

I was surprised she'd taken this long to get here. She must've only just found out. I was also surprised that Hansen was able to keep this shit under wraps for as long as he had. This woman had him wrapped around her little finger.

Heels slammed against the floor of the clubhouse as I contemplated my drink. It was the same one I'd been staring at all day. I'd only held a glass in my hand so my brothers assumed I was actually drinking and left me the hell alone. Not that I'd really needed the glass. They'd steered clear of me when I was sober or drunk; they knew I was a loose cannon. They were all afraid of me now. Even I was fucking afraid of me.

But this five-foot-nothing woman in platform heels was not afraid of me.

"You've got to be fucking *kidding* me," she snapped from right beside me.

I still didn't look up.

"Yeah, I'd have a little trouble looking me in the eye too," she sassed, venom in her tone. "I bet it's a fuck of a lot harder looking at yourself knowing that your woman, your *pregnant fucking woman,* is alone in another state, most likely scared, swollen and heartbroken. I'd wager my entire shoe collection that she hasn't checked out of life to drown herself in a bottle."

She chuckled sardonically before starting in on me again. "You know, since she technically can't drink her troubles away on account of her pregnancy. But she could wallow. She could refuse to get out of bed, threaten to kill people who look at her wrong, pretty much turn into a toxic, bad person. But she won't do any of that either. You know why? Because she's tougher than you. With your enforcer patch and your deadly glower. She's so much fucking tougher than you. And—"

"Macy, enough."

Both of us turned to stare at Hansen, standing at the door to church. Even I was fucking shocked. Hansen had never spoken to his wife like that, and the motherfucker never interrupted her when she was on a roll like that.

Hansen's expression was grave.

He only looked that way when someone was dead. I tried to get myself to care. A brother? A member from another chapter? Someone I'd drank with? Fucked? Not sure why I even asked myself those questions since my reaction was the same regardless. I was totally fucking apathetic.

I abandoned my drink. "Tell me who I have to kill," I told Hansen without emotion, not bothering to acknowledge Macy. Her words had all hit fucking true. Freya was fucking better than me. Which was why I'd stayed away. I would do nothing but ruin her and that child's lives if I hadn't.

"No, fuck." Hansen ran his hand over his head, eyes flickering to Macy in something that resembled panic. I felt a reaction then. Something deep and carnal. "It's Freya."

———

"You tell me what the fuck you have right now, or I won't be responsible for my actions," I seethed in Hansen's face.

We were in church. He hadn't told me jack shit since her name had come out of his mouth in that flat fucking way that had terrified me.

We were in church, with a full table. "Careful, brother. That's your president," Jagger bit out. He was right up against me. I knew his hand was on his gun. Swiss was on my other side. His hand was also on his gun. All my other brothers were preparing to take me down if need be. They'd correctly pegged me as a man apart. In fucking pieces. The patch on my back was nothing but decoration at this moment.

"Stand down," Hansen commanded. He wasn't talking to me.

After a loaded pause, both Jagger and Swiss retreated. The air was still tense.

Hansen kept his eyes on me. "Her aunt reported her missing about an hour ago. Wire has been keeping tabs, so he picked it up quick"

My heart stilled.

"Missing?" I repeated.

Hansen nodded gravely. "Waitin' on Wire to get back to me, but that's all I know right now."

"All you know?" I repeated again, my voice still, cold.

Swiss moved closer to me, correctly clocking that I was seconds away from losing it.

"Okay, if that's all you know, let me get you caught up on some shit," I spat.

"She loves disaster movies," I gritted out, pacing, unable to be still. "The cornier the better. The more destruction the better. She's seen most of them at least three times but still sobs her heart out at the ending. Every damn time." I kept pacing because if I stood still, if I stopped, the weight of my memories would settle too heavily. I would not be able to stand under the weight of them. I would have to kill someone. "She loves sugar. Fucking loves it. She's a vegan who eats cheeseburgers once a month because she can't deprive herself. She bakes when she's nervous. People meet her and worship at her feet because they feel compelled to, like they have no other choice."

Everyone in the room was staring at me. I didn't give a fuck. I couldn't stop. If I stopped, someone was dead.

"One of her best friends is a sixty-eight-year-old man. She met him at the grocery store, saw that he was sad and lonely in a way that most people don't notice. Or people who pretend they don't notice, not giving enough fucks to do anything about it. But she did. She did what no one else would do, she did something about it. She invited him to her home for dinner. Not once out of pity. She brought that man back to fucking life. Because that's who she is. *And she's carrying my fucking kid!*"

The last part I roared because it was tearing me apart.

No one spoke. No one dared touch me. No one dared fucking breathe.

I had no idea what I would've done if Hansen's phone hadn't rung when it did. Not taking his eyes off me, Hansen turned it on speakerphone. "You've got the full table, brother, and you better have some fuckin' news."

"I've got the footage from the grocery store parking lot," Wire's voice announced, the tapping of keys also coming through. "She was either lucky or smart enough to park in full view of the cameras which were recently updated, so the picture is clear." He cleared his throat. "The man who took her was either stupid or cocky 'cause he also parked in full view of the camera."

I clenched my fists against the table, forcing myself to remain still even after hearing 'the man who took her.' The man who took my woman and my unborn fucking child. The man who was not long for this world.

"Got his plate number then hacked into the computer system of his vehicle and tracked him to a place in the mountains owned by a man named Conrad Ashton," Wire added.

"Fuck," I hissed.

Everyone recognized the last name.

"The father?" Hansen guessed.

"Yeah, the father of that rich scumbag we took care of months ago. One who isn't as stupid as we thought," Wire grumbled.

"The father who is fucking about to be *dead*," I seethed.

Swiss banged his knife on the table in agreement.

"We know anyone with a plane?" Hansen asked the table. The

location was about a six-hour drive, and a lot could happen in six hours.

My skin crawled.

A lot could happen in six fucking minutes.

"Rosie will know someone," Wire offered.

Hansen nodded once, not even questioning him. No one questioned Rosie's ability to get a private plane on the closest airstrip within an hour.

"We just need a pilot," Hansen added.

"I can do it."

Everyone at the table looked at Swiss.

He shrugged. "Had some time on my hands, figured learning how to fly would come in handy. And it has."

After a beat of silence, Hansen nodded. "Yeah, it's come in handy. But you better fuckin' know what you're doin'. I don't plan on dying in a plane crash."

Swiss looked offended. "I don't plan on dying in a plane crash either. I've got a pussy appointment in two days that I've been looking forward to for *months*." His eyes flickered to mine, instantly sobering. "And no fuckin' way would *I* do that to Freya."

That was the closest anyone had come to an accusation. To laying the blame for this shit at my feet. And he knew I couldn't do shit about it because he was the pilot. He was the only way I'd get to Freya before some shit happened that we could never come back from.

If it hadn't already happened.

FREYA

The man wasn't rough with me when he got me out of the car. Just a hand on my upper arm, firm but not painful. He kept glancing to the swell of my stomach. He was obviously uncomfortable with it.

"You don't have to do this," I told him as he walked us through the high-ceilinged rooms of the mansion. It smelled like expensive candles and cleaning products. There was a fire roaring in a great room, and it certainly looked impressive, but the entire house was freezing cold.

The man walking me hadn't responded. He also had not taken me back to the car then drove me back to the grocery store parking lot, so I'd figured he didn't feel overly bad about kidnapping a pregnant woman.

I'd been wracking my brain as to who would be kidnapping me in the middle of the week, in the middle of my quiet, peaceful little town. The town I'd only been in for just over a month. I hadn't run into any kind of trouble there. Which meant it was trouble linked to what I'd left behind. Or at least thought I'd left behind.

The first and most obvious choice was trouble in the form of a man. In the form of a man wearing a cut who still owned my wretched, broken heart.

It hurt to even think about him, even here, in my captor's home. Or lair. Although I could be wrong, I got the feeling that these were not the kind of people the Sons of Templar did business with. Which left me stumped as to who, or what, I could be connected to.

Until I walked into the study.

"Mr. Ashton," I gasped, stopping in place.

Derek's father looked just like him. He was handsome with only a peppering of gray in his hair and subtle creases to his face that did not betray his age. Men did tend to age better than women because the universe was cruel, but I'd always suspected he got Botox. It wasn't obvious, especially when he was standing next to his wife who was a poster girl for plastic surgery.

He hadn't looked at me, his focus on the man no longer holding my arm. "That'll be all, Sanderson" he dismissed him. Like the man had brought him his dry cleaning instead of the pregnant ex-girlfriend of his now dead son.

I wondered if he knew his son was dead. Maybe, since he'd had me dragged here.

He had been standing behind his fancy, rich guy, oak desk that was meticulously clean and organized, just like the rest of this house. Like the other one in Texas that I'd visited for a dinner party. The kind where you were afraid to breathe for fear of spilling or messing something up. There was no 'welcome to our home', it was more, 'we're rich, and if you break anything, we'll sue you until you're bankrupt.'

My hand protectively cradled my stomach as he rounded the desk, undoing the buttons on his Stuart Hughes suit. I'd seen him on a handful of occasions, and he'd never worn anything else. Never a hair out of place. The same was true now while committing a federal crime.

His lips curled into a sneer when his eyes landed on my belly. It was a look so ugly that it made me take a step back. I'd never been scared of this man before. Intimidated, yes. Scared, no.

But in that moment, I was scared.

"Is that my son's bastard?"

I flinched. Then I remembered the way he'd looked down on me every time Derek had brought me home. Every time he'd talked down to me. How clear he'd made it that he thought I was trash. The only true trash were people who thought they had the right to judge others because they were a little bit different than them.

As he stepped toward me, I lifted my chin in defiance and steeled myself against his approach, refusing to take a step back. Luckily, he didn't come any closer than a few feet. as if he thought trailer trash was contagious.

"Your son hasn't done anything to me that would result in a child in years," I sneered. "Thank God."

My words did nothing to brighten his disposition. "You always were a stupid slut," he scoffed, his eyes full of derision. "I bet you have no idea who the father is."

"Ah, calling the stripper a slut. Very original. I thought you were supposed to be some intelligent, rich guy," I replied, putting my hand on my hip.

"You're trash," he snapped.

"And you're a narcissistic, entitled, misogynistic asshole," I replied sweetly.

I hadn't expected the backhand because as much of an asshole as he was, I hadn't thought he was a violent one. Then again, he was a very small man who thought that hitting women—pregnant women at that—made him bigger, more important.

He hadn't hit me hard enough to make me fall to the ground. He'd done it to demean me. It hadn't been a soft hit, though, so my cheek burned as I straightened, one hand on my stomach, the other on my face.

"Like father like son," I tsked, voice low and stable. He would not hear the fear in my voice. I felt like that would've made my situation even more precarious.

His eyes darkened at the mention of Derek. "Well, a woman like you deserves to be taught a lesson."

"A woman *never* deserves to be hit," I rebuked. "Never. It's men like you who really deserve to be hit. But I'm not petty or insecure enough to do that." That was a lie. I would've clawed his face off right then if I'd thought I could manage it. If doing so wouldn't have put my baby in danger.

"Derek is missing," he gritted out, folding his arms in front of him. Obviously, he'd decided not to continue with our back and forth. Hopefully we were also done with the violence portion of the evening.

Once Hades had told me the truth about what happened to Derek, I'd combed through the articles covering his disappearance. His family had offered rewards of all kinds. But there hadn't been any evidence. He'd just vanished. Without a trace. The Sons of Templar did not leave traces. No matter how much money he spent, he would never find anything, I knew that. He must've known that too because he'd had me dragged all the way up here, thinking he'd get answers.

I was not a good liar. Not in the slightest. This was not a good man, but I would hazard a guess that he was an experienced liar and that he knew how to spot one.

But my life, my *baby's life,* might depend on me being believable, so I was going to lie my fucking ass off.

"I saw that online," I replied truthfully.

"You're not surprised?"

I raised a brow at him. "Your son was an entitled asshole who thought that his name would get him everywhere, that he was untouchable and that he could treat people however he wanted. Including beating up women who told him no. So no, I'm not at all surprised."

His face turned hard, eyes full of contempt and hatred. I didn't know whether that meant he believed me or not.

"Tell me where my son is," he demanded, obviously not believing me.

"I have no idea where your son is," I said honestly. "We broke up, remember? You probably had some kind of party to celebrate."

A frown crumpled his brows. "You broke something in him. Made him weak. Pitiful. I know he followed you around. I know he followed you to New Mexico."

I pursed my lips. Derek's family had money, a lot of it. Not enough to make the police cross state lines and look for someone who was not of this world anymore, but enough to pay someone to do that.

"He did," I agreed. "He followed me there, then he beat me almost to death when I told him I wanted nothing to do with him. Stellar job you did raising him, by the way. After that, I never saw him again. And I for one could not be happier about that."

Again, none of that was a lie.

Conrad was silent for a long time, glaring at me. I glared right back.

"You had something to do with this, I know it," he eventually sneered.

"I had nothing to do with this," I shot back.

"You're not leaving this house until you tell me where my son is," he warned me, his voice even now. Almost reasonable. Or it would have been if what he'd said wasn't absolutely insane.

"I am definitely leaving. Now." As much as I wanted to turn around and walk out the door, I was not stupid enough to turn my back on a man like him. You didn't turn your back on a predator, did you?

"I'm afraid not. The men in my employ have been instructed to use any and all force necessary to convince you that staying is in your," his eyes flickered down to my stomach, "and your child's best interests."

It was a physical feat to keep the very large breakfast I'd eaten down. My morning sickness had all but disappeared, so I'd been making the most of it. As much as I would've relished ruining something of his, I was not going to vomit all over his no doubt expensive rug. He would not get that satisfaction.

"You own a chain of banks," I recalled with a frown. "You're not some kind of mob boss. You cannot have 'guys' willing to use excessive force on a pregnant woman." I spoke with a lot more bravado than I felt.

He stepped forward, and it took every cell in my body not to flinch back. I almost gagged at his expensive aftershave. He wore the same one as Derek.

His eyes were the same blue as Derek's too.

"I couldn't expect someone like you to understand this, but enough money can buy you any kind of man willing to do anything." He grinned, sending chills up and down my spine. "And, honey, your life is worth less than my watch."

For a horrible moment, I thought he was going to touch me. Or hit me again. Maybe do something worse than that. My bravado failed. Just a little, but he saw it. I knew because his grin stretched wider until he wore a satisfied smile.

He stepped back, having achieved what he'd intended. He'd wanted to scare me. To remind me that he was in control of everything here, that he'd taken away all of my power and agency.

"Martin will show you to your room," he stated, moving around me to open the door. "You'll have food brought up to you. And we'll speak when you're rested and hopefully a little clearer-headed."

CHAPTER NINETEEN

My room was nice.

For a cell.

Martin held onto my arm the entire walk, squeezing it so hard, I let out a little whimper. He'd liked that, so he squeezed it harder.

I didn't fight him because I'd suspected he'd like that too. I was actually relieved when he shoved me into the room, and I heard the click of the lock behind me. I tried my best not to think about the fact that he had the key and could unlock it any time he saw fit.

Of course I tried the windows, even though I was on the second story and there was nothing below but polished concrete. The windows were locked. There was no phone in the room. Nothing I could effectively use as a weapon.

There was a bathroom complete with a claw-footed tub, walk-in shower and a large four-poster bed. One that I was never going to be able to sleep in, no matter how long they left me in here. I had to keep my wits about me.

I woke with a start.

The kind of way you saw people wake up in movies that seemed ridiculously dramatic and unrealistic. Where they sat up with an audible gasp, hand at their throat.

Yeah, I woke like that.

I woke up in a bed in a house where I was being held hostage by my dead ex-boyfriend's crazy, violent father. While almost five months pregnant. No one knew where I was, no one was going to be able to find me.

Save me.

I could very well die here. My hand went to my stomach. *We* could very well die here.

Yes, those were some pretty good fucking reasons to wake with a start. I chastised myself for falling asleep in the first place. I really had underestimated how tired I would get, especially after eating the large—and surprisingly delicious—meal that was delivered to me after the sun went down. Thankfully, it hadn't been Martin who'd delivered it. Nor was it my driver, Sanderson. It had been someone else entirely, a man who wouldn't meet my eyes.

"Yeah, I would be pretty ashamed of myself too," I snarled, imprinting his face into my memory, taking in every detail like I had with the other two. It was a very hopeful thing to do, something that was riding on a long shot. A really fucking long shot. I wanted to be able to describe every single detail of their faces if I escaped. If I needed to identify them in a lineup.

Or describe them to a very angry, possessive, deadly biker.

Like I said, a long shot.

I'd figured that the food wasn't poisoned. What would be the point in bringing me all the way out here if they were going to poison the food? Plus, I was pregnant and starving and needed my strength.

I'd been dying for a shower, to scrub the touch of foreign men off my skin, but I hadn't wanted to be that vulnerable. Hadn't wanted Martin to walk by, possibly hearing the water running then getting ideas. So I settled for splashing water on my face, frowning at the angry red mark high on my cheek. Another Ashton man who had left a bruise on my face.

Then I got bored. It was kind of insane to get bored when you were a kidnapping victim, but they hadn't left any reading material around. I didn't have a phone to scroll through, no TV to watch. Again, I was pregnant, so I was exhausted all the time. In my life, before this happened, I took two-hour naps daily. There had been no nap today—or I guessed that was yesterday, squinting at the pitch black beyond the windows. There was no clock in here, but something told me it was around three. The night felt thick, heavy, foreboding.

My skin crawled with something.

It wasn't just the unfamiliar bed, the unfamiliar sheets, or the overall situation. Something had woken me up. I threw the blankets off me and leapt out of bed, holding my stomach protectively.

The floorboards creaked as I tiptoed around the room, the sound puncturing the thick quiet. I froze when I heard it. A loud thump. Like a body hitting the floor. Even though I'd held my breath to listen better, my heart drowned out whatever sounds there might've been.

A footstep. I was certain I'd heard a footstep. Was that the low thump of motorcycle boots across Persian rugs? That was insane. It was close to impossible that he knew I was here. That he even knew I was missing in the first place.

But still, I hoped.

The chances of it being him were slim, which meant I was standing frozen and defenseless in the middle of the room while the footsteps got louder. They had definitely gotten louder. And they were coming my way.

Fuck.

I darted to the door at the last second, standing so that when it opened, I would be hidden. There wasn't much purpose behind this, considering I wasn't holding a weapon of any kind. But there was a chance I could quietly dart out the door while the person was walking farther into the room, looking for me. Or did that only happen in the movies?

My heart was a roar as the click of the lock echoed through the room, the jangle of the handle rattling my insides. The door opened with a squeak, and my body tensed even more. There it was. The thump. Of heavy footwear. Familiar footwear. But I couldn't gamble my life and my child's life on my talent for recognizing shoes by their thump. The door opened wider, and the wood got closer to me, masking me from whoever was entering. The air moved a little, and I inhaled. Musk. Cigarettes. Leather. *Him.*

I was frozen in place as the scents entered my nostrils. My sense of smell had rivaled a superhero's lately, which had not been a good thing until this very moment. Until I smelled something that did not make my stomach roil.

Hades.

I still didn't move from my spot behind the door. My mind could be playing tricks on me. The trauma could've caused a break in reality. Or I could be smelling what I wanted to smell, hearing what I wished to hear. Maybe it was really Martin coming to do what his eyes had promised earlier.

So I waited. For him to speak. For something else to confirm it was him. But he didn't speak as he stepped farther into the room, and there wasn't any light to make him anything other than a large, black shape.

I tasted blood as my teeth sank into my lip, desperate to call out to him.

There was a swish of blankets as he searched the bed. Then there were other thumps from farther down the hallway. I heard heavy items, or possibly bodies, hitting the floor. A whisper that sounded familiar. One that gave my heart a little more hope.

My attention shifted back to the shape in the room as he

moved to the bathroom. I prayed that he would turn on the light, illuminating the room just enough for me to see him.

But he kept skulking in the dark, barely making a sound.

More thumps sounded, coming from the hallway. Then coming through the door. I held my breath.

"You get her?"

My entire body sagged at the voice. But I still couldn't make myself move.

"She's not fuckin' here."

I almost collapsed at the sound of that voice. *The* voice. *His* voice.

"Well, how do you think you're gonna see her stumbling around in the dark?" Swiss scoffed. "You think you're fuckin' Batman or something."

I squinted as light flooded the room, momentarily blinding me.

"She's not fuckin' here."

He was angry. Furious. Terrified. Spectacular.

"I'm here," I whispered. My voice was scratchy and raw. It was almost nonexistent. My limbs were lead as I stepped out from behind the door.

Hades and Swiss were standing in the middle of the room, both of them staring at me. Swiss was grinning. Hades was not. When his eyes zeroed in on my stomach, they flared slightly, his only visible reaction. Then his gaze moved upward to my face. Then there was a reaction.

He stormed forward with such force that I reflexively slammed myself flat against the wall behind me.

Hades stood as close as he could without actually touching me.

"Who hit you?"

The words were ground out. Torn out from somewhere deep within him.

"Who fucking *hit you*, Freya?" He asked louder now. Almost a shout, but something more guttural than that.

My skin prickled, and I shivered visibly.

Swiss stepped forward, eyes fixed on me, filled with concern, full of rage. But there was also something softer.

There was nothing soft in Hades's eyes.

"Brother, you wanna get your shit together? Freya—"

"Freya has been *hit in the face*," Hades seethed, interrupting Swiss but not looking at him. He wouldn't take his eyes off me. I'd been craving his stare for the longest time, but now I wasn't sure I could continue to breathe under it.

"Someone hit my woman." He was even louder now. "I won't get shit together. And if you don't step the fuck back, I won't be responsible for what I do to you."

Swiss's expression turned steely, dangerous. I feared that there was going to be some altercation between the two of them, with me just standing there like a fucking scarecrow.

Unlike me, Swiss had full use of his limbs and stepped back. Not all the way back, though. He hung there, poised, taut, ready to do something, to jump in. As if Hades was going to do something to me.

I didn't know a lot right in that moment. In fact, it seemed like my head was a big, white, vacant space full of nothingness. But there was one thing I was absolutely certain about, which was that Hades would never lay a hand on me. I had nothing to be afraid of. Conrad, on the other hand, had a whole fucking lot to be afraid of.

"Freya," Hades warned.

"It was, Conrad," I said, my voice a breath above a whisper. "He slapped me."

I'd sentenced him then. Not to death, no. He was already dead the moment he'd made the decision to do this to me. I had sentenced him to something else entirely. I had sentenced him to *Hades*.

"They..." Hades trailed off and sucked in an audible breath. "Did they do anything else to you?" The words dripped ice, as though that was the only way he could speak them.

Anything else. Rape.

"No," I reassured him quickly. "No one did anything else."

"Need the names of everyone who touched you," he demanded, recovering quickly. But I saw the relief that washed over him, the slight softening of his jaw.

"No one else hit me," I told him.

His hands were fists at his sides. "But other men touched you."

I frowned. "Yeah, they just ... squeezed my arm."

Fuck, wrong thing to say.

Hades's eyes zeroed in on my biceps. Then they blazed. I looked down at the reddish purplish fingerprints on my upper arms.

"Martin," I whispered. Then I hesitated, thinking of Sanderson, how uncomfortable he'd been with this. "Sanderson."

He'd been uncomfortable, but he'd still done it. He'd damned himself. I could've saved him, maybe. Maybe not.

"Find them. Ashton first. Bring him to me," Hades spoke to Swiss but still looked at me. "Find Anderson, tell him to get Freya the fuck out of here."

"No," I jumped in, much louder than a whisper now.

Hades stared at me. Just stared. He hadn't needed to say a word. His eyes told me that this was not up for discussion. I figured he'd been doing that a lot lately. Staring at people with eyes full of menace, threatening people without speaking. It worked on everyone else because I knew he wouldn't hesitate to hurt anyone else. But not me. I straightened ever so slightly, his eyes panning down to my stomach as I did.

I swallowed at something I thought I might've ... maybe had seen there. But it was too fleeting to catch, his eyes quickly returning back to mine, full of that cold menace.

"I'm not going anywhere," I proclaimed.

"Yes, you fuckin' are," Hades refuted. "What I've got in mind is going to take a long time."

I crossed my arms. "Then I'll wait."

"Like fuck you will. I want you checked out by a doctor as soon as fucking possible."

I wasn't going to argue about the doctor. I knew that I wouldn't win that. "Well, then you better rethink how long you're going to take with Conrad," I challenged.

Swiss was no longer glowering behind Hades. He was smirking.

Hades was nowhere near smirking. He was furious. At me for deigning to argue with him. And at himself, because he was carrying the blame for letting another man lay his hands on me.

I was pretty furious too. At myself for letting him push me away, for running. At him for pushing me away in the first place, for not chasing after me. I was also determined. No way was I leaving the room I was sharing with Hades after spending months apart.

"You will have to get Anderson to drag me out kicking and screaming if you want me to leave," I advised.

A muscle in Hades's jaw twitched. He was pissed. Beyond pissed.

He took one more look at me, in my eyes, not my stomach, then he stormed out of the room.

Swiss wasn't smirking anymore. He had a full-blown smile. "Oh, darlin', have I missed you."

Although it was shaky, I did my best to smile back. "Right back at you."

———

I didn't hear any screaming. I didn't know why I'd expected to. This was a fucking big house, and Swiss had urged me out of the bedroom to a ginormous room with insanely priced rugs and a floor-to-ceiling fireplace. He shielded me from the blood, the bodies, but I still knew what was happening so it was like I witnessed it all anyway, my imagination running wild. I'd blinked at it all, emotionless. In shock, surely.

The whole club was there—Hansen, Jagger, Elden, Anderson, various prospects and a couple of patches I didn't recognize. Their cuts read 'Colorado', which made sense. The men stared at me and the red mark on my face with varying degrees of fury. It was comforting, their anger insulating me from the reality of it all.

Swiss sat me in front of the fire then disappeared, presumably to help with the torture. No one touched me. I'd figured that had something to do with Hades going around torturing all of the people in this house who had touched me.

Someone brought me water. I sipped it thoughtlessly, staring at the flames, waiting.

Then Hades was there, kneeling in between my legs, his hands on my bare thighs. They were covered in blood. It was the first time he'd touched me in months, wearing the blood of the men who'd hurt me.

I didn't know if that was him apologizing or trying to scare me away. I didn't care. Hades was touching me. My body could relax, finally. I could breathe again. My hand covered his without hesitation, the other reaching up to cradle his jaw. His entire body was granite, but he didn't flinch away from my touch.

"Will you take me home?" I whispered.

His eyes stayed locked on mine. I hadn't needed to say that I didn't mean the house full of boxes in Falcon Springs. I said *home*. I'd only ever had one of those. We'd only had one of those.

———

As much as I'd wanted to go back to New Mexico tonight, logistically, it didn't work. Hades wanted me to see a doctor, and the Colorado charter had already arranged for me to see theirs which happened to be less than an hour from Falcon Springs.

Then there was Aunt V who had been expecting me to come back with groceries hours ago. Who would've been worried sick. And Sirius.

Home had to wait.

The club doctor in Colorado checked me over then said I seemed healthy, the baby too. He advised that we do a sonogram to be sure, but I knew that the baby was fine. I'd do it for Hades, who had been quiet and brooding during the entire drive. As much as I had wanted to, I couldn't ride on the back of his bike. So he'd driven a fancy SUV, just the two of us. We didn't say anything the entire drive. His hand remained on my thigh the entire drive, though. The sun was shining by the time we pulled up to the small house Aunt V and I had been occupying. There was no police car, so I guessed the Sons had taken care of that like they took care of everything.

Aunt V and Sirius met us at the door, Aunt V crying and hugging both of us. Sirius pressed heavily into my leg, looking up at Hades with accusation.

Aunt V had forgiven Hades for whatever pain he'd caused me the second he brought me back. She hadn't said so in words, but if she hadn't forgiven him, there would've been a lot of words. We sat with her, letting her lead the conversation while she cooked us breakfast. I was so tired I could've fallen over, but I knew that Aunt V needed this, so I leaned heavily against Hades as I ate. He ate one-handed, palm still resting on my thigh as if it was glued there. Eventually, Aunt V saw through the grief and worry, registering my exhaustion, the thick tension between Hades and me. She ushered us into my bedroom, telling us she had a gym class to get to and wouldn't be back for hours.

Hades closed the door quietly, with a gentleness I hadn't seen from him the entire night. There was still blood on his knuckles. He didn't turn to face me straight away, keeping his back to me as if he couldn't handle looking at me. As if he couldn't face me.

I was grateful for it. For his back. For a moment to contemplate the familiar cut and try to regain some courage. He hadn't given me enough time, though. I still didn't have enough courage, enough oxygen.

Hades didn't look familiar. There was something different about his face. Something about the way he held himself as he just stood there, almost plastered to the door, staring at me.

He didn't have enough courage either. Hades was scared.

Hades.

Something about that made it all melt away. The months. The pain. The details of it all. I crossed the distance between us quickly, then without hesitating, I threw my arms around his neck and pressed my body to his. My body relaxed as I drowned in his scent, as his warmth seeped into my bones.

He didn't hesitate either, his arms encircling me the second I touched him. It was a relief to know that despite everything we didn't have right now, despite everything we had to figure out, we still had this.

We stood there for a long time, hugging. It was strange. I didn't think I'd simply hugged Hades ... ever. Not without his hand in my hair or his lips on my neck. It felt like the most intimate thing we'd ever done, despite all of the very intimate things he'd done to me.

Eventually, it had to end. There was a small swell to my belly that was pressing into his flat abs. Small but it took up the entire room. It filled up all of the cracks we had inside of us.

Hades put his hands on my shoulders, pushing me back gently. Even more gently than he had closed the door.

My breath emptied from my lungs as his eyes locked on mine, as I searched the angles and the ridges of his face, tracing his full lips with my eyes. His lips didn't part, he didn't speak. Instead, he moved a hand from my shoulder and placed it down on my belly. His hand spanned the entire bump, covering our baby with his bloodstained palm.

We both froze as a very small and very determined foot kicked against his palm.

I'd never seen Hades open his eyes so wide, never seen his expression change so dramatically. I'd never seen them filled with marvel.

"Was that?" his voice was croaky, rough, full of holes.

It was the first time I'd heard him speak words that weren't reinforced with iron.

"The baby," I whispered. "That was the first time she's done that."

His hand twitched on my shoulder, the only movement in his entire body.

"She?" His words were even more ragged this time.

I nodded. "I found out three weeks ago."

"A girl," he breathed.

"Our girl," I corrected, my heart beating in my throat.

"Our girl," he repeated.

Then, I saw something I'd never thought I'd see in my life.

A tear ran down the porcelain cheek of the man I loved. A tear for our daughter. For us. A tear that said everything that I knew he couldn't say.

———

I fell asleep naked in his arms that night.

We'd showered together, the tiny shower stall barely holding us, but that was fine since neither of us wanted any distance of any sort. Blood ran quickly down the drain then disappeared. Hades soaped up and washed every inch of me. He must've spent three times as long on my belly as he did anywhere else. He was fascinated with it, captivated by the small bump.

We stayed in there until the water ran cold, then Hades got me out, wrapped me in a towel and dried me like I was a child. We both fell into the bed.

We didn't have sex; we just fell asleep holding each other.

I woke up to his lips at my neck, his fingers parting my legs. Still half asleep, I opened for him, completely.

My body writhed when his fingers entered me. I let out a moan of pleasure, my eyes fluttering open. Hades was there, right above me, staring at me.

"Hades," I whispered. It was a moan. It was a plea.

"I know, baby," he murmured, adding another finger, coating himself with me, coaxing my climax forward.

"I need you to fuck me," I begged.

His eyes flared. "I need to watch you, Freya. Just for a little while longer." He kept his fingers moving, the cords in his neck tight with restraint. With need.

Just when I was about to explode around him, his fingers left me. He moved quickly, sensing my desperation, meeting it with his own.

He hovered above me, his torso brushing against my bump. I was glad that had not freaked him out, his cock pressed against my pussy.

"Seeing you growing my baby," he rasped. "Fuck." He let out a growl from the back of his throat. "Never seen anything more fucking beautiful in my life. Mine," he murmured against my lips as he surged inside me.

My nails raked down his back as he filled me up, replenishing all the empty fucking spaces.

I reached up to hold his face in my hands, to still him. Our eyes were locked. "Don't you ever fucking walk away from me again," I whispered.

His eyes burned as his hard cock flexed inside of me. "Never."

His words were an oath.

CHAPTER TWENTY

"What the fuck are you doin', carryin' that?" a voice boomed.

Two seconds after the boom—two seconds exactly—a very large and very pissed off biker snatched the box from me and glared. "What the fuck, Freya?"

I rolled my eyes. "Hades, that box is full of nothing but lingerie. You could literally hold that with your pinky finger."

I didn't know why I was even bothering.

"I don't give a fuck," he snapped. "You are not to carry a single box, or I swear to fuck I'll put you over my knee."

My stomach dipped delightfully, my body pulsing with need. Pregnancy hormones and Hades made it impossible to think of much else other than sex. I did my best to distract myself with unpacking, decorating the nursery, catching up with everyone and starting a new series on YouTube about pregnancy.

It was obvious I couldn't go back to work for Kallum. Or stripping in general. I hadn't technically needed the money for a couple of years anyway, but I'd made it while I could, saving it for a rainy day. Or a market crash. Or whatever.

My income from day trading and the channel was more than

enough. Plenty, in fact. Enough money for ten years of mortgage payments was stored in a high yield bank account.

So I was sorted.

We were sorted.

It meant something to me, to be able to do that. To give us a home. Our family.

It meant something to Hades too.

Some of the boxes we were moving belonged to Hades. To be fair, about three percent of them were his, considering all he valued was his cut, his motorcycle and a wardrobe full of black.

"What am I supposed to do while you unpack boxes?" I whined, feeling almost petty enough to stomp my foot. "Stay in the kitchen, barefoot and pregnant?"

His eyes twinkled. "I wouldn't object to that."

"Nuh uh," I scoffed. "I'm not giving up everything to be a stay-at-home mom. This is the twenty-first century, I can do both. I'll be raising our child and bringing home the bacon."

Something flashed in Hades's eyes. Something that said he was not amused by my teasing. "We will both be raisin' this baby." His palm was on my stomach. "And I am taking care of the other shit now."

Though I was pretty sure I knew what he meant, I really hoped I was wrong. "What shit?" I asked slowly.

"I'm takin' care of the mortgage. Household expenses"

I was not wrong. "What?"

A crinkle formed between Hades's brows. "Sold my house, Freya. Didn't make a ton, but I made decent coin. Lived my life pretty fuckin' simple, which means I do have a ton saved. Enough to pay off the mortgage. Add some more rooms."

Although I was pretty pissed, I just stared at him. "Add on more rooms?" .

Hades nodded, putting his hands on my belly. "Thought you wanted to fill this place with kids. It's plenty big, but I know you won't give up your filming room. Don't want you to. Also know that with more kids and your shopping habits, there's gonna be a lot more shit in this house. It's plenty big now, but not once we're finished... Kids can share when they're young, but it's good for them to have their own space when they get older."

I continued to stare at Hades. No, it was safe to say I was gaping. "You went from no kids to multiple kids in the space of *six months?*"

"I went from having a wasteland to a fuckin' world, Freya," he corrected.

My heart did a flip. "You're making it really hard to be mad at you," I snapped.

His eyes kept fucking twinkling. "Be mad all you like, Freya, it's happenin'."

My eyes narrowed. "Just because you grunt 'it's happenin' ' without using the letter g doesn't mean your word turns into law."

"I think it can," he argued.

Now I was pissed. I stepped away so he wasn't touching me anymore. I couldn't think with him touching me.

"Hades, I've worked my entire fucking life to be able to take care of myself," I huffed. "I've worked hard. You can't just take all of that away from me because you're an alpha male who needs to feel manly by paying for everything."

"Fuck," he muttered as he thrust a hand through his hair. "I don't want to take shit away from you, Freya. What you've done, what you've built ... it's fucking magnificent." His eyes went around the house, our house, which was almost completely unpacked. "I've built nothing in my life except a pile of fuckin' bodies. Me taking care of you isn't about feeling like a man, or fuck, maybe part of it is. Most of it is me meeting the reaper, knowin' that I helped build something magnificent."

Tears filled my eyes as he stepped forward again, pulling me to him until our bodies met. The process was rather different now with my growing belly, but it worked. No complaints here.

"Now, let me fuck you so you're not mad at me," he murmured.

And he did just that.

I wasn't mad at him anymore.

He also took over the mortgage.

I'd caught up with everyone in town and had re-established my weekly dates with Des, which Hades came to sporadically. He wasn't allowed to attend every single time since Des said he 'fucked with his mojo and killed his game.' There was one person who had been scarce since I came back into town. Someone who finally turned up at our door over a month after we moved back. We'd had a welcome home party which he'd been invited to but hadn't attended. I didn't know if it was because the entire club was there, or if he was just being petty.

I was too happy to see him. He was sitting at the breakfast bar, coffee and a plate of cookies in front of him. I'd already eaten five of my own. We had been chatting about nothing and everything. Natasha was doing well at the club. His mom. His sisters. Everything except the elephant in the room.

Kallum's eyes went up and down my body, pausing at my belly. "You're happy."

It wasn't a question, but I answered anyway, cradling my stomach. "Yeah, I really, really am."

He sighed, long and heavy. "That makes it that much harder to hate him." He nodded to where Hades was speaking on the phone outside. He hung out there a lot, even though he'd given up smoking. At that moment, I knew he was out there because Kallum was in here.

"Come on, you can't hate the father of my child," I teased.

Kallum's jaw tightened, and he rubbed the back of his neck. "I can't," he agreed.

"Why do you hate them so much?" I asked. "The Sons?"

It was the question that had been on my mind for a long time, one that felt much heavier since I'd met Hades.

He shrugged. "Fuck, Freya, I don't know. I guess because they remind me of the gang I used to run with, all the shit I got tangled up in. Fuck, they remind me of what I wanted from that. A brotherhood, yet all I got was a fuck-load of blood and death." He paused, looking into his coffee like he'd find the answers there. "I still don't know whether they're really that much different. There's gonna be blood and death in your future, being involved with them, Freya, and I fucking hate that."

"Maybe," I agreed, thinking of everything that Hades had told me the night I found out my father died. "But I'm going to have a family. One that loves fiercely. Who fight for each other. We both know I never would've been able to have a normal, white picket fence life."

Kallum chuckled. "No, you'd be bored shitless."

I examined Kallum then. The lines at the corners of his eyes seemed to have deepened since the last time I saw him, only making him more handsome.

"What about you?" I asked. "Where's your happiness?"

He contemplated that for a long time, but he never answered me.

Because my happiness walked in from outside, nodding to Kallum once before wrapping his arms around me.

Kallum downed his coffee, gave me a peck on the cheek in goodbye, grabbed a handful of cookies then all but ran out the door.

"He doesn't like me," Hades commented, nuzzling my neck.

I relaxed into him. "He doesn't know you. Once he does, he'll love you."

"No, babe. No one loves me once they get to know me. Only you."

I smiled up at him. "Because I'm the only one you show the real you to."

His eyes glittered. "Plan on you being the only one for the rest of my life, Freya."

My entire body thrummed, and our daughter kicked his hand. "We're happy with that," I whispered.

And I was. Happy. Home. Barefoot and pregnant in the kitchen. Not long after, my biker and I were both naked in that kitchen.

CHAPTER TWENTY-ONE

Evangeline 'Eva' Cooke came into the world with drama, pain and a heck of a lot of blood loss.

Cooke, that was Hades's last name. I hadn't known that until I saw Eva's birth certificate. I didn't know his first name until then either. Brian. Fucking Brian. "I get why you go by Hades," I teased.

He tried his best to glower at me, but with everything that had happened, he wasn't physically able to glower at me.

It was three weeks before my due date, so labor hadn't even been on my mind. Our OB-GYN had assured us that first-time mothers almost always went past their due date.

Our OB-GYN had obviously never dealt with the fruit of Hades's loins.

My water broke in the Trader Joe's parking lot.

"You've got to be fucking *kidding* me," I hissed at my drenched panties.

Hades, who never let me do anything alone anymore, most especially grocery shopping with all the lifting of the bags and my history of parking lot drama, was at my side in an instant.

"I fucking *knew* those were contractions," he chided.

I glared at him. "Really, you're choosing *now* as an 'I told you so' moment?"

Hades examined my face then realized what a mistake it would be to lord his triumph all over me at this particular moment. I'd been in pain all day, but I'd been convinced that they were Braxton Hicks, especially since Hades and I had done the dramatic run to the hospital two times before that, and I was not going for three. I thought some cookie butter ice cream would serve as a distraction, hence us being at Trader Joe's.

"At least now we get a positive experience in regard to parking lots," I joked as he gathered me into his arms and carried me the ten feet to the car. "Of course, I couldn't possibly walk the rest of the distance," I muttered.

Hades chose to ignore that.

He did not ignore my curses and the contortions of my body as my contractions intensified during drive, though. He counted the time between them, and it was confirmed that he had correctly ascertained that my labor was pretty damn advanced when they sent me straight to the delivery suite upon our arrival.

"This is not how it's supposed to be," I whined in between pushing. "We don't have the oil diffuser, the crystals, the Bluetooth speaker."

Hades arched his brow ever so slightly. "You think I'm leavin' your side to get a fuckin' oil diffuser then you're—"

My turn to raise my brows. "Then I'm *what?*"

He was pretty fucking lucky about Eva's timing, since she chose that exact moment to save her father's ass by making her entrance.

She made an entrance, and I *almost* made an exit.

I didn't remember much from the whole process aside from the pain. There was no fucking way in hell I could forget the pain. Nor could I forget Hades, carved in black against the stark white walls of the hospital room, murmuring in my ear, kissing my head and never letting go of my hand. I could never forget the weight of our daughter on our chest, her warmth.

Then, to be horribly cliché, everything went black.

HADES

It was the best day of my life.

Until it wasn't.

Freya had never been stronger. Her small hand crushing the bones in mine, her beautiful face dewy with sweat, with the effort that it took to bring our little girl into the world.

Our daughter.

Freya had not screamed as she pushed, she muttered curses, she squeezed my hand and she talked about how fucking stupid she was to refuse the drugs. She was Freya. She pushed. She *fought*.

Until the screams of our daughter drowned everything else out.

Her hand went slack in mine. I hadn't noticed at first because I was enraptured by the world that the doctor had placed on Freya's chest. I steadied the little body with my hand, my hand covering her entire body. She was fucking tiny and she was fucking everything.

Freya's eyes were wide in wonder. With love.

Then, as the doctor took the baby to be cleaned, I noticed Freya's hand, limp in mine.

"Freya!" My voice was dull to my own ears, all sharp edges.

"We need to get her into surgery, now," someone yelled. Things moved quickly after that. Freya was surrounded by doctors; they had to get Swiss, Hansen and Jagger in from the waiting room to hold me back as they wheeled her away.

They weren't the ones who had me locking it down. It was the small pink bundle the nurse had finished cleaning.

"Let me go," I demanded.

There was a long moment of hesitation before my brothers let go of me.

I stepped over the blood. *Freya's blood.*

The only thing that kept me from tearing this whole place

apart was her, Eva. She had Freya's eyes. She was my fucking anchor.

EIGHT HOURS LATER

They tried to take her from me, the nurses. *My fucking baby.* They tried to take her out of my arms, spouting shit about feeding her, putting her down to sleep, changing her. I barked at them to get me the fuckin' bottle. She didn't need to be put down to sleep. She slept in my arms. When she needed changing, I changed her. Not one single person touched our baby. The next person who touched her would be Freya.

Had to be.

I'd been sure, fucking certain that I'd never hold a baby in my arms, especially not my own. My resolve was iron-clad. I had been and would've been if I had continued getting in my own fucking way. Freya had given me this, she'd given me fucking her, she'd given me fatherhood. It terrified me and filled me up at the same time.

"She's beautiful."

Swiss sat down beside me. He wasn't technically allowed in here, but the hospital had given up on their rules with the Sons of Templar. My brothers had set up camp in the waiting room as a show of support. I didn't give a fuck. It hadn't meant shit. Freya opening her eyes and holding our daughter ... that was all that mattered.

She'd come out of surgery. Lost a lot of blood, the doctor had said. They couldn't tell me when she'd wake up, and I couldn't shake it out of him because I was holding my daughter.

"Yeah, she is."

I kept my eyes on Freya, my mind focused only on the steady beating, signifying that she was still alive, that my world was still whole.

"I only got to hold mine in my arms once."

That almost had my eyes moving from Freya.

Almost.

No one knew about Swiss's past. All we knew was that his current life was plenty fucked up, so some fucked up shit must've happened,

"My wife, she died at eight months," Swiss continued. His words were fucking daggers. Dripping with blood. His own blood.

That's why I let him place his hand on Eva's beanie-covered head.

"They tried to save the baby," he added, his hand settling on Eva with a barely-there touch. "They didn't. I got to hold her, though. So beautiful. And heavy. Like I was carrying a universe. Walkin' around with empty arms, well, it's a special kind of hell." His hand stayed on Eva's head for a moment longer. "You've got the future in your arms, brother. And in that bed." I saw the jerk of his head in my periphery as he nodded to Freya. "She's gonna wake up."

"I know," I bit out, unable to say a fuckin' word to him about what he'd just told me.

He slapped me on the shoulder then walked out. With empty fucking arms.

I held Eva tighter.

A couple of hours later, Freya woke up.

And I could fucking breathe again. Because I had my world.

FREYA

Hades didn't talk about what happened after Eva's birth. He couldn't.

With tears in her eyes, Macy had told me enough to raise the hairs on the backs of my arms. As did Marilyn when she clutched my hand in a death grip and ordered me to never have another fucking child as long as I lived.

Aunt V hadn't said much, nor had she shed a tear, but she held onto my hand for a very long time when she entered the hospital room.

Hades barely left my side. And the only time he wasn't holding Eva was when I was holding her or nursing her. She didn't even sleep in her crib. Hades was completely and perfectly content with letting our infant daughter sleep in his arms.

My Old Man loved his daughter so much that he couldn't stand the idea of her sleeping without feeling his arms around her. He cradled our daughter with the same hands he'd ended lives with. I didn't care whether it made me completely insane, but that meant so much to me. It meant fucking everything.

For a man who had been so convinced that he was a monster, he was an incredible father. He took care of almost everything while I recovered, despite the numerous hands available to help at all times. Our house was never empty. Aunt V had decided to move to Garnett, purchasing the closest house to ours. One that very conveniently went up for sale the second that Aunt V announced she was moving—about one hour after I was discharged from the hospital.

Marilyn and Jed were around constantly, the fridge full of amazing meals he'd cooked. Macy and Caroline constantly stopped in, and the entire Amber chapter had driven up for the party Macy had insisted we have for the baby, and to celebrate me not dying while having said baby. She'd said that as a joke, but I think the only thing that saved her from Hades's wrath was the fact she was his president's wife and one of my closest friends.

I was utterly spoiled. I knew that the first few months of a new mother's life were usually hell. Full of uncertainty, of sleepless nights, of a crying child. Sure, I was terrified I'd do something wrong and accidentally kill or maim my daughter. And my body had gone through hell. Hormones made it so I cried at the drop of a hat.

But for the most part, it was magical. My atypical sleep schedule meant that things didn't change all that much. It was like

I'd already unwittingly trained myself for a newborn and nightly feedings. Eva herself was a magical baby. She was unexpectedly placid. Sure, she fussed when she was gassy or hungry, but she never screamed. Not once. And if she seemed like she was getting upset, whoever held her just handed her to her ever-present father.

Although I didn't think it was possible, I fell more in love with Hades in the six weeks after Eva was born. He was patient, gentle, unyielding, devoted. To both of us.

The six weeks without sex was fucking torture, though.

Given everything that had happened down there, I'd figured that I wouldn't be interested in anything happening down there for a *long* time.

I'd figured wrong. Very wrong.

Hades, interestingly, was very adamant about the rules the doctors had communicated.

"Baby, that's one of my favorite areas on your body, so I'm not going in there until cleared by a medical professional," he'd murmured when I'd tried to seduce him one particularly frustrating evening. Right after he'd burped Eva. Shirtless.

No woman could resist that. Not even a woman recovering from a particularly traumatic birth.

"I thought you were an outlaw, that you didn't let any kind of professional tell you what to do," I'd griped in frustration.

His lips turned up, gifting me with one of his rare smiles. "When it comes to your cunt, Freya, I'm following the rules." He'd moved closer to kiss me. "Once we're clear, I'll bury myself in that cunt for weeks. Don't you worry about that."

Frustrated, I'd placed my palm against his chest and pushed him down on the bed. "Fine, if I can't get off, then I'm getting you off."

Hades had not argued about that.

EPILOGUE

Macy had been very excited about the party for the baby. And very insistent that we go shopping for the perfect dress. Apparently with Gwen and Amy coming, they'd decided to make it a little classier than the usual Sons of Templar parties. It was black and white themed.

I had no idea how the women had managed to get their badass husbands to agree to a theme, but then again, most wore black like it was the only shade that existed, so it wasn't like they had to do anything different.

It was obvious then, according to Macy, that the women would all wear white. I'd tried to argue with Macy on this, self-conscious of my six-week post-partum body and the unforgiving shade of white.

But then we'd found *the* dress. A bias-cut, long-sleeved, maxi dress. It skimmed over the bits that I was self-conscious about and clung to the curves I was now proud of. Especially with the lingerie that Macy had found that was sexy and flattering at the same time. A white, strapless bustier which pushed up my new, gigantic breasts. Panties that revealed my entire ass and a garter belt that clipped onto my lace topped stockings.

"Why aren't you buying anything?" I asked, struggling with my many bags. I'd had to get shoes to go with the dress. Louboutins. I'd also had to get new shoes because my feet had not shrunk back down to their regular size.

It was a good thing that I could afford to replace the majority of them. My pregnancy series on my YouTube channel had generated more views than ever, and I had sponsorships and income like never before. Hades had, as promised, paid for all the household expenses. I, as promised, had done a lot of shopping for our household. And for Hades.

"My dress already arrived yesterday," Macy replied to my question with a wink.

I hadn't thought about the fanfare of the party. There were too many wonderful things happening in my life.

It was only then, on the day, in that moment, that I realized what the party was.

A wedding.

My wedding.

Our house was full of people because I'd insisted we'd have the party there. Macy had quickly agreed to that, and I understood why when I walked into our backyard.

The backyard that, in the space of the two hours it took me to get ready—thanks to Marilyn, Macy, Caroline and Aunt V distracting me and plying me with drinks—had transformed into a wedding venue.

Hades and I had been separated, which meant that Eva and I had been separated. The next time I saw them, Hades was wearing a dress shirt and slacks, and his cut of course. Eva was wearing the most beautiful little dress that Gwen had bought for her—I found that out later.

They were standing at the end of an aisle. In our backyard. There was an arch covered in flowers, the desert a perfect backdrop. Seats had been set up on either side of an aisle constructed with lanterns.

Everyone we knew and loved was there. A sea of Sons of Templar cuts. Des, grinning from ear to ear, wearing a tan suit complete with elbow patches. Marilyn and Jed. All the girls from Fate. Oliver from the coffee shop. All of the Sons of Templar Old Ladies.

All of our family.

Aunt V walked me down the aisle, her hand tight in mine as I stared at Hades and my daughter. Hansen was standing there, too, because who else officiated an outlaw wedding but the president of said outlaws.

Aunt V pulled me in for a tight hug when we reached the end. "You did it, my sunshine," she murmured in my ear. "You got the exact life you deserve."

She let me go, smiled at Hades and Eva then went to sit down in the front row beside Des. Though almost all of my attention was focused forward, I didn't miss how Des placed his hand on Aunt V's thigh before she covered it with her own.

Then my focus went to Hades and my daughter.

"Only *you* would propose to me with a wedding," I teased, fighting back tears.

Like the expert he was, Hades nestled Eva in one of his large arms to reach into his jacket and retrieve a ring. No box.

By the look of the cut and carat, it needed a box. That should not have been roaming around in the pocket of his cut. But then again, it was safe with Hades. As were me and Eva.

I held out a shaking hand to let Hades slide the diamond onto my finger. It was black.

It was perfection.

"You're gonna marry me," he murmured. "You're gonna spend the rest of your life with me."

My heart thundered. "Yes sir," I whispered.

Then we got married.

———

The rest of the night was euphoric. Our home full of people, laughter and love. Eva settled in her father's arms, happy and content as music filtered softly through the speaker. All of the surfaces in our living room were covered with either food or flowers. It was casual, relaxed and exactly how I wanted my wedding reception to be.

I would've been happy for it to last the entire night, but Hades promptly kicked everybody out after only a handful of hours.

I knew why after we'd put Eva to sleep in her crib. Sirius promptly curled up at the base of it, the other male who was never far from her side.

It had been six weeks.

Exactly.

And Hades had made it clear just how long those six weeks had been for the both of us when the buttons of my dress went clattering to the floor.

I forgot about everything else but Hades and his hands. He let out a low hiss when he revealed my lingerie.

He stepped back, rubbing his hand over his mouth, cock straining through his slacks. "Turn around," he rasped, his voice husky.

Trembling with desire, I did as he ordered.

When I turned around, his eyes were burning. "Never seen anything more fucking perfect in my life, Freya."

My entire body flushed.

"Lie down on the bed, baby," he ordered.

I did as I was told.

Then I went up on my elbows, watching as Hades slowly undressed, my entire body coiled with need, with excitement.

Once he was naked, he climbed on the bed. My eyes feasted on his cock. Long. Thick. Hard. Magnificent. Then my eyes went to the space above his heart. Up until six weeks ago, it had been the only place on his body where there was naked skin. Now, mine and Eva's names were inked on top of his heart.

"Lift your hips for me, baby," he murmured, his hands running up my stocking-covered legs.

"You arranged this whole wedding because it's the first night we could fuck?" I moaned, my mind working slowly thanks to all the desire flooding it.

His hands at my hips, pulling down my panties answered that particular question. My body relaxed against his touch, desperate for him, until he pushed apart my legs.

Then I froze.

Hades noticed immediately, his eyes darting to mine. "Freya?"

I pursed my lips, my cheeks suddenly hot.

He moved up so he was laying on top of me. The weight of his body was comforting, but not comforting enough.

"Freya," he repeated, my name a warning.

"It's stupid," I whispered. "And embarrassing."

"I don't give a fuck," Hades snapped. "Talk."

"I'm just worried..." I trailed off, suddenly unable to look him in the eye. I inspected the ceiling.

For about two point five seconds.

"You look at me, Freya," he demanded.

I took a deep breath then met his eyes. My *husband's* eyes. "I'm worried it won't be the same, I won't be the same. Down there." I swallowed, mortified. "That I'll feel different. That it won't be as good."

There it was, a shameful admission, one that I shouldn't have even voiced. My body had done exactly what it was designed to do. It had birthed our amazing daughter, and it had healed how it was supposed to heal. Yet because I was a coward, I hadn't looked too closely at *that* area.

"You're serious," Hades remarked, surprise in his tone.

I pursed my lips and nodded.

"Freya, I didn't think I could love your pussy anymore until six weeks ago." He kissed my neck. "Whatever has changed down there is only going to make me love it more because it's evidence of what you've given me." His lips trailed lower, encircling my nipple.

I cried out, my hands tearing through his hair. My breasts were still swollen and full of milk, much more tender than they'd ever been.

"Your pussy has given me the fuckin' world, Freya," he added, lifting his head to look into my eyes. Then they slid down my stomach, the one that bore stretchmarks and was nowhere near as flat as it used to be. Hades worshipped it.

Then he continued his descent lower, to my pussy, and he worshipped that too. His lips moved slowly, with reverence, exploring every inch of me. My body reacted in that exact same way as it had before Eva, savoring the pure ecstasy he gifted me with.

I fisted the sheets as my body writhed in pleasure, every nerve ending singing for Hades, desperate for more, for release. Just as I was about to topple into oblivion, Hades stopped. My entire body protested as he climbed upward, his lips brushing mine with the taste of me as his cock pressed up against me.

"First time you come is going to be around my cock, Freya. The baby is asleep, so your gonna have to come quietly," he murmured against my lips, poised at my entrance.

My nails clawed at the skin of his back, willing him to start working on that orgasm he'd promised. "I'll be quiet." My voice was low, desperate, feral.

The cords in Hades's neck stood out with the effort it was taking him to stay there, right there, and not surge inside.

"There will be time, when we have the house to ourselves, when I'll make you scream, don't you worry baby. I'll take care of you."

It was another oath I looked forward to him fulfilling.

I lifted my hands to cup his cheek. "I know, Hades," I whispered.

Then he surged inside of me.

There was a time when the house had been empty and he'd made me scream. But those times were just memories for the next twenty-three years. Although we always found the time, even when, as time went on, our house was rarely empty. Not just with Eva then later with her friends. But after much convincing and reassuring, the house was later filled with the twins, Carver and Miles. And after that, it was Victoria. Then we were done.

Because our home was plenty full.

ACKNOWLEDGMENTS

It felt so wonderful being back with our favorite MC, even if it's in New Mexico instead of Amber. I hope you enjoyed meeting some new characters.

There were many late nights with this book, many moments when I felt like I might not be able to finish. Which is where the people below come in. Although writing is a solitary act, I couldn't produce a book alone. I'm so so lucky to have wonderful people in my life to support me and cheer me on.

Taylor. My partner, my best friend, my soulmate. You endure my moods, my ups and downs, my demons. Thank you for keeping me safe. For making me laugh. For letting me cry. For going on any adventure with me.

Dad. You can't read this. But nonetheless, you are the reason I'm here. You taught me how to be a badass, how to believe in myself, how to leave my manners on the side of the court when I was playing netball. To be kind. And you're the reason I have such expensive taste.

Mum. You are my hero. My best friend. I am always so surprised when everyone doesn't list their mother as one of their best friends. Because not everyone is lucky like me. Thank you for taking my calls, for never judging me for buying shoes that I don't need, for urging me to get the matching bag. I know what a strong woman looks like because of you.

Polly, Emma, Harriet. My girls. You're still over on the other side of the world, but you're always there if I need an opinion on a selfie, or to have some form of breakdown.

Jessica Gadziala. My #sisterqueen. You are the reason I get through many of my writing blocks and general anxieties. You are a selfless friend, a kickass author and an all around queen.

Amo Jones. My ride or die. You tell me when I'm being crazy, you support me no matter what.

Michelle Clay. I am so lucky that you came into my life. You are such a special human. You're so precious to me. In short, you're family.

Annette Brignac. I'm so glad my books brought us together. I honestly don't know where I'd be without you. My books would not be the same. My life would not be the same. Thank you for being you.

Ginny. You are so important to my books. To my life. You know my characters almost as well as you know me. You know when I need a kick up the butt or some kind words. Thank you for being there for me always.

Kim. Thank you not only for being an amazing editor, but being there as a friend too. You are such a special human and I'm so so lucky to have found you.

You. The reader. I would not be typing this without you. Without your support. You are the reason I get to live my dream. Why I get to write stories and call it a job. Thank you for making my dreams come true.

ABOUT THE AUTHOR

ANNE MALCOM has been an avid reader since before she can remember, her mother responsible for her love of reading. It started with magical journeys into the world of Hogwarts and Middle Earth, then as she grew up her reading tastes grew with her. Her love of reading doesn't discriminate, she reads across many genres, although classics like Little Women and Gone with the Wind will hold special places in her heart. She also can't get enough romance, especially when some possessive alpha males throw their weight around.

One day, in a reading slump, Cade and Gwen's story came to her and started taking up space in her head until she put their story into words. Now that she has started, it doesn't look like she's going to stop anytime soon, with many more characters demanding their story be told as well.

Raised in small town New Zealand, Anne had a truly special childhood, growing up in one of the most beautiful countries in the world. She has backpacked across Europe, ridden camels in the Sahara and eaten her way through Italy, loving every moment. She has settled down with her fiancé, their dogs and happy to be in one place ... for a while at least.

Want to get in touch with Anne? She loves to hear from her readers.
You can email her: annemalcomauthor@hotmail.com
Or join her reader group on Facebook.

ALSO BY ANNE MALCOM

THE SONS OF TEMPLAR SERIES

Making the Cut

Firestorm

Outside the Lines

Out of the Ashes

Beyond the Horizon

Dauntless

Battles of the Broken

Hollow Hearts

Deadline to Damnation

Scars of Yesterday

THE UNQUIET MIND SERIES

Echoes of Silence

Skeletons of Us

Broken Shelves

Mistake's Melody

Censored Soul

GREENSTONE SECURITY

Still Waters

Shield

The Problem With Peace

Chaos Remains

Resonance of Stars

THE VEIN CHRONICLES

Fatal Harmony

Deathless

Faults in Fate

Eternity's Awakening

Buried Destiny

RETIRED SINNERS

Splinters of You

THE KLUTCH DUET

Lies That Sinners Tell

Truths That Saints Believe

STANDALONES

Birds of Paradise

Doyenne

Midnight Sommelier

Hush - co-written

Printed in Great Britain
by Amazon

83720458R00192